These players will capture your heart

They're not quite ready for the big league, but these hot hockey hunks are ready to give their hearts.

Includes:
Netting the Goalie
Pucking the Grinder
Falling for the Enforcer

Offside Hearts

Offside Hearts

Volume 1

Stephanie Julian

Moonlit Night Publishing

Netting the Goalie

I need to get my head in the game...

Shane

I'm a goaltender in a slump but, when I meet a redhead who raises more than my blood pressure, it's game on. One steamy night with Bliss, and I'm winning games again. Our affair is on fire and so is my game. But we both know it can't last. I want to move up to the NHL, and Bliss has her roots planted in a small town.

...not let my heart call the shots.

Bliss

I'm not looking for a relationship, especially not with an intense, driven athlete who's chasing his dreams. My ex's need for control nearly made me his emotional slave. I'm never going to give another man that kind of hold over me again. But a one-night stand with a hot hockey player who won't be around forever? Absolutely. But Shane's off-beat humor and killer smile might be more than I can withstand. And when Shane gets the call he's been waiting for his whole life, I realize I've been fooling myself about giving him up. And Shane isn't giving up without a fight.

Chapter 1

Shane

"Son-of-a-mother-fucking bitch."

Stalking into the empty locker room of the Reading Civic Arena, I tossed my helmet, swearing even more when it smashed into the wall. Something cracked, either the wall or my goalie helmet and I didn't much care either way.

One more nick in the cinderblock meant shit. One more ding in my helmet... Well, my game was fucked at the moment. I probably wouldn't need the goddamn helmet much longer anyway.

Not the way I was playing.

"Fuck."

The rest of the team was still on the ice, though they'd be making their way back here in a few minutes. This was our last practice before our last game before the three-day Christmas holiday.

And it looked like I'd be riding the bench tonight.

Which made me feel like I was back in high school—the fat,

awkward kid at the school dance, sitting alone on the bleachers while my friends danced with the hot chicks. The ones who only gave me the time of day because I had a wicked sense of humor and I'd led my high school hockey team to three straight victories.

Throwing myself onto the bench, I ripped open the laces on my skates then threw them on the ground for good measure.

Fucking hell, this sucked.

Get your damn head out of your ass.

Good advice. Wish I knew how to do it.

Frustration burning through me like lit gasoline, I started stripping off the rest of my gear, careful not to rip my practice jersey and shorts. Didn't give a shit about the rest. I hung my pads in my locker out of habit before I grabbed a towel and stalked naked to the showers.

I stood there for at least five minutes, let the scalding hot water pour over my head and back, trying to get the frustration and the anger to roll away with it.

So far, not working.

And didn't that just make me want to suck down a gallon of Jack Daniels?

"Shane."

I stiffened as my teammate Cary Lenville's voice penetrated the fog in my head. I considered ignoring him, but no one ignored Cary.

The assistant captain of the Reading Redtails Hockey Club, Cary was the glue that held the team together. At thirty-six, he was the oldest player with the most experience. And, even if he wasn't the most skilled player, he was the one everyone went to when they had problems. Cary always had an answer, didn't matter what the question was. And even if it wasn't the completely right answer, it was better than anything you'd come up with on your own.

But I knew Cary couldn't help with this problem. Not when I was pretty damn sure it was all in my messed-up head.

Shutting off the water, I grabbed my towel. "What's up?"

I didn't meet Cary's gaze and I tried to keep the edge out of my tone but couldn't manage it. Not when frustrated embarrassment threatened to choke me.

Goddammit, I was supposed to be the team's number one goalie. They'd nicknamed me the Brick Wall, for fuck's sake. So why the fuck wasn't I playing like it?

The guys were depending on me to help them get to the Calder Cup championships this year. They'd been playing well enough to consider it a real possibility. But I had to pull my head out of my ass…like, now.

"Coach said you're not going home for the break."

Huh?

I turned to give Cary a look before heading back to my locker. Luckily, no one else was off the ice yet so I had time to pull myself together.

"Yeah, that's right."

I didn't add that I couldn't bear to go home to Minnesota, where Mom would fuss over me like I was still in high school and Pop would lecture me like he was still my coach.

I loved my parents but if I had to deal with them for an extended period of time, it would totally fuck with my head.

And that just made me feel worse.

Could I be *any* more screwed up? If I continued like this, Coach would trade my ass to Alaska or send me down to the ECHL.

"Then what're you doing tomorrow night?" Cary asked.

I snorted with disgust and shook my head. "Besides drinking myself into a coma? Not one goddamn thing. Why?"

"Come to my place. Lori and I are having some people over."

I automatically shook my head. "Nah, man. I don't think I'd be good company. Thanks anyway."

Cary went silent but he didn't move. And that was never a good thing. The six-foot-two, two-hundred-plus defenseman not only was built like a brick shithouse but was pretty much as immoveable as one.

As the silence stretched on, I sighed and turned, forcing myself to look directly into Cary's eyes.

"What?"

Cary had crossed his arms over his chest, emphasizing just how broad the fucker really was. "You're strung tighter than a drum and you need to decompress or you're gonna explode. And that won't be good for you or the team. Won't be anybody there you know and we won't talk hockey all night, unless Lori goes on a bender. Besides, I could use the backup." He grimaced. "Lori's always collecting strays. I swear I won't know half the people there. And her cousins are crazy."

Hearing Cary talk about the love of his life coaxed a smirk out of me. The guy was married to an abso-fucking-lutely gorgeous woman who seemed to think Cary hung the moon and stars. Cary apparently thought the same of her.

It'd be sickening if they weren't so perfect for each other.

But… *Christ*. Cary wanted me to spend a few hours making small talk with a bunch of people I didn't know? I opened my mouth to say no again but Cary just stared at me.

Shit. My resolve crumbled.

With a sigh, I began to pull on my clothes. "How crazy?"

Cary's shit-eating grin made me want to smile back but I squashed the impulse. Didn't want to give the guy the impression he'd won. Even if he had.

"Let's just say they have some holiday traditions that'd put the Addams family to shame."

I tried not to sigh but couldn't help it. "As long as there's alcohol, I guess you can count me in."

Cary nodded, his grin disappearing. "You find it helps?"

I didn't bother to misunderstand him and shook my head.

"Not really. And no, I don't have a problem. At least, not with alcohol."

Cary took me at my word. Another thing that made every single one of the guys worship him like he was the goddamn King of Hockey.

"Good to hear it. And yeah, I know you've been having a few bad weeks. It happens. The break'll be good for you. Get your head on straight. If you want, we can run some drills tomorrow, just the two of us."

And *this* was why Cary was rumored to be the front runner for the next Redtails Coach. The gossip mill outside the locker room had been working overtime lately. Our current coach, according to gossip, had a lock on an NHL job. Everyone expected Cary to step into the vacated position.

The players loved him. The front office loved him. The fans thought he walked on water.

I found myself nodding. "Yeah. That'd be… That'd be helpful." I hoped.

Cary grinned then punched me on the shoulder and practically knocked me off the bench.

"Good. And come to the party. You'll have a good time."

Chapter 2

Bliss

"So I told him, he needed to pick one pattern or the other. Honestly, how hard is it? I mean, it's not like I'm the only one getting married. It's his wedding, too. Shouldn't he at least be a little interested in the china we're going to be using for the rest of our lives?"

I sat on a loveseat in a corner of Lori Lenville's comfortable living room, sipping champagne and nodding sympathetically at the two women sitting across from me on the couch.

They seemed like nice women and, when they'd discovered I worked at With This Ring Bridal Boutique… Well, you would've thought they'd found a long-lost soulmate.

At any other time, I would've been thrilled to talk weddings. I actually enjoyed them, even when I had to handle the occasional bridezilla, momzilla, bitchy sister-in-law-to-be, drunken sorority-sister bridesmaid and snotty five-year-old flower girl. I knew how to deal with them all.

My boss, Aunt Rosie, called me a godsend. I actually thought my aunt was the godsend for giving me a career when I'd had no idea what the hell I was going to do with a degree in business.

And even after my own wedding had fallen apart two years ago, I still got teary when I helped a bride-to-be find that perfect dress for her walk down the aisle to the man she'd decided to spend her life with, even if I had no time or inclination for a life partner.

But a one-night stand? That would be just fine. And, oh please, could he be good in bed? Hell, I wouldn't even wish for great. Just good enough with his hands to get me off at least once.

I'd had no such luck lately.

And it didn't look like tonight would be any better. Not one of the guys here tonight made me want to go to the trouble of giving up a few hours of sleep.

Jeez, what's wrong with you? You're only twenty-six, not eighty.

But between working with my aunt, whose business was steadily growing, and the fact that my friends were either married or hooked up with Mr. Right Now… Well, I didn't get out much.

And when I did, I had to wonder if there were any decent guys left in the world. Most were dicks with attitude problems or nerdy man-children who lived in their parents' basements, played video games until three in the morning and spent their weekends drinking with their buddies who were lucky or mature enough to have an apartment.

And… *Oh my god.* Was I really this much of bitch? No wonder I couldn't find anyone to screw. Honestly, I wouldn't want me either.

"Lori's been *amazing.*" One of the women gushed, drawing me back into the conversation. "She helped us smooth over the problem with the zoning and made sure we had all the right permits. She'd been our guardian angel…"

I nodded, completely in agreement with my new friends on this.

I'd met Lori at a local Chamber of Commerce mixer. Aunt Josie hadn't been able to attend but she'd begged me to go in her place. I couldn't even remember why my aunt had sent me. I only knew I hadn't wanted to go. But then I'd met Lori and we'd bonded over a few drinks and a mutual admiration of hockey.

Lori's husband played for the local professional hockey team and, though I had only been to a few games, I'd gained an appreciation of the sport from my dad. It'd been the one thing the two of us enjoyed watching together. If it hadn't been for hockey, me and my great, hulking bear of a father might never have held a conversation that didn't begin and end with "How was school?"

My dad loved me and he tried but I'd always been a girly girl and that had been mom's domain.

"So I told him if he didn't at least attempt to get along with my cousin, we might as well call off the wedding. I mean, my family is so important to me and…"

Yep, I totally got that. Family was important. I'd seen more than one wedding disintegrate into factions more fierce than anything in the Hunger Games during the planning stages.

And anyone who said words would never hurt you had never dealt with a Bridezilla whose mother-in-law dared to have an opinion on what color napkin should be used on the cake table.

I swallowed a sigh.

What the hell are you doing here anyway?

I should be mingling, flirting, having a good time. It wasn't like there weren't any good-looking guys here. A few of them had even made eye contact and two had tried to start conversations.

Until five minutes later and I realized they only wanted to talk about what they did and how much that should impress me. Sure, they had decent jobs and wore decent clothes and were attractive but—

What's wrong with you?

"And who tells your mother her dress makes her look fat? You know what I mean? I just wanted to punch…"

Yep, I knew exactly how the bride-to-be felt. I wanted to punch someone, too.

Except I didn't do physical violence. I was no tough cookie. More like a cupcake with fluffy frosting. And who didn't love cupcakes, right?

Sighing again, I took another sip of my drink and tried to wipe the pissy look off of my face.

I knew I was no great beauty but I certainly didn't look like an ogre. Sure, my nose was a little too big and my body a little too curvy. But I still managed to attract guys who liked big tits and a decent ass. I knew that because most guys I talked to couldn't stop checking out either one long enough to hold a rational conversation.

Then again, I hadn't exactly allowed any guys close enough to get to know me better. A vicious cycle, one I didn't know how to break.

So, here I sat. Smiling and nodding through a conversation with two women I barely knew.

This had been a mistake. I should just take my pitiful self home and—

The front door opened, catching my attention simply because it was directly in my line of sight.

But then *he* walked through.

And I actually felt my mouth drop open. Like, literally, my jaw dropped. Then my lips parted and I sucked in a sharp breath that I immediately tried to cover with a slight cough.

I assured my new friends, who interrupted their conversation about guest lists to make sure I wasn't choking, that I was fine and managed to come up with a question to get them back on their conversational track.

So I could go back to checking out the newcomer.

The really *big* newcomer.

And I didn't mean fat. I meant *built*. Big as in broad. Wide. He looked like a—

Hockey player.

Like Lori's husband, Cary, who greeted the newcomer with a big smile and a firm handshake as he pulled him farther into the house.

Cary led the new guy right into the great room, where I sat against the far wall, and walked him straight to the bar.

I tried not to stare. Really, I did. But how could I *not* when this guy ticked off every box on my Yummy Meter, including a few I hadn't known I had.

Like his dark, wavy hair. Everyone in my huge Italian family had dark hair so every boyfriend I'd ever had had been blond, pretty and clean cut, like he'd just walked off a magazine shoot.

Like my ex-fiancé, the prick.

Nope, not thinking about him.

This guy looked like he hadn't cut his hair in months or seen a razor in days, if the dark stubble on his strong, square jaw was anything to go by. He looked scruffy but not like he was trying to be trendy.

Now, the bright blue eyes… Yeah, I absolutely had a thing for those. And his were a perfect ocean blue I could see from across the room. Combined with that nose that looked as if it'd been broken a few times…

Damn. My mouth watered.

And when my gaze slipped south… Hell, I was pretty sure my thighs just clenched.

The guy had to be at least a five inches over six feet, which means he'd tower over me. And his clothes couldn't hide the fact that he had muscles in places all men should have muscles. Like in their thighs. And their abs. And their arms—

When he took off his coat to let Cary hang it in the closet, I had to swallow because… Oh my god. The man's arms bulged beneath his blue dress shirt.

With black dress pants and that blue shirt, he looked good enough to eat.

And wouldn't you love to get your mouth on him?

Yes, please. Anywhere he had skin.

And when he turned to walk with Cary to the makeshift bar on the other side of the room, I thought I might have actually squeaked at the wonder of his ass.

Ho-lee shit.

"Bliss, are you okay?"

Blinking, I turned my attention back to the two women, now staring at me with identical expressions of knowing amusement.

Damn. Had I been that obvious?

I forced a smile. "Yes, I'm fine. Sorry, I, uh…"

"Got a glimpse of Shane Conrad." The bride-to-be, whose name was Crista, smiled with commiseration. "He certainly is nice-looking. Kind of shy, though. Lori's tried to set him up with a few girls before but nothing's stuck. He's apparently a really nice guy but doesn't talk much. Or he doesn't like girls." Crista shrugged. "No one's been able to figure out which yet. Would you like to meet him? I'm sure Lori would be thrilled to introduce you. He's kind of become her pet project."

Is that why Lori had invited me tonight? To introduce me to Shane? Not that that would be a bad thing but…

But what?

"I think I need a drink. Anyone need another?"

Both Crista and her friend shook their heads, their grins widening.

I didn't care. For the first time in months, I wanted to jump a guy's bones. I'd be damned if I didn't follow up on it.

And maybe later, I'd get to strip off his pants and shirt and rub against his naked body like a cat in heat.

Just as long as I didn't stick my foot in my mouth first.

Chapter 3

Shane

Why the hell are you here? You're a goddamn glutton for punishment.

I knew my strengths and my weaknesses. I could be the life of the party but only if I felt comfortable with the audience.

I didn't know a single person here, except Cary and Lori, and I had the almost overwhelming urge to slink back to the door and make my getaway.

Dork. Get a grip.

I glanced around for Cary but the guy had disappeared not long after introducing me to Damien and Lynton. I'd make him pay for that. Somehow.

"...must be amazing to get paid to be an athlete. You have like...what? Two games a week? Better than working in an office ten hours a day, six days a week."

I nodded and agreed, letting the guys continue to tell me how amazing my life must be.

Of course, they didn't have a fucking clue what they were talking about.

If they did, they wouldn't be giving me those sly smiles when they talked about all the "fun" I must have on the road.

Oh, yeah, I was just swimming in pussy all the fucking time. Between daily practice and three or four games a week and travel and—

Yeah, I loved playing hockey. Couldn't think of anything I'd rather do. But like everything else, it had a downside.

Playing in the AHL meant I didn't move around as much as when I'd been in the ECHL but it wasn't the easiest way to make a living.

Hockey was tough on the body. Plus, I had a shelf-life. Goalies, especially had knee problems. I might last until thirty-three. If I was lucky, my knees would hold out until I was forty. But eventually I'd have to leave the ice and find something else to do to make money. Especially if I continued playing the way I was and never made it to the NHL.

Damn, what I wouldn't give to be home binge-watching "Daredevil" and drinking beer.

"So I told him I could work that weekend just so I wouldn't have to be home when her parents showed up. I know I was being kind of a dick but if I had to listen her dad..."

I nodded like I knew what Lynton—what the fuck kind of name was Lynton anway?—was talking about but I really had no clue. I hadn't been in a serious relationship...well, ever.

I'd had no time and no opportunity.

Shit, where the hell had Cary disappeared to? Maybe I could slip away and no one would notice?

Out of the corner of my eye, I saw Cary coming toward me. *Oh, thank Christ.* This had been a mistake. I'd make my excuses and—

"Hey, Shane." Cary turned and smiled at the smallish redhead by his side. "This is Bliss Vescovi. Bliss, this is Shane Conrad. He's the goalie for the Redtails. And—" Another knock at the door and Cary grimaced. "Sorry, I gotta get the door again. Hang tight, I'll be back."

I barely noticed Cary's departure as Bliss smiled and held out her hand, "Hi. Nice to meet you."

Her voice made the hair on my arms stand straight up. And sent a shock straight to my cock.

Holy shit. Pure fucking sex.

If I believed in heaven, I figured I'd just died and gone there because, Jesus Christ, this woman was a fucking angel.

Red hair so deep it had to be fake and hazel eyes that were a swirl of green, blue and brown. A face that belonged on a billboard and a body slapped together like a porn star.

And damn, if I wasn't standing there with my mouth hanging open.

I shut my trap and took her hand. "Shane Conrad. Nice to meet you."

Then I glanced down and as her fingers wrapped around mine.

Warm. And soft. Damn, she's soft.

My cock sprang to attention before I could rein in my response. I'd be sporting one hell of a boner in a few seconds. I couldn't remember ever getting hard just by shaking a woman's hand, not even as a horny teenager who hadn't had a chance in hell of getting laid by even the sweetest cheerleader in my high school.

I couldn't believe I hadn't noticed her when I'd come in a few minutes ago. Then again, I hadn't really been interested in anything other than grabbing a beer and something to eat. Since I'd been in this slump, I'd fallen into old habits of using food for comfort. If I wasn't careful I'd be putting on pounds that'd slow me down. And I definitely didn't need that.

But, damn, wouldn't it be great to work them off in bed with her?

When she didn't say anything else, just stood there staring at me with a smile that made my balls tighten, I forced myself to release her and think of something to say. Anything at all, just to keep her here. But she beat me to it.

"Nice to meet you, too. So Cary said you're a hockey player?"

"Yeah, I am. So how do you know Cary?"

Her head tilted to the side, silky red hair sliding along her shoulder. "I don't really. I know his wife, Lori. We met at a chamber mixer a few months ago and we've kept in touch."

Oh, hell, that voice. It made me want to beg her to take pity on me and get naked. To let me put my mouth all over her until she melted into a puddle of lust on the ground.

On the ice, I was known for my flexibility and my ability to work well with both hands. I'd show her I had just as how well that translated in the bed.

"Lori's really sweet and Cary's a great guy."

Her smile regained a little of its former brightness. "He must be. Lori can't say enough good things about him. And Lori's amazing. I swear she knows everyone in the county. Unlike me. I have to confess," she leaned closer and I bent my head. "I really don't know anyone except Lori."

"Then we're pretty much in the same boat." I couldn't stop staring into those gorgeous eyes. "I don't know anyone except Cary and Lori. And right now, I don't care if I don't meet another person in the room."

Shit, probably shouldn't have said that. But Bliss—damn but I loved her name—smiled again, brighter this time. Then she laughed. Holy fucking hell, did I love her laugh. Low and husky, it sank straight into my gut and made my blood heat like lava.

And when she leaned closer, I caught a whiff of the sexiest perfume I'd ever smelled. Christ, if I wasn't careful, I'd throw this woman over my shoulder and make a break for the nearest bedroom.

I was pretty sure she'd be pissed off about that but I didn't have much experience with a woman who looked like she'd stepped off the pages of a fashion magazine, even if she was only wearing a slim black skirt and some sexy-as-hell shirt that showed off enough cleavage to make me drool.

My fingers twitched and I stuffed them in my pockets to keep them from flexing. Or from reaching out to touch her again.

Fuck.

But then she stepped closer and I sucked in another breath, laced with her scent.

Damn, maybe I'd hit my head at practice today and was passed out on the ice, hallucinating.

And wouldn't that fucking suck?

Then again, if I was having a hallucination, maybe I needed to hit my head more often because, holy hell, she was only inches away and my heart revved like a muscle car.

And when she put her fingertips on my chest and tapped twice, my heart actually answered by pounding against my ribs.

Strangely enough, I knew what she wanted me to do, even though my teammates accused me of being the most clueless guy around.

I bent down, turning my head so she could whisper in my ear.

"I know exactly what you mean. I'm really glad we met."

My abs clenched and, when I straightened so I could look into her eyes again, her expression made my lungs seize up.

Her lips curved in a smile I wanted to taste.

Christ Almighty, I hoped I was reading her right. She was flirting with me, wasn't she?

I'd been making all the wrong moves on the ice lately. Maybe I couldn't trust my instincts.

Even so, I couldn't stop myself from blurting out the words on the tip of my tongue. "Maybe you and I could slip out of here and get to know each other better."

She blinked, her eyes widening as her smile froze.

Jesus, I was a fucking idiot. Why the hell—

"I would love that." Her smile nearly took me to my knees. "But maybe we could wait until after dinner? I have a feeling I'm going to need fuel for later."

Chapter 4

Bliss

I watched Shane's mouth drop open and my grin widened as anticipation made my body tingle like I'd taken shots of grain alcohol.

It'd been a long time since I'd tingled over anything. And that had sucked.

But so far, tonight didn't suck at all. Not while there was the possibility that I would take this man home with me, strip him down to his skin then run my hands all over every hard muscle in his body.

While I contemplated that scenario, Shane continued to stare at me until finally he shook his head.

"Damn, I didn't… I mean, yeah. Sure. After dinner." Then he shook his head again and his lips curved in a kind of rueful smile. "So can I get you a drink?"

Was he actually embarrassed? Yeah, he'd shocked me by being blunt, but the way he'd said it hadn't made me feel like a piece of meat. No, I'd felt desired.

Adorable. The guy was freaking adorable.

"I'd love one, thanks."

The relief on his face made my smile widen. "Anything you don't like?"

"Not much." Totally the truth. I had three older brothers with a healthy admiration for alcohol in any form. They'd given me a wide breadth of knowledge to pull from.

Shane started to shake his head again but stopped when a bemused smile twisted his lips.

Oh, please tell me this man wasn't one of those closet cretins who thought women shouldn't enjoy sex and alcohol. Chauvinists who believed simply because they had a dick, they were entitled to pass judgment on women?

I'd leave him with a serious case of blue balls—

"So you want it sweet or hard?"

Oh my.

Heat lit through me at the deep, suggestive tone of his voice and I had to take a quick breath before I could answer.

"Can't I have both?"

The curve of his lips made my thighs clench and, when he spoke, I went wet between my thighs.

"Honey, you can have whatever the hell you want."

My answering smile made my face hurt, it was so wide. "Then I'll have a shot of tequila and a beer."

"Coming right up." He took a step away but looked back over his shoulder, those blue eyes shining as if lit from within. "Don't go anywhere."

I raised an eyebrow and made an X over the exposed flesh above my breasts drawing his gaze down before he snapped it back up. "I'll be right here when you get back."

"I'm gonna hold you to that."

"I hope that's not the only thing you're going to hold me to."

His gaze darkened with sexual intent. "Wherever and whenever."

Then he turned and headed for the makeshift bar on the other side of the room.

I sucked air into my starved lungs. Damn, I felt light-headed.

It'd been so damn long since a guy had had this response to me. Or that I'd had a response like this to a guy. I liked it

Across the room, I watched Shane handle two tall bottles and two shot glasses as he made his way back to me. He didn't stop to talk to anyone and he didn't seem to notice the looks the women in the room were giving him. Looks that I sincerely hoped he'd never see because I wanted him all to myself.

When he stood in front of me again, I took a glass and a shot off his hands and immediately downed the shot. *Nice.*

Setting the shot glass on the table beside me, I took a sip of beer, aware that Shane watched my every move. When I lowered the bottle, his gaze slipped to my mouth then down to my breasts, which I'd displayed to their full potential tonight. What good was having a decent body if you couldn't dress to please yourself? The lace bra and panty set I'd decided on tonight would be worth the expense, especially if Shane got a look at them.

"So you're a goalie. How's the team this year?"

He blinked and his gaze popped back up to mine. I actually thought he blushed at being caught staring at my chest.

"We're doing good." Then he grimaced. "Mostly."

He looked like he wanted to say something else but stayed silent.

Since I pretty much couldn't, I asked, "And you play with Cary?"

Shane nodded and kept his gaze glued to mine. "He's a great guy. He'll make a great coach."

The reverence in Shane's voice made me smile again. He obviously looked up to Cary.

"And are you from the area?"

He shook his head. "Minnesota. Didn't feel like going home for Christmas this year." Something crossed his expression but passed quickly. "We have a game the day after Christmas and I didn't want to do all that traveling. What about you? You're local?"

Apparently, he didn't want to talk about his family. No problem. Everybody had family issues. "Yep. Born and raised. My whole family's still here, including all four older brothers. We're disgustingly close."

Just how close… Yeah, I typically didn't go into that, especially not when I first met someone.

His eyebrows raised at the mention of my four brothers and I almost expected him to back away slowly. Some guys did. And when I mentioned that one was a cop… Well, that thinned the herd even more.

Then he smiled…and stole my breath. "Sounds like my family. Even though I'm not home anymore, my parents and my sister and brother still need to know every little thing about my life."

"Is it hard being away from them at the holidays?"

Nodding, his smile slid toward a grimace. "Yeah. But I've been traveling for hockey since I was twelve so I'm used to it."

"That seems really young."

He shrugged. "Not really. At least not where I come from."

"I have to admit…I've only been to two Redtails games and mostly I sat in a box and talked to my friends. It's not that I don't like the game. I do. I just always have something else going on."

Now, his grin widened. "I can take care of that problem. Let me get you a ticket to our next home game."

Chapter 5

Shane

Holy hell, when this woman smiled, which she did a lot, I had the almost overwhelming instinct to fall to my knees at her feet and repeat, "I'm not worthy."

No clue why but I knew exactly what I'd do when I was down there. I'd shove those pants down around her ankles, put my hands on her naked thighs and pull her closer. Then I'd put my mouth—

Holy shit. I needed to stop before I had no hope at all of hiding my boner.

"Sure." Her smile brightened. "I'd like that. Is the team having a good season?"

Grimacing, I shrugged. I'd been having a great year until recently. The past few weeks, though…

Damn it, I'd sucked. And I needed to get her off the topic of hockey.

"Yeah, we're doing pretty well. So what do you do?"

"I help my aunt run her bridal shop in West Reading. She has all boys and none of them wanted to work in the shop. I've been helping her since I was fifteen. Now it's a full-time job. My uncle retired last year and they like to travel so I'm alone there a lot of the time."

"You run it all by yourself?"

Her eyebrows raised and I wondered if I'd stuck my foot in my mouth.

"It's not that big so, yeah. On the weekends another one of my cousins helps out. My dad was one of ten so I've got a lot of cousins. I actually love helping brides pick out their dresses. We also do bridesmaids and mothers' dresses and prom and special occasions. It's actually really fun." She leaned in and I bent closer. "Don't tell my aunt but I'd work for free if I didn't need to pay my rent."

"Where do you live?"

"In an apartment in West Reading."

"Me, too. I live with one of the guys on my team. But he's home for the holiday."

Something sparked in her eyes. "So I guess, if we wanted to go back to your place for drinks later…"

I tried not to let my mouth drop open but… Damn, this girl made me feel like I won the fucking lottery. I needed to thank Cary for twisting my arm to come to tonight.

"There'd be no problem with that."

Her smile made me want to ask her if she wanted to leave now but that'd be rude. Totally worth it but rude.

Besides, she hadn't exactly said she wanted to go home with me. She could be flirting and not mean it. I honestly didn't have enough experience with girls to know.

Maybe I should just resign myself to a few hours of foreplay and eventual blue balls. At least I wouldn't be disappointed.

Luckily, Lori announced that dinner was ready and everyone headed into the kitchen for food.

Small talk got a little easier then, mainly because there were other people around to carry the load. I wasn't good at making conversation unless they were talking about golf, working out, TF2 or, of course, hockey.

Which made the fan meet-and-greets torture. I'd learned to cover my awkwardness to some extent but most people still found it hard to draw me out.

But Bliss didn't seem to be put off. I didn't think she had trouble talking to anyone.

As everyone came together to fill their plates then retreated back to the living or dining rooms to find somewhere to sit and eat, she chatted up several people but never left my side.

By unspoken agreement, Bliss and I found space in the living room, where another woman sat next to Bliss and began to run at the mouth about her upcoming wedding.

Bliss didn't seem to mind. Probably because they were talking about wedding stuff. A subject I had absolutely no interest in. At least, not at this point in my life.

No way did I have time for a wife or even a steady girlfriend. I had to concentrate on my game. Or I'd be ending my career sooner than I expected.

But I definitely wanted to spend a few hours with Bliss.

"So, Shane, how's it going?"

I turned with a smile for Lori, who'd sat on the arm of my chair.

"I'm pretty sure you know the answer to that already." I grimaced. "I pretty much suck right now."

"I know that's not true." Lori smiled that cool, mysterious smile that had reeled in Cary like a trout with a hook in its mouth. "I've seen you play. You're just having a rough patch. It'll pass. You need to get out of your own head for a while. Enjoy life a little and not always be so focused on work."

If only it was that easy.

Nodding, I forced a smile for her. "You're right. Cary's always telling me to keep my head up. But when you play, your moves have to be instinctive. The game's too fast to stop and think. I need to be able to see the move before it happens and react before I think about it."

"Very true." Then she leaned closer and her voice dropped to a whisper. "But the advice wasn't only for hockey."

Ah.

I might not be the sharpest blade on the ice but I was no fool.

Lori squeezed my shoulder but Bliss' laughter grabbed my attention. She was still talking to the other girl but now it was about veils and lace and some other shit I had no clue about.

Didn't much matter, though, so long as I could listen to Bliss talk. The sound of her voice made me hard. Maybe I *had* been concentrating a little too hard on hockey lately, especially if I got a boner just listening to a girl talk.

As if Bliss had heard me thinking about her, she turned and smiled at me.

I nearly swallowed my tongue.

When the hell could we leave without looking suspicious?

Now. Ask her back to your place for a drink.

Yeah, all I had to do was open my mouth and get the words out.

But I kept getting distracted by the sight of all that red hair falling down her back in perfect waves and a pretty face that put some actresses to shame.

And her body… Christ, I was salivating. I wanted to put my hands on her breasts then slide them down her body to her gorgeous ass. Then I'd lift her so she could wrap her legs around my waist.

Naked. I wanted her naked and under me. Or over me. I wasn't picky.

Lori made a soft sound, almost like a muffled laugh, and my gaze shot back to hers.

Shit. She knows exactly what you're thinking.

"Have a good time tonight, Shane." Lori stood, smiling down at me. "Tomorrow will take care of itself."

Then she left, but not before ruffling my hair with her fingers. Like my mom would've done. Made me feel like a kid but not in a bad way.

Smiling, I turned back to Bliss and found her watching me.

"Are you enjoying yourself?"

Her question barely registered because her expression made every muscle in my body tense in anticipation and a strange hum sounded in my ears.

Then her adorable nose crinkled. "I know I've been monopolizing your time and—"

"Please." My smile disappeared, replaced with deadly serious intent. "Monopolize me. All night. I'm begging you."

Her smile faded but I saw the heat in her gaze increase.

Leaning closer, she put her hand on the cushion between us, almost touching my thigh but not quite. "I'm going to take you at your word."

"I really fu—hope you do."

Her smile returned, slowly, and with enough sexual heat to make my heart pound against my ribs.

"Um, I think my fiancé needs me." The woman who'd been talking to Bliss also had a smile on her face as she rose to her feet. "Nice talking to you."

Bliss' nose wrinkled as the other woman walked away but did nothing to stop her.

And when she turned back to me, her lips had curved in a tiny smile that made my heart race.

Okay, maybe I really had gotten banged around at practice and this was a hallucination. And wouldn't that totally suck.

Then Bliss put her hand on my knee and a jolt of electricity poured through me. Nope, definitely not a hallucination.

"So how many are on your team?"

Amazingly, I could still talk. "We've got twenty-two guys on the roster."

"Does everyone get along? I can't imagine that many guys spending that much time together and getting along all of the time. My brothers were always fighting over something and there were only four of them."

"For the most part, yeah. We've got a good group of guys."

And that was no bullshit. I really enjoyed the hell out of my teammates. At least, the ones that'd been around for most of the season. There'd been a few guys who'd been traded or moved up or down but mostly, we'd hung together. And were a stronger team because of it.

"Sounds like you enjoy what you do."

"Can't imagine doing anything else. Even when—" Shit. Probably better not to finish that sentence, especially to a girl I'd just met. She didn't want to hear about all the gross shit guys did to one another in the locker room. "Even after we've lost three straight on the road and the coach is chewing our asses and we've got a seven-hour bus ride home."

She laughed, low and soft. "You're right. That sounds like hell."

"Yeah. You don't want to be in a locker room full of hockey players after a losing game. We're barely human."

Bliss laughed and I swore every guy in the room turned to look. I knew if I wasn't sitting here with her, I would have looked because, damn, her laugh made my gut clench with lust.

I was pretty sure I could fight off anyone who attempted to poach her. I was one of the biggest goalies in the league. I looked like a brawler and I wasn't afraid to take a hit if I needed to.

And if I had to move someone out of my crease…

"I'm sure that's an exaggeration. Some men look great sweaty." Bliss leaned closer, her voice dropping into bedroom territory. "Makes a girl want to lick him. All over."

I had to fight hard to swallow my groan but I couldn't do

anything about my rock-hard erection. That bastard refused to stand down.

Staring into Bliss' beautiful hazel eyes, I said the first thing that came to mind. "You can lick me anywhere you want."

Jesus Christ, I hoped like hell no one else had heard that. Not exactly dinner party conversation.

Good thing Bliss didn't seem to mind. In fact, I thought her gaze actually got hotter.

"Don't be surprised if I take you up on that."

Her voice had dropped to a husky whisper and her breath brushed against my cheek.

Oh, fuck.

With one last, hot look in my direction, Bliss turned her attention back to her meal.

Since I couldn't take my eyes off her, I watched as she slid her fork from between her lips. Moaning, her eyes closed and the look of utter…well, bliss on her face made my lungs feel like they'd been gripped in a vise.

"Oh, my gosh." Her eyes snapped open. "This is amazing. Have you tried this?"

I had no idea what she was talking about because I had no idea what she'd put in her mouth.

"I can't wait to see what's for dessert."

I seriously hoped I was on the menu.

Chapter 6

Shane

Half an hour later, I was ready to climb the walls to get to the door.

I'd spent the last half hour talking to Cary, who'd been true to his word. They hadn't mentioned hockey once. Instead, they'd been tasting and discussing the new beers Lori was considering adding to the taps in the bar she ran.

Well, Cary was talking. I was pretending to listen but was really obsessing over Bliss, who was talking to Lori.

Until a few seconds ago when she turned to me with a smile as Lori walked in the opposite direction.

Now I fucking ached.

And beside me, Cary laughed under his breath, like he knew exactly what I was thinking. He probably did.

"Have a good night, Shane." Cary clapped me on the shoulder and gave me a little shove in Bliss' direction. "Call me tomorrow and let me know you survived. I'll let you know about the ice time."

I held onto my manners long enough to say thanks to Cary before I walked to Bliss' side.

When she looked up at me and her lips curved in a smile, I swore everyone else in the room vanished.

"Do you want to come back to my place for a drink?"

I wanted to smack myself on the forehead for just blurting that out but at least I hadn't been stupid enough to add "and hot monkey sex" to the end of that question.

Yeah, it's exactly what I hoped would happen but still. Three hours of foreplay had given me a massive case of perma-erection and I knew exactly how I wanted to lose it. Buried deep inside Bliss.

My hands itched to touch her and I practically had to bite my tongue so I wouldn't lean down and kiss her. Like I'd been fantasizing about for the past hour.

And then I'd strip her down to her skin and—

"Would you like to leave now?"

Bliss' quiet question and her slight smile hit me low in the gut and nearly made me groan.

Holy fuck. I wasn't sure I'd make it all the way back to my place without embarrassing the hell out of myself.

This girl brought out something in me I wasn't sure I could control. And I was all about control. It's what made me a good goalie.

But I'd loosen the reins a little if it meant she came home with me.

"Or," she continued, "we can wait—"

"I'm ready to leave whenever you are." Damn but her smile slayed me. "Do you want to follow me?"

"Sure. That'd be great."

I wanted to pump my fist in the air. "Great. Just let me say goodbye to Lori."

She put her hand on my arm and my pulse thumped through

my veins. "We can do that together. Let me get my coat and purse. Be right back."

Ten minutes later, she followed behind my truck in her little red Jeep Renegade and I had to keep from speeding the entire way. The drive wasn't long but I kept looking in the rearview mirror to make sure she was still there.

By the time we parked in the lot behind my building, I had clenched my jaw so tight, I was afraid it'd crack.

With my roommate home in Ottawa for the holidays, we'd have the place to themselves. Luckily, CJ was anal about everything and I had learned to be a little less of a mess while we'd been living together this season. So, the apartment wasn't in bad shape.

And I'd actually changed the sheets on my bed yesterday. How was that for blind dumb luck?

Stepping out of her car, Bliss shivered a little as she put her hand on my arm as we walked to the building's entrance.

"My car didn't even have time to warm up on the drive," she said. "You're probably used to the cold, aren't you?"

"Pretty much. When you spend as much time on the ice as we do, this is nothing."

"When did you start playing hockey?"

I opened the door to the building and waved her in ahead of me. "Honestly, I don't remember a time when I wasn't on skates. My mom says I was born with them strapped to my feet. Where I grew up, you either skated or you spent a hell of a lot of time cooped up inside from November 'til April."

"So you've played all your life?"

A short walk down the hall to my apartment and I had the door open as I answered.

"Never wanted to do anything else. I love the game."

She slipped by me as I reached inside to turn on the light. "I don't know much about the game."

"I'll teach you whatever you want to know."

She stopped just inside the door as I continued into the living room, shrugging out of my coat so I could put it in the small closet next to the kitchen.

"My own personal player. Hmm, I think I'd like that."

The husky tone in her voice made my head snap around to her.

"What do you want to know? Ask me anything."

"Well, now." Her eyes widened. "That's almost too good to pass up."

The teasing note in her voice, combined with that private little grin, made another shiver run up my spine.

"What do you want to know?"

Her head tipped to the side, as if she were thinking. "Do you enjoy what you do?"

Too easy. "Love it. It's all I've ever wanted to do."

"That's amazing. So many people have jobs they hate just so they can eat. But you get to do what you love."

Something in her voice made me ask, "Don't you enjoy what you do?"

She shook her head as she unbuttoned her coat. "Oh, don't get me wrong. I love working for my aunt. And I love what I do. It's just…"

I walked back to take her coat, trying not to salivate as she stripped it off. "What?"

She shrugged, drawing my gaze down to her chest. Then I gave myself a figurative slap upside the head and dragged my gaze back up.

"It's kind of isolating." She shrugged. "It must be nice knowing you've got an entire team at your back."

I laughed. Couldn't help myself. "Well, it's kind of like having this huge family of brothers. You spend so much time together that you get to know everybody really well. That also means you get to know them *too* well. We've got a good group of guys this season but there's always a few, you know? The ones you want to strangle when they tell the same damn joke for the thousandth time. Or is always borrowing something and never returning it. And they all know just what to do to get under your skin."

Her smile made my cock twitch. "*That* I totally understand. I have a big family and there are days I want to strangle them all and days I wouldn't know what to do without them. It's tough growing up with four older brothers."

She seemed to want to say something else but never finished.

"Were you ever able to date? I figure with that many brothers, they'd scare off anyone who tried."

I waved her toward the couch. She took the hint and sat, toeing off her shoes before curling her feet under her legs.

"My two older brothers were away at college when I started dating and my younger brothers… well, they had their own stuff to deal with. But my dad… He used to be a cop. Want to get rid of a guy fast? Have your dad tell your date he'll throw his ass in jail if he dared lay a hand on me. Of course, when I told my mom, she read him the riot act. After that, he just glared at every guy I brought home and then my mom would do something to distract him. They're pretty much the perfect couple. Always have been."

I laughed. "Yeah, my parents were pretty freaking perfect, too. My mom worked at home so she was always there. Dinner on the table every night, homemade cookies after practice. My dad worked days at the paper plant so he coached all of my teams from the time I was five until I went to high school."

"Sounds like the American dream."

I grimaced at how perfect it'd been. "Yeah. I can look back on it now and know that but back then… Man, it felt like I never had a minute to myself."

She propped her arm on the back of the shoulder and rested her head on her hand. "Do you have siblings?"

"Younger brother and sister. Twins."

But I'd been the focus of my parents' life for seven years

before my mom had gotten pregnant again. And when it'd become evident that I had enough talent to actually make a career out of hockey, my parents had done everything they could to get me where I needed to be.

"My brother plays too but my sister spent most of her childhoods in hockey rinks and doesn't play. She's actually a damn good ice skater but…"

"But what?"

She sounded genuinely interested and I couldn't not answer.

"Sometimes I think my parents invested a little too much time into me and my sister got the short end of the stick."

"Has she ever said that?"

Bliss' voice held a sweet concern that made me want to kiss her.

"No. But I still wonder."

"Does she still skate?"

I shrugged. "Not a lot. She's in college. Going for her veterinarian's degree."

My brother and I teased Giselle relentless about the fact that she was the only one of them to go to college. But I was damn proud of her.

"Sounds like a smart girl."

"She is."

"So if she'd wanted to skate, she would've found a way. Right?"

A grin caught me off guard. Giselle wasn't the only smart woman I knew, apparently.

"Probably, yeah. She's always known how to get what she wants. Guess she had to with two brothers."

"What about you, Shane? Do you get what you want?"

I thought about how shitty I'd been playing lately, about how I was letting down my team. About the fact that she'd agreed to come home with me.

"Not always, no. But I hope I will tonight."

And there was her smile again. "I don't think you have to worry about that."

Grinning, I shook my head. "I love that you're not afraid to say what's in your head."

She shrugged. "No one should be."

"You're absolutely right. I'd much rather hear you speak your mind than not say anything at all."

I swore I felt the heat of her smile as she leaned closer and laid her hand on my arm, muscles bunching at her touch.

"Then let me tell you how much I look forward to kissing you." Her head tilted to the side. "And touching you. And… anything else that might come up along the way."

Chapter 7

I pulled back far enough that I could see Shane's face in the room's low light. Saw the deep breath he sucked in and the way his throat convulsed as he swallowed. Then he ran one hand through his dark, shaggy waves and I wanted to do the same. I knew it'd feel like silk against my skin.

"Great. That's great." He paused, frowned, then shook his head like he was trying to get something to fall back into place. "I just don't want you to think I'm trying to take advantage of you."

Wow, was he for real? He seemed too damn sweet. Not at all what I'd been expecting. Not that that was a bad thing. But it made me wonder if I was starting to come off a little too strong.

Then I looked into his eyes and saw an inferno of lust. And realized Shane was the real deal. An actual, genuinely nice guy.

I'd begun to believe they were pure myth.

My thighs clenched and I sucked in air, suddenly finding it hard to breathe.

Holy hell, when had the temperature risen to the point that I wanted to start shedding clothes? Okay, maybe I just wanted him to start shedding clothes.

But first I needed to ask him a very important question. "What if I want you to take advantage?"

That heat in his eyes burned even brighter and the wry grin that curved his beautiful mouth made my thighs clench.

"Maybe I'd rather you take advantage of me."

Oh, yes, please. I could *so* work with that.

As his bright blue eyes narrowed to slits and his mouth flattened into a straight line, I swore I felt sexual intensity coming off me like heat.

Then he moved closer and, as I had to crane my head to look up at him, I realized just how much bigger he was. Broader and heavier and more muscled.

But I felt no fear. I knew instinctively this man wouldn't harm me. Of course, if I asked him to slap his hand across my ass…

Oh hell, just thinking about it made heat flush across my cheeks.

What would he say if I asked him? Maybe he didn't do kinky? Not that spanking was really kinky but——

Fuck it.

Reaching for him, I wrapped my hands around his neck and pulled him forward, meeting him halfway and pressing my lips against his.

I needed him to have no doubt about what I wanted. That I wanted whatever he had to give.

And when he kissed me back, I realized not only was he a really good kisser, but what I'd thought was shyness was really reserve. And I'd just given him permission to release his restraints.

His hands wrapped around my shoulders, tight but not threatening. And it definitely didn't hurt. But he wasn't going to release me unless I asked.

My heart beat just a little faster.

So strong. So…demanding.

With a soft moan, I shifted closer as his mouth opened over mine and his tongue slid between my lips.

I might've been the one to initiate the kiss but I realized I wouldn't be the one who controlled it. I was okay with that. Totally okay.

With a sigh, I tilted my head so he could kiss me more deeply. He didn't need any more encouragement than that.

His kiss became more intense, threatened to burn. Heat flashed through me, making my nipples tighten and my thighs clench.

His tongue slid against mine, tangling with mine. No teasing, no hinting. Just flat-out demand.

Shane had gone straight from zero to a hundred in record time.

And though I didn't have a problem with that, it took a few seconds for my body to catch up. To allow him to take control

And when I did…

My lungs froze as his lips moved over mine with a skill I hadn't expected. A skill that made my brain fuzzy when he stroked his tongue along mine then sucked with a sexy demand that made me want to agree to anything he asked.

How had that happened? How had he gone from slightly awkward and adorable to hot and demanding?

And honestly…who cared? Especially when lust thrummed through my body, making my sex slick with desire and… Holy hell, when had he flattened those huge hands across my back to urge me closer?

I felt each finger through my shirt as he pressed them into my skin. He wasn't hurting me but I certainly wasn't going anywhere unless he allowed it.

Oh my god, did I love that.

Wrapping my arms around his neck, I arched my back, mashing my chest against his, trying to ease the ache in breasts. I wanted him to put his hands on them and squeeze, not to hurt, just…

God, I *hurt*.

With a little moan, I rose to my knees, cursing my tight skirt. I couldn't spread my legs without rutching up my skirt and I couldn't do that without actually reaching down and pulling it up.

Maybe he'd just tear the damn thing off of me.

My heart began to double-time and it got harder to breathe as his hands began to move.

Stroking down my back with a heavy hand, he cupped my ass in his palms and pulled.

I had a second to wonder if my skirt was going to split at the seams before he leaned back and took them horizontal. Without releasing my mouth.

The man was talented. He stole my breath and never gave me time to regain it. His hands never stopped touching me, cupping me, molding me.

Not a shy bone in his body now. Which just meant I couldn't think straight.

Especially not when lying flat-out on top of him and feeling his impressive erection pressed against my stomach.

Wow.

I wanted to slip my hands in his pants and wrap my fingers around him but I'd have to maneuver to get a hand between us and I didn't want to distract him from…whatever spell he was weaving over my body.

His hands seemed to be everywhere. Stroking down my back, petting my ass, sinking into my hair to twist my head a certain way so he could kiss me harder, hotter. A lot harder.

I wanted to move. I didn't want to move. I wished we could get rid of our clothes and skip to the good part.

Although there definitely wasn't anything wrong with this part.

He kissed me like he was starved for me. Like he couldn't get enough and I was the only person in the world who could give it to him.

His intensity threatened to overpower me. Stole my breath and sapped my will to move. It'd be so easy to give him the control he wanted.

But it wasn't in my nature.

I began to battle my way back to the surface. Not fighting him but slowly giving more than I was getting.

When his tongue retreated the next time, I followed him, flicking against his teeth and teasing him until I heard him groan.

His hands smoothed over my ass then cupped me and held me to him so he could thrust against me. Hard. As if he could penetrate me through our clothes.

A split second later, he released me and pulled away.

"Shit, I didn't— Sorry. I mean— *Fuck.*"

The heated look on his face made my pelvis rock against his.

I slide my hands up his body to cup his jaw, the stubble rough and enticing beneath my palms. "Don't be. Please don't be sorry. Trust me, I'm right here with you."

I watched him swallow hard, his eyes narrowing slightly. Had I come on too strong?

Then his mouth curved in that little grin again and I swore my bones went liquid. Or at least, I did between my thighs.

In the next second, he twisted our bodies in a move I couldn't quite follow, his body so incredibly agile.

I found myself on my back looking up at him, slightly stunned. Not frightened. Too turned on to be frightened.

But damn, the guy was big. He blocked out everything. The light. The surroundings. Made me feel as if I was the only thing in his world right now.

Sweet heaven.

And when his head descended to kiss me again, I met him

halfway, his mouth crushing against my lips in a clash of teeth and tongues.

Shoving one hand into his hair and winding my fingers around the almost-shoulder-length strands, I held him close, sucking in air through my nose as our tongues dueled.

God, I could do this for hours. Just let him kiss me until I honestly thought I might pass out from a lack of oxygen. I'd never been with a guy who could kiss this well.

Where the hell had he learned to do this? And was he just as talented in other areas?

The thought hit me like a punch to the gut as he began to gentle the kiss, withdrawing his tongue until finally he pulled away.

Propped on his elbows, he stared down at me. Those bright blue eyes, so intent and focused on me, made me want to pet him. All over. While he was naked.

"If I'm moving too fast, just smack me, okay?"

No way. "If you were moving too fast, my knee would be in your groin. I told you I grew up with four older brothers, right?"

His gaze narrowed. "Yeah, you did." He paused and he got a look in his eye that made me want to lick his throat. Or anywhere I could reach. "So if I ask if I can take your clothes off, am I gonna find your knee somewhere I don't want it?"

Letting my hands stroke from his shoulders to his waist, I began to pull his shirt out of his waistband as I smiled up at him.

"No. I don't want to…damage you. In any way."

There was that blush again, the one that made me grin. Then he wove one of his hands through my hair and tugged. Not enough to hurt. Just enough to make my sex clench.

"I'm pretty tough. I can take a lot of damage."

Heat flashed through me as I thought about just what he could do with that body. "I have no doubt."

With his shirt separated from his pants, I slid my hands under the fabric to press against his sides, just above the waistband of his pants.

The definition of his muscles made my fingers itch to bare him completely.

While he held himself above me on stiff arms, I reached for the buttons of his dress shirt.

Before I started, though, I glanced up and had to swallow at the lust defining the sharp angles of his face.

Oh my.

I'd never been the recipient of that much pure desire from anyone. Ever. It was intoxicating. It made me want to strip naked and give him free rein.

Dangerous. Way too dangerous.

Why? It wasn't like I was going to marry the guy. I was going to have hot sex for one night.

"I think you need to take your clothes off now."

His only outward response to my husky demand words was the ripple of his throat as he swallowed. Then he pushed up onto his knees above me and went to work on his shirt buttons.

My fingers actually twitched to help him but I kept them curled into the couch cushions. I'd never seen anything as sexy as this man taking off his shirt to reveal the amazing body beneath.

Wide shoulders, broad chest bulky with muscle. Freaking washboard abs that would've made an underwear model salivate.

But this man was no model. His collar bone showed the long scar of an incision and he had a bruise on his left arm that covered most of his bicep and another just above his right hip.

"Do those hurt?"

His gaze never left mine. "Does what hurt?"

I reached out to trail my fingers just above the bruise on his hip. He looked down, watching with narrowed eyes as I barely touched him.

"No." His voice held a deep note of control that made me want to whimper. "But I'll show you what does."

I swallowed convulsively as his hands dropped to the waist-band on his pants then flashed him a grin when he stopped after popping the button.

"Do you need some help?"

His eyes narrowed and I had to suck in a quick breath before I started to pant. "I'd say yes but it might derail my plans."

"And what plans are those?"

"Making you come at least twice before I get inside you."

Holy shit. Adrenaline drop-loaded into my bloodstream and my lips parted but nothing emerged. I was at a loss for words and that didn't happen often. If he knew me better, he'd know just how amazing my silence was.

That thought was obliterated a second later when he pulled down the zipper and shoved his pants off his hips.

I had a quick glimpse of his thick, rock-hard erection before he reached for my shirt and began to pull it up my body.

As I wiggled beneath him to help get the shirt over my head, I had a quick second to think, *Damn, I'm glad I wore the green satin bra and panty set this morning.*

And if the look on Shane's face was anything to go by, he liked it, too.

Then he bent and put his mouth on the exposed curve of my upper left breast, pressing kisses along the lace-edged cup before opening his mouth over the thin satin covering my nipple and sucking it into his mouth.

My back arched as I gasped, the sensation so sharp, all of my muscles tensed. I reached for his head, sliding my fingers into his hair to hold him to me. The soft strands felt like silk against my palms and I wanted to rub my cheek against the crown of his head. Or better yet, have him brush the longer strands against my breasts, my stomach. The inside of my thighs.

Sucking in much needed air, I pressed his head closer. Shane took direction well. He bit at me, laved my nipple though the material then blew a cool breath across it to make it pucker.

He moved to do the exact same thing to my other nipple and, for the next several minutes, proceeded to drive me more than a little crazy.

With my other lovers—at least the ones after I'd broken up with my ex—I'd been the one in control. Maybe I'd unconsciously chosen men who allowed me to be in control.

Maybe it wasn't that unconscious.

But not Shane. He had his own plan, apparently, and I was more than happy to go along with it.

His tongue flicked at my nipples, which I'd never considered all that sensitive. Tonight…they ached with sensation, almost painfully. I squirmed so much, I realized he'd moved his hands to my ribs to hold me down.

I liked that. Oh, hell, I liked that a lot.

And when he began to kiss his way down my body, my hands dropped to his shoulders. Just to make sure he didn't stray.

But Shane had a definite purpose in mind.

His fingers didn't fumble at all with my skirt, just slid down the zipper with a move so smooth I had a second to wonder if I got a lot of practice.

Then he tugged on the skirt and had it down around my ankles in seconds. Now all I wore were a pair of barely there panties and my bra. And a smile.

A really big smile as he pulled a condom out of the wallet he grabbed out of his pants, still hanging around his hips.

"I'm gonna take these off now." He stuck the fingers of his right hand in the string holding the two sides of my panties together and tugged. I had to lift my bottom to help him get them off, my feet braced on his thighs until he had them down around my ankles.

As soon as he'd dropped them, I reached for him. Wrapped my hand around his cock and stroked him.

His eyes closed as I pumped him from root to tip. Damn, he

was thick. Not stubby, though. Just long enough. Mouth-watering. Perfect.

A smile curved my lips and I watched his gaze narrow as he leaned forward, planting his hands on the cushions just above my shoulders.

His lips were close enough that I could lift my head and kiss him. And I could tell that's what he expected.

Instead, I leaned back…and lifted my hips to brush the tip of his cock against my labia.

His jaw clenched, eyes narrowing until I could barely see any blue at all. I loved the feel of his hot flesh against mine, could have teased him for the next hour at least.

Or not. Because when he deliberately slipped the tip between labia, my brain short-circuited. I arched my back and sought to get him deeper.

Instead, he pulled away and pushed back up onto his knees.

Moaning, I reached for his hips but he leaned back, out of my grasp. And made sure I watched as he rolled the condom down his length.

His intense focus made my lungs struggle for air. I'd never had another man affect me like this. It was almost too much to take.

I wanted to close my eyes, take back a little bit of control, but I didn't want to break the connection between us.

So I saw the way his expression tightened when he leaned forward again and rubbed the tip of his cock against my clit. Biting back a moan, I reached for his forearms, fingers digging into taut muscles as the ache between my legs built.

My hips rose to meet his and his lips covered mine again for a kiss that fuzzed my brain.

I needed him inside, to fill the aching void and make me come.

But the damn man wouldn't move.

Not that his kisses weren't amazing. They were. I just needed more.

Sliding my hands up his arms as he worked his mouth over mine, I stopped for a few seconds to pet his shoulders before gliding down his back.

His skin heated beneath my palms, so smooth. And then I had my hands on his ass. Jesus, the man had muscles everywhere.

As my hands smoothed down to his thighs then back up again, teasing closer to the seam splitting his cheeks, I felt his groan rumble in his chest as his hips rocked forward.

Yes, that's what I want.

Hands on his hips, I tugged him closer. Or tried to. The man was immoveable.

With a moan, I pulled away from his lips, one hand rising to sink into his hair. I tugged, not hard enough to hurt but enough to get his attention.

Or so I thought.

Apparently when Shane was set on a course, he didn't falter.

Instead of pulling back, he bent to put his mouth on my neck. He laid a string of kisses down my neck to my collarbone then followed that to my shoulder. And then he bit me.

The sting made me gasp and lit my entire body on fire, a blazing hot lust eating me up from the inside. And then I felt his fingers rubbing between my thighs, testing my readiness.

If I was any more ready, I'd be really freaking embarrassed.

"Oh my god. Shane."

"I like hearing you say my name. Do it again."

"Shane, please."

"I think I want to hear you scream it."

Which I did when he pulled his hand away. But he immediately replaced it with his cock and slid inside, fast and hard and all the way.

My scream wasn't exactly his name but he must've been satisfied because he gave me exactly what I wanted. What I needed.

His hips thrust with a controlled speed that teased the possibility of more, even if I didn't think I was capable of taking any more.

I already felt wound too tightly but unable to get off.

Because Shane kept me on the edge. Every time I thought I might come, he adjusted his pace or the angle to keep me on the brink.

He'd lowered his body until we were pressed together but his height meant my face was pressed against his shoulder so he had to hold himself up on one elbow so I didn't suffocate.

Not that I would've noticed. And I was too far gone to care.

I came with a shudder and a moan, my teeth sinking in his pec as he rode me through it.

Only when I'd gone limp beneath him did he thrust one last time before holding still and letting his cock pump inside me.

Several minutes later, still panting, he wrapped his arms around me.

"Next time, you're on top."

Next time? Oh god, please let that be soon.

He kept his word.

Chapter 8

Shane

I woke the next morning—

No, wait.

I peeled open my eyes and looked at the clock. One in the afternoon.

Damn, how the hell had I slept so late?

Duh, asshole. A few drinks and about five hours of the best sex of your whole frickin' life, that's how.

Luckily, I didn't have a hangover, which was kind of amazing, because I was a lightweight when it came to alcohol.

But, holy hell, I was wiped. If I could, I'd go back to sleep but now that I was awake, I knew that wouldn't happen.

Why hadn't she stayed?

With a groan, I sat up, glancing over at the empty space beside me. The pillow she'd used still had an indent from her head. She'd left sometime after that last round when she'd climbed on top of me and made my eyes roll back in my head. Which had been after the two times I'd made her scream.

So why the hell hadn't she stayed for breakfast?

Sliding my legs off the side of the bed, I ran a hand through my hair, adjusted my morning wood out of habit so it wasn't poking through my shorts, and headed for the bathroom across the hall before making my way down the stairs to forage for food. I was fucking starving.

And I wished like hell I was eating something other than bagels and peanut butter, two pears and a half gallon of chocolate milk. What I wouldn't give to be sliding down her body and putting my mouth over her—

My cock throbbed.

Fuck.

With a sigh, I lifted the chocolate milk container to my lips, practically able to feel my mom's hand smacking me on the back of my head.

Why the hell had she snuck out?

She hadn't seemed like the kind to fuck and run. Then again, I didn't know her. Like…at all.

Hey, dude. I could practically hear CJ's voice in my head. *You got laid. She saved you the hassle of getting rid of her this morning.*

The problem was, I wasn't a dick who would've smacked her on the ass, said thanks for the great night and called her a taxi.

No, I would've made her breakfast or at least taken her out to eat before saying, "Can I get your number? I'd like to see you again."

Because, yeah, I really wanted to see her again.

Who wouldn't want to see her again? She'd rocked my fucking world last night. Of course, I wanted to do it again. And again.

Maybe she doesn't want to see you again.

A very real possibility.

Bliss had her shit together, had a life and a career and didn't move every six months or so to whatever team needed a goalie that particular day. This stint with the Redtails had been the longest in my career. I'd actually allowed myself to think maybe I'd finally found a niche where I could prove myself. And I had been. Until I'd hit this slump—

My cell phone rang and I grabbed for it, hoping…

Nope.

Shit.

"Hey, Cary." I forced myself to sound normal. And probably failed miserably. "What's up?"

A slight pause. "Just wondering if you're up for a few drills today."

I wanted to groan. Wanted to crawl back to bed and spend a few more hours wallowing. Which was stupid.

"Yeah, sure. That'd be great."

Cary laughed. "I can tell you're really into it. Long night?"

"Uh…" What the hell did I say to that?

Now Cary really started to laugh. "How 'bout we forget I asked that question and you meet me in an hour on the ice. Then you can tell me all about it."

A grin pulled at my lips. "What are you, now? My priest?"

Cary snorted. "Worse. I'm your fucking captain. Get your ass to the arena."

Forty-five minutes and a fifteen-minute shower later, I parked beside Cary's truck in the side lot and walked to the door where Cary waited for me.

The guy had a shit-eating grin on his face that made me want to punch him.

"Well, you look like you can walk okay, but can you skate?"

I gave Cary the finger as I walked by him into the lower level of the arena, headed for the locker room. There was enough light to see where I was going but I spent enough time here that I could do this walk blindfolded.

"Still faster than you, old man. And who gave you a key to the arena? I can't believe management's letting just the two of us use the ice."

"Called in a favor. Besides, it's not that big a deal. That ice show's coming in tomorrow and they're gonna be using the ice to practice. So no big deal."

"Sweet."

We walked the last few yards to the locker room in silence. I had been expecting Cary to cross examine me about last night, but surprisingly, he didn't way a word. And when I stepped out on the ice to warm up, Cary still in the locker room gearing up, I felt my muscles relax as I made a few circuits around the boards.

Yes.

I sucked in a deep breath, drawing in the cold air rising off the ice. Just the feel of the smooth surface under my blades and the sound they made as I circled the rink was enough to drop my blood pressure. Always had been. I stepped onto the ice and it felt like home.

Having the ice to myself, even for these few seconds, was like being in my own private paradise.

My mom had always complained that hell wasn't hot. Hell was cold.

I didn't have an opinion on that but I did know the cold helped me feel things more intensely and see things more clearly.

"So, you have a good time last night? At dinner."

Cary matched his pace to mine but I kept my gaze forward.

"Yeah, the food was great. Thanks again for inviting me. Really appreciate the home-cooked meal."

"You left with Bliss."

"Yeah."

No way was I adding more. Cary was a friend but Bliss was friends with Lucy. I wasn't about to diss Bliss. No fucking way. And I couldn't bring myself to drill Cary for information.

Besides, I didn't fuck and tell like some of the team. A few of the guys were worse than high school kids the morning after a date, spouting off about shit I never wanted to know. At least, not and be able to look the girl in the eyes the next day.

"Everything…okay?"

I shot my teammate a look. Cary sounded worried about something.

"Yeah." I frowned. "Wait, why? Did Bliss—"

"Nope." Cary held up his free hand. "Not why I'm asking. Lucy hasn't heard from her. I'm just…kinda worried about you."

Okay, this conversation was heading off the rails fast. "What the hell?"

Cary shrugged. "Never mind. So, you ready to do some work?"

Because I didn't want to talk about what'd happened, at least not yet, I grabbed my helmet and stick from the bench and headed for the goal.

For the next half hour, Cary and I ran through a series of drills meant to increase my acuity.

Cary was one hell of an offensive defenseman so he was no stranger to scoring goals and he got a few by me early, which just frustrated the hell out of me.

Cary skated in from the left circle, where he'd scored his last one. "You're leaving that top corner open every time. You gotta get that glove up."

I swung my stick from side to side, clearing the ice out of the crease. "I know." Frustration made my tone sharp. "It's always been one of my weaknesses."

"Then we'll work on it until it's not. But you gotta retrain your brain so you're not constantly thinking about that as a weakness."

For another twenty minutes, that's all we worked on until I knew I was gonna have to ice my right shoulder for the rest of the fucking week.

But by the time we headed for the showers, I thought I might actually have a little better handle on that corner.

"Hey, thanks, man. I really appreciate you taking the time for this."

I was already dressed while Cary pulled on his jeans. I was ready to leave but couldn't force myself to get off the bench and head for the door.

I'd been able to keep Bliss out of my head for the past hour while Cary and I had been on the ice but now…

Fuck, now I was having to bite my tongue to keep from asking about her.

"All right, Shane." Cary finally lifted his head, a wry grin on his lips. "Spit it out. You should know by now that nothing you tell me goes anywhere."

I knew it. It was part of the reason Cary had the trust of every guy on the team.

But damn, I hated the fact that I was gonna come out of this looking like a dick. I must've done something wrong for her to sneak out in the middle of the night.

But since I didn't even know how to get in touch with her and I didn't want to put her on the spot by walking into the shop where she worked…

"Can you give me Bliss' number. I didn't get it last night and I want to call her."

Okay, that didn't sound too creepy stalkerish. I hoped.

"I thought you left with her."

I forced myself to hold Cary's steady gaze.

"I did. But she left before I could ask for it."

Cary's brows lifted slightly. "Any reason for that?"

My back straightened. "No. I thought… No."

Now Cary nodded. "I knew that, Shane. Just had to ask. Yeah, I can get her number for you. Let me text Lori."

I almost bit my tongue through, trying not to ask the next question. But finally, I couldn't help myself. "So is she seeing someone?"

"Do you think she would've left with you if she were?"

Fuck. "No. Shit. It's just…" Jesus, what could I say that wouldn't make me seem even more like an ass? I sighed. "You know what? Never mind. She left while I was sleeping, didn't leave me a number. If she wants to see me, I guess she knows how to find me."

Now Cary started to laugh. "Damn, kid. How the hell do manage to be so damn clueless?" He whipped out his phone and started to text. "Hang tight. I'll get you the number. Then you need to call her. And Shane?"

"Yeah?"

Now Cary looked serious as all hell. "We're heading into the stretch. Don't let anything fuck with your focus."

Shit. "You don't think I should call her?"

Cary's shit-eating grin made a return. "I think you'd be an idiot not to. And you're no idiot."

Chapter 9

Bliss

"I can't believe you didn't leave him your phone number? What the hell were you thinking?"

I groaned between sips of my too-hot coffee, which I needed to mainline if I was going to be any good today.

"I wasn't thinking. Remember? Too much mind-blowing sex. My brain was stuck somewhere between 'Oh my god, I'm never going to get any sleep tonight and be worthless tomorrow' and 'Oh god, I want to stay all night and lick his pecs.' I mean, come on, my brain wasn't exactly functioning correctly. Not after he—"

Faith Donovan took one hand off the arm of her wheelchair and held it in the air. "Nope. Don't wanna hear it again. The first time was more than enough."

Grimacing, I fluffed the skirt of Faith's wedding dress hanging on the stand, waiting for its big day, which happened to be tomorrow.

A Christmas Eve wedding. Just thinking about it made me teary.

Too bad the groom—

Nope, not going there.

"Sorry, sorry. But now I don't know what to do. Should I ask Lori for his number? I mean, I snuck out of his apartment like I was embarrassed to be there. He probably thinks I'm a bitch. Or worse, he doesn't care and was happy I left and didn't have to deal with the morning-after bullshit."

"From what you were telling me about him, that doesn't sound like something he'd do. But I never met him so…" Faith shrugged and sipped her own coffee.

"I know. *Ugh.* Maybe I just have to let this one go. I mean, last night was amazing but I know from talking to Lori that these guys are always on the move. The good ones barely ever stay in one place more than a few months. And from what I've heard, Shane's good enough for an NHL slot. He won't be here long."

Faith's eyebrows rose. "Sounds like you've been doing some online creeping."

A sigh as I picked up Faith's veil from the chair and hung it on the rack with her dress. "Maybe a little. Just to depress myself even more." With a huff, I sank into the seat across from Faith. "All right, no more. So, is everything ready for tomorrow night?"

Faith laughed, though I swore I heard a little strain that hadn't been there before.

"You've met my mom so you know the answer to that."

I had met Faith's mom, Shelly, at the same time I'd met Faith. A year ago, just after Faith had gotten her chair. My shop had been the third one Faith and Shelly had visited. Faith had been near tears but unwilling to give up in pursuit of the perfect dress. Shelly had been ready to strangle the next person who treated Faith like an invalid.

I had shaken their hands, asked Faith her size and started to pull out dresses, never once mentioning that they could be altered to take her "condition" into consideration.

Faith had smiled and Shelly had burst into tears. And I had

gained a new friend who didn't let her disability define her. Something I had a little experience with.

"So then everything's been checked at least five times."

"You know it." And there was that look on Faith's face again. "I just…"

I set my coffee cup on the table and leaned forward, concerned. "Just what?"

With a shake of her head, Faith smiled. "Jitters. They suck. You know what, I think I do want to hear more about this amazing guy you met last night."

Since Faith was getting married tomorrow, I decided not to push. Every bride had jitters before her wedding. They came with the territory.

"There's really nothing else to tell. Except I think I made a really stupid mistake by not leaving my number."

"It's not like you don't know how to get his."

I rolled my eyes. "Then I look pathetic and, if he really doesn't want to hear from me, then I'm being clingy."

Faith's nose scrunched. "Yeah, I get it. But still, if you want to see the guy again, and I think you do, then get his number. You never know, he could be the one."

And there was that tone in Faith's voice again and I couldn't ignore it this time.

"Hey." I reached over and grabbed Faith's hand. "Is something going on? I mean, other than the fact that you're getting married tomorrow?"

Faith didn't answer right away, wouldn't meet my gaze for several seconds. When she finally did, I knew my friend was having more than jitters.

"I'm afraid Jimmy doesn't want to get married."

I didn't say anything…mainly because I wasn't sure Faith's fiancé deserved her.

I'd only met Jimmy Collins a few times but hadn't been impressed. Yes, he'd stuck by Faith after the accident that had put her in the chair. Faith's spine had been badly damaged, to the point that the doctors had told her she'd never walk again.

But between Faith's will and Shelly's determination, Faith had been working her ass off at physical therapy with the goal of being able to walk down the aisle at her wedding.

I had no doubt Faith would manage it. But I wasn't sure Jimmy was worth that effort from her. Faith needed to walk again for herself. Not because she thought her fiancé would feel better about himself because she could.

And maybe I was being a total bitch to a man she really didn't know. Then again—

No. I was damn good at reading people. And Jimmy Collins didn't deserve this woman. Not one bit. But no way would I ever say that to Faith.

"Why do you think that?"

Faith made a wry grimace. "I'm probably being stupid."

Faith sounded as if she wanted me to agree but I couldn't bring myself to lie, not even to set my friend's mind at rest the night before her wedding. There was still time for Faith to call it off. But it had to be her decision and not something I advocated in any way.

"You're one of the smartest people I know." Actually, Faith was *the* smartest person I knew. She designed rockets for a living, for chrissake.

"Well, I don't feel smart at the moment. I think I've been really, really stupid. Or maybe just blind. He's been so distant lately and I think..." She took a deep breath. "I think he wants to tell me he doesn't want to get married but doesn't know how to say it. And I'm afraid..."

Faith's expression made me want to punch Jimmy right in his perfect nose. The guy had walked away from the accident with barely a scratch. He'd been going too fast for conditions and had sailed off the road around a sharp curve. And then there was the matter of a few drinks at dinner...

Yes, he'd stuck with Faith through her long recovery. But there was just something about the guy that made me want to scratch at him every time he came toward me.

"What are you afraid of?"

Faith's fingers tightened around mine. "That I'm making a horrible mistake."

I practically bit my tongue in half not to speak my mind.

"Why do you think that?"

"He's been…quiet." She paused. "Dismissive."

Bastard. I would cheerfully cut Jimmy's balls off with a dull spoon.

"Have you talked to him about it?"

Faith nodded slowly. "He says everything's fine. And it is. For a little while. And then it's not again. I just…don't know what to think."

I knew exactly what to think. I just couldn't bring myself to say it to my friend's face. Maybe my personal dislike of Jimmy was coloring my judgment. Maybe he really was just having cold feet and everything would be fine.

Maybe…not.

I had made more than one mistake in the past few hours, including sneaking out of Shane's apartment this morning. I didn't want to make a completely horrendous one now.

"I think you need to talk to him again. Tell him exactly what you just told me and see what he says."

Maybe the bastard would actually man up and make things right for this incredible person.

And maybe, just maybe he'd completely screw Faith over. And the I would cheerfully find that spoon.

Faith's lips lifted in a completely fake smile that broke my heart and I tightened my grip on Faith's hand.

"I'm sure I'm just being paranoid. And I guess I should try on my dress one last time."

Which was the reason for Faith's visit today. Her final fitting.

Tomorrow, I would help her dress at the church then attend the wedding and reception as a friend.

"And speaking of tomorrow, did you decide to bring anyone to the wedding?"

I knew Faith had closed the door on our other conversation. And really, what more was there to say?

"I told you not to hold that spot open. I just don't have anyone in my life right now."

Immediately, images from last night popped into my head. Shane, naked and braced over my body on strong arms, his hips pounding against mine, his mouth on my breasts.

Damn. If I wasn't careful, I'd have a hot flash and need to change my panties.

"Uh huh." Faith's tone definitely held a hint of laughter so at least I had been able to lighten my friend's mood. Even if it was at my expense. "I'm thinking maybe you wish there was."

Nope, not touching that. "All right, lady. Let's see—"

My cell rang and my heart gave a little extra thump.

Stupid.

I picked it up, checked the number and didn't recognize it. But that didn't mean anything. I used this as my work number and I got calls all the time from vendors.

Swiping it into voice mail, I refocused all of my attention on Faith. Where it should be. And not on a random hookup that would never go anywhere.

Shane

My call went straight to voicemail and I was all set to end it when I heard her voice.

"Hi there. You've reached With This Ring Bridal Salon. We can't get to the phone right now but we want to help you find that perfect dress. Please leave us a message and we'll call you back."

And damn if I didn't get hard.

So, yeah, I waited through the recorded message, trying to figure out what the hell I should say.

"Uh, hey, Bliss. This is Shane…from last night." Christ, I sounded like a fucking teenager. "I'd like to see you again. I'm free tonight or tomorrow night. Oh wait, tomorrow's Christmas Eve. You're probably busy. I could do the day after Christmas but then I'll be gone for a few days after that. Road trip." Which she probably didn't care about. "Anyway, give me a call. If you want. I had a great time last night."

I cut off before I sounded like even more of an idiot.

So now what?

Blowing out frustrated breath, I pushed away from the dining room table and tried to think of something else to do today that didn't involve sitting in front of a screen alone.

Only a couple of guys from my team were still in the area, including the Russians. Actually, only Vladislav Marchenko was Russian. Jakub Mozik was Czech and got super pissed if you called him Russian. So, of course, they all did.

They held the first-line defensive positions and were pretty much inseparable. Had been since being drafted by the Redtails NHL affiliate, the Philadelphia Colonials, when they were eighteen and sent to the Colonials' ECHL affiliate before being called up to the Redtails last season.

Those two would probably play video games all day, order in pizza and sleep off a couple bottles of vodka. They had the ability to drink men twice their age and size under the table.

Not exactly how I wanted to spend the day.

No, I wanted to spend the day with Bliss.

With a sigh, figured I could at least do something worthwhile.

I hadn't done wash for a couple weeks. Might as well get that out of the way.

So I was in the basement, where I got totally shitty reception, when my phone rang.

I didn't recognize the number at first glance but then my brain kicked in and I started to grin.

"Hey, Bliss. I'm glad you called me back."

"Hi, Sha…How are you do…I was hop…tonight. I know it's…but—"

Shit. The reception down here sucked. I ran for the stairs.

I got to the first floor in time to hear her say, "Shane? Are you—"

"I'm here." I had to take a quick breath because I'd taken the stairs two at a time. At least that's what I told myself. "Sorry. Bad reception in the basement."

She laughed and my cock jerked.

"Is that where you keep the bodies?"

"Only the ones I can't fit in the walls."

She paused and I wanted to smack my head. Jesus, could I be any more of an idiot—

Then she laughed even harder and…

Holy shit, she got my sarcastic sense of humor and didn't think I was a serial killer.

Even more amazing? I didn't feel like a complete ass.

"So," she drew the word out for several seconds, making my heart beat faster in anticipation, "I was wondering what you're doing tomorrow night?"

"Nothing at all." Please, god, let that be what she wanted to hear. Or was that pitiful? Oh wait. It was Christmas Eve. I'd forgotten.

A light huff of laughter came through the line and I hoped like hell she wasn't laughing at my pathetic lack of a life.

"Well, I actually do have something and…I was wondering if maybe you wanted to go with me?"

The question in her voice should've rung a warning bell but I knew I'd do anything she asked, just to spend time with her. Did that make me creepy or pathetic? Or both?

Then she continued. "I've got a wedding tomorrow night and I was wondering if you'd like to go with me?"

My brain short-circuited for a second. "Did you say wedding?"

Her laugh was softer and sweeter this time and made my muscles tighten.

"Yeah. I told you I work in a bridal salon, right? Well, one of my clients is getting married and she invited me to the wedding and I was wondering… Would you like to go with me?"

She wanted me to go with her to a wedding? Like as her date?

My brain kicked into gear, tossing out danger signals.

Take a girl to a wedding and she'll get ideas.

Which was total bullshit.

Dude, you're not that great a catch. Seriously, get over yourself.

"Uh, sure."

Somewhere in Ottawa, my roommate CJ was shaking his head and he had no idea why.

"I mean," she quickly started to talk, "if you have something else, I'd totally understand—"

"No, no. I've got nothing to do. I'd like—love to go with you."

Another pause and then, "Okay, great. That's…good."

I swore I heard a smile in her voice now and that made me smile, too. "So this is a formal thing, right? Suit and tie?"

"Yeah. Oh, is that a problem?"

"Nah. We're required to dress for games. Unless I need a tux. Then you're out of luck."

"Really?"

"Yeah. So what time should I pick you up?"

"I have to be there early to help the bride with her dress."

"No problem. I've got nothing to do and nowhere to be."

"Okay then, can you pick me up at four-thirty? I'll text you the address. The wedding's at six. I told her I'd be at the church by five but I want to be there early."

"Great. I'll see you tomorrow."

"Thanks, Shane."

When the call disconnected, I took a deep breath and couldn't stop grinning.

Bliss

I hung up with a smile.

That was either the stupidest thing I'd ever done or the bravest. Guess I'd find out which tomorrow night.

But…there was something about Shane. Something about how quiet he could be and not seem withdrawn. Or how his humor was a little goofy, a little sarcastic and sometimes just plain weird.

And how I knew all of that just from spending one night with him was weird. And a little scary. And a little exciting.

So I wasn't surprised by the flutter in my stomach. Or the pulse between my thighs because, holy hell, the man had been amazing in bed.

The kind of guy a girl could fall for and who could break her heart.

With a sigh, I tried to shake some sense into my head.

"Completely getting ahead of yourself. It's just sex."

Really great sex. And a seemingly great guy.

Too good to be true.

Weren't they all?

I'd found that out the hard way when I found the man I thought was the one, in bed with another woman.

Oh, Rich had sworn up and down that nothing had happened between him and the ex-girlfriend passed out on his bed. Sworn he'd only allowed her to sleep in his bed because he hadn't wanted her to drive home in her condition.

I had wanted to believe him.

I couldn't. Couldn't bring myself to trust him. Couldn't help feeling like a fool. Apparently I'd been right because when I'd got rid of him, he'd immediately started dating the ex.

So much for trust.

No, Shane would be a great diversion while it lasted. And when he moved on… No harm, no foul. But in the meantime, I'd enjoy the smoking hot sex.

"Liss! Hey, Liss. Guess what?"

I jumped as my door slammed open but smiled when I saw my older brother, Mike, in my living room.

"Hey, Mike. We've talked about knocking before, remember? You're supposed to knock before you come into my apartment. Or anyone else's."

Mike's sweet face screwed up into a frown and I had to bite my tongue against the words that wanted to escape.

But I knew if I said, "Never mind, it's okay," it wouldn't help Mike. The therapist had been crystal clear about that. He'd stressed, when my parents and I had first talked to him about Mike moving into his own apartment, that they had to hold him to the same standards as they would a person who didn't have his disabilities.

Mike had to be held accountable, Dr. Farouk had said.

"Damn. I'm sorry, Lis." He hung his head, ginger hair shades lighter than my own, hanging over his forehead. "I'll remember for next time. I promise."

Now I smiled. "I know you will, bud. Now what's so important you forgot your manners?"

And that fast, his grin returned. My parents swore Mike had taken one look at me after I'd been born and hadn't stopped smiling since. And I'd hadn't known a time when my brother wasn't a fixture in my life.

"My boss told me I'm getting a raise!"

My brother's infectious joy made everything in life just a little brighter.

Throwing my arms open, I hugged my brother tight and said a silent "fuck you" to the few so-called friends who'd told me I was crazy to agree to have my "disabled" brother move in next to me. Mike wasn't disabled. He was differently abled. In my mind, the distinction was huge.

"That's great! I'm so happy for you."

Mike pulled back, but not before putting a smacking kiss on my cheek.

As he told me about his day at the grocery store where he worked, I let myself get caught up in his joy. Since we'd moved into their side-by-side apartments, I'd watched him gain so much confidence.

My parents had never tried to hold him back but even they'd been worried about his plan to move out on his own. But when my former neighbor had told me he needed to sublet his apartment immediately because he'd gotten a new job out of state, I'd gone straight to my parents and Mike.

I'd known Mike would be fine. My parents had taken some convincing but, in the end, Mike had moved in next to me and I'd never regretted the decision.

My ex had never understood why I'd want to "chain" myself to my brother, "with all his problems."

With an internal sigh, I knew that should've been a question I'd asked myself about Rich at the time.

I learned my lesson. Wouldn't make the same mistake twice. You never knew who was going to turn out to be a dick.

I really hoped Shane proved to be the decent guy he seemed
to be.

Chapter 10

Shane

"Seriously? You're going to a wedding with a girl you just met? Are you insane or just stupid?"

I showed off my dexterity by giving Lad the finger without losing my grip on the game controller or getting my character killed.

"Leave the guy alone." Jake knocked his controller against mine in a show of solidarity as we sat on the floor, backs against the couch. "He's obviously taken too many shots to the head. Addled his brain."

With the press of a button, I killed off Jake's character. "Yeah, fuck you, too, Jake."

With a burst of Czech that probably called my parentage into question, Jake tossed his controller over his shoulder to Lad. Jake had no doubt Lad would catch it. The guys were more in sync than an old married couple. It made them a great defensive team on the ice.

"So I take it the sex was amazing." Joey Constantino sat on

the couch beside Lad. "Why else would you subject yourself to a wedding, especially when you won't know anybody there?"

I elbowed Joey's thigh, hard enough for the guy to flinch. "I didn't say anything about sex. And…what the fuck, man? I thought you were on my side."

Joey smirked as he got his character up and running. The wiry forward skated with a blinding speed that totally contradicted his laidback personality.

"I *am* on your side. But not if you're gonna be a total dickhead. You haven't stopped talking about her since you got here. You only met her last night. You got laid. The sex was obviously great or you wouldn't have agreed to go to a wedding with her because, yeah, who goes to a wedding with a girl they just met unless they're expecting more awesome sex?"

Okay, Joey might have a point but still… "Fuck that. I haven't talk about her that much."

Had he?

When the other three guys exchanged a look then started laughing, I wanted to grab the nearest stick and slash the hell out of all of them.

"Yeah, fuck you, assholes. Just because you aren't getting any—"

"Who says we're not getting laid?" Lad punched him on the arm.

I snorted. "You spend most of the time we're not on the ice here playing videogames like twelve year olds."

Jake stuck his elbow in my side. "And aren't you sitting here, right now?"

"Visual acuity exercise."

Joey burst out laughing. "You're so full of shit. You don't have anything better to do than sit around with us. Why didn't you go home anyway?"

I shrugged. Didn't want to admit that I was avoiding my Hallmark parents.

Lad and Jake wouldn't understand. They would've been on the first plane out if they'd had enough time to fly home and get back in time for the next game.

Joey… Well, Joey's parents were a living nightmare so he didn't go home. Ever. He wouldn't understand why I wanted to avoid my perfect family.

"I needed to work on some things and Cary said he'd help. So I stayed. I need the practice."

"Don't sweat the past few games, man." Jake shrugged. "This shit will work itself out."

Jesus, I hoped so. Otherwise… "I just want to stay focused on the game and not get caught up in all the family stuff."

Jake snorted. "And nothing says focus like screwing around with some girl you don't know."

"It's not like that. She's…" Amazing. Sexy. Smart. "Nice."

Silence.

I looked over my shoulder to see Joey staring at me with wide eyes. When I looked at the other guys, they had identical expressions of what-the-fuck.

"What?"

"Nice?" Jake said. "This girl is so *nice*, you told her you would go to a wedding with her?"

Jake's accent got thicker with each word and his blond eyebrows rose until they were hidden by the fringe of pale hair that fell over his forehead.

I shrugged, feeling a little WTF myself over the guys' reaction. "Yeah, she's nice. So what?"

Jake and Lad exchanged a glance then they both looked at Joey, who started to shake his dark head.

"Nice girls are the ones you really have to watch out for, "Joey said. "They'll screw with your head and you'll never know what hit you. Seriously. You should run now. Before you're totally fucked."

I adjusted my tie, grabbed my coat and headed out the door.

For some stupid reason, I was having trouble breathing. It wasn't like I hadn't been on a first date before but it'd been a while. At least six months, maybe more.

Damn, I couldn't even remember. Had to have been after last season, when I'd been home. Couldn't even remember the girl's name. Did that make me a dick? Probably.

Pitiful. Fucking pitiful.

Sliding into my truck, I doubled checked the address Bliss had texted me, took a look at the map to make sure I knew where I was going, then headed out of the parking lot.

My phone rang seconds later and I answered through the truck's Bluetooth system when I recognized the number.

"Hey, what's up?"

"Yo, Brick. We are checked up on you before your date tonight. Jakub and I are planning to get shitfaced and watch… that show. What's that show?"

The last of that sentence had faded, probably because Lad had turned away from the phone to talk to Jake.

"I have no idea what the hell you're talking about." That was Jake, hard to make out because he must have been farther from the phone. "Shane, please come save this asshole's ass before I fucking kill him out of boredom."

Lad responded in Russian, some of which I understood but only the swear words, and then Czech, which I didn't understand at all. And then what sounded like a scuffle.

I started to laugh but the other two guys didn't hear me until at least a minute had passed.

"Bastard laughs at us." Jake's voice, closer to the phone now. "But we are not the ones going to a wedding tonight."

Still laughing, I shook my head. "At least I'll be drinking for free."

"It is not the drinking you go for." Lad's voice got sly.

Very true. "Fuck you, Drac. It's a date. You remember those, don't you? Or are you and Jake still playing with each other on and off the ice?"

Despite the language barrier they'd faced when they'd first arrived in the states three years ago, Lad and Jake had picked up English quick. But they still fell back on their native languages when they wanted to insult you.

So when Jake spouted off something in Czech and Lad started to laugh, I figured I didn't want to know what Jake had said.

"Well, then, fuck you," Jake finally said in English, disgust in his tone. "Ignore your buddies for a slice of ass cake."

"If I had the chance to get some of that," Lad added, "I'd leave you at home, too."

I laughed so hard, my chest started to hurt.

"You two are fucking assholes, you know that, right? You deserve each other."

"Dude, you definitely need to get laid more often." Lad sounded serious now, such an abrupt switch that I had to shake my head. "This will help you get your head out of your own ass. You need some…what's the word?"

"Ass!" Jake yelled from the background again.

"No, not— He's an asshole. Don't listen to him. No. Distraction. You need distraction. So go be distracted. We call you tomorrow. Or maybe you call us if you're not busy, yes?"

Shaking my head and trying not to laugh, I agreed then hung up to the sounds of Jake singing Smoky Robinson's "Let's Get It On." Bastard had a decent voice.

I still had a smile on my face when I pulled up to Bliss' apartment building, which turned out to be a renovated school building on a side street not far from my place.

Since she'd also texted her apartment number, I parked on

the street and buzzed her from the lobby to let her know I was there.

"Bliss, hey—"

"Oh, wow. You're here. Come on up. I just need a minute."

She sounded distracted and maybe a little out of breath and I didn't even get a chance to respond when the intercom cut off and the door buzzed.

I found her apartment on the second floor and knocked, hearing the faintest trace of heels clicking against wood before the door flew open.

My mouth dropped open and my brain literally froze for a second. Then I practically swallowed my tongue.

Holy shit.

"Hi, sorry, I'm running just a minute behind." She took a step back and waved me in, but not before her gaze dropped and she checked me out from head to toe. "Um. You look…great."

I could've sworn her cheeks flushed but she turned away before I could be sure.

One thing I did know…she looked fucking spectacular. If I'd thought she looked edible last night…

Now, I wished like hell we could skip the wedding so I could strip off her dress, throw her over my shoulder and toss her on her bed…wherever that might be.

"I hope you don't mind if we take my car tonight," she called over her shoulder as she hurried toward the back of the apartment. Her legs looked amazingly long in high heels.

The open floorplan allowed me to watch her as she headed for an alcove where a long, white bag hung from the top of an open door.

"I have an SUV so I can lay the dress out in the back and my sewing kit's in there already."

"No problem."

As long as I got to spend time with her, I didn't care how we got where we were going.

With the dress bag now in her hand, she walked back to me with a wry grin. "You're awfully agreeable. Are you always going to tell me yes?"

"I guess it depends on the question." I thought about letting her respond to that but wasn't sure my cock would behave if she started to tease me. "You want me to get the door?"

She blinked and nodded. "Yes. Please. The keys are on the table."

Grabbing the key ring, I opened the door, waited until she walked through, then followed her and locked the door.

Walking behind her down the hall, I marveled at the view.

Jesus, her ass was perfect, outlined in that tight dress.

"You look amazing."

Looking over her shoulder, she smiled, sweet and hot. Christ, I nearly tripped over my own feet.

How the fuck did she do that? How did she make me feel like a fucking teenager, tongue-tied and horny and clumsy?

"Thank you. You clean up pretty well, too. But then I knew that last night."

I would've continued to simply stare at her gorgeous ass as we walked through the building to her car but that'd be a dick move so I looked up—and found my gaze caught on her breasts as she stopped next to her SUV.

I knew how soft those breasts were because I'd had my hands and mouth all over them last night.

Fuck.

I was going to spend the entire night with a hard-on in front of a couple hundred people I didn't know.

Fuck.

And…crap. I'd totally missed what she'd said. Something about how I cleaned up…

"Uh, thanks. We dress for games so…yeah, you get used to wearing suits pretty fast."

"Doesn't hurt that you look good in it."

My turn to smile. I really liked that she wasn't afraid to flirt but didn't come off too abrasive. Basically, I liked everything about her.

A lot of women I'd met after becoming a professional threw themselves at me. I'd felt more like a conquest rather than someone they really wanted to get to know.

"I'd say the same about you," I spoke slowly so she heard every word, "but it wouldn't do you justice."

As I clicked the remote to open the car, she threw another smile my way as she hung the dress on a bar she had rigged beneath the roof. Then she moved to the back, opened the gate and arranged the bag so it looked like a white waterfall.

"Looks like you've done this a few times."

She huffed out a laugh as she closed the door then took the keys I held out to her. "You learn a few tricks. My aunt's been in the business for thirty years."

As she walked back to the driver's side, I walked with her then offered her a hand getting into the car. She looked surprised at first but let me help her in. I'd seen my dad do this a hundred times for my mom, who only stood five-three.

In those heels and that tight dress, Bliss would've had to do some fancy maneuvering to get into that seat. Besides, I got to put his hands on her.

Win-win.

And the smile she gave me—part heat, part sweet—made my gut clench.

"Thank you."

Her tone had dialed down a notch, low and a little husky. And damn, if that didn't make my balls tighten and my cock throb.

Only another six hours of foreplay.

I nodded but before I moved away, she reached out, stroking her fingers along my jaw. I froze, my lungs catching at the sizzle along my nerve endings.

When she let them play across my lips, I couldn't help myself. I opened and bit lightly on the tip of her index finger.

And watched her eyes narrow and darken and her smile turn a little more wicked.

I flicked the tip with my tongue, heard her suck in a sharp breath, then let her slide her finger away.

"I can see you're going to be a handful."

Damn, but her voice made me want to shove her skirt around her hips and put my face between her legs so I could lick her until she came. I hadn't gotten around to that last night. Tonight, it'd be first on my to-do list.

"I know how to behave in public." Then I shrugged. "But all bets are off later."

Chapter 11

Bliss

Maybe I should've packed an extra pair of panties because, oh my god, the man made me wet.

If I hadn't needed to be at the church with the dress, I might've said fuck it and taken him back to my bed. Or maybe we would've gotten as far as the door. I could've pulled up my dress and dropped my panties and he could've undone his belt—

Oh wow.

Sucking in a breath, I pulled my hand away from his mouth, and the tempting scruff on his jaw, and dropped my gaze on the pretense of putting the key in the ignition.

Because I couldn't think of one sane thing to say, I said, "We should get going."

Shane didn't miss a beat. Stepping back, he made sure my dress was safely out of the way of the door before he closed it. My heart gave a serious flutter.

Then he walked around to get in the passenger side, his knees nearly hitting his chin before he adjusted the seat back.

When he buckled himself in, I put the car in gear and headed for the church, trying to ignore the way he took up so much space in my car.

Damn, he was *big*.

Yes, I'd known from being in bed with him last night. But here, now, enclosed in the car together… He took up so much space, it almost felt like there wasn't enough air.

Of course, that could just be from the way I couldn't catch her breath when he was around.

"So is the bride a friend or a client?"

Ridiculously relieved that he'd asked a question I didn't have to think about, I said, "Both, really. I mean, she started out as a client but became a really good friend. She has mobility issues and," *I have a brother with mental disabilities that I'm not going to mention because you could still turn out to be a dick,* "I told her I'd help her get dressed."

"What kind of mobility issues?"

The kind caused by a fiancé who got careless and flipped the car he was driving and crushed Faith's spine.

"She was injured in a car accident and needs a wheelchair."

"Damn, that sucks."

The true emotion in his voice hit me somewhere in the middle of my chest.

"It does. But Faith's amazing. They told her she'd probably never walk again but she's not giving up. I have no doubt she'll be able to get rid of that chair. But for now, she knows she needs it and doesn't take shit or pity from anyone."

"She sounds amazing. Can't wait to meet her. Gotta say I noticed you haven't said anything about the guy she's marrying."

I tried not to grimace and barely managed it.

"He's…fine."

Shane laughed. "Damned by faint praise."

Grimacing, I shot a quick glance at Shane as I stopped for a red light. "Is it that obvious?"

"That you don't like the guy? Yeah, kinda."

I huffed. "Well, the feeling's probably mutual. I just don't think he's good enough for her. Honestly, I'm not sure anyone's good enough for Faith. She's just one of those people, you know? She's almost too good to be true. But she's absolutely the nicest person you'll ever meet. I just think…"

"He's not worthy."

I slid him another look and found him watching me. God, I really hoped I wasn't coming off as a self-righteous bitch. "Yeah. And please, just tell me to shut up. I can't believe I'm bad-mouthing a groom on his wedding day."

"I don't want you to shut up. You can talk all night. I love the sound of your voice."

Oh my god, was he really for real? Every word out of his mouth made me want to pull over, put my car in park and crawl all over him. That suit fit him like a glove, an extra-large glove.

Suit-porn was *so* a real thing.

Shaking my head, I huffed out a laugh. "You're dangerous."

Luckily, I couldn't see his smile but I heard it in his quick laugh. If I'd glanced over at him, I might've driven off the road.

"Glad you think so." A pause. "Be nice if the other teams thought so, too."

I slid him a quick glance. "Why do you say that?"

His shoulders barely moved in a shrug. "Just…having a little trouble lately. I've been—" Another pause. "In a slump."

"What does that mean?"

I heard him suck in a breath and, when I glanced his way again, saw him shake his head, his beautiful mouth a flat line.

"It means I'm letting my team down."

I heard his anger and frustration so clearly, I wanted to soothe him in some way but didn't know him well enough to know how. But I couldn't stop myself from trying.

"Is that why you didn't go home?"

Everything about this man intrigued me and I wanted to know every little thing about him.

Which was foolish. He wouldn't be around long enough for me to get to know him that well. This…whatever we were doing, was just for fun. He wouldn't in Reading forever.

And I certainly wasn't in the market for an emotional attachment to a guy who could pick up and move across the country at the flick of a coach's fingers.

That didn't mean I didn't want him to talk to me.

After a few, long seconds, he finally said, "A little, yeah. I just need some time to think. Get my head straight."

I almost said, "I'm sure you'll be fine," but knew that was bullshit. Sometimes things weren't fine and you needed to work through your issues before they got better. And sometimes they never got better and you just learned to handle them.

So I reached for his hand, resting on his knee, and laced my fingers through his.

"So you thought a Christmas Eve wedding was just the thing to take your mind off your game."

I glanced his way again, made sure he saw me smile.

But he didn't return it. Instead, he stared at me, even after I returned my attention to the road. I felt his gaze on me.

"Actually, you're the one taking my mind off my game. You're a distraction. A good one."

Heat shot through me and I had to suck in air. "Then I'm glad I asked."

"Yeah, me, too."

We fell silent then but we were only a few minutes from the church so it didn't have a chance to get awkward.

By the time I parked, we were a few minutes early but Faith's mom's car was on the street so I parked behind it.

Shane was already waiting at the back of my car.

"You want some help?"

I smiled again. My ex would've watched me struggle with my

purse and the dress and my kit before asking me if I'd needed help.

What the hell had I ever seen in Rich? And why the hell was I even thinking about him now?

Shoving those thoughts aside, I nodded. "If you don't mind, could you grab my kit? And…"

The ultimate test. I held out my clutch with an apologetic grin.

He didn't even blink. Just took it and grabbed my kit.

"Jesus, my gear bag's heavy but it's huge. This thing's half its size and weighs more. What do you have in here? A sewing machine and a weight bench?"

His wry smile made me laugh but I hoped he didn't hear the breathiness in it. Damn him. Every time he smiled at me, my lungs reacted like I'd just finished a marathon.

I wanted to fan my face with my hand. Instead, I reached for the dress.

"I never know what I'm going to need so I make sure I have everything."

"Gotta love a girl who's prepared."

My mouth twisted in a grimace that I quickly wiped away. The last man who'd said something similar hadn't been complimenting me.

Shane's not Rich.

Maybe I should just keep chanting that little mantra for the next few hours.

Especially when I was pretty sure this man had meant it as a tease. A sexy tease.

"I try my best. Besides, I think you can handle it."

I wanted to say something else, something that would make him as hot for me as I was for him but couldn't think of one damn thing. And that wasn't like me. I wasn't usually at a loss for words.

"Nice to know you have faith in me."

That almost stopped me cold because I realized I did. After spending only a few hours talking and a few hours rolling around in bed together, I *did* trust him.

Bad idea.

Telling myself to shut up, I smiled over my shoulder at him and continued into the church.

Since I'd been here before, I knew I'd find Faith in the basement. Faith had decided to get ready in the church instead of arrive dressed. With her chair, there was always the possibility that the dress could get caught in the wheels and that would be a disaster.

Kinda like this wedding.

I really needed to stop with the negativity. It wouldn't do Faith any good and it would only make me feel bad when Jimmy turned out to be a decent guy.

Ha.

"Watch your head," I said as I headed down the stairs.

"Holy— Uh, yeah. You gotta be a hobbit to work here."

Stifling a laugh, I shook my head instead and stopped at the bottom of the stairs to make sure he didn't hurt himself.

When he'd made it out of the stairs in one piece and stood beside me, towering over me in the narrow hall, I met his gaze.

"Thank you."

He shook his head, his mouth curved in a confused grin. "Why?"

"Because you're here."

Chapter 12

Shane

I wasn't exactly sure what Bliss meant but I couldn't miss the sincerity in her voice.

I could've blown her off and told her I had nothing better to do tonight. Which would've been true. I had absolutely nothing better to do tonight than spend it with her. And I didn't mean that this was better than doing nothing.

No, I honestly meant I couldn't think of anything I'd rather be doing than spending the night with her. Even if it meant going to the wedding of two people I didn't know.

But that wasn't something you blurted out to a girl you'd just met. It went against the guy code…whatever the hell that meant.

"Well, I'm here for whatever you need. Just point me in the right direction."

And there was her smile again. The one that made me remember exactly how she'd looked in my bed last night before—

Fuck, I needed to think about something other than her naked body.

"I'm going to take you up on that offer." Then she scrunched up her nose and shook her head. "But not now. Right now, I have to get Faith ready. Let me introduce you and then I'm going to abandon you for about half an hour. Sorry."

"No problem. I know how to amuse myself and not get into too much trouble."

She laughed and my gut tensed. Hell, I might embarrass myself standing here listening to her.

Then she did something I wasn't expecting. She crooked her index finger at me, her lips curved and a playful gleam in her eyes.

I bent because I didn't want to deny her.

When our noses were almost touching, she closed the last few centimeters separating us and brushed a kiss across my lips.

My lungs fucking froze in my chest and I was pretty sure I had an erection no one would be able to miss.

All because she'd barely kissed me.

The only good thing… When she pulled back, she looked like how I felt.

Like I'd taken a wicked slapshot off my helmet and got my bell rung.

Damn, I liked this girl. A lot.

"I'm just gonna go find a place to hang until you're finished. I can meet your friend later. You probably have a lot to do."

She nodded, still looking shell-shocked.

"Sure. That's…" She took a breath. "That sounds like a plan."

Then she smiled and I couldn't think of one damn thing to say. So I nodded and turned to walk back down the hallway before I leaned forward and kissed her way harder than she'd kissed me.

Bliss

"Marcia, I need to talk to you."

I knew something was wrong the second Faith's dad stuck his head through the door and stared at his wife. Frank's expression made my stomach clench.

Luckily, Faith was facing way from the door and couldn't see her dad. Her mom's eyes narrowed for a quick second before she smiled in Faith's general direction and hurried out of the room.

"If my brother's kids are causing problems, I'm gonna strangle them myself. Those little demons are adorable but they're spoiled rotten." Faith paused, her expression solemn. "I can't thank you enough for everything you've done."

"It's been my pleasure. I just—"

"Faith, honey." Her parents walked back into the room together and I knew something had just hit the fan.

Because they looked pissed. Not angry. Not upset.

They looked pissed off and holding it together by a thread.

Shit.

Sheer terror flashed through Faith's expression before she wiped it away and turned to face her parents.

"What's wrong?"

Her parents paused and I squeezed her hand before making a break for the door. Whatever was going down, I figured Faith's parents would want to break it to her alone.

As soon as the door closed behind me, I headed back down the hall, figuring I'd find Shane upstairs. He surprised me by straightening away from the wall at the base of the stairs.

"So I guess you heard." He shook his head, disgust plain on his face. "What a douche."

I shook my head. "Actually, I don't have a clue what's going on. But you do, obviously."

"Shit. Yeah." He grimaced. "I wasn't eavesdropping but they weren't trying to be quiet so…" He sighed. "I'm pretty sure the groom took a powder."

I flashed cold then hot.

That bastard. That absolute bastard. I'm going to hunt him down and—

"Uh, Bliss? You gonna be okay? You look a little…"

"Furious? Yeah, you could say that."

Shaking my head, I sucked in a deep breath and tried to tamp down my anger. But…oh my god, if Jimmy ever dared to show his face—

"No, I mean you look like you took a puck to the balls."

I laughed. I couldn't help myself. And then I shook my head because that's probably what it would feel like. If I, you know, had the right equipment.

Shaking my head, I looked up into his eyes and smiled, though a second ago, I wouldn't have thought I'd be able to smile at all tonight.

Dangerous man.

My smile faded and I really hoped he couldn't read my mind.

"I'm not sure what's going to happen but if you want to go…" I shrugged. "I can call you a taxi?"

"Nah. I'll wait with you."

He waved at a bench along the wall and, when we sat, his thigh pressed against me and radiating heat into my body. If I leaned close, I'd be able to lay my head against his upper arm. Snuggle into his side.

It surprised me how much I wanted to do just that.

Instead, I distracted myself by asking, "When's your next game."

"Day after Christmas." He paused. "Not sure I'll be playing. Coach had me on the bench last game."

Since that seemed like a touchy subject, I asked another question. "What are you doing for Christmas?"

He shrugged. "Sleep. Eat. Hang out with the guys who didn't go home. A couple of the booster club members invited us over for dinner so I'll probably do that. Then I need to get a good night's sleep so I'm ready to play. If Coach puts me in."

"I think…I'd like to come to the game."

I felt him shift beside me. "You want me to get you tickets?"

"I can do—"

"Nah, it's no problem. We get comps. How many do you need?"

I thought about my answer for several seconds. "Is two okay?"

"As long as you're not bringing a date, that's not a problem."

Smiling at his wry tone, I did rest my head against his arm for a few seconds. "I will be bringing a man. But he's related to me."

He tensed. "Your dad's a cop, right? Am I gonna need bail money?"

I laughed, just a quick huff of sound. "I'm not bringing my dad. I'd like to bring my nephew. He's sports crazy."

"Sure, no problem."

I had the sense that, with Shane, that was no bullshit. That he honestly meant what he'd said. I was so used to guys who lied to get what they wanted or told me what they thought I wanted to hear.

This guy seemed so genuine.

So what are you missing?

Hopefully nothing that would come back to bite me.

Down the hall, door hinges squealed and my head swiveled to see Faith's dad emerge. His chin almost rested on his chest but I could see his hands clenched in fists at his sides.

The man was pissed. And heartbroken.

Touching Shane on the shoulder, I leaned in. "I'm just going to see if Faith needs me."

"No problem. Don't worry about me. I'll be waiting here when you're ready to go."

I flashed him a smile and got caught for a second in the sincerity of those blue eyes.

You are in so much trouble. This man is dangerous.

But it would be so much fun while it lasted.

"Do you want to come in for a drink?" Bliss looked over her shoulder at me as she opened the door to her apartment. "I'm afraid I might drink an entire bottle of rum by myself tonight and that wouldn't be a good idea. I don't want to be hungover at dinner at my parents' tomorrow."

I had been hoping she'd invite me in but I hadn't wanted to get my hopes up. And I really didn't want her to feel like she had to entertain me.

Bliss was upset. And yeah, I totally got why. I didn't even know Faith and I wanted to punch her douchebag former fiancé.

I also didn't want to make Bliss' night any tougher than it already had been.

But I didn't want to leave, either.

"Sure."

Smiling, she opened the door and waved me inside.

I hadn't gotten a real look at her place before but now I let myself look as she headed toward the back of the apartment.

"I'm going to change. Give me a minute."

"No problem."

As I took off my jacket and loosened my tie, I glanced around. The open floor plan was pretty cool and the higher ceiling meant the bedroom area was a loft accessed by a short flight of stairs.

She'd hung fabric from the ceiling so I couldn't see her but I heard her rustling around. My brain supplied images of her naked body and my dick took the hint and got hard.

Shit.

"There's beer in the fridge if you want one," she called down. "Or wine. Help yourself."

Sounded like a plan.

"Do you want one?" I called back.

"I'll have wine. There's an open bottle in the door and glasses are in the cabinet next to the fridge."

I'd poured her a glass and had just opened my beer when I felt her come up behind me.

Turning, I held her glass out…and nearly dropped the damn thing.

I'd thought she looked amazing all dressed up but… *Holy shit.*

She'd pulled her hair back in a pony tail that hung over her shoulder, washed off all her makeup and wore a sweatshirt with the neck cut out over a tank top and a pair of yoga pants that clung to every curve.

My fucking dick was gonna have the imprint of a zipper.

Damn, I wanted to grab that hair and wrap it around my hand then I'd pull her close and kiss her until she melted. And then I'd lay her out on the bed and put my mouth between her legs.

I'd wanted to go down on her two nights ago but we just hadn't gotten around to it.

Tonight, if she let me into her bed…

As if she could read my mind, her cheeks turned pink and she swallowed hard.

Her gaze flicked away from me as she took the wine glass out of my hand. "Thanks. I need this. I can't believe—" She cut off with a grimace. "Sorry. I don't mean to keep talking about what happened tonight."

"I guess it's better he called it off at the last second. Other-wise, she'd be stuck with the dick."

Her eyebrows rose as her lips curved. "You're absolutely right." Then she started to laugh. "I glad she didn't marry him. I just hope someday he realizes just what he lost when he decided not to show up tonight. And I hope he regrets it for the rest of his life."

"You're tough. I'd hate to get on your bad side."

Her nose wrinkled as she took a sip of her wine. "I'm really not. My family all think I'm a marshmallow."

Looking at her now, I could see why. Soft. She looked so damn soft, I wanted to curl my hand around her neck and pull her against me. Put my mouth over hers and let myself sink into the kiss.

Something niggled at the back of my brain but I ignored whatever it was trying to tell me.

Especially because she was looking into my eyes with a heat I recognized from the last time we'd been alone together.

My hand had moved before I realized. And when I grabbed the end of her ponytail and began to wind it around my palm, I knew why my lungs suddenly felt like I'd done a half hour of sprints.

Because I was going to be inside her again.

"I happen to love marshmallows."

Her lips parted and I took that as all the encouragement I needed.

Setting my beer on the counter, I took the wine glass out of her hand and set it beside my beer.

We could drink it warm later.

Right now…

I cupped her face in my hands, tilted her face up and kissed her.

I expected her to meet me halfway. I didn't expect her to come at me with such unbridled lust.

But damn, I appreciated it.

Her enthusiasm released my own constraints.

Wrapping my arms around her, now that my mouth had engaged hers in a deep, wet kiss, I pulled her against me. Her pelvis flattened against me, rubbing against my hard on in a way that let me know she was with me all the way.

My dick got even harder and jerked against her as she wriggled against me.

Fuck.

I tore away from her mouth so I could look into her eyes. "Fast and hard first time. I promise I'll make you come. Slower the second time."

Her cheeks went red but her eyes burned as she nodded.

"Absolutely."

Her hands were at my waistband in the next second while I grabbed the sides of her yoga pants and shoved them down her hips. I covered her mouth again, my tongue sinking into her mouth and rubbing against hers.

Then she pulled down my zipper and wrapped her hands around my dick.

Holy fuck.

She immediately started to stroke me as she wriggled her hips while I pushed her stretchy pants farther down her legs.

I had them to her knees when they finally started to fall on their own and I could use my hands for other things.

Like petting her between her thighs.

Her sex lips were silky soft and wet. So fucking wet. I let my fingers play there for several seconds, heard her moan deep in her chest and her fingers pause.

When I flicked at her clit, she shuddered and her fingers clutched around my cock.

Fuck, yes.

I pulled away and turned her around before she realized what I was doing. I caught a quick glimpse of her slack mouth and surprised eyes before I plastered myself against her back and grabbed her wrists, stretching her arms out in front of her.

"Hands on the counter. Hold on."

She obeyed me, bending forward at just the right angle to let me know she was on board with my plans.

Whipping out my wallet, I grabbed the condom, dropped the wallet and covered my dick in record time.

Then I put one hand on her hip, rubbed the head of my cock between those wet lips while I slipped two fingers inside her.

Tight. Hot and wet.

His.

Pushing back onto my fingers, Bliss moaned again. "Shane. No teasing."

Hell, I wasn't. I couldn't. Not now.

I took one step closer, angled my cock and thrust home in one motion.

Her back bowed as she took me in. And I nearly lost it at the feel of her wrapped around me.

Running my hand along her spine, I began to move. Short, jerky thrusts that had her gasping, her hands clenching at the edge of the counter, her ass tilting up to take me deeper.

Yes.

I hadn't been kidding. It was gonna be fast. But she hadn't come yet.

Keeping up the pace, I leaned forward until I could reach around and get one finger on her clit.

Rubbing in time with my thrusts, I found what she liked fast enough and worked her until she gasped out my name and her pussy milked me as hard as a fist.

I managed to hold out for a few more seconds but the temptation was too much.

My cock jerked and I came with a grunt, one arm wrapped around her waist, the other on her shoulder.

I let myself stay inside her for a long minute until my cock stopped.

But I was still hard.

Without warning, I pulled out, her moan an aphrodisiac. And I wasn't done yet.

Before she could speak, I spun her around again and lifted her onto the ladderback stool next to her.

"Wha—"

I was on my knees and my mouth on her before she could finish.

"Oh my god. *Shane.*"

My tongue licked through her folds, slick and puffy. Her hand pushed into my hair, gripping the strands tight as I flicked the tip of my tongue against her click. Moaning when I pushed inside her, tilting her hips up so I could reach more of her.

She tasted fucking amazing and I couldn't stop tasting her, especially as she shifted and let me know exactly what she liked. Which seemed to be everything I was doing.

It made me cocky, made me hot as hell.

I wanted her again.

Luckily, I'd stuck two condoms in my wallet.

Pulling away, I looked up to find her staring down at me with dazed eyes.

I wanted to beat my chest like Tarzan.

Standing, I kept my gaze locked on hers as I reached for my wallet.

I saw her gaze dip to my crotch, watched her eyes widen slightly and her lips curl in a smile as I covered himself again.

But she didn't say anything until I finished with the condom and lifted her off the chair.

Then she swallowed hard. "Shane."

I didn't say anything, just let her slide down until my cock hit her mound. It only took a little adjustment for me to have her right where I needed her.

The tip split her lips and I let her sink onto my cock, filling her.

"Fuck, yes," I muttered. "So hot."

I felt her hands slide into my hair and her lips clung to mine as I moved her up and down my cock. Her rounded ass against my palms made my heart pound harder and every time I let her slide down my cock, she sighed into my mouth.

And I couldn't get enough.

I wanted to feel her pussy clinging to me all fucking night. Would stand here and hold her until my arms gave out but I wouldn't let her fall. I'd never let her fall.

Heaven. Absolute heaven.

Chapter 13

Shane

"Remember what we've been working on, Shane. Cut down on those corners. Lock up that five hole. Get out of your head and don't overthink. Eyes on the puck and keep your crease clear."

I nodded at each of my goalie coach's points, making sure Paul Collins knew I was listening even as I went through my pre-ice routine.

To my surprise, I was the starting goalie for tonight's game. Coach was giving me this shot to prove to myself and my team that I deserved it and I wasn't going to screw it up.

I'd already checked my stick and made sure my catcher and blocker were in good shape. Same with my helmet.

I had a system and god forbid anyone fucked with my system before a game.

Standing at the front of the line, where I'd been most of the season, I allowed myself five seconds to think about Bliss in the crowd. To let myself remember the scorching sex we'd had Christmas Eve.

Then I shoved it all back into that box where I kept everything that wasn't hockey.

I'd deliberately not asked where her seats were located when
I'd requested them to be left at Will Call. I didn't want to know.

"And Shane?"

I turned my full attention back to the coach, blocking out
everything else. It was almost time to head down the hall to
the ice.

"Don't be so focused on the outcome. Handle each moment
as it happens. Don't try to think too far ahead."

Yeah. I could do that.

Deep breath.

The music hit my cue and I started walking, vaguely hearing
the other guys behind me.

But I knew they were there. Knew they had faith in me to see
us through the night. And knew we had a damn good team.

My skates hit the ice to the cheers of the fans. I heard the
cowbells from the crew directly behind me, heard the chant from
the group to the right of my net.

As always, I took a lap around, tapped my blade on the blue
line as I passed by then skated straight to my net.

Here. This was my home. My ice. My net.

My game.

Bliss

"That was a great game, Lissy. Thanks for bringing me. Are we
going to meet Shane now?"

Mike hadn't stopped talking all night, at least not since we'd
taken their seats in the section just off center ice.

I'd been a little worried the other people sitting around us would get frustrated with the constant chatter. But I'd realized after about five minutes that our seats were in the middle of a large group of season ticket holders—who'd been just as talkative as my brother. And as friendly.

They'd set me at ease immediately and that had allowed me to enjoy the game.

And it had been a great game. The Redtails had scored four goals against the other team, which had only scored once.

And Shane had played a great game.

For the past two months, I'd been at every home game. Sometimes I brought my nephew, Dillon. Sometimes I brought a girlfriend. Shane never asked but he made sure I had two tickets.

And every game, I watched Shane get better.

Not that he won every game but now he was on a five-game winning streak.

I didn't kid myself into believing I had anything to do with it, except allow Shane to use sex to get out of his head between games and blow off steam.

And make me scream his name as I came, sometimes twice a night.

Just thinking about last night made me blush.

Today, I'd brought Mike. Because last night, Shane had asked, almost too casually, if I wanted to get something to eat after the game today.

I'd taken a few seconds to think before saying, "Sure," in the most nonchalant way I could.

As if he wasn't changing the unspoken rules of our affair without discussing them with me first.

So I'd brought Mike. But not because introducing Shane to my brother was a test. One a lot of guys failed.

Not at all.

I turned to Mike with a smile. "Yep. Shane's going to meet us and then we're going to go to dinner." I looked around to make sure we had everything. Mike was notoriously forgetful, especially when he was excited. "We have to go downstairs now."

Mike kept up a steady flow of conversation as we made our way to the stairs Shane had told me about and gave our names to the guard. After checking us off his list, he nodded and waved us down.

Heading down the stairs felt like getting a peek behind the curtain and I couldn't help but be a little excited.

When we reached the bottom of the stairs, I noticed pockets of people standing around.

Several other girls my age stood in a cluster, all of them checking their phones and talking without looking at each other. Players' girlfriends, I assumed. A slightly older girl leaned against the wall, gently rocking a baby carriage, alternating her gaze between the baby and the hallway, where I assumed the guys would appear.

A couple who looked like parents talked quietly at the mouth of the hall and a trio of younger guys leaned against the opposite wall from the new mother, laughing at something and shaking their heads.

Mike's conversation had stalled as we'd descended but now he couldn't contain his excitement.

"Is the locker room down here? Are we gonna meet all the guys? Is this where they keep that machine that cleans the ice? I wonder if you can drive that on the street."

Usually I didn't mind Mike's constant stream of questions. I'd had my entire life to get used to it but I knew it could drive other people a little crazy.

The player's mom smiled at Mike then flashed me a smile I recognized. The commiseration smile. The father didn't even glance our way. I'd bet they had a disabled family member, if not their own child then a niece or nephew or a sibling.

A few of the girls glanced our way but only one of them

made eye contact and smiled. The others dismissed us immediately.

Mike never noticed. I'd learned to shrug it off over the years.
Mike wasn't the one with the problem. They were.

"Look, Lissy, they're coming."

He'd spoken a little louder than normal and I winced at the
volume.

"Yeah, but you don't need to shout, buddy. I can hear you."

Mike made a face. "Sorry." Then he pointed toward the hall.
"Is that Shane?"

"Not yet. He's got a lot of equipment to take care off. He'll
probably be one of the last guys out. Let's just wait over here out
of the way."

The guys trickled out a few at a time. Several left together, a
few paired off with the girls and headed out. Finally Shane and
another player walked out together.

He caught sight of me right away and his grin made my body
flush with heat.

What the hell do you think you're doing, introducing your brother to him?
Good question.

His gaze cut to my side, to Mike, and his grin faltered, but
only for a second, then it actually seemed to widen.

"Hey." Shane stuck his hand out to my brother. "I'm Shane."

Mike lit up and his smile stretched until I thought his lips
would crack.

"Hey, Shane. I'm Mike. I'm Lissy's brother. Great game. It
was so much fun…"

As Mike continued to ramble on, Shane kept eye contact and
managed to keep up with Mike's conversation. And I realized,
right then, that I could be in really deep trouble.

Shane was the kind of guy a girl wanted to keep. But he was
going to leave one day. And I couldn't.

No, not couldn't leave. I *wouldn't*. If I left…

Mike turned to me with a smile that made my heart ache. For all of Mike's developmental delays, the one thing he had no trouble with was sensing insincerity in another person. He'd been the first to realize my ex hadn't been the decent guy he seemed to be.

No one had noticed Mike's reticence whenever Rich had been around. Probably because Rich hadn't been around Mike often. Looking back, I blamed myself for not seeing the warning signs.

But I'd been blinded by Rich's smile and by how much attention he'd paid to me. Luckily, I'd gotten out of the relationship before he'd managed to isolate me from my family and friends and hijack my life.

It'd taken me six months and, finally, the threat of a restraining order to get him to leave me alone.

I'd blamed myself for being gullible and letting that man into my life. And even though I knew, absolutely *knew* Shane was nothing like my ex, there was always the fear that I was missing something.

All because of one asshole.

Which Shane *definitely* was not.

Continuing to keep up his conversation with Mike, Shane got us moving toward the door.

Just before we left the building, Shane grabbed my hand, lacing our fingers together.

Tightening my own fingers around his, I returned the quick grin Shane gave me over his shoulder.

My heart flip-flopped in my chest.

And I realized I might've made a huge error in judgment.

Shane

. . .

"So, your brother. He's a nice guy."

I kept my eyes on Bliss as she walked through her apartment, setting her purse on the counter by the small kitchen then setting her coat on one of the chairs at the island.

"He is." She smiled over her shoulder at me. "One of the best I know."

"Was he in an accident or was he born disabled?"

She shook her head, her smile dimming a little as I walked closer. "He developed normally until he was around 18 months old. And then my mom noticed certain things he wasn't doing. By that time, she was pregnant with me. All we know is, it's not genetic."

When I reached the counter I stopped a few inches away from where she stood, back straight and her eyes sharp on mine.

I knew tonight had been a test. Knew instinctively that she didn't introduce Mike to most of the men she dated. And I knew that because Mike had told me when Bliss had gone to the restroom during dinner.

"He seems…pretty self-aware."

Nodding, her smile reappeared. "Sometimes I think he's the smartest person I know. There's no pretense with Mike. What you see it what you get. He's definitely the sweetest person I know. And he's a great judge of character."

Something about the way she said that pinged my radar.

Since the wedding that wasn't, I'd realized that despite her openness, she had a wall around her heart. A wall she only seemed to let her family behind.

I didn't know why the wall was there but I could guess. She'd been hurt before. Probably pretty badly.

And if I wanted to get closer to her, I'd have to break through that wall.

The question was, did I want to?

I'd thought I'd known the answer.

Yesterday, that answer had been no. This affair was supposed to be fun. Not a lifetime commitment. Hot while it lasted but over and done when it'd run its course.

And yet…

I'd asked her to go to dinner with me tonight. And she'd brought her brother.

"Shane?" She frowned up at me. "Is everything okay?"

It had been.

Until last night when I'd realized I wanted to take her out to dinner after the game. I'd wanted to see her waiting in the hall for me.

And I'd wondered what it would be like seeing her there every night. No matter what arena I was playing in, what city, what state. I wanted her face to be the first thing I saw after a game.

I shook my head.

Shit.

"Shane?" Her head cocked to the side. "What's wrong?"

I shook my head. "How long has Mike lived next door?"

Her smile popped out again. "Almost a year. He's done better than anyone expected him to. I mean, I knew he'd be fine but my parents…they were worried."

"You make sure he's okay, don't you?"

She shrugged like it was nothing. "Of course. That's what family's for. I can't imagine being so far away from them all the time. Do you miss your family?"

I nodded. "But I know they're just a phone call away if I need them."

Her chin lifted slightly. "I like knowing mine are twenty minutes away."

I leaned my hip against the counter and watched her take a deep breath, as if my nearness affected her.

Good to know.

"Don't you want to travel?" I asked. "Get out and see the world?"

"Sure. Some day."

"If I don't get called up next year, I've given some thought to playing overseas."

She blinked. "Really? I guess...I didn't realize that was an option. I mean, I'd love to travel but being away from my family that long… How long do you go for?"

"The seasons are shorter over there and you play fewer games but at least seven, eight months."

I saw her search for an appropriate response, saw how she forced a smile when she realized I was watching her.

"Sounds like a great opportunity, especially if you like to travel."

"And you don't?"

Her smile turned bittersweet. "Sure. Some day. But right now, I've got a job and an apartment and bills to pay."

Ties I wasn't sure she'd ever want to break.

Maybe that's a sign you're getting in over your head.

And maybe it was time I started facing my own problems instead of making new ones with a girl who was never meant to be nothing more than a distraction.

I was getting my game back on track. The team was close to clinching a playoff spot. The parent club's goalie coach had been down to work with Nate and I a couple times in the past month and had seemed happy with what he saw.

Now was not the time to get hung up on a hometown girl.

And what if you're already hung up?

"Shane?"

I snapped back to attention. Damn it. I'd fucked this up. Like, seriously screwed our no-strings affair to the point that I didn't have a clue how to fix it.

But I knew one thing.

Reaching out, I curled my hand around her neck, brought her close and kissed her until neither of us were thinking straight.

When I pulled away, finally needing to breathe, I made sure

she was looking at me before I said, "I hope you got enough sleep last night, babe. Because I don't think you're going to get any tonight."

She didn't say anything but she got that look in her eyes, the one that said she'd just accepted my challenge.

Putting her hand over my hard on, she made sure I maintained eye contact as she went to her knees in front of me.

And proceeded to show me exactly why she had me tied around her little finger.

Chapter 14

Shane

"Conrad. Coach wants you."

My head snapped up as assistant coach Novak's voice punched through the noise in the locker room.

The guys were stoked. Jake had scored the only goal of tonight's game and I had had my first AHL shut-out. My face hurt from grinning but I wasn't about to stop.

The Redtails were going to clinch a playoff spot. I could practically taste it.

The guys planned to go to Third and Spruce to celebrate and I would be there.

And I didn't want to go alone. I wanted Bliss with me.

The problem was I didn't know if I should ask her. I hadn't seen her since the last game, when we'd gone out to eat with her brother.

And where she'd blown my fucking mind when she'd gone down on me.

But we hadn't seen each other since then.

The team had been on a five-game road trip, so we'd been gone most of two weeks.

We texted and talked a couple of times but things had felt different.

She seemed distant. Like she was pulling away.

Fuck.

"Be there in a minute," I shouted back and watched Novak nod before disappearing out the door.

I didn't know what Coach wanted but the trade deadline had passed so I didn't figure I was going anywhere. Especially not after tonight's game. I'd been in the zone. Focused. Prepared. I'd lived up to my nickname, Brick Wall.

I'd already taken a shower so I only needed to pull on my clothes and shove my wet hair out of my face when I walked to the office.

And froze in the doorway when I saw Mark Arrons, the team's GM, in addition to the coach.

"Shane. Come in." Coach motioned me forward. "Close the door."

I followed orders without a word but my heart pounded against my ribs. "Hey. What's up?"

When Mark started to smile, I began to breathe again.

"Just got off the phone with Coach Angstadt. You need to be in Philly tomorrow morning. Gragnani's hurt. You're backing up Stanton in tomorrow's game. Congratulations, Shane."

Two thoughts flashed through my head.

Holy shit was the first.

This was the call I'd been dreaming about since I'd been old enough to know what the NHL was.

The second…*Fuck, I don't want to leave my team.*

Snapping out of my thoughts, I took Mark's hand then shook Coach Scott's.

"Thank you. Do you know how long I'll be up?"

Coach started to grin. "Honestly, I don't know. I only know

Gragnani's injury is lower body. You could be up for one game, you could be up for a few weeks. No way to know."

Weeks? Shit. "Yes, sir."

"You'll probably be riding the bench the entire time but take it all in. Listen. Learn. Watch. Even if you don't get to play, it's a chance to show your commitment. When you come back, I expect you to be that much better. Good luck."

"Thank you, sir."

Coach clapped me on the shoulder. "Now go out and celebrate. You played a damn good game tonight. Just don't be late for morning skate."

Bliss

I knew by the look on Shane's face. Something had changed.

I hadn't seen him for two weeks and I tried to tell myself it hadn't mattered.

Liar.

Swallowing hard, I sucked in a breath and forced a smile.

When he reached for me in the arena hall, I went into his arms immediately, hugging him tight before stepping away.

And if he didn't release me right away… Well, I had to be wrong.

"You were amazing tonight. Congratulations."

"Thanks. I felt…pretty damn good tonight."

And he'd felt pretty damn good pressed against me. But something was up.

"Hey," he said. "Can we talk for a second?"

My chest felt like someone had just stuck me in a vise and started to crank.

No, I refused to let myself get worked up over something I'd known was coming.

And this was it. I could sense it. He was going to tell me he didn't want to see me anymore. That the team had to come first and he needed to focus on the playoffs and that he didn't have room for me. Not now.

And I'd nod and smile and say I understood completely. Because I did.

I'd known this relationship was going nowhere when we'd started. I hadn't let myself get involved so I wouldn't be devastated.

"Sure. Do you want to…?" I pointed to a quiet corner away from the other girlfriends.

"Yeah. That's good."

Putting his hand on my elbow, he drew me deeper into the hallway, until the only sound I could hear was the hum of the cooling units.

Then we stopped and I looked up.

And the smile on his face stole my breath.

"I got called up. I have to be in Philly for morning skate then I'm backing up Stanton for the game."

Time froze for one very short second while I thought about those simple words.

I got called up.

I blinked and sucked in a breath I hoped he would interpret as surprise. Because it was. But it was a whole lot more.

And even as my smile came naturally, I couldn't help but feel as if I'd been kicked.

"Oh, my god. Shane. That's wonderful."

And it was. It was amazing.

I wrapped my arms around his shoulders and hugged him tight. And when his arms came around me and clung, I knew why I felt like I was losing him.

Because this felt like goodbye.

Drawing back, I kept my smile pinned in place, though I didn't have to force it.

I was so damn happy for him. And so miserably sorry for myself.

Which totally sucked. I'd known this affair had an expiration date. I just hadn't expected it to be before the end of the season.

Stupid.

"So when do you leave?"

"I have to be in Philly tomorrow for the morning skate then I'll be on the bench for the game. I won't play unless something happens to Stanton. I probably won't see any ice time during the game but it's a chance for me to practice with the team, get to know the coaches a little better. I know it won't be permanent, at least not now. I mean, I really want to be back in a week for the next game here. As it stands now, the Colonials aren't going to make the playoffs so I'd probably be back anyway but..."

"This is your team." I understood. At least, I understood him. How he thought. In the short time we'd been together, I'd learned to read him remarkably well.

Hell, a danger sign should've been flashing over his head.

Can't fall apart now.

That wasn't the deal I'd made myself. It'd been fun. That's all. We hadn't made promises, had never spoken about what happened after the season. For all I knew, he hadn't even considered it. Just figured we'd go their own separate ways.

He nodded. "Yeah. This is my team. I think we're gonna go all the way to the Calder Cup this year."

"Then you need to go celebrate with the team."

His gaze narrowed. "I want you there."

My heart melted at his insistence. "Of course. Are you ready to go?"

"Yeah. I told the rest of the guys we'd meet them at the bar."

I brightened my smile. "Then let's go and have a good time."

He leaned in to kiss me, taking me a little off guard and taking my breath away.

"Always do with you."

My heart stuttered but I refused to give into the ache that wanted to bloom.

He'd never been mine to keep. I had to start letting him go.

Now.

Shane stroked inside me with that steady intoxication I was afraid I'd grown addicted to.

"Faster. Shane, please."

"No fucking way." If possible, he slowed even more. "You're gonna come again."

Considering he'd already made me come twice in the past fifteen minutes, I knew it wasn't an idle boast.

Sometimes, all it took for him to push me over the edge was a couple of words spoken in that deep, gruff way he had when he was inside me.

Digging my fingernails into his shoulders, I scraped them down his back, eliciting a groan but no increase in his rhythm.

The man's patience exhausted me. And his stamina... I might as well give in and admit defeat.

But not just yet.

Turning my head, I bit at his neck, a nip that made me hunger for more.

"*Fuck.*"

His hips pushed forward, pressing his cock deeper inside and making my thighs tighten against his side.

Moaning, I bit him again, this time on his chin. He took the hint and bent his head to kiss me.

His mouth sealed over mine, stealing my breath as his tongue slid against mine, coaxing me to play with him.

Overwhelmed by sensation, I broke apart on his next thrust as he pressed against my clit.

As I squeezed around him, I felt his cock flex and throb deep inside me.

With a groan, he bent until our foreheads touched and stayed there for several seconds, breathing heavily.

When he finally seemed to catch his breath, he rolled to the side, taking me with him until I lay on his chest. His softening cock remained inside me, as if my body was unwilling to give up any part of him.

Spread across him, all I wanted was to stay there for the rest of the night.

"I should go," I said instead. "You need to be up early. You can't be late tomorrow."

He stayed silent for a few more seconds. "Stay."

How could he ask that?

Blinking away the hot tears that popped into my eyes, I pressed a kiss to his left pec and forced a smile, even though I wasn't sure he could see it. "I can't. You need to get a decent night's sleep. Tomorrow's a big day for you."

"It's not like I'm gonna be playing. The only time I'll see the ice'll be at morning skate and warmups. Then I'll be on the bench for the entire game."

"And you know it doesn't matter. You need to make a good impression and you won't if you'll be distracted by me all night."

Now I did look up, forcing myself to smile and hoping he didn't see the nerves behind it in the dark. Then, because I couldn't help myself, I rubbed my nose against his then pressed my lips to his for a quick kiss.

With a sigh I didn't have feign, I rolled to the side and slid off the side of the bed, grabbing my underwear from the bottom of the bed.

As I dressed, I felt his gaze on me.

"I should be back day after tomorrow," he said. "Thursday. We've got a game Friday. I'll leave tickets for you and Mike."

"Sounds good."

Even though I probably wouldn't claim them. Something would come up. I'd make sure of it.

"Bliss."

Shane was on his knees and leaning forward to catch my arm before I could get away.

"You'll watch the game tomorrow night?"

Because he sounded as if he didn't think I would, I turned, cupping his jaw in my hand and rubbing my thumb over the scruff he hadn't shaved in days. I had to admit I liked it.

"Of course I'll be watching. I wouldn't miss it for anything."

"And I'll see you when I get back."

I held my smile. "Yep."

Because I couldn't help myself, I leaned in to kiss him again.

"Good luck tomorrow, even though you don't need it. You wouldn't have gotten the call if they didn't already know how good you are."

In the dim light, I could just see the curve of his lips as I stepped away from the bed.

"Have fun, Shane. And don't forget to breathe."

Chapter 15

I woke the next morning with a knot in my gut and the most incredible urge to call Bliss and tell her I wanted her to come with me to Philly.

Which was stupid. She had to work and I needed no distractions.

I ate, checked my gear twice, loaded everything into my truck then went back inside to make sure I hadn't forgotten anything.

I knew I hadn't but I needed to be sure.

I was at the front door, ready to head out with a second water bottle in my hand when I heard CJ.

"Hey, man. Kick some ass today."

CJ stood in the doorway to my room, boxer shorts barely covering his junk, hair standing up all over the place on one side and flat on the other.

"Not gonna play, you know that. But thanks."

"Yeah, I know. But still. And man, don't take this the wrong, but I hope like hell they send you back for the weekend."

Nodding, I held out my hand and waited for him to walk over and bump my knuckles.

"Did you actually set your alarm to see me before I left?"

CJ grimaced and I thought he might've actually blushed.

"Fuck you."

"Dude. I'm touched."

"Uh huh. Have fun. I'll see you when you get back."

I turned back to the door but before I left, CJ said, "Wait."

"What's up?"

"Is Bliss in your room? I mean, I don't want her to, you know, catch a glimpse of me and throw you over."

Fuck. "Nah, you're safe. She went home last night. Before you stumbled in."

CJ's eyes narrowed but he didn't say anything.

"All right. Safe travels, man. And don't let shit fuck with your head."

I left with a smile on my face but it vanished minutes later.

My stomach ground in on itself as nerves started to hit me but I pulled on my years of training to steady myself.

By the time I reached the team's training facility in northeast Philly, I had myself under control.

This was what I'd been working for since I was five.

Since I'd been down for pre-season training camp, I knew where to park. After I'd checked in with the guard, I grabbed my gear from the back of the truck and headed for the locker room.

I wasn't the first one there.

"Conrad. Nice to see you. How's it going?"

Stanton turned away from his locker, where he'd been pulling up his compression pants, and came forward with a smile and his hand out.

I took it with a nod. "Not bad."

"The Reds are having a hell of a year and so are you. Congrats."

At six-three, Stanton was an inch shorter than me but the guy had almost 20 pounds on me, all of it muscle. He'd come by his nickname Tank for his methodical play.

"Thanks. The team's come together this year. We're looking forward to the playoffs."

Stanton's grin turned lopsided. "Gonna suck if you're stuck up here riding the bench. Between you and me, Gragnani's injury's not gonna keep him out longer than tonight so you'll be back. He's being a pussy about pulling a muscle in his leg." Stanton shook his head. "But you didn't hear that from me. Christ, the guy's nearly thirty-three. Guess I should cut him some slack."

I nodded, smiling. "Thanks for the heads up."

"No problem." Stanton turned back to his locker and began pulling on his pads. "When you get back, tell Coach Scott I said hello."

That's right. Stanton had been the Redtails top goalie before being called up to the Colonials two years ago.

"I will."

"Good." A voice came from the door. "You're here early. You and me are gonna spend a little time together this morning. I caught up on your tapes last night. Got a few things to go over. Get dressed and I'll see you on the ice."

I turned to see goalie coach Gary Ellis. The five-foot-eight bulldog had produced some of the best net minders in the league. A former goalie, he had a Stanley Cup ring and a reputation for being gruff, uncompromising and arguably the best ever.

Then he disappeared back into the hall.

And I took a deep breath. And another.

Then I started to shed my clothes so I could get ready for my first practice in the NHL.

Bliss

"Lissy, hurry up, the game's starting!"

"I'm coming, Mike. And my apartment's not that big. You don't have to yell. Besides, the game doesn't start for another half hour."

"Yeah, but they're talking about the players and they might say something about Shane."

My heart fluttered at the thought. I was so damn excited for him.

And so damn sorry for myself. Something I would never admit to anyone else.

As I sat next to my brother on the couch in front of the TV, listening to Mike's almost breathless chatter about everything from how the Redtails' uniforms used the same colors as the Colonials to the way the announcers were dressed.

"And with Gragnani out, backing up Stanton tonight will be Shane Conrad, brought up this morning from the AHL Reading Redtails."

As Mike let out a whoop, I turned up the volume to make sure we didn't miss anything.

"Conrad's been having a great year but I doubt we'll get to see him at all tonight as Stanton will be in net…"

And that was all they heard about Shane. But I couldn't help the tears that pooled in my eyes hearing his name. I actually had to take a deep breath and hoped like hell that Mike wouldn't look over and see me trying to brush the tears away.

Damn it. I'd broken my own damn rule.

That whole not-getting-involved thing? Hadn't really worked, had it?

Now I had no one to blame but myself.

And what if he's the one?

I slid a glance at Mike. What happened if Shane and I actually did try to make a relationship work? His career might take him anywhere in North America. What happened to me when he got called up? If they traded him to Winnipeg or Los Angeles or Dallas?

Did I give up my apartment, my job, my life and follow him?

And aren't you jumping ahead of yourself? The guy hasn't even asked you move in with him, much less spend the rest of your life with him?

And was that part of the problem? Is that what I expected him to do? Is it what I wanted?

Maybe I needed to figure that out for myself first.

Bliss

"Hey, Bliss. I'll be home tonight. I missed you. What are you doing for dinner? I'd really like to see you."

I had missed Shane's call. I'd been with a customer and hadn't been able to get to my phone. That customer had been there until fifteen minutes after closing and I had been late for my dinner date.

Which didn't explain why I hadn't texted him back last night. Oh, I'd congratulated him after the game. I'd called and left him a message right after the game. When I knew he'd still be in the locker room and unable to answer his phone.

Coward.

But I hadn't responded to the call he'd left around ten-thirty last night. I could easily explain. I'd been in bed early. And I had been. And if I'd also maybe been trying not to cry, well, no one needed to know that.

Tonight, I had the perfect excuse. I was "out with friends"

and if he was smart, he wouldn't interrupt. That was part of the guy handbook, wasn't it? Rule No. 1: Don't interrupt a girl when she's out with friends.

"Whoa. I know why I get blamed for resting bitch face, but I can't say I've ever seen that look on your face."

Faith lifted an eyebrow at me across the table at the Greek tavern down the street from the bridal salon.

I sighed and took a sip of my wine. "I know. But can we wait for Sophie so I don't have to repeat myself? She and her dad should be done arguing in a minute."

I had helped Sophie Tsoukalos, the tavern owner's daughter, find a dress for the tavern's grand opening a few months ago and, since then, I stopped in for a glass of wine whenever I could to talk to Sophie. The other girl's sunny personality drew people to her like bears to honey.

The only person she ever fought with was her dad, Spiro. They were arguing in the kitchen in Greek, which they did at least twice a day. That might've been an exaggeration but I didn't think it was. And when it blew over, as it did in a matter of minutes, life went back to normal.

I could never live like that. Sophie seemed to thrive on it.

"That bad, huh?"

I winced, knowing my problems were nothing compared to Faith's, who'd made it perfectly clear if she caught even a whiff of pity from me, she was leaving.

So I sighed again. "It's just—"

"I swear that man is going to have a coronary and my sisters will all blame me." Sophie pushed through the swinging door from the kitchen then hurried over to lean on the bar in front of Faith and I. Her long, dark hair fell over one shoulder, dark eyes wide and inquisitive. "Now, what's going on. I can tell you're not happy. What'd the man do?"

My nose wrinkled. "How do you know it's a man?"

Sophie rolled her eyes. "Oh please. That's definitely not your 'Had to deal with Bridezilla' face. That's definitely a 'Man did me wrong' face. Spill it."

My expression crumbled. "Honestly? I think I'm the one that did him wrong. I need to break it off with Shane and I don't know how."

Sophie and Faith went totally silent, their expressions shocked.

"What? Why are you both looking at me like that."

The other women exchanged a glance then Sophie reached across the bar and patted me on the hand.

"What did he do? He must've done something if you want to break it off. I mean…seriously, I thought you liked him. I mean, really liked him. Why would you want to break it off?"

"Because the season's going to end and he's going to leave. Maybe he'll be back next year. Maybe he won't. And I just can't follow him around like a groupie. I mean, I've got a job and an apartment and what would happen with Mike if I moved away? My life is here."

I looked up to find my friends staring at me with raised eyebrows.

So I pushed on. "And it's not like he asked me to give up everything and follow him all the hell over the place. I mean, he's probably just in it for the sex and when the season's over he'll dump me anyway. So if I dump him now, I'm saving him the hassle."

Sophie and Faith exchanged another glance before Faith said, "Sounds like you've given this a lot of thought."

Shrugging, I avoided their gaze by taking another sip…okay, a gulp of wine. "Maybe. Maybe more than I should have."

Sophie reached beneath the bar for the wine and topped off my glass. "I didn't realize you'd gotten that serious."

I frowned. "We're not. I mean… I don't… Oh hell." I closed

my eyes and dropped my head. "I don't have a clue. I just know it's better to end it now before either of us gets too involved."

Faith huffed, wry amusement in her expression. "Yeah. *Before* you get too involved. I think you're past that point, hon. But you're probably not wrong. If you know you're going to end it, better to do it before you really get hurt."

Sophie looked between Faith and I, shaking her head. "Wow, you two are enough to make me swear off relationships forever. And I get it. I mean, I get Faith's reason. I totally think you should castrate that bastard if you ever see the prick again," Faith's statement was all the more shocking for the smile she had while speaking, "but Bliss…damn, what made you so cynical?"

Resting my hand on my cheek, I grimaced at Sophie. "I may have dated a guy who might have turned into an emotionally abusive asshole."

At Sophie's gasp, I held up my hand. "In all fairness, he didn't start out that way. He had everyone fooled. Except my brother. Mike figured him out right away. It took me a little longer to realize but when I did, I got out."

And I hadn't had a serious relationship since. But that didn't mean I wasn't right about ending my relationship with Shane. It wasn't because I was scared. It was because it was the right thing to do.

Bullshit.

I wanted to tell that sarcastic little voice in my brain to go fuck itself but that might prove I really was wrong in the head.

And wrong about giving up Shane.

Shit.

"Well, I haven't met the guy, so I don't have a clue what he's like." Sophie acknowledged the group who pushed through the front door with a wave. "But Bliss, the way you talk about the guy…maybe you need to think this through a little more."

Sophie moved to seat the new party, leaving Faith and I alone.

"And what do you think?"

"I think all men are pricks who will cut your heart out." Faith shrugged. "But that's just me."

After a few seconds, I nodded. "No, I'm right about this. Better to break it off now before it goes any farther."

And hope I didn't regret the hell out of my decision later.

Chapter 16

Shane

"Hi Shane, sorry I didn't get back to you sooner. I've had a million things to do."

And apparently I wasn't one of them.

I nodded though I knew she couldn't see me. I also knew something was up.

I'd gotten a bad feeling in my gut two nights when she hadn't called back after the game. Yeah, she'd texted but I'd wanted to hear her voice.

And then yesterday, she'd blown me off again with a text.

Now she'd finally called and I realized I didn't actually want to talk to her. Because I knew what she was doing.

I just didn't know why. I had a few ideas but…

Damn it. My jaw clenched.

"I thought maybe we could get some dinner after the game tonight."

Silence. Then, "I don't think I can make the game tonight."

Goddammit. Was she really going to do this now?

I sucked in a breath. "Something wrong?"

Another pause. "No, nothing's wrong. I just…I can't make it tonight. Aunt Rosie and I are getting ready for a bridal show on Sunday and there's so much we need to do before then. And the shop's open tomorrow and of course we've got three fittings and a consultation with a new client. And Sunday's going to be crazy. One of the models backed out and if we can't find anyone, I'll have to step in which means altering the dress and… well, it's just crazy right now. I'm sure you understand. I mean, you've only got two weeks left before the playoffs and I know you're going to clinch a spot so you're going to be busy too and…"

She finally stopped to take a breath but I felt like I couldn't catch mine.

"Bliss. What—"

"I just don't know when I'm going to be free." She rushed to cut me off. "And I'm not sure—"

"Bliss. Don't."

I wouldn't beg. No fucking way would I beg for her not to do this.

But…

Hell, everything she said was right. I was going to be busy. Making it to the playoffs had to come first. I knew I needed to concentrate on winning the Calder Cup. Hell, I should be thanking her for making this easy on me.

Except, this didn't feel easy. It felt the exact opposite.

"I've had a really great time with you these past few months," Bliss pushed on like I hadn't said anything. "But I know your life is going to get crazy and I don't want to feel like I'm getting in the way."

"Have I ever said that? Have I ever even mentioned that?"

Another pause and then a deep breath. "We both knew this wasn't going to last."

"And what if that's not what I want?"

Bliss

For a moment, my heart rose into my throat.

An old memory, one from my former relationship rose up.

I'd made the decision to break up with my ex and I'd asked him to meet me at a restaurant to talk. A public space, where there was no way he would do anything…physically to me.

But the look in his eyes when I told him I was leaving him and I never wanted to see him again? That look had made me want to run. It had made every muscle in my body tense, ready to flee.

And I'd felt like I was going to be sick.

Like I felt now.

But now it was the thought that I'd lumped Shane into the same mold as my ex that made me ill.

Shane was nothing like that bastard. He was a decent guy. A great guy, actually.

And you're just throwing him away.

No. It was better to end this now before either of us really got hurt.

"I know you're going to have a great run in the playoffs."

"Wait—"

"And you've made a superfan out of Mike. But I really have to go. Good luck. With everything. And…Bye."

Shane

.   .   .

The line went dead and I took a second to look at the screen to make sure she'd actually hung up on me.

She had.

What the fuck just happened?

I felt like I'd gotten taken out by Rager Bolden, the league's biggest linesman. Shaking my head, I reached for my keys but stopped when the front door opened and CJ, Jake and Lad stormed in.

"Shane!" CJ rushed me, grabbing around the shoulders and hugging me. "You cocksucker. You're back. We are *so* fucking happy to see you!"

Lad and Jake smacked me on the back hard enough to make me wince.

"How was that NHL bench?" Jake headed for the fridge. "Feel different on your ass?"

It took me a second to switch gears, to shove the hurt down and concentrate on my friends.

"Felt the same to me and I was on it all night."

Lad grabbed my shoulder and squeezed. "Yeah, but you got the call."

For the next fifteen minutes, I answered a barrage of questions. Mostly from CJ. This was his first year playing in the AHL after spending two years in the ECHL. CJ might've been more excited than me about getting called up.

But even as I told the guys about my time in Philly, I couldn't stop thinking about Bliss.

Jake noticed my distraction first. His gaze narrowed as I talked about the strength of the shots.

When CJ would've asked another question, Jake held up his hand.

"What is wrong? Something is not right with you."

"Nothing." I shrugged. "Just tired. I took practice with the team this morning."

Jake wasn't buying it and now Lad and CJ were looking more closely at me.

"No, that ain't it." CJ crossed his arms over his chest and leaned back against the kitchen counter. "What happened?"

Taking my beer, I headed for the sofa. Might as well be comfortable if they were going to cross-examine me.

"Nothing happened. Everything's fine. What'd I miss—"

"Why are you not going to see Bliss?"

Fucking Lad. The bastard could read other players like he had ESP.

"Because she doesn't want to see me. It's not a problem. With the playoffs coming up, I need to be focused. I don't need a woman fucking with my head."

The guys exchanged looks.

"Bullshit," said Lad and Jake in perfect unison.

CJ shook his head. "Damn. I don't get it. I thought she really liked you."

Shrugging, I sucked down more beer. "Guess not."

"That is bullshit." Lad cocked his head to the side. "What did you do?"

I frowned. "What the fuck? I didn't do anything."

"You must have done something." Lad exchanged a glance with Jake. "That girl had it bad for you."

Shrugging, I forced myself not to rub at the ache in my chest. "Obviously she didn't or she wouldn't have dumped me."

"This is not good." Lad looked at Jake. "We must do something."

"What? No." I shook my head. "Hell no. Just leave it."

"Oh, we definitely have to do something." Jake nodded. "We will help you with this."

"Jesus...I don't need any fucking help. It's over."

Jake's gaze narrowed. "Can you honestly tell us you don't want her back?"

No. "Yes. I have more important things to focus on."

"Yes, I'm sure you do." Lad snorted. "Fine. So tell us more about the game."

Trying not to sigh in relief, I recounted everything I could remember.

And tried not to let Bliss totally dominate my thoughts.

Bliss

The tickets showed up the next morning.

But not at my door.

No, they showed up at Mike's. And they didn't come from Shane.

"Lissy, look what Jake sent. Tickets for the game tonight. Can we go?"

My heart pounding in my chest, I took the envelope, hating the fact that I'd almost wanted them to come from Shane. "How do you know they're from Jake?"

"He sent a note."

Hey, buddy. I hope you can make it. If you need a ride, just let me know. Jake.

Definitely not Shane's handwriting.

Damn it.

Not that I wanted it to be from Shane. I was glad he wasn't making this hard on me.

But I couldn't say no to Mike. Not when he looked at me with so much excitement.

"Sure. But Mike…"

I hadn't had a chance to tell him I'd broken up with Shane. I told myself it wasn't because I regretted my decision. I didn't. I'd done the right thing.

But…

Shit.

"Mike…Shane and I broke up."

The shock on my brother's face made my heart hurt. And my stomach clench.

He looked the way I still felt. And I'd been the one to break up.

Which had been for the best, damn it.

"Why? What happened?"

Yeah, what did happen?

I'd gotten scared, that's what happened.

But it was still for the best. Better to hurt a little now than be heartbroken later.

A little?

I wanted to tell myself to shut up but didn't want Mike to think I was talking to him.

Forcing a quick smile, I shook my head. "Nothing. It just wasn't going to work out between us."

Mike's head cocked to the side. "How do you know?"

I shrugged. "It's just wasn't. It's better this way."

Mike frowned hard. "Why?"

Because he would've left me anyway. "Sometimes relationships just don't work out."

"Was he…" Mike frowned even harder, "like your ex?"

"God, no! No, Mike. Shane is nothing like Rich."

"Then…" With a sigh, Mike shook his head. "I guess I just don't understand."

Christ, now I'd dragged my brother down into the dumps with me.

"There's really nothing to understand. It just wasn't going to work out."

After a few seconds, Mike finally nodded slowly. "Like me working at that restaurant. That's what the manager told me, that it wasn't going to work out. He didn't like working with me. So you didn't like Shane enough."

Blindsided, I went blank. The real reason the manager had fired Mike was because he was a prejudiced asshole and hadn't been comfortable around my brother.

"No, that's not it. I like Shane. It's just…"

"Complicated."

Looking into Mike's eyes, I saw an understanding I hadn't expected him to have. I shouldn't have been surprised, though. My brother's brain functioned differently than most people but he was practically empathic when it came to reading people's feelings.

"Yeah. It's really complicated. Especially for me."

"Because of your ex."

I wanted to deny it but I wouldn't lie to Mike.

"Kind of. I just…don't want to be left behind when he moves on."

The truth rushed out but it finally felt good to admit it to someone who wouldn't judge me. It truly sucked that I knew it was my own screwed-up emotions that had pushed Shane away. It also sucked that I couldn't think of another way to handle it.

Because the truth still remained. He would eventually leave and I would stay. And nothing either of us could do would change that fact.

Mike reached for my hand and squeezed. "We don't have to go to the game."

"Of course we do. Jake wants you to come. And I know you want to go."

"But—"

"No buts. We'll have a good time."

Keep telling yourself that. Maybe you'll believe it in a year or so.

Chapter 17

Shane

"Holy shit, we fucking *destroyed* those fucking gerbils," CJ shouted as I walked into the locker room after taking a bow for being the first star of the game. "The Brick Wall lives!"

I smiled at my teammates as they started to chant, "Brick! Brick! Brick!" and bumped gloves with Nate as I passed the other goalie on the way to my locker.

We'd clinched a playoff spot tonight with the win against the Maine Flying Foxes, whose mascot looked like the unfortunate mating of a chihuahua and a gerbil.

The game had been sweeter still because we'd played on home ice and the fans had gone crazy. The team had missed the playoff the last couple of years so this was icing on the fucking cake.

"You played like a man possessed tonight, Conrad." Cary smacked me on the back on his way to the showers. "Keep it up and we'll have that cup."

"Dude, you shut them *down*." Jake dropped onto the bench

next to me and watched as I pulled off my gear. "Guess getting dumped was actually good for you, yes?"

Shaking off my blocker, I gave Jake the finger without bothering to look at him. I wasn't about to respond to that.

"You had a great game," I tossed over my shoulder. "Congrats."

"Ah, so we're still not discussing her. Okay. Yes, I did have a great game, thank you."

Shaking my head, I listened to the other guys on the team razz Jake about his almost non-existent humility while managing to compliment him at the same time.

Thinking I was safe from any more of Jake's reminders of Bliss, I headed for the showers, where I stood under a scalding hot shower for at least five minutes.

It was part of my post-game ritual, which I'd let slide while I was with Bliss.

Should've been your first clue. Don't change the routine for a girl.

My dad had drilled that one into my head all through high school. Not that I'd been in danger of that but it'd stuck with me through juniors and into my years in the ECHL.

But I'd done it for Bliss and not noticed any harm. In fact—

I shook my head. Didn't. Matter. Not one fucking bit because Bliss was gone.

And I was back to my routine and the team was winning and would continue to win.

"Hey, you heading straight home?" CJ stuck his head into the shower room, already showered and dressed. "I'm leaving now."

"Yeah, I'll be out in a few. Need a decent night's sleep before the game tomorrow."

We had another game against the Wolves tomorrow and the other team would be out for payback.

"Okay. Oh, and, just a head's up. Bliss and Mike are in the hall. I'll make sure Jake gets them out before you come through."

My head shot up. "What the fuck?"

Justin Perry, the defenseman they'd just brought up from the ECHL after losing Joey Constantino to an injury last game, shot me a wary glance.

I knew I had a rep for being intense. Knew it was warranted. I also knew there was a fine line between intense and being an arrogant bastard. I'd always managed to walk it before. The tide could turn though.

Especially when I thought about Jake hitting on Bliss.

"No need to go psycho, dude. Jake sent the tickets to Mike. He didn't know Bliss would be here."

No fucking way did Jake not expect Mike to come without Bliss.

Bastard. I was gonna kill Jake. If he so much as laid a finger on her—

Shit. *Shit.*

I took a deep breath. That wasn't fair. I knew Jake and Mike had hit it off. Jake had a brother with Down syndrome, who he missed more than he'd ever admit to anyone. Except to me, one drunken night a few months ago.

"Sorry." I shook my head. "Just…never mind. You don't have to do anything. I'm fine."

Shrugging, CJ waved. "Okay. See you at home."

CJ disappeared and I hung my head, letting the water pound against the suddenly tense muscles of my back.

It'd been three days since she'd told me she didn't want to see me again. Three days since I'd let her go without a fight.

Because she'd been right.

Our relationship had been going nowhere.

"Fuck."

"Uh, you okay?"

Justin shut off his shower and rubbed a towel over himself, carefully not looking me in the eyes.

I let out a big sigh. "Yeah. I'm fine. Good game tonight."

"Thanks. You, too. It's good to be here."

I didn't want to be a dick but I had no interest in conversation. No, I was much more interested in what was going on in the hall.

"Glad to have you."

Luckily, the new guy didn't say anything else and walked away a second later. Leaving me alone in the showers.

I told myself I wasn't standing here just so I could avoid her. I was soaking my tight muscles.

Yeah, right.

With a muttered curse, I shut off the water, toweled off and headed back to the locker room.

I glanced at the clock, figuring I'd give Jake another five minutes to say goodbye to Mike and Bliss.

And give myself another five minutes to tell myself I really didn't want to see her.

Bliss

"Do you mind, Lissy?"

I smiled and shook my head. "Of course, I don't mind. Have fun."

Jake touched me on the shoulder. "We're just going to get something to eat at the West Reading Diner. We won't be out late. We have a game tomorrow. If you guys can make it, I'll make sure you've got tickets."

Mike's smile widened and I knew I couldn't say no. It was almost like they were ganging up on me. But I couldn't deny the friendship that had developed between Mike and Jake. I'd be suspicious of Jake's motives if I hadn't seen the way he treated Mike. There was no way I was going to throw up roadblocks to their friendship.

"I can get the bus in if you don't want to come tomorrow, Lis."

Because I was weak, I said, "No, I've got nothing going on. I can bring you."

Jake nodded, his expression serious but I could've sworn he was hiding a smile.

And then my brain fuzzed over. Because Shane walked out of the locker room.

Damn it. I'd wanted to be gone before he got out. He was typically one of the last guys to leave.

And my heart hurt to look at him because… Oh my god, the man took my breath away.

Tall and broad, dressed in the gray suit that fit him like a glove and the blue shirt that matched his eyes. He hadn't bothered with his tie, which I was sure he had rolled up in his pocket.

His hair was still wet and he'd brushed it back from his face, which still bore the marks from his mask.

I had the opposing urges to run in the other direction and brush my fingers across those marks.

God, I'd been so stupid. I'd fallen for him. Hard. And I had no one to blame but myself.

As he came closer, I found myself sucking in a breath and holding it.

Which was so stupid because he barely nodded at me. He did stop to say hi to Mike and shake his hand but he left seconds later.

My heart felt like he'd taken a knife and sliced right through it.

Still think giving him up was a good idea?

Absolutely. Because if it hurt this much after only a couple of months of dating, just think how much worse it would be after five or six months? Or a year?

Maybe…

I turned to watch him leave. Couldn't help myself. Just like I'd been unable to take my eyes off him throughout the entire game.

Why are you torturing yourself?

Because I was an idiot. But that didn't mean I wasn't right.

Shane

"Jesus, Shane, you're on fire. Dude, I don't know what the fuck you took but whatever it is, I want some."

I gave Nicky Thompson an acknowledging grin over my shoulder. The rookie forward from Ottawa had been a great addition to the team mid-season. The kid wouldn't turn twenty-one for another six months but he played like a ten-year pro.

"That's what happens when you don't have a life." Lad was already on his way to the showers after their final game of the season. "The Brick Wall eats, sleeps and breathes hockey, son. Take notes."

I had a response on the tip of my tongue, one that would've made everyone laugh. But I just couldn't come up with the energy to care.

So I acknowledged the catcalls from the rest of the guys with a wave but stayed silent as I stripped off my gear.

The noise of the locker room faded in and out as the guys moved from here to the showers and back. Coach had already told me the local reporter and the AP stringer wanted to talk to me so I hustled. I knew the writers would wait however long it took but I hated to keep them waiting. They had deadlines and I...would go home to a lonely bed and try to sleep without dreaming about Bliss.

Shit.

When I got out of the shower, only a few guys remained, including Jake.

"You should probably not go into the green room looking like you just ate puppies and kittens for dinner. You'll scare the pretty blonde with the tape recorder. New AP stringer. Much better looking than the old dude they used to send."

Jake was already dressed as I hung the last of my equipment and wrapped a towel around my waist.

I spared him a glance, noting the bag he held in his hands. "You going out?"

"Yes. Mike and I are going to get some dinner and then I will meet the guys at that bar in West Reading. The one that's always empty. I can never remember its name."

Jake couldn't remember its name because it had some weird Native American spelling that no one but people from the area could pronounce properly.

"You want to meet us there?" Jake asked.

I automatically shook my head. "I'm tired. Need to get some sleep."

Jake didn't move but he didn't say anything either. Most of the other guys had already left.

"What?" I shot Jake a glance, frowning. "What's wrong?"

"You are." Jake crossed his arms over his chest, looking like he was digging in for a fight. "You need to snap out of this."

"Snap out of what? Christ, I'm playing the best I've played in years."

"I'm not arguing with that. But Shane, you are miserable. Everyone can see it. No one wants to say anything because you are playing amazing. But man, there's more to life than hockey. Even during the playoffs. I mean, what good is winning if you sleep alone every night."

"Jesus, Jake. Just leave it the hell alone."

I yanked my undershirt over my head…and ripped the damn neckline out.

The few guys left in the locker room gave me sidelong glances but quickly looked away again.

"Fuck."

Jake rocked back on his heels, his expression unchanged as I finished dressing…without the t-shirt.

"She misses you, too. And the way you're playing… Well, she's sure she made the right decision."

"So what? I'm supposed to lose a few games so she'll come back to me? That's the stupidest fucking thing——"

"Damn, you are blind. You only need to show her how much you love her. And play like you're playing now. Show her you can do both."

How much you love her.

Were my feelings that fucking obvious? They must be if Jake had picked up on them. But no way in hell was I about to admit it.

"Jake…Jesus."

"No, I am not. But I do know what I'm talking about. You have to make sure you show her you're worth it. And then you have to be."

Chapter 18

Bliss

The flowers showed up at the shop Monday. A bouquet of daisies.

No card. Just two tickets to the first playoff game. The Redtails opened at home this Saturday. Mike already had his ticket. Jake had hooked him up. Mike had asked if I wanted to go with him, that he would ask Jake for another ticket. I said no.

Mike didn't need me to get to the games. He was perfectly capable of getting there himself.

That didn't mean I didn't want to go.

"Ooh, Bliss, honey. Those are beautiful. Got a new beau I haven't heard about?"

I gave my Aunt Rosie a distracted smile. "No. I'm pretty sure they're from Shane."

"Oh. Did you two get back together?"

"No. I haven't seen him since we…since I broke up with him."

"So why the flowers?"

"There're tickets to the first play-off game."

"Ah. The flowers are beautiful. And there's so many of them."

Rosie was right. There were fifteen total.

"That's an odd number." Rosie looked at me with a frown, her short, dark hair swinging around her face. "Does the number mean anything?"

I shook my head. "Not that I can think of."

"Huh. Well, obviously it means something to Shane."

Rosie was right. It did mean something to Shane. I just wasn't sure what and what it might have to do with me.

"So are you going to the game?" Rosie asked.

"I don't know."

With a sigh, Rosie finished hanging the dress for a first fitting later this morning before she turned to me. "Honey, I know you said you don't want to talk about it but…you know you can tell me anything right? It seemed like you really liked Shane. Did he do something? Was he——"

"No. No, it was nothing Shane did. It was me."

Rosie reached across the counter and patted me on the hand. "Tell me, hon. You've been walking around here like a ghost for the past few weeks. What happened?"

I shook my head. "Nothing happened. I just realized I needed to break it off before…" I sighed. "Before he leaves. He's eventually going to move on. And I'll still be here."

"And why do you think you need to stay here?"

"My life's here. My job, my family."

Rosie made a face. "Oh, hon. You're smart enough to get a job anywhere. And your family will always be here for you. There's no reason you have to stay tied to this little corner of the world. I love working with you and you know you'll always have a job with me but I don't remember hearing you talk about wanting to run a bridal salon when you were young."

"I was always changing my mind about what I wanted to do

when I was young. I went to college and got a business degree because…"

"Because what?"

Because I'd had no idea what I wanted to do with my life. Except I'd known I needed to be able to support myself. Especially after I'd gotten untangled from my ex.

Had I been hiding here? Afraid to go out and do something else?

No, that wasn't it. I loved living here, in this town. Where my parents lived fifteen minutes away and my nieces and nephews ran to hug me when I babysat. Where I lived next door to my brother.

"Because I didn't know what else to do with myself."

Rosie humphed. "I don't believe that for a second. You're no little lost girl. Maybe you just haven't found what you want to do with your life yet but that doesn't mean you won't ever. And don't get me wrong. I'm not saying having a man will fix all your problems. I just don't want you to count them out of the equation totally."

Shane

"So have you figured out where she's sitting yet?"

Lad sat next to me on the bench, watching me lace my skates. My teammate had waited until I took out my earbuds before speaking. Everyone knew not to talk to me until I'd finished my pre-game routine.

The noise of the sold-out crowd reached us back in the locker room, stoking the players' excitement even higher.

The final series started tonight. We'd won the first series with a sweep. The second series had gone five games. The semi-finals had gone six.

I was praying we broke the pattern and took this series in five games. That allowed for the other team to win one and for the Redtails to win at home. Of course, a sweep would be nice, too.

"No. I only know she's using the tickets." He shrugged. "Don't wanna know."

"You sure? Jake could ask Mike—"

"No. I know she's here. That's good enough."

"You really like her, don't you?"

I pulled my jersey over my head then gave Lad a look, which had Lad holding up his hands.

"Just an observation. Don't take my head off."

"Don't be fucking with his head before the game." CJ smacked his glove across Lad's shins. "He doesn't need to be thinking about anything but the game."

Actually, I'd been thinking about Bliss a lot lately and it hadn't affected my game at all. As a matter of fact, thinking about Bliss got me out of my head when I started getting too wrapped up in the game.

I didn't get to tell the guys that though, because the coach came in to give his last remarks before the game started.

Then I heard the crowd begin to roar and knew we only had a few seconds before I needed to lead the guys onto the ice.

Standing, I walked to the door, hearing the guys line up behind me. Nobody spoke but I heard Lad praying under his breath in Russian directly behind me. I had no idea what Lad was saying but I crossed myself when he muttered "Amen."

And started down the hall.

Bliss

. . .

"Holy crap, I didn't think this place could get any louder but damn." Faith had to raise her voice to be heard. "I think my ears are going to bleed."

I nodded and leaned in to speak closer to Faith's ear. "I know. It's amazing, isn't it?"

The sold-out crowd had been cheering since the start of the video showing highlights of the previous season and ending with solo shots of the team. My heart stuttered every time Shane's picture appeared on the Jumbotron above the ice.

"I'm so glad you forced me to come to these games with you."

Faith's smile made me put my arm around my friend's shoulders. "I'm glad you're enjoying it."

I had had to exchange the tickets Shane had sent me for handicapped access seats but the ticket office rep had been more than happy to make that happen.

"Yeah, well, the guys aren't hard on the eyes," Faith continued, "and the game *moves*. I love that."

Yes, Faith would. Before her accident, she'd been a soccer player and a runner. And if I thought about that much longer, my good mood would evaporate.

Instead, I shoved the thought out of my mind and watched Shane step onto the ice. In his gear with his mask on, he should've been indistinguishable from the other goalie. But I would've been able to pick him out of a lineup of men in the exact uniform. Something about the way he held himself captured my complete attention.

I didn't take my eyes off of him as he went through his pre-face-off routine, roughing the ice in front of his net, taking a drink, then tapping the posts with his stick in a certain rhythm. Every goalie had their own routine. But I only ever had eyes for Shane.

Dangerous. He was so dangerous.

And yet, when the first tickets had arrived, I knew immediately I was going to use them.

He'd sent me tickets to every home game with a bouquet of flowers. The first bouquet had had fifteen daisies.

The second had had fourteen. They'd continued to get smaller. It had taken me until the start of the second series to realize that the flowers signified how many games they needed to win to capture the championship.

I couldn't help but feel like it was also a countdown and that made my heart ache.

He would still be leaving at the end of the season, going home to Minnesota or elsewhere to train until training camp started late this summer. And then he'd be in Philadelphia.

Which isn't that far away.

I shook the thought out of my head. I couldn't go down that path. Not if I wanted to keep my distance.

And do you?

Snapped out of my thoughts by everyone around me standing, I shot to my feet as a group of school kids sang the anthem but I couldn't take my eyes off Shane. He wasn't wearing his mask, of course, and I had the almost overwhelming urge to run my fingers along his jaw, covered by a thick beard. Not even his playoff beard could disguise the handsome lines of his face.

I wanted to feel his beard against my skin, preferably between my thighs—

Shit.

Luckily, the ref dropped the puck.

And I sucked in a breath and held it.

Shane

. . .

Second period.

2-1 game.

The Redtails were up by one but we'd been losing at the end of the first period.

The defense had scrambled after a broken play in the other end and Pittsburgh Spikes' Greg Bruecker had shot off on a breakaway and scored the first goal of the game.

It'd been a beautiful shot and I would've been able to admire it—if it hadn't been against me.

As it was, I allowed myself to be pissed off for five seconds and then I shut it out and reset.

Between periods, the defensemen had apologized before the coach ripped our asses for getting dominated that first period.

And the Redtails had come out flying at the beginning of the second period.

CJ had scored the first goal, which had lit a fire under the crowd's ass. And then our top goal scorer, Tyler Richardson, had scored a short-hander after a questionable penalty on Lad.

And just that fast, the ice tilted back in the Redtails favor.

I watched the play at the opposite end, never taking my eye off the puck. So I saw Riley whiff on a one-timer from the top of the left circle and watched the Spikes' first line break away toward me with speed. The Redtails defensemen scrambled to catch up and, as ten players raced toward me, I had a split second to set.

Skating out to meet the onrushing players, I kept my eye on the puck as the right winger passed to the left winger setting up on my right.

I lost sight of the right winger but saw the way my guys were moving and knew that winger now had to be behind me.

Which meant I was blindsided by the crash.

All I felt was the rush of bodies crashing into me at high speed.

I went down, my head hit the ice and bodies fell on top of me.

Everything went black for a second and I had the terrifying thought that I'd blacked out.

Then I realized someone's arm had covered my mask. But my fight response had already kicked in and I was trying to toss players off me as my ears began to ring.

Fuck.

As I struggled to my knees, lungs working to replace the air that'd gotten knocked out of me, I saw my guys ripping opposing players away from me. Saw the linesmen jump in to separate bodies.

But it was all a little blurry.

Fuck. Fuck. Fuck.

Shaking my head, I tried to bring everything into focus. And that was when I heard Lad shout for the trainer.

I wanted to wave him off, wanted to get off my damn knees and get my skates under me.

But I wasn't sure I could do it without falling over.

So I stayed down and waited for the trainer.

And hoped like hell that I could finish the game.

Bliss

I saw Shane go down under a pile of bodies and, around me, the crowd gasped and shouted.

I could do neither. I could barely breathe as my heart jumped into my throat.

I watched as his head hit the ice right before he disappeared from view as the teams swarmed around the net.

Several players paired up to fight but I only had eyes for Shane.

Rising slowly, too slowly, to his knees, he sat with his head down, unmoving.

My lungs seized and I had to force air into my lungs.

"Oh, my god," Faith muttered. "Is he okay?"

I couldn't answer. I could only watch as CJ leaned down to check on Shane then made a beeline for the bench, where the trainer took CJ's arm so he could race to Shane's side.

As the linesmen and refs got the fighting under control, everyone's attention turned to Shane. The crowd seemed to hold its breath waiting for him to get up.

The longer it took, the harder it was for me to breathe.

I didn't realize I was on my feet until Faith took my hand.

And when it took two players to help him to his feet, I wanted to run for the stairs.

But I knew I wouldn't be allowed downstairs. I wasn't family. I wasn't even his girlfriend.

And still, I couldn't take my eyes off him. I watched as CJ and Lad helped him off the ice, watched him disappeared down the hall to the locker room, the trainer on his heels.

I only returned to my seat when Nate came onto the ice to take Shane's position.

"Hey, hon, are you okay?" Faith had leaned in to speak into my ear because the crowd had erupted into boos as the announcer listed the penalties, including one for goaltender interference.

I had the totally insane urge to walk down the stairs to the penalty box and coldcock the player who'd taken out Shane.

Shaking my head, I turned to Faith. "I don't even know who to ask to make sure he's okay."

Faith's lips turned up in a bittersweet smile. "He'll be back. He's tough."

But he didn't return by the end of the second period.

And I honestly thought I might sit there and cry.

Until my phone vibrated.

I grabbed it before I considered the fact that it might not have anything to do with Shane. And slapped a hand over my mouth to stop my cry of joy when I realized who it was from.

JAKE

He is fine. Be back third period. Name on list to come down. Be there.

I was going to kiss Jake when I saw him.

After I hugged the hell out of Shane.

"So are you gonna tell me what you're smiling like a loon about or just leave me in the dark?"

Faith's wry voice drew my attention away from my phone.

"He's okay."

Faith smiled. "Glad to hear it. But are you?"

I didn't even have to think about it. "No. I think I screwed up."

"Yeah," Faith nodded. "I'm pretty sure you did. But I don't think it's unfixable."

"We still have the same problem, though. He's eventually going to leave."

"And you'll go with him. And when he's done playing hockey in ten or fifteen years and you want to come back, then you do. But if you love the guy, and you must because you don't get this upset over someone you don't love, then you've got to make a choice."

Faith made it sound so easy. I knew it wasn't.

I only knew I didn't want to be on the outside again.

Shane

· · ·

After spending time in the dark room to assess for a concussion, I was pronounced okay to play by the doctor.

Damn right. I'd started this. I was finishing it.

"Guess you really are made of brick." Jake bumped my shoulder as we lined up for the start of the third period. "You okay?"

"I'm good. Ready to get this done."

Behind me, the rest of the team shuffled on their skates, sticks tapping.

"She's here." Jake leaned in to speak directly into my ear. "In case you wanted to know."

The music queued up, the fans began to scream and my adrenaline began to pump. I could've said it wasn't because she was watching. I would've been lying.

So I turned to Jake and smiled.

"Yes, now that is the face we need." Jake nodded. "And so we go."

I shook my helmet into place and led my team out.

I'd win the game and then I'd get the girl.

Seemed like a plan.

Chapter 19

Bliss

I gave my name to the guard at the stairs and practically held my breath. But he didn't even need to check his list. He just waved me through.

So I could have a momentary panic attack as I walked down the stairs.

What if Jake was wrong? What if Shane didn't want to see me?

Then why was he sending you the tickets?

Letting him go the first time had been heart-wrenching. If I was wrong about this now, my heart might just break.

Faith had assured me she'd be fine taking a taxi home. So here I stood, smiling at the small talk between the wives and girl-friends but not saying much. I knew most of them by name now and, for the most part, they were sweethearts.

They didn't say anything about the fact that I hadn't been here for the past couple of games. They just welcomed me back with smiles and continued on as if nothing had happened.

Which left me alone to gnaw over every little worry.

My head popped up when I heard Chrissy squeak as her boyfriend, forward Colin Johnson, snuck up behind her and wrapped his arms around her.

I looked down the hall, hoping to see Shane. A few other guys made their way out of the locker room but not mine.

He's not yours. You pushed him away.

And if he gave me another chance, I'd make it up to him.

"Hey, Liss, I didn't know you'd be down here."

I turned away from the locker room to smile at my brother. "Hey, Mike. You waiting for Jake?"

He nodded, his smile bright. "Yeah, we're gonna go eat." Then he looked over my shoulder for a second. "See you later, Lissy."

I figured Jake had appeared but a second later I heard my name in a familiar voice. A voice that made my thighs clench and my inside quiver.

"Bliss."

Sucking in a breath, I turned and had to bite my lips against the huge grin that wanted to escape.

"Hi."

"How'd you get down?"

And just that fast, I panicked again. "Jake put me on the list. I'm sorry. I should've warned you. I didn't mean to put you on the spot. I just wanted—"

He leaned forward and sealed his mouth over mine, kissing me until I could barely breathe.

When he pulled away, long seconds later, I vaguely heard the catcalls from a few of the other guys and laughter from the girls.

But nothing could take my attention from Shane.

"I'm glad you're here. And I'll thank Jake later—"

"You are welcome." Jake smacked Shane on the back as he walked past to bump his fist with Mike. "Just don't wear yourself out tonight. We have a game tomorrow. Be nice to him, Bliss. He might still not be right in the head. Considering he let you go way too easily the first time, he definitely is not thinking straight."

Shane's lips curved, making my heart beat faster. "I'm a fast learner. And I try not to make the same mistake twice."

I shook my head, wrapping my arms around his waist. "I was the one who made the mistake. Can we—"

"Go? Absolutely."

Shane got me turned around and headed for the door in a split second, his arm around my shoulders. I had to walk fast to keep up as he made for the door to the side lot where the players parked.

"My car—"

"We'll pick it up— Shit. I brought CJ." He stopped, turned and tossed his keys at Jake, whose lightning-fast reflexes allowed him to catch them.

"Give those to CJ. Tell him not to ding my truck."

Jake's laughter followed us out of the building but Shane didn't slow. But he didn't talk either as we hurried to my car in the lot across the street from the arena. I figured that was because there were still fans heading the same way.

A few of them recognized him, called out congratulations and encouragement for the next game. He acknowledged every one with a smile and a wave but he didn't slow.

It wasn't until he folded himself into my front seat and I got us on the street did he speak.

"We're going back to your place to work this out, right? Because I don't want there to be any misunderstandings."

I swallowed hard. "Yes, we are."

"And we're going to work this out. Because I love you, Bliss. I don't want you to have any doubt about that."

My hands clenched around the steering wheel at the absolute authority in his voice and I nodded, not sure I could answer coherently and still drive.

"I missed you. You know that, right? I never wanted to give you up but I didn't want you to think I was like your ex."

"I know. Shane—"

"You got the flowers."

"Yes. Shane—"

"When there were no more games, I would've shown up at your door and we would've talked. And I would've told you just what I'm telling you now."

Stopped at a red light, I turned to see him watching me.

I smiled and his expression lightened enough for me to see the heat in his eyes.

Then the light changed and I stepped on the gas. He didn't say anything else as I drove the last few miles back to my apartment.

He unfolded his big body from the front seat as soon as I put the car in park. Which meant he was at my door as soon as I opened it.

He took my hand to help me out and didn't release me as he hustled me toward my apartment building.

By the time we reached my door, I was laughing. I couldn't help it. I could barely keep up with him when he walked fast and, right now, he was practically running.

As I went to fit the key into the lock, he pressed himself against my back, short-circuiting my brain, and I dropped the keys.

"Let me get those," he grumbled, "because if you bend over…"

I went wet at the deep note in his voice and I might have whimpered as he scooped up the keys and opened my door.

With his hands on my hips, he hurried me through and, in the next second, he had me plastered against the door. His big body held mine against the door, so much hard muscle I wanted to bite him. Then his mouth sealed over mine. His full beard was a new sensation that only added to my sensory pleasure.

As the fury of his kiss infected me, I shoved my hands into his hair and held on tight. I'd already toed off my sneakers and locked my legs around his waist when he lifted me off my feet.

Tilting his head, he kissed me deeper, sank his tongue into my mouth and made me moan as his hands worked at my jeans.

With a groan, he pulled away for a second. "I'm making it a rule that you always wear skirts."

I huffed out a short laugh but, at the moment, I couldn't agree with him more. "I may actually agree to that. But for now, just hurry."

His mouth slipped back over mine as his fingers worked at my jeans.

"Drop your legs."

I obeyed without thought, wrapping my arms around his shoulders so my legs could hang free and he could work my jeans down my legs.

It took a little maneuvering because that damn denim clung but finally I felt cooler air brush against my bare thighs and my mound.

My moan sounded loud enough that I feared my brother might be able to hear it through the walls.

And then he slid his hand between my legs and flicked at my clit with two fingers and I didn't care who heard me.

I only wanted Shane to hurry.

Hips writhing against him, I felt him fumble with his pants.

"Fuck." He growled. "Condom."

"Good thing you're so good with your hands."

He sucked in a sharp breath then let out a sharp bark of laughter. "I fucking love you, Bliss."

He'd said it earlier in the car but here, now, I melted. Completely. Totally.

"I love you, too."

He kissed me hard enough to press my head back against the door.

Then he let me slide down until my feet hit the floor.

And handed me the condom.

Smiling, I looked down to see his cock pressing out of his open zipper. Hard, dark and oh so enticing.

"Put the condom on, sweetheart. And then I'm going to fuck you against the door because I don't think I can make it to the damn couch."

I took the condom from his hand, hands shaking with need, and rolled it down his hard shaft.

Then I wrapped my arms around his shoulders again and would have climbed him like a pole if he hadn't put his hands on my hips and lifted me.

The next time we did this, I wanted us to both be naked and standing in front of a mirror so I could see his arms.

Then he lifted me like I weighed nothing and the only thought my brain was able to process was *Now. Right freaking now.*

As if he'd read my thoughts, he settled me on the tip of his cock and let me slid down the shaft at an excruciatingly slow pace.

In this position, he felt huge and my arms tightened around his neck until I figured he might not be able to breathe. But I didn't let go.

And his hands tightened on my hips as his chest rose and fell with each gasping inhale.

When he was seated deep inside me, he held there until I couldn't take the anticipation any longer.

Turning my face into his neck, I bit him. And as he shuddered against me, his hips pulled back.

And he gave me exactly what I wanted.

All of him.

Epilogue

Shane

The crowd had begun the countdown at twenty seconds.

I heard them but kept my eye on the puck. The play was at the other end of the ice. The Redtails were winning one-nothing but the Arizona Rattlers weren't giving up.

We were battling in the corner for the puck, trying to make one last play to push the series to six games.

The Reds were doing everything they could to make sure this series ended here at home with the Calder Cup in their hands.

Ten. Nine. Eight.

The Rattlers' left winger dug the puck out and made a break for center ice.

I set, catcher up, stick down. The massive roar of the crowd barely registered.

Five. Four. Three…

From the blue line, the winger took his shot.

And I cleared it just like I had every shot this game.

I roared along with the crowd as the horns blared, signaling the end of the game.

And the Redtails won the Calder Cup.

My team rushed toward me from the opposite end of the ice, sticks forgotten, helmets torn off and tossed.

We met in a crush at the center of the ice, hugging, jumping, screaming.

And in the center, I grinned until I thought my face would break.

Life was good. Life was really fucking good.

Pucking the Grinder

I go in deep and make the plays...

Riley

I'm a fast-talking minor-league hockey player with a reputation as a grinder. I go in deep, hit hard and come out with the puck. I'm not known for giving up and, when I meet a cool blonde who trips all my switches, I fall hard and fast. I'm going to need more than determination to break down Aly's reservations. But will my lifelong dream of making it to the NHL cost me the woman of my dreams?

...but she's not going to fall for my game.

Aly

My aversion to professional athletes falters when faced with Riley, a six-foot-four hockey god. He's everything I never wanted in a man: sexy, rough around the edges and pushy as all hell. And absolutely irresistible. But I'm not going to give him my heart because he's going to leave. And I don't want my heart to follow.

Chapter 1

Aly

The door to the billing office of the Reading Health Center squeaked open, causing me to do two things.

First, I cringed because I was currently bent over at the waist trying to find the cord that'd fallen between two desks, and my ass would be the first thing anyone walking through the door would see.

And second, I hoped like hell whoever had just walked through that door was a coworker and not someone I'd actually have to talk to.

"Uh, hey. How's it going?"

Shit, shit, shit.

No such luck. The voice was male and unknown, deep, with just enough of a husky edge that my heart kicked up a beat.

And, of course, I'd been caught with my ass in the air.

With a sigh, I began to wiggle my way out from between the desks.

"I'll be with you in a second."

"Yeah, sure. No problem. Take your time."

Great, just great. He was a perv, too, which meant he was going to watch my ass the entire way.

And, since I was the only person in the office, I'd have to smile and pretend to be pleasant while he berated me for a bill he probably didn't understand.

Today, smiling would require a superhuman effort. The hospital's internet had been spotty all day, and the program the office used to bill patients had been glitchy since it'd been updated last week.

I'd just gotten off the phone with the tech guys, who'd told me to try the old unplug-replug method for fixing the connection. If that didn't work, I'd have to wait my turn because apparently every other department in the hospital had had the same problem today. Which meant I'd probably embarrassed myself for no reason.

Sucking in a deep breath, I finally freed myself and stood, pushing the hair that had escaped my pristine twist out of my face.

Then I forced a smile and hoped I didn't look like a rabid dog.

"Hello, can I help…you?"

Holy crap.

The man leaning his elbows on the counter had definitely been checking out my ass.

Quite frankly, I wasn't sure I minded.

Specimens like this didn't typically pass through my door, much less stare at any part of me. No, I usually only saw guys like this in memes about eye candy and fantasies.

He had to be at least six-two and probably weighed more than two hundred pounds. All of it muscle. Thick, bulging muscle that made his faded gray t-shirt stretch at its seams.

I felt small standing in front of him, which was a minor miracle because I wasn't. I stood five-seven and carried a few more pounds than I'd like. In heels, I could stare down most men I knew.

But not this one.

I had to look up, even as his gaze dropped to my feet then made its way up until he finally met my eyes. And when we did…

Holy freaking crap.

I had to bite my bottom lip to make sure my mouth didn't hang open. He was quite possibly the hottest guy I'd ever seen in real life. Seriously, he should be modeling underwear.

I had the urge to pick up the nearest stack of papers and fan myself. I couldn't remember ever meeting a guy who made my body flush with heat from my toes to my scalp. And everywhere in between.

Rugged features that reminded me a little of a young Brad Pitt but even more handsome. Damn, I never would've thought that possible.

His brown hair had a wave to it, and his eyes were a dark greenish-brown that made me want to lean over the counter and get really close so I could see them better. Like, maybe flat-on-his-back-lying-on-top-of-him close. With our noses almost touching and our lips only centimeters apart—

"Hey, yeah, I'm hoping you can."

Can what? flashed through my mind, but luckily I couldn't get my mouth to work right away. Oh yeah, I was at work.

When he reached behind his back to take something out of his back pocket, all the muscles in those arms shifted and bunched and generally made me feel like I was watching a porn movie. Which I never did.

"I got this bill…"

He grinned at me as he unfolded a piece of paper and set it on the counter.

And holy crap, I nearly swallowed my tongue.

Down, girl. He wants you to fix his bill, not lick him from head to toe.

"I'm not sure why I got it. It should've gone to my former team."

Swallowing hard, I smiled and reached across the counter for the paper. Tearing my gaze away from his, I focused instead on scanning the bill. After I'd taken a look at his hands. The man had huge hands, with long fingers covered in scars.

"Of course, Mister…" I looked down at the name, "Hatch. Let me take a look."

"It's Riley. And thanks, Miss…?"

"Martin. Aly Martin."

I happened to look up at that moment and found him smiling down at me. Not a full-out grin, but one of those half grins guys did so well.

"Nice to meet you, Miss Aly Martin."

I blinked and sucked in a breath. "Nice to meet you, too. I'll, ah, just take a look at your bill."

He leaned his forearms on the counter, getting even closer. "Got it a week or so ago but we've had practice every day and I haven't been able to get over here. I figured it was better to do this in person than try to explain over the phone."

And I was so grateful he had. "Practice?"

His smile widened and my ovaries practically exploded.

"I play for the Redtails."

"Redtails?"

I cringed as I parroted him for a second time, just as I realized that he must be a hockey player for the local Reading Redtails.

"Sorry. Stupid question." I shook my head and focused my attention on the paper in front of me. "Let me take a look at this."

"Are you a hockey fan?"

The bill was standard and nothing looked out of the ordinary. The only thing that didn't make sense was that the bill was from this hospital for services at a hospital in another state that was in the same network. "You were treated for a shoulder injury last July?"

I looked up to find him watching me with a slight smile, the kind of smile that invited me to smile back. Which I did.

"Yeah. Took a hit into the boards." He reached for his left shoulder and rubbed it with one of those big hands. I couldn't help but follow the movement before I blinked and snapped out of it.

"Does it still hurt?"

I wanted to take it back the second the words were out of my mouth and barely managed not to roll my eyes at my own words.

Damn it, I wasn't my younger sister, Vivi, who'd never met a guy she didn't want to sleep with. Although no one would blame me for wanting to see this man stripped down to nothing because, *holy crap*, he was hot.

His smile widened as he shook his head. "Not anymore, no. I just rub it out of habit. So what do you think?"

"That maybe you want to get another job? This one seems dangerous to your health."

He burst into laughter and, Jesus, if I'd thought he was hot before, now he was off-the-charts drool-worthy. His mouth alone made me want to grab him and kiss the hell out of him.

And since that was completely out of the question, I could only smile back when he stopped laughing.

"Yeah, it kinda is, but it's still fun and I love to play so I'm gonna until I physically can't."

He certainly looked physically able at the moment.

My gaze dropped to his broad shoulders then to his muscular chest. I'd never been this up close and personal with a hockey player before. The only other professional athlete I'd ever been this close to before had been Vivi's ex, a football player. And he'd been a cocky asshole I had hated on sight.

This guy looked just as cocky. I'd reserve judgment on the asshole part.

Which doesn't matter because you'll never see him again.

I didn't go to hockey games, didn't think I'd like them. From what I'd seen on TV when my dad used to watch, the sport was rough and loud. Two things I tried to avoid as much as possible in my life.

I usually dated nice guys, nerds who spent hours in front of a computer every day and considered Hacky Sack a sport. The ones who took off the day the new Marvel movie released.

Nice, regular guys. Who left me completely cold.

Tearing my gaze away from his chest, I looked over his bill again.

Luckily, there was no one else here to see me make a fool out of myself. The five other women who worked in this office would have never let me live this down.

"So, what's the problem with your bill?"

"Well, it should've been paid by my previous team. The injury happened during a game so I figure it should've been covered under their policy. I don't know why it wouldn't."

"Which team?"

"The Colonials' ECHL team in Lancaster."

"How long have you played hockey?"

Okay, technically, that had nothing to do with his bill but, sue me, curiosity had taken hold.

Leaning his elbows on the counter, he cocked his head to the side. "For as long as I can remember. Have you been to a game?"

I shook my head. "No."

His eyebrows rose. "Would you like to? I could get you tickets. We have a game tomorrow night."

Yes and *No* popped onto my tongue at the exact same time.

Yes, because *hello*, hot guy. No, because, well, I didn't accept random offers of hockey tickets from unknown men. At least, I never had before.

I blinked, trying to reboot my brain. "I don't think I'm available."

Which was total bullshit. I didn't have a date. Me and my last boyfriend had parted ways six months ago. He'd wanted more than a few dates a week and sex whenever we could squeeze it in. I'd been perfectly content with the arrangement.

It wasn't like I'd been planning to marry Paul.

And didn't that make you a stone-cold bitch?

Probably.

Still, I'd thought we'd been happy. Not in love but there'd been sparks. Well, more like a warm ember or two. But, really, wasn't all that chemistry stuff just a big lie to explain away the stupid stuff you wanted to do because you were in lust?

I wasn't some hopeless romantic who was waiting for "the thunderbolt," that lightning strike from out of the blue that was supposed to hit you when you met the man you were supposed to marry.

"Got a date?" Riley asked.

Was he teasing or fishing for information? And really, how badly was I deluding myself?

I wasn't some hideous troll but guys like this didn't ask out girls like me, with my reading glasses hanging around my neck and my skirt a safe two inches below my knees and my buttoned-up blouse.

I resisted the urge to look down at myself to see if I'd actually buttoned it all the way to my neck this morning.

Besides, professional athletes had bad reputations. Not that I'd ever dated one. But my sister had dated an NFL player I'd met at a party during training camp at a local college. And he'd been a huge asshole.

"No, I don't. But I—"

"Then I'll leave two tickets for you at the door." His smile widened. "Bring a friend."

"I'm not sure I can. I've—"

"Come on, you'll have a great time. We're playing the second-best team in the league. It'll be a good game."

He grinned and…oh wow. That smile should be illegal. It made my thighs…and other parts…clench.

And I couldn't resist asking, "So who's the best team in the league?"

"We are." His smile widened even more and I felt my insides tighten and heat. "Our team won the Calder Cup last year and we're looking to repeat this year."

I nodded like I knew what winning a Calder Cup meant.

Then I resisted the urge to bat my eyes at him and pet his chest.

"So, Miss Martin, wanna come to a game tomorrow night?"

Riley

I watched the woman in front of me think really hard about her answer to my question.

And I had to admit, my pride was taking a hit.

Usually, women jumped at the chance to accept whatever I was offering. Tickets, dinner, sex…

Then again, most of those women knew who I was and what I did. Most of them sought me out and, even if they didn't, I didn't have to do much chasing.

This girl was nothing like those others who went out of their way to catch my eye, except for one—she was *hot*. From the top of her blonde head to the tips of her toes in those little heels and everything in between, this girl flipped all of my switches.

But she didn't seem to want anything to do with me.

Well, damn. Wasn't that just par for my fucking course this year?

I hadn't really wanted to do this today, hadn't wanted to have to fight through the bullshit of medical bills and be reminded of the injury that'd nearly killed my career last season.

I'd figured I'd be up against some middle-aged battle-ax who'd question me for five minutes, make me feel like a criminal for daring to question the mighty hospital's bill, and make me fill out a shit-ton of forms.

But when I'd stepped into the office and seen that beautiful ass in that tight black skirt sticking up in the air, I'd been understandably turned on.

Then she'd stood and every naughty librarian fantasy I'd ever had flashed through my brain.

Hell, my mouth had gone dry.

"Um," she finally said, "I'm really not sure if I can get there tomorrow night."

Well, at least it wasn't a flat-out no. I could work with that.

Toning down my smile by a few watts, I leaned my arms on the counter separating them. "Well, how about this? I'll leave the tickets at will-call, and if you can come, you can pick them up there. Then maybe we can go out for a drink afterward."

Her pale-blue eyes widened and she didn't answer right away. Shit, maybe I should've waited to ask her out for that drink. But I wasn't known for keeping my mouth shut, on or off the ice.

"A bunch of us usually go out after the game."

"So… it'd be a group thing?"

I'd make it whatever she wanted. "Yeah, a group."

Her teeth sank into her bottom lip and I had to swallow a groan.

"I'd really hate to say yes and then not show up. The tickets will go to waste. I should really just—"

"The tickets won't go to waste," I assured her, knowing she'd been about to turn me down. "We never sell out. I'll leave two. Bring a friend."

Now her tongue came out to lick at her lips, and it was all I could do not to reach out and let my finger run over that plump bottom lip.

"Well, my sister loves sports."

There were more where she came from? Someone on the team was going to owe me big time. "Bring her along. The more, the merrier." Then my smile toned down even more. "Don't say no. I'll leave the tickets at the will-call window, and I'll give the guard your name so you and your sister can meet me downstairs after the game. I'll give you my number and you can text me for directions."

It took a second, but finally she smiled. "Okay. I'll see if my sister can go."

Our gazes held for a few more seconds and, for the first time in my life, I found myself without a single thing to say.

If she hadn't looked down at the bill she still held in her hands, I wasn't sure how long we would've stood there, staring into each other's eyes. And I wouldn't have minded.

Then she sighed. "And I hate to say this but I think I'm going to have to get back to you about your bill. Our system is messed up and I can't get online at the moment."

"No problem." Just meant I'd have an excuse to talk to her again if I didn't see her tomorrow night. Grabbing a piece of paper and a pen from the counter, I wrote my name and number and slid it across the counter.

She took it, our fingertips brushing as the paper exchanged hands.

I didn't know how long we would've stood there, barely touching, me grinning like an idiot and her looking a little shell-shocked, if the door hadn't opened.

"Dude, you ready, yes? I need—oh, hello."

Controlling the urge to roll my eyes, I shook my head instead and turned to see Jake grinning at Aly.

The Czech player had a reputation as a manwhore, and with his looks it was easy to see why. Tall, blond and ripped, the guy smiled and women threw their panties at him.

Apparently, Aly wasn't immune. Her eyes widened as she stared at the Redtails' best defenseman.

Which made me want to kick the ever-loving shit out of Jake if the kid so much as hinted at making a move on her. Okay, Jake wasn't exactly a kid at twenty-three, but I was twenty-eight and had a few pounds on me, which I would use to kick Jake's ass if he didn't turn down that smile.

Luckily for Jake, Aly barely glanced at him and said "Hello" before staring at me again.

Take that, kid.

"I need a few seconds yet."

Sliding a glance over my shoulder, I saw Jake's mouth twist into a shit-eating grin. Oh, I would *so* make the kid pay for that at practice tomorrow.

"Yes, I see that. Fine. I will be in hall. You come get me when you are ready. Hopefully in the next hour."

If I had my way, I would spend at least another hour talking to this woman but she was obviously working and wouldn't be able to leave in the middle of the day.

Damn, I couldn't wait until tomorrow night.

"I guess you need to leave," she said, although she looked a little depressed at the thought.

"Unfortunately, yeah. I'm hosting the team dinner tonight. Twenty-two hockey players in one enclosed space. Always good for a few laughs."

Her lips curved in a flat-out smile that almost made me pant. "I don't know. Sounds like the setup for a sitcom."

"Not one they could show on TV."

The door to the office opened again and we both turned to look. This time, a short guy with a wrinkled dress shirt, black pants, and a mop of unruly black hair hustled through the door.

"Hey, Aly. Just gonna check out your terminal—"

"Wait! I haven't—damn it." She sighed. "I'm sorry. I really have to go."

"No problem. I'll see you tomorrow."

When she smiled, it gave me hope that I actually would. "I'll try. I just—"

"Hey, Aly," the guy in her office called out. "Can you come close out your programs?"

With a little grimace, she turned and hustled toward the office in the back. Giving me another look at her great ass, which I watched until I couldn't see her anymore.

Then I turned and walked out of the office with a smile, which I knew would set off Jake.

Fuck it. I couldn't care less.

Sure enough, Jake fell into step beside me, still wearing that shit-eating grin.

"Dude, you look like the cat that ate that bird. I don't think I have ever seen you look this way. You know, like you are happy. You asked her out on a date, yes? I assume she said yes or you wouldn't be smiling. Good for you. I was worried about your skills with the women. I thought maybe you were still virgin."

With a sigh, I stuck my elbow in Jake's side, making me flinch.

"Hey, kid. We're in public. Tone it down a little."

But, of course, Jake couldn't contain himself. Or he just didn't care. I had never met anyone with less of a filter than Jake.

"What is to tone down? Since you are not virgin, you should not be ashamed. You did ask her out, right?"

I shook my head, knowing I wasn't going to be able to ignore Jake. The guy's focus was legendary on and off the ice. But I hadn't gotten where I was on skill alone. I'd been a sports management major in college and not far from the top of my class. If I hadn't been so damn determined to play professional hockey, I probably would've become an agent, which I still might do some day. I was good at talking.

"Yeah, I did. She'll be at the game tomorrow night."

Jake clapped me on the back. "And that is what we like to hear. Maybe you get laid now. Be good for you."

I couldn't contain my laughter. It rang through the parking garage as we reached my car.

"Dude, do you ever shut up?"

Jake just shrugged. "You talk on the ice. I talk off the ice. We make a good team, yes?"

Shaking my head, I had to agree.

"Yeah, we make a good team."

"Good. That is settled. Now, what are you going to make for dinner? Lad can't handle dairy and Tyler can't handle anything green…"

As Jake ran at the mouth again, I nodded at the appropriate spots, but my brain had latched on to something Jake had said and wouldn't let go.

It'd been a while since I'd gotten laid. Like, since before the beginning of the season.

Holy shit, how the hell had *that* happened?

For the past seven years of my professional career, I'd played hard, on and off the ice. I'd been through ten times as many women as I had teams. I didn't brag about it and I tried not to be a dick about it but it'd been a fact of my life.

But for the past five months, I'd been a monk.

I'd always been dedicated to the game, always showed up to win. But this year…well, this year, I was twenty-eight.

I was one of the oldest guys on the team. Still six years younger than Cary Lenville, who was probably playing his last season as he was groomed to become the Redtails' assistant coach, but a lot of the guys I'd come up with had either moved up to the NHL or had retired.

Retired. The word alone was enough to make me shudder. Hell, I wasn't ready to retire.

Which was why I was working so damn hard this season. This was my year to make it. I couldn't afford any distractions.

And yet…I hadn't been able to resist the blonde behind the counter.

Jake punched me on the shoulder hard enough to make me flinch. Luckily, we were stopped for a red light.

I shot Jake a glare. "What the fuck?"

"You have not listened to one word I said this entire time, have you?"

"How could I *not* be listening? You haven't shut up since we left the hospital."

Rolling his eyes, Jake sighed. "I supposed you are to be forgiven considering the hot girl you scored."

"That's not who I was thinking about."

Jake smirked. "So what are you thinking about? You don't look happy whatever it is. What is wrong? Tell me. I am good listener."

Then the guy fell totally silent. A minor miracle. No one on the team would believe it.

"Nothing's wrong. Just thinking about the season."

"Should be a good one. You are a good addition to the team since we lost our last grinder."

I shook my head, smiling. "Happy to be of service."

"And we are happy to have you. You and CJ make a good team."

"Yeah, well, I'm not on the first line." Which rankled, like a splinter in my heel. Damn it, I wanted to be on that first line but Coach had me on the second. Of course, it just made me work that much harder, which Coach knew would happen.

"Word is Knapper will not be here long. Duchene is having problems."

Dickie Duchene was the Philadelphia Colonials' third-line right-winger, notorious for playing as hard as he partied. Problem was, sometimes he didn't know where the line was and he crossed it more than he should.

"Yeah, I heard the same."

Sure, I'd briefly entertained the thought that maybe I'd be the one called up. Totally unrealistic considering I'd only been with the team since the beginning of this season and Sam Knapp had been a Colonials prospect since his draft four years ago.

"But this is an opportunity for you, yes? You will get Knapper's spot on the first line."

I just shook my head. "Life doesn't always work the way you want it."

Jake shrugged, the arrogance of youth written all over his face. "Then you just have to make it work for you. What is saying? When a door closes, you climb out the window. Sometimes you just have to make your own window by breaking down the wall."

When Jake looked at me with a smile, I laughed all the way to grocery store.

Chapter 2

Aly

"So...I've got two tickets to the hockey game Friday night. Wanna go with me?"

Vivi looked up from her drawing table, shock written all over my sister's face.

"Did you just say *hockey*? As in ice hockey? As in, you're going to go to a Redtails game? With actual hockey fans all around you screaming and yelling and having a good time and possibly spilling their beer all over you?"

I rolled my eyes at my sister, unwilling to concede that Vivi had a good reason for her shock.

"Yes, I am. And I thought you could come with me since you don't work tomorrow night."

Sitting back in her drafting chair, Vivi narrowed her gaze at me and gave me a once-over, pushing rainbow-hued, waist-length hair over her shoulder. "You look like my sister but you're speaking in tongues. Who are you and what have you done with her?"

Flipping Vivi the bird, I spun my sister away from her desk, where she'd been drawing something that looked like erotic fan art of… "Is that the Tenth Doctor and Ianto? Why is the Tenth Doctor kissing Ianto?"

Vivi shrugged. "Why shouldn't they kiss? I'd watch at least two episodes of them kissing, wouldn't you? And you're not getting out of this conversation that easily. Why do you have tickets for a hockey game tomorrow night? You hate hockey."

I wrinkled my nose. "I never said I hated hockey."

Vivi's stunning aquamarine eyes widened even more. "I distinctly remember having a conversation where you said something about hockey being a sport played by illiterate farm boys."

Wincing, I shook my head. "I did not."

Vivi nodded as she turned back to her drawing and picked up her pencil. "Yes, you did. I think you were dating that lawyer wannabe at the time. He was a total douche, by the way."

That much was totally true. He had been a douche.

"So what if I did. I'm a girl." I pulled the covers up on Vivi's unmade bed then sat on the edge. "I can change my mind. Come to the game with me Friday night."

"Why the sudden interest in hockey?"

I didn't answer the question right away. Instead, I let myself look around my sister's room.

The home we shared technically belonged to our parents, but Vivi and I now paid the second mortgage our parents had taken out so they could buy a home in Florida, which was where they now lived full time. Leaving us with a very nice cottage home in a good neighborhood not far from the hospital where I worked. My decent salary and Vivi's fluctuating salary as a freelance graphic artist, part-time tattoo artist and part-time waitress allowed us to pay that mortgage and all the bills with no problem.

And the fact that our parents lived a thousand miles away in Florida made it that much sweeter.

"Aly? What's going on?"

Vivi had abandoned her drawing again and now watched me with narrowed eyes.

"Nothing's going on."

Vivi snorted. "Yeah, right."

I finally looked at my sister. "So…I met this guy today."

A knowing expression now crossed my sister's face. "Ah. That's where you got the tickets. Let me guess. He works for the team. He's their…what? Their accountant? Their lawyer? Their marketing guy?"

I couldn't wait to wipe that smirk off her face. "Second-line right wing."

My sister's stunned expression made me smile.

"Holy fuck. Seriously?"

I shrugged, as if hockey players asked me out all the time. "He came into the office today with a problem with his bill."

"Well, damn." Scrambling up from her chair, Vivi grabbed her laptop off her desk and hopped onto the bed beside me.

Like two teenagers, we spread out on the bed with the laptop between us as we Googled Riley and clicked on the first listing for a site called hockeydb.com.

Vivi whistled as soon as the site came up. "Damn. He's *hot*."

I grinned at the breathless appreciation in my sister's voice.

"And he's even hotter in person."

Which he totally was. Tall. Dark. Handsome. Wicked grin and green eyes that made me want to kiss him…which made no sense at all.

I'd gone back and forth all day about accepting the tickets, had tried to tell myself I really shouldn't accept them.

I hadn't been kidding when I told him I'd never been to a game. And Vivi had every right to be shocked about her wanting to go. It definitely wasn't something I'd ever thought I'd do. And especially not as the guest of one of the players. Who wanted to take me out for a drink after the game.

I should've told him no and stuck to my answer. But there'd been something about him…

I'd already checked out his page on the Redtails site at work this afternoon, but now I read over his stats again.

Riley Hatch. Six-two. Two-ten. Just turned twenty-nine a month ago. He'd played for five different leagues, including Boston University. I hadn't expected that, which made me wrinkle my nose at my own arrogance.

"*This* is the guy who gave you tickets to the game? What did he want?"

"What do you mean?"

Vivi rolled her eyes. "I mean, what does he want from you?"

"He wants us to go out with the team after the game for drinks."

Vivi's eyes got even bigger. "No fucking way. Seriously?"

All right, now Vivi was starting to get on my nerves. I adored my younger sister but sometimes…

"Hey!" I smacked Vivi on the arm. "Why wouldn't he?"

Vivi knocked her shoulder against me in retaliation. "You know that's not what I meant. I just mean, athletes have never been your thing. I can't believe you said yes."

"I didn't exactly say yes. Yet. I told him I might have plans."

I snorted. "Which, of course, you don't."

My sister knew me too well. "I know, but…I'm not sure what he wants."

Vivi's eyebrows rose. "He wants what they all want. The question is, what do you want? If you want to go out with the guy, then do it. It's not like you have to sleep with him. I don't think he expects sex for a pair of tickets."

"I know that. He seems really nice. And when he smiles… No lie, I swear my ovaries exploded. Seriously hot."

Vivi raised her hand as if to testify. "No argument from me. The guy is totally fuckable. You should jump his bones, which I know you won't, but still."

Was I really that much of a puritan? No, I didn't sleep around. Never had. I had to have a connection with a guy before I fell into bed with him. Otherwise, there was no point.

Yes, I'd felt an immediate reaction to Riley, but that didn't mean I had to jump into bed with him right away.

Then again, I probably jumped in bed with every girl he asked out for drinks, and when I told him no, I'd never see him again.

"I'm not going to jump his bones tomorrow night."

Vivi rolled her eyes again. "Obviously. Just don't expect to hear from him again when you don't put out, you know?"

I heard the bitterness in my sister's voice and had the urge to go completely against my nature and beat the living shit out of Vivi's ex-asshole of a boyfriend who'd crushed her heart and her spirit. Jamie Dunbar might have a multimillion-deal with the NFL, but the prick had made my sister cry for weeks, and if I ever saw him again, I'd smack the shit out of him.

Yes, every girl had that one guy who broke her heart into a thousand pieces. Well, every girl except me. I'd never fallen that hard for a guy. And yes, I secretly worried that maybe there was something wrong with me.

But I never wanted to be like Vivi, bitter and crushed because of a guy.. Or like my mother, stuck with a man I couldn't stand but wouldn't leave.

"So are you coming with me Friday night or not?"

My sister rolled her eyes. "Of course. Gotta see this guy for myself. Besides, you won't go if I don't, and you need to get out and have some fun. You're starting to remind me a little of Mom and that's scary."

My brows knit together. "What do you mean?"

Vivi rolled onto her side and propped her hand under her head. I mimicked her position.

"You know. You never have any fun and you're always worried about something."

"I'm not always worried."

Vivi's brows rose. "I notice you didn't say anything about having fun."

Now I rolled my eyes. "Work's been crazy lately and I haven't had a lot of time—"

"Excuses, excuses." Vivi waved her hand in front of me. "Just like Mom. She always has an explanation for why she doesn't do anything, and you're starting to act like that, too."

I opened my mouth to deny it…then closed it because I couldn't.

"That's a low blow."

"No, it's true. And you know it. But you have a *date*. With a real hottie." Vivi's smile widened. "Maybe you'll actually get to find out if he's good in bed."

"It's just a date. Don't get ahead of yourself."

"So you've never had sex on a first date?"

"Not since college. Older and wiser."

Vivi rolled her eyes. "Oh please. Live a little. Get what you can out of the guy before you dump him."

The flat tone of Vivi's voice worried me but I didn't say anything because, god forbid, I didn't want to sound like our mother, who I tried so hard not to be like.

"We haven't even gone out for a drink. Maybe he'll turn out to be a dick and I won't see him again."

"Oh, he'll turn into a dick sooner or later. Probably sooner."

I couldn't let that pass. "Viv, are you okay?"

My sister's gaze dropped for a few seconds before she shrugged. "I'm fine."

"No, you're not. You haven't been for a while and I'm worried about you."

Vivi sighed heavily. "You don't need to worry about me. I'm fine. Honestly."

"But you haven't been yourself lately."

"Maybe I'm finally growing up."

"You're twenty-four and you're making ends meet working three freaking jobs. I think that's adult enough."

"But you're the one working fifty hours a week in an office where you have to wear grown-up clothes."

"And have no social life at all. Don't forget that."

"I guess that makes us both pitiful losers."

"Yeah, but I'm a pitiful loser with a date with a hot hockey player. And if you come along, I'm sure you'll meet lots of other hot hockey players."

Damn it, I shouldn't have said that. Vivi's expression hardened and her mouth pursed in a way that only happened when she thought about the former asshole boyfriend.

"Never gonna happen. But I will totally be there tomorrow to make sure he's not a complete dick."

"Gee, when you put it like that, maybe it's not even worth it."

"I'm not sure any guy's worth it."

Trying to lighten the mood, I grinned at Vivi. "I guess you really do want to live with me forever. We'll be known as the Spinster Sisters and have twenty cats."

Vivi rolled her eyes again and finally started to laugh. "All right, all right. I'll stop being such a downer. And no, I do *not* want to live with you for the rest of my life. We'd probably kill each other after twenty years or so. Doesn't mean there has to be a man involved. One of these days, I'm going to backpack across Europe and I'm going to hike Everest and…"

As my sister continued to rattle off all the things she wanted to do with her life, I considered the fact that I didn't really think about stuff like that.

Sure, I'd love to travel and see the world, but my sister wanted to escape.

And what's so bad about that?

I hated to admit it, and wouldn't never admit it to my sister, but I wanted to find a guy, someone to spend time with and do things with. Someone with mutual goals and—

Oh my god. I sounded like my mother.

"Hey, Aly?"

My attention snapped back to my sister, who stared at me like I might have accidentally said all that out loud.

"Yeah?"

"I totally think you should do him."

With a laugh, I grabbed the pillow and smacked her across the head.

"I totally think that's *not* going to happen."

Riley

"We have a game tonight and you are taking a girl out on a first date? We have a streak going and you must fuck with it?"

Taking laps around the rink before the start of practice, I ignored Vladimir "Lad" Marchenko's taunt and kept skating.

I refused to allow any of the kids to get in my head. As the second-oldest player on the team, I sometimes was reminded that I'd actually grown up some since I'd been Lad's age.

"Seriously?" Defenseman Derek Flaherty flew by then turned to skate backward so he could get in my face. "Chickie got someone to go out with him? How the hell'd that happen, old man?"

Restraining the urge to check the little shit into the boards for using that stupid-ass nickname and for commenting on my age, I once again took the high road and ignored the six-foot, hundred-and-eighty-pound redhead who couldn't keep his mouth shut, no matter how many times he took a fist to the face for opening it.

Okay, Derek and I had a lot in common, but I would never admit it.

"Yes, unlike you." Lad pounced on Derek with the same droll

wit he'd used on me. "Who cannot get a date because you open your mouth and speak."

Instead of taking offense, Derek grinned. According to his roommate, Adam Zappala, that grin got Derek laid more than a rabbit in mating season.

"Don't need to date if all you wanna do is get laid. Don't need a girlfriend, either. They just fuck with your head."

"Yeah, well, we all know he doesn't have a brain so they don't fuck with that."

I turned to smile at Cary, who'd skated up beside me.

"Hey. How goes it? So you got a date tonight?"

I let my head drop back. "Christ, not you, too? Seriously, you're all a bunch of teenage girls, I swear."

Cary laughed, a deep sound no one heard much. The guy had earned his reputation as a brawler almost twenty years ago when the game had been a lot different. Now, the skill players got most of the spotlight.

Kids like CJ Young, the twenty-one-year-old forward who'd started the first five games of the season with two points per game. And Robbie Lindback, the nineteen-year-old first-round draft pick from Sweden, who'd probably get called up the next time the Colonials needed a forward.

"At least they don't scream and giggle. Much. How's it going? Haven't had much time to talk since you got here. You need to come over and have dinner again with Lori and me. Does next Tuesday work?"

"Yeah, it should. Thanks."

"How's the roommate situation working out?"

I had to laugh. "Is this your way of trying to figure out if I'm pissed off at you for pointing me toward Pigpen?"

There was Cary's laugh again, this time even louder. "Yeah, maybe I shoulda warned you about that."

"A heads-up that the guy is basically a walking haz-mat spill would've been helpful."

Justin Perry, or "Pigpen," had been the only guy who'd needed a roommate when I had signed. I'd never talked to Justin except on the ice before so I hadn't known much about him personally.

The guy was really nice and skated like he'd been born on blades, but off the ice Justin was one big accident waiting to happen. Kind of like a twenty-four-year-old toddler. If he held it, he spilled it. If he ate it, he wore it, and if he was walking, sure as shit he knocked something over.

"So you really have a date tonight?"

I slashed Cary across the shins, not hard enough to hurt, of course. We had a game tonight. "Why is that such a shock?"

"Maybe because you haven't done it much since your divorce."

Ah, yes. I'd almost forgotten I'd known Cary that long.

"Been almost seven years since it was final. I've dated a few times since then."

"Yeah, no shit."

Okay, maybe more than a few times, but fuck it. I wasn't married. Not anymore. "Hey, just 'cause you're old and married doesn't mean the rest of us should be."

"Okay, if you're gonna insult me—"

Luckily, Coach blew his whistle, calling the team in to talk about the game tonight and what we needed to work on.

But Cary's remark about my divorce stuck in the back of my brain. I hadn't thought about Ann for months. At least, not since I'd left my parents' place in June. I'd gone home for a few weeks between the end of last season and the start of training camp. I hadn't seen my ex the entire time I'd been back, and my parents hadn't mentioned her at all. But I had seen her new husband, Thad, and their two kids.

Thad and I had graduated high school together. Ann had been a year behind us. We'd been close back then. Hell, Thad had been one of the groomsmen in our wedding. Now, she and

Thad were happily married with kids and a house and a mortgage.

And I still ping-ponged around North America playing a game I loved. A game Ann had come to hate because I'd loved it more than her.

But now...I had to admit I was getting a little sick of never really having anywhere to call my own.

Maybe I needed to think about hanging up the skates after this season.

The problem was...what the hell would I do if I didn't play hockey?

Chapter 3

Aly

"So that's the guy. Damn, he's huge."

I could barely hear Vivi over the roar of the crowd and pumping music. We'd gotten to the arena only five minutes before the game had started and had barely gotten into our seats before the lights dimmed and the teams skated onto the ice.

I'd had to wait until the lights came up to see the program and find out what number Riley wore so I could find him on the ice.

But as soon as I spotted him, I knew I'd never mistake him for another man. There was something about Riley that made every single hormone in my body tingle and take notice.

"They're all huge. I think some of it's the gear."

"Maybe. But he's *really* big." Vivi looked over and grinned. "So not your type. I like."

Knocking my shoulder against Vivi's, I shook my head. "Don't even go there. Jesus, we haven't even gone out yet. And I talked to him for, like, ten minutes."

"Yeah, but you're going out with him tonight. Guess I shouldn't be surprised if you don't come home, huh?"

I felt a blush heat my cheeks. "Jeez. Tell the entire arena."

Vivi rolled her eyes. "Oh please. No one can hear us over this noise."

Probably true. The arena wasn't completely sold out but there had to be at least seven thousand people in the building, most of them standing and clapping for their team while they waited for the referee to drop the puck to start the game.

Since I'd never been to a game before, I wasn't really sure what to expect.

The speed was exhilarating but, oh my god, the game was *physical*. Players slammed each other into the boards so hard, the glass around the ice shook. They fell or were tripped and hit the ice so hard, I flinched, unable to believe they didn't break bones.

But milliseconds later, they were back on their feet and skating off after the puck.

After a particularly brutal-looking hit by an opposing player against one of the Redtails, the man sitting a few rows down yell, "Get off your knees, ref! You're blowing the game."

Vivi and I turned to each other and started to laugh.

As we continued to laugh, the buzzer sounded and the players exited the ice. Music started to play and everyone around us rose and stretched or headed toward the aisles.

Vivi and I stood but didn't leave.

"I think I might love hockey." Vivi grinned at me, no hint of sarcasm to be found. "I can't believe we haven't come to a game before."

I smiled back, happy to see my sister smiling. "I'm enjoying it but, oh my god, every time they get hit, I want to cringe. How do they take so much damage? It's brutal. They must be one big bruise afterward."

"Usually, yes, they are."

The friendly voice came from behind us, and I turned to find a pretty redhead smiling at us.

"Sorry, couldn't help but overhear. Hi, I'm Bliss." She stuck out her hand, which I immediately shook. "You obviously haven't been to a game before and we are *so* loving your commentary."

Immediately on my guard, my smile dimmed as I transferred it to the brunette standing next to Bliss.

"Hey, I'm Lori." She stuck out her hand, too. "And honestly, we're not being catty. My husband and Bliss's boyfriend are players. I've been living and breathing hockey for a few years so whenever I meet someone who doesn't, I love watching them fall in love with the game the way I did."

"I'm fairly new to the sport, too," Bliss said. "My boyfriend, Shane, is the goalie. Lori's husband, Cary, is a forward."

Then Lori and Bliss exchanged a glance before Lori's smile widened. "So I hope you don't mind me asking but…which one of you is dating Riley?"

Stunned, my eyes widened.

What the hell?

Obviously, Lori read my expression because the other woman held up a hand. "Yes, I know we're being really intrusive, but you're sitting in the wives and girlfriends section so we figured we'd say hi. And since hockey players are almost as bad as teenage girls about gossip, everyone knows Riley has a date after the game. We just wanted to say hi. If you have any questions, feel free to ask us. We've probably had the same ones."

Since they seemed nice, I decided to take them up on the offer. "Is the game always so…rough?"

Both women's smiles warmed, and I felt my internal walls slipping even more.

"Sometimes, it's worse." Lori shook her head. "This game's actually been pretty tame."

"Since Shane's the goalie, he doesn't get hit a lot but Riley's a pretty physical player," Bliss continued. "He'll probably have more than a few cuts and bruises when he takes off his gear tonight. Just don't be shocked. The guys are used to it. You will be, too, when you're around the game long enough."

I had the almost overwhelming urge to reiterate the fact that Riley and I had just met and were having our first date tonight then decided against it when Lori continued.

"The first time I met Cary after a game, I thought he'd been in a fight in the locker room. He had a black eye from a fight in the second period and a huge bruise on his side. I was afraid to touch him." She exchanged a glance with Bliss. "He didn't have the same problem."

Bliss rolled her eyes while Lori laughed. She was a little older than the rest of us, probably mid-thirties, but her laughter was warm and inviting and I couldn't help but like her. Even Vivi, who didn't always warm up to people right away, smiled at Lori.

"Yeah, I'm not going there." Bliss shook her head. "But I will say they're usually a little…hyper after a game, especially if they win."

"Do they win a lot?"

"Well, we're two months into the season and they're twelve and three. Last year, they won the championship and this year, they're predicted to get to the finals again."

"So they're good?" Vivi asked.

Lori smiled. "Yeah, they're really good. Riley wasn't here last year but he's been a great addition to the team. Cary thinks this could be Riley's year to get called up."

I shook my head. "I don't—"

"Sorry, sorry." Lori made a face. "Forgot you don't speak hockey yet. Called up means he'd get to play in the NHL."

Okay, now that I understood. "And that's where he wants to be, right?"

"That's the ultimate goal, yes." Bliss nodded. "Not all of them make it, though."

Lori put her arm around Bliss's shoulders and hugged. "And

some are destined. They don't call Shane 'Brick Wall' for nothing."

Aly was fascinated. "Does Riley have a nickname?"

Bliss grinned. "Well, some of the guys call him 'Chickie' because he chirps. It means he likes to talk shit to the other players, throw them off their game, draw a penalty. He's pretty well known for it."

"Cary swears Riley could get a saint to take a swing at him." Lori shook her head. "But he's mainly known as a grinder. He doesn't make a lot of goals but he makes sure his teammates have the puck so they can score."

Chirp. Grinder. The lingo was making my head spin.

Lori must have seen her brain misfiring because the other woman reached out and squeezed my shoulder. "Stick with us, ladies. By the end of the game, you'll be experts."

Riley

"So your woman showed up. See, I told you. No need for worry."

Jake stopped beside me as I buckled my belt then grabbed my coat. We'd won the game so the noise level in the locker room approached deafening, but it barely registered.

I had played hard tonight. I had one fight because one of the Lynx players had gotten in my face, and had three assists on four goals.

A good night. And hopefully about to get better.

"I wasn't worried," I told Jake as I headed for the hall where I'd told Aly I'd meet her after the game. I hadn't thought about her at all during the game. I never let anyone—not a girl, not another player, no one—mess with my head before or during a game.

But now… Yeah, maybe I had been a little worried she wouldn't show.

I'd purposely not looked into the stands to see if she was there tonight. I'd kept my mind on the game and it'd paid off. This season was off to a good start and I hoped to hell it continued.

"I know you do not worry during game. You are machine out there. Damn good game tonight."

"Thanks. I—"

Damn, there she was. And, holy shit, was she gorgeous.

Vaguely, I heard Jake laugh, but I dismissed him as the uncontrollable urge to grab her and kiss her nearly overtook me. The urge was so strong, my fingers clenched.

She didn't see me right away. She stood next to Cary's wife, Lori, and Shane's girlfriend, Bliss. They looked to be in deep conversation.

And then she smiled and, holy shit, I swore I was back in high school when a girl just had to look at me and I got hard.

Back then, my only desire had been to get laid. Until I'd met Ann and things had changed.

Damn, I'd have to stop thinking about my ex. That'd been a hell of a long time ago. I let myself stare at Aly instead.

Fuck, was she gorgeous. Sure, I'd noticed yesterday but now, in tight jeans and boots with heels, a tight white shirt and a blue cardigan, she looked so fucking hot, I thought I might break out in a sweat.

How the hell did she manage that looking like a kindergarten teacher?

Probably because the jeans fit her long legs like a second skin and the shirt had a v-neck that hinted at just enough cleavage to make me drool.

And her hair was down, nearly reaching the small of her back. Holy fuck. I wanted to wrap my hands in it and tug her head back so I could kiss her. And do other, less polite things to her.

Not that the way I wanted to kiss her was polite. No, what I wanted to do to her should be done in private. And naked.

I really wanted to do naked things with her.

A grin formed and she looked up at that moment, caught me staring at her.

Her smile softened a little as our gazes connected, but it was the look in her eyes that made my dick hard. Hot. Sweet. But definitely heat there.

I knew she wasn't like any other girl I'd dated in the past five years. And that meant I'd need to take this slow. It'd be a first for me but I'd do whatever it took to make sure Miss Aly hung around.

"You, my friend, should be very glad you saw her first." Jake bumped my sore shoulder as he walked by but the shooting pain from the injury sustained in a late-third-period collision with the boards couldn't deflate my dick.

"There's no way a woman that gorgeous would give you a second look," Shane spoke from behind us. "Though why she thought Riley was a better option, I'll never know."

Shane gave Jake a shove as he came up behind the other guy. Jake barely moved and didn't even look at Shane. "Is too bad for her. I suppose Lad and I will go spread our joy to the women at West Reading. Have a good time, Chickie."

I let the hated nickname flow right past me.

"Oh I plan to, Jake. I definitely plan to."

Chapter 4

Will

"You deliberately baited a man who weighed fifty pounds more than you to take a swing at you? Are you crazy?"

I shrugged, a grin reappearing on his lips.

"Some people say so, yeah. But he was killing us so we needed him off the ice. Took me until the third period but I finally got to him. While we were in the bin for five, my guys scored twice and tied up the game. We won in overtime."

"Is that where you got the nickname?"

"What nickname?"

The wince gave me away.

"Chickie."

I rolled my eyes as I turned onto the street where she lived. We'd spent the last three hours talking at the bar and I was a little amazed we hadn't run out of things to discuss.

Then again, everything seemed easy with this woman.

"Hockey players think they're funny."

"Aren't they?"

"Not most of them."

"Then I guess you're not like most of them."

I slid her a glance. "You think I'm funny?"

Her smile made my cock twitch in anticipation. "I think you're avoiding telling me how you got the nickname."

I laughed. "I got it in college. One of the guys on my team was a farm boy from Pennsylvania, and after a game he told me how I reminded him of this chicken he had that never shut up. The other players started calling me Chickie and it stuck."

"Did you play in high school, too?"

"My dad says I grabbed a stick when I was about four and never let go. It's been my life ever since."

"How long do you plan to play?"

I shrugged, not yet ready to admit my defeat aloud. "Not sure. When I'm done, I'll figure out what to do with the rest of my life. I have a degree in sports management. The plan is to work with kids when I get out, but beyond that, I don't really know. I've been too focused on playing for the past twenty years."

Her eyes widened. "Twenty years? You've been playing since you were eight?"

The shock in her voice kind of surprised me. "Well, more than that really, but yeah."

"Do you really love the game that much?"

"Yeah." Something my ex had accused me of more than once. That I'd loved the game more than I loved her. It'd stung at the time…mostly because she'd been right. I'd been selfish. "You have to or what's the point?"

After a short pause, she said, "You're absolutely right."

"Could you say that again so I can record it and play it for my mom? I swear, no matter what I do, she thinks it's wrong. So, did you and your sister have a good time tonight? She was welcome to come with us tonight, you know."

She laughed quietly and nodded. "I know but she, ah, had plans come up. But we did enjoy the game. I can't believe how physical it is. How are you still able to walk? I saw you get hit really hard a few times."

Shrugging, I automatically rolled my shoulder, happy there was no pain. "You get used to it. Besides, I knew I had a date to look forward to and I wasn't missing it because of a few bumps and bruises."

I slid her a glance and caught her smiling again.

"You're kind of a flirt, aren't you?"

"Just kind of?"

She laughed, as I'd hoped she would, and shook her head. "Okay, definitely a flirt."

"Thank you. Would hate to think I was half-assing something."

She was still laughing when I parked at the sidewalk in front of the address she'd given me.

"Is this yours?"

It looked so…suburban. I almost expected two-point-five kids to run out, screaming, "Mommy!"

"Mm-hmm. Technically, it belongs to my parents, but when they moved to Florida a few years ago, they asked my sister and me if we wanted to stay here. It was a no-brainer. My parents took out a second mortgage, bought a condo in Florida, and now my sister and I pay that mortgage and live here and my parents have their place in the sun and everyone's happy."

"You are *way* more adult than me."

She sighed. "So I've been told."

I looked back at her but couldn't figure out her expression. I wanted to ask her if I could come in but I didn't want to push her. We'd spent the past three hours talking, and even though I'd expected to carry the conversation, she'd held up her end. She was quietly funny, her laughter a husky rasp that bit me low in the gut.

And she seemed to think I was hilarious. She laughed at my

jokes, which meant I'd had a constant hard-on. Still had one, as a matter of fact.

And when she bit her lip then said, "Do you want to come in?" I wanted nothing more than to say yes.

So why didn't I?

"Yeah, I do. But...we've got practice tomorrow. Well, this morning, actually. And if I come in with you, I won't want to leave."

She blinked and her lips parted and I had to bite back the urge to groan. So I did what I did best. I kept talking.

"But Coach gets pissy when we don't show up, especially the morning before a game. I might find myself riding the bench tomorrow night and that'd be a problem."

I was expecting a pout. A lot of other women would've been pissed off. This woman smiled, which made me want to kick myself in the ass for saying no, even though I knew it was the right decision.

Because for the first time, I didn't want to rush. Maybe I was growing up. Maybe I was learning some control. Whatever.

"And you would hate that, wouldn't you?"

"It would suck, yeah. I don't like riding the bench."

"You're too good to do it much."

"Now who's the flirt?"

And there was that smile again, the one that made me want to take a bite out of her. Her breast, her ass, the inside of her thigh... That smile wasn't shy. Aly was a little reserved, yeah, but not shy.

"Come to the game tomorrow night. I'll leave tickets for you."

That smile made me want to rethink my decision.

"Okay, thanks. My sister has to work, but I'll be there."

"Good."

We sat there for a few more seconds, smiling at each other until she dropped my gaze and grabbed her purse.

Taking the hint, I got out and walked around to open her door. Without thinking about it, I wrapped an arm around her shoulders and drew her into my body. Her arms slipped around my waist, and when she put her hand on my hip, I tugged her even closer.

Walking her to the door, I stood by while she got her keys out of her purse and opened the lock. Then she turned and looked up at me with those blue eyes and no one could fault me for being unable to resist her.

I leaned in and kissed her. With my hand cupping the back of her head and the other on her hip, I pulled her in and didn't hold anything back.

I'd been so damn good all night and I wasn't going to follow her in that house. But I had to have a taste.

Her heat shocked me—in a good way. Her response nearly made me forget my resolution to take this slow.

And when her arms slid around my waist and she stood on her toes to kiss me, I might've groaned. Okay, I did groan. And then I opened my mouth over hers and inhaled her.

She opened to me immediately, her tongue meeting mine without hesitation.

Holy Christ. Lust surged as our tongues tangled. Every nerve ending in my body lit up, and I pressed her mouth open even farther. Sucking in air through my nose, I sealed our lips together, my fingers spreading through her hair to hold her.

She didn't balk at my possessive hold. Instead, she went soft against me, and I got even harder.

If I hadn't been trying to be good, I would've lifted her against the door and pressed my aching cock into her soft mound.

It took every ounce of restraint I had not to grind against her or run my hands down her body. Her curves had taunted me all night. The woman had no sharp angles. She was made to be petted.

But not tonight.

I began to pull back but she followed me, going up on her toes to prolong the kiss until I was about to break my resolution to take this slow.

We were both breathing heavy when she took a step back.

Forcing myself to do the same, I fisted my hands so I wouldn't reach for her again.

She swallowed hard and licked her lips before tilting her head to the side and all that silky hair slid over her shoulder, making me want to groan. Christ, I wanted to feel that hair against my skin. Preferably against my chest and my thighs—

I sucked in air. "So…I'll see you tomorrow night."

She nodded. "Will I sit with Lori and Bliss again?"

"If you want, yeah, I can arrange that."

Her smile widened. "That'd be great. Since Vivi can't go, I'd rather not sit alone."

"No problem." I'd make sure to give a huge thank-you to Cary's wife and Shane's girlfriend the next time I saw them.

Another quick smile. "Good night."

I had to suck in air before I could answer. "Night."

Then I waited until she closed the door and I heard it lock.

I was still smiling when I got back in my truck. Hell, I was still smiling when I walked into my apartment.

"Dude. Didn't expect to see you back here tonight. Bad night? No luck, huh?"

I smacked Justin on the back of the head as I walked by on the way to my room.

"Fuck you. Great night. Going to bed."

"Damn, thought you were too old for quickies. Although at your advanced age, I guess if you can keep it up longer than a minute, that's pretty good."

As I kept walking through I shot Justin the finger over my shoulder. No way was I getting drawn into a conversation now.

"It's past your bedtime, kid. You need to get your beauty sleep. St. John's is fast."

"Wait, are you really going to bed? You're not gonna share at all?"

"Night, Justin."

As I closed the door to my bedroom behind me, I smiled as I heard Justin bitch, "Dude, you suck."

Chapter 5

Aly

"So." Vivi drew the word out to about fifteen syllables the second I stepped into the kitchen Saturday morning. "How'd it go?"

I didn't bother to answer right away. Yes, I was one of those disgustingly cheerful morning people though I did need coffee before I became fully functional for the day.

So I walked past my sister, got my mug and poured coffee that Vivi, amazingly, had already brewed. Since I was almost always the first one up in the morning, I usually made the first pot.

Bracing myself, I sipped…and managed to avoid a full-body shudder. Vivi made legendarily strong coffee. I was a little surprised I didn't immediately sprout hair on my chest.

"Holy. Shit." I managed to suck in a gasp of air before sliding into a seat at the little table by the window where Vivi sat. "How the hell do you drink this?"

"With my mouth." With a sarcastic grin, Vivi lifted her mug and saluted me before gulping down half of her mug. "And what'd you do with your mouth last night? Not much, I'm guessing, because he left without coming in."

I smiled, thinking about exactly what I had done with my mouth last night. And yes, all we'd done was kiss.

"But," Vivi continued, "I guess something happened or you wouldn't be smiling like a lunatic."

I wrinkled my nose. "I'm not smiling like a lunatic. I'm just smiling. It was a nice night."

"Nice?" Vivi hmphed. "How 'nice' could it've been if he didn't even come in the house? What's wrong with him?"

I took another sip of coffee and glared at my sister over the rim of my mug. "There's absolutely nothing wrong with him. He was a total gentleman."

"So he didn't touch you." Vivi shrugged. "Sorry."

With a huff and a roll of my eyes, I set my mug down. "Not every guy's just looking to get laid, you know. Sometimes, the foreplay's just as much fun as the actual sex."

Vivi's turn to roll her eyes. "And maybe the guy's got…" She held up her pinkie and wiggled it.

I laughed, shaking my head. "Yeah, no. I don't think Riley has to worry about that. From what I could feel, that's not even remotely a problem."

"So what happened?" Vivi leaned on the table. "Why'd he leave? Did you not invite him in?"

"I did but he had practice this morning and he needed to sleep. He has another game tonight and I'm going to that and meeting him afterward again. He's an actual nice guy, Viv."

"Did he even kiss you?"

I smiled and let Vivi figure out the answer to that on her own. "I'm starving. I think I'll make pancakes. You want some?"

"Sure, if you're making. But I gotta leave in an hour. Double shift at the studio today and I'm picking up a shift at the bar tonight. Hey, why don't you guys come over after the game? Chet won't be there tonight so you won't have to deal with his shit. And tell Riley to bring his team. The girls will love me if you do."

One of Vivi's three jobs was waitressing at The Bomb Shelter, one of the most popular bars in the area.

I didn't usually go there. The music sucked, it was always crowded on the weekends, and a lot of the guys who went there were douchebags who thought women existed for their personal pleasure.

"I'll check but I don't know what he'll want to do tonight."

On the other hand, I had some great ideas about what I wanted to do tonight. Last night, I hadn't been ready for anything really physical and somehow Riley had known that. I'd been a little worried, not that he'd force me, but that he'd push for something I wasn't ready to give.

We'd been so in tune and I'd almost convinced myself to give him whatever he wanted.

Or maybe I was kidding myself and he'd decided he didn't really want me and he'd text me today and tell me something had come up and—

Okay, I needed to stop.

Shaking my head, I ladled batter onto the skillet just as my phone rang.

I grabbed it off the counter, ignoring my sister's laughter, then sighed when I saw the screen.

"Oh, I know that look." Vivi shook her head. "You better answer it because if you don't, she'll call me and you know I'm not picking it up. Then she'll call the police because she'll think we were murdered in our sleep or some other horrible thing and I'm not dealing with it."

Because my sister was right, I took a deep breath and answered.

"Hey, Mom. How's it going?"

"Did I wake you? It's almost ten. I figured you'd be up by

now. Were you out late last night? I know it's Saturday but I know you don't sleep in. Now, your sister…"

I rolled my eyes and sucked in a deep breath, hoping for patience as my mom continued to talk for the next thirty minutes.

I finished the pancakes while mom relayed every ailment she and dad had endured that week, in more detail than I ever wanted to know. Unfortunately, I was used to it because this was how almost every week's call went.

Mom would start with the health update. Sometime she'd stick to just her and Dad's health. If it was a slow week for them, Mom would throw in an update on the neighbors, all of whom were around the same age. The condo complex they lived in was mostly seniors but there were a few younger people. Younger being a relative term. Anyone younger than fifty was a kid to my mom.

After the health update, Mom would complain about the weather. Too hot, too windy, too rainy, or, oh my god, hurricane season. I would counter with the fact that, hey, it was Florida and they didn't have to deal with snow or cold.

Then Mom would ask what was going on at home, and if I didn't have enough to talk about, my mom would want to know what was wrong. Sometimes she'd ask specifics, like about work or she'd want to know what trouble Vivi was getting into.

If Vivi happened to be around, my sister would sigh, shake her head, and conveniently have somewhere else to be.

And sometimes, if I was *really* lucky, my mom would ask if I'd met anyone.

Yeah, that was fun. Especially when mom decided she'd found the perfect guy for me. All I'd need to do was move down with them.

Apparently, it was my lucky day.

"Oh, and I met finally met Susan's son. You remember Susan, right? She lives at the end of the first floor. Lost her husband to cancer a few years ago. Her son moved down here to be closer to her. He's got a job with some insurance outfit in Tampa. Seems like a nice guy. When you come down, you should meet him. I think you'll like him. He's only a few years older and he's handsome…"

I let my mom talk, replying when necessary. My mom meant well but, oh my god, I was tired of this constant pushing. Mom was convinced I would eventually move to Florida, marry some nice man—whom she would find for me, since I apparently couldn't meet nice guys on my own—and provide grandchildren.

I wasn't sure I even *wanted* to have kids. Especially not if I became just like my mom someday.

Sighing, I turned to Vivi, who was shaking her head and had her hand over her mouth so mom wouldn't hear her laughing and want to talk to her.

Vivi never got the "I met this man you should meet" speech from our mom. Vivi was convinced our mom was afraid she would actually procreate and her children would be just like her.

I had always been the "good one." Good grades, never in trouble, college degree and job right out of college.

Vivi… Well, the local cops knew Vivi by name. And after the third or fourth time they'd shown up at the door asking to talk to our parents, Vivi had become the "difficult one."

It was a distinction that still pissed me off, even though Vivi had gotten past it years ago. Hell, she'd pretty much embraced it.

Which left me as the one our parents relied on. The one to visit the sick aunt in the hospital and help the cousin move into her dorm room and be sure I remembered everyone's birthday and went to every wedding and anniversary to represent "the family."

Everything I would've done anyway because that's what family meant to me. Hell, I didn't even know why being considered reliable pissed me off.

Maybe…maybe I secretly wanted to be a little less reliable and a little more wild. Like Vivi.

Maybe that's why I liked Riley. Because he wasn't a guy my mom would ever think I'd date.

"And I told him when you come down at Christmas—"

"Whoa, wait. Mom, I'm not sure I can come down at Christmas. I told you. Julie's probably getting married around the holidays so I can't make any plans."

"Oh." My mom paused. "Well, I didn't honestly think that would last. Julie's always been so flighty."

Oh my god, mom was going to drive me crazy.

My friend, Julie, was marrying a smart, handsome guy who happened to be black. My parents hadn't raised me and my sister to be prejudiced, but their own prejudices were deeply ingrained.

"Well, we still hope you and your sister will be able to get down for a few days around the holidays. It'd be so nice to have everyone together for Christmas."

"We'll have to wait and see how everything works out. You know Vivi's work schedule is a mess around the holidays and there's always something going on at the hospital."

Thankfully, my mom let that go and we chatted for another few minutes before finally saying good-bye.

And when my phone screen finally went black, I drew in a deep breath and released it on a heavy sigh. I felt like I'd run a marathon.

"And this is why I try not to talk to Mom more than a few minutes at a time." Vivi shook her head, waving her fork like a wand. "You look like you're about to heave. What'd she say about Julie?"

I grimaced. "That she didn't think 'that' would work. And I'm not sure but I think the only reason she called was to see when we were coming down so I could meet some guy, marry him, and move down there."

Vivi rolled her eyes. "Oh my god, I can't believe she still thinks she can get you to do it. Thank God they gave up on me. I don't know why you just don't tell them it's never gonna happen."

Because I wasn't sure I wouldn't. Which, of course, I couldn't tell my sister. Vivi would freak and tell me I'd be making a huge mistake. Which I probably would be.

But I also knew my parents weren't getting any younger and eventually would need help. But that would leave Vivi alone here.

"Aly?"

"Hmm?"

Vivi sighed and shook her head. "You need to stop thinking about everyone else and put yourself first for a change."

"I don't know what you're talking about."

"Bullshit." Vivi held her gaze. "Are you *seriously* thinking about moving to Florida with Mom and Dad? Because if you waffle even a little, Mom will put on the full-court press and you'll find yourself living in Florida married to some guy named Tad with two-point-five kids, a mortgage you can't afford, and Mom in your house every day 'just to help out.'"

I had to hold back a shudder at the thought. "I'm not. At least, not now." She rolled her eyes and huffed. "Okay, *maybe* I might've thought about it. Maybe I feel like I've been in a rut lately. I've had the same job for five years. I still live in the house I grew up in. Last night was the first time in months I've had a date because I'm so freaking boring. All my friends are married or getting married, and some of them have kids or they've moved away. So yeah, I'm thinking about it."

Vivi's eyes widened. "Wow. Aly, I didn't realize—"

"Sorry." I shook my head, grimacing. "Sorry, sorry, sorry. I don't mean to take out my frustration on you. I've just been… restless lately."

"Don't be sorry. You hide stuff so well. I had no idea you were so…"

"Bitchy?"

Vivi's mouth twisted in a rueful grin. "Conflicted."

Conflicted. Yeah, that was a good description.

I shook my head. "Don't mind me. PMS. I'll be fine."

Vivi's grin gained a wicked edge. "I think you might have found the cure for that. You can work out some of your frustrations with Riley tonight. Have some fun, sis. Try not to worry so much. And take the guy to bed tonight, for chrissake. Seriously. Get naked and get laid."

Was a night of sex with a hot guy the answer to everything?

Could it really be that easy?

Chapter 6

Riley

"Riley, sweetheart, how are you? Season going well so far?"

"Hey, Mom. So far, so good, yeah. What's doing at home?"

Kicking back into the recliner, I shoveled food. Practice hadn't been difficult but I needed to refuel before the game tonight.

"Oh, nothing much." She paused. "Well, not too much, anyway."

I put down the fork that was halfway to my mouth. "What's wrong?"

"Nothing's wrong." Another pause. "Nothing serious, anyway. Oh, your dad's been having some trouble with his leg again and I keep telling him he needs to go to the doctor, but you know your father. I thought you could talk to him, maybe convince him he needs to get it checked. You know you're the only one he listens to. When I talk to him, it goes in one ear and out the other. I don't think anything's seriously wrong but… Well, I was hoping you'd talk to him."

I closed my eyes for a second and took a deep breath. Being an only child had its perks but I'd been a late baby. My parents had been over forty when I'd been born.

Which made them almost seventy now. Not ancient but more prone to health problems, especially this past year when my dad had had pneumonia twice and my mom had had two biopsies on her breasts. Neither had been cancerous, but still. And of course, all of it had happened during the season.

"Have you gotten Julie over to see him?"

My parents' neighbor was an emergency room nurse who'd been our first stop for all things medical for as long as I could remember.

"I've tried. He says he doesn't need to talk to her because he's perfectly fine. Which makes me think he isn't. Can you talk to him, Rye? I know you probably have a game tonight but—"

"Mom, it's no problem. Where is he?"

"Thank you, honey." My mom sounded so relieved, I pressed my fingers against my temples, rubbing against the ache I felt starting there. "I'll take the phone to your dad."

My mom fell silent but I heard her footsteps as she made her way upstairs. I knew she couldn't navigate the stairs and continue to hold a conversation because her balance wasn't great. Another sign of her age.

Setting my plate on the table in front of me, I drew in a deep breath, trying not to let my deeply buried guilt rise any further.

Damn it, there was no reason for me to feel guilty. My parents wouldn't want me to feel guilty. They'd never played that card with me, had never made me feel like I owed them anything.

And yet…

"Harry." My mom's voice sounded muffled. "Your son's on the phone."

"Rye, everything okay?"

"Everything's fine, Dad. How're you doing?"

"I'm good, I'm good. How's the team? Saw you had three points last night."

I shook my head. The only way my dad could have known that was if he'd looked it up on the computer, which dad hated but used so he could keep up with me.

I gave my dad a rundown of the past couple of games and gave him a preview of tonight's game. My dad had never played beyond the club level and didn't really understand my consuming love of the game. But my dad had never told me to give up hockey and get a real job. Not even when I had taken that year off in college.

Finally, the conversation wound down and I took the opening.

"So, Dad, what's up with your leg?"

"There's nothing wrong with my leg. Your mother doesn't know what she's talking about. My leg's fine."

"No, your leg is *not* fine." I heard my mom in the background. "Tell him about the other day when you couldn't even stand."

"The damn thing just fell asleep. There's nothing wrong."

From almost two thousand miles away, I spent the next ten minutes refereeing my parents' argument while trying to figure out if my mom was overreacting or if my dad was downplaying.

By the time I ended the call, I'd convinced my dad to get his legs checked out and told my mom I'd call later this week to make sure my dad had gone.

Setting my phone on the table, I picked up my plate but my appetite was gone.

Fuck. What the hell was I supposed to do? I couldn't go home. I had a game tonight and I needed to have my head on straight. I already had Aly in there, fucking with my concentration. And now this stuff with my parents.

Shit.

"Dude, everything okay?"

Justin walked into the living room with a sandwich in one hand and a glass of chocolate milk in the other.

"Yeah. It's fine. It's just…my parents."

"They sick?" Justin sat in the chair opposite me, munching away, oblivious to the fact that he was already wearing some of the mayo from this sandwich.

"No. I don't know." I shrugged. "My dad's having trouble with his leg. My mom's worried. I'm not there."

"Hey, man. They were adults before you were born. I think they can take care of themselves."

The simplicity of Justin's statement made me blink. And then grin as I shook my head.

"So you going out with that girl again tonight?" Justin asked. "She was fucking hot, man."

Before I could answer, Justin continued. "You think Coach is gonna switch up the lines tonight? A few of the guys were talking about it— Why are you laughing?"

It took me almost a minute to rein in my laughter while Justin looked at me like I'd lost my mind.

"You gonna tell me what the hell you were laughing at?"

I shook my head. "Man, does your brain ever shut off?"

Justin shrugged, not offended at all. "Nope. So you seeing her again?"

"Yeah, I am."

And tonight, I wasn't stopping until she asked me to.

"Hey, fucknugget. I'm gonna fucking put you on your ass the next time."

"Fuck you, asswipe." I baited the opposing player as he came out of the corner. "Try not to play with yourself in the box, kid. Don't want everyone to see how small your dick is."

For a second, I thought I'd managed to piss off the opposing player enough to take another swing at me, but the linesman had a good grip on the kid's arm and they skated toward the penalty box before I could say anything else.

Probably a good thing since the Redtails were going on the power play and I needed to get off the ice. There were eleven minutes left in the third period and the scoreboard read that the Redtails were down by one. The St. John's team was fucking fast, but they were young and a little undisciplined. They'd managed to get two goals in the first period, but they'd taken five penalties, two of them drawn by me. Now, we needed to capitalize on this one and tie the game. Then we needed to get our heads out of our asses and win this game.

We'd played like shit tonight, our first line sluggish and out of sync. The defense had broken down more times than I could count and we were lucky to only be losing the game by one goal.

"Good job, Hatch." Coach smacked me on the back as I sat on the bench then shifted down with the other guys to make room for the next line.

"Yes. Nice job, Chickie." Jake leaned over and bumped shoulders. "Now if only we make it count."

Chapter 7

Riley

Our power play team hadn't been doing so well this year. We'd been working on our special teams hard the past week but they still hadn't gelled. Two minutes later, we hadn't scored and I skated back on the ice for my shift.

But the ice never tilted back in our favor and we lost the game two to one.

The mood in the locker room was subdued. Coming off last night's win, we'd been expecting another two points. Having our asses handed to us tonight sucked. And now I needed to throw off the pissy attitude because I had a date.

For a split second, I considered texting Aly to call it off. Then I realized that was a shitty solution and took myself into the showers to soak my head.

By the time I came back out, I felt a hell of lot better because I hadn't been able to stop thinking about Aly.

Christ, I had half a chub now and I hadn't even seen her yet. And when I walked out into the hall and caught sight of her, I had an instant hard-on and the rest of the night's disappointments faded.

All because she smiled at me.

Tonight, I had no intention of being good. Tonight, I planned to be as bad as I could convince her to be.

"Hi." I almost had to strain to hear her, even though the mood in the hall was pretty quiet as the guys left the locker room and headed for the parking lot.

I wanted to grab her and repeat that kiss from last night. Just thinking about it made my muscles tense in anticipation.

"Hey. You ready to get out of here?"

Her smile dimmed a little and I cursed myself for the pissed-off tone in my voice.

I was about to apologize when she reached for my hand and squeezed. "Sure. Tough game tonight."

"Yeah, you could say that."

Her teeth lodged into her bottom lip for a second before she spoke again. "Would you like to come back to my place for a drink instead of going somewhere? Vivi's working late and—"

"Yeah. I would. That'd be great."

Her smile warmed again. "Then let's go."

We walked in silence to her car in the lot across the street, her hand in mine. I'd caught a ride in with Justin. If I needed to, I'd Uber it home tonight. I was hoping I wouldn't need to. Hoped like hell that her smile was an invitation I had no intention of turning down tonight.

"So do you have practice tomorrow morning?"

"Not in the morning, no. We've got an optional skate in the afternoon that I'll probably go to. We had our asses handed to us tonight. We're lucky the score wasn't ten to one."

"They seemed like a tough team."

"They're one of the worst in the league. A bunch of fucking kids with no— Shit. Sorry. Don't mean to take my frustration out on you."

She squeezed my hand as we reached her car, a sensible four-door gray sedan that would be a tight fit for me. I'd suffer through it for her.

The lot was mostly deserted now, the fans already on their way home. She'd parked her car in a dark corner and the next thing I knew, I had her backed up against her car with my mouth sealed over hers.

I hadn't wanted to wait another second to kiss her. Couldn't wait another second to kiss her.

And when she wrapped her arms around my waist and pressed against me, I wasn't sure we'd make it back to her place before I stuck my hand up her shirt so I could get my hands on her skin.

Christ, I felt like a teenager, all hormones and lust. But, holy fuck, she was hot and right there with me.

Her fingers bit into me, pulling me closer, showing me how much she wanted me. Damn good thing, too, because I had a burning ache deep in my gut that intensified with every passing second.

For the first time in months, maybe years, I felt wanted, not because of what I did but for who I was.

And how fucking awesome was that?

Her lips moved with mine, opening for me to slide my tongue into her mouth. She tasted hot and sweet and made me want to suck all that sweetness into my own body. Her natural reserve melted away under the heat of that kiss and she snuggled in closer, her stomach pressing even tighter against my cock.

Oh, fuck yes.

Sucking in air, I kissed her harder, more intensely, wanting her to be as crazy as I felt myself getting. I didn't want to be the only one out of control.

Sliding one hand into her hair, I tugged her head back even farther and spread my other hand across her back. She wasn't going anywhere unless I allowed it.

The thought made me want to growl, made me want to put my hands on her ass and lift her into me.

I wanted to strip off her clothes and—

Hell, that definitely wasn't happening here.

I stepped away, breathing hard, gratified to hear her gasp.

"I think we should probably get out of here."

She nodded, sucking in a deep breath. "I think you're right. Are you hungry? We could—"

"I'm not thinking about food."

And there was that smile again, the one that made every muscle in my body clench with anticipation.

"Then I guess we better go."

I didn't move for another few seconds, sifting my fingers through her hair before reluctantly releasing her.

But I didn't move away, my gaze locked with hers. Her eyes mesmerized, such a calm, tranquil blue.

"Riley?"

And her voice… Damn, I could listen to her for hours. Preferably while she screamed my name as I made her come.

After a few more seconds, I took a step back, just enough for her to slip out from between me and the car and head for the driver's door.

"I guess you don't want to talk about the game," she asked after I folded myself into her car.

I shrugged. "Bad night. Wasn't the first. Won't be the last."

She slid me a glance before putting the car in gear and putting us on the road. "You seem…like there's something else on your mind."

"The only thing on my mind right now is you."

Which was totally true. I'd worry about my game tomorrow. Tonight, I only wanted to think about her.

"Tell me what you did today." I honestly wanted to know. I wanted to know everything about her.

Her soft laughter did crazy things to my insides.

"Not a damn thing that isn't totally boring."

"Why don't you let me be the judge of that."

"Seriously, I cooked, I cleaned…I kept looking at the clock to see if it was time to leave for the game."

She looked at me and smiled, and I had to keep telling myself I couldn't touch her. Because if I did, we'd wind up in an accident.

"Glad to hear you're enjoying the games."

"I enjoy watching you."

Oh fuck. The things I wanted to say to her right now could get me arrested in some states and would definitely involve putting my hands on her. And then we'd be in real trouble.

"You can watch me whenever you want."

"I think I might like to watch you skate with a few less clothes on."

She startled a laugh out of me. "You're a little kinkier than you like to pretend, aren't you?"

"I never have been before. And I didn't say I wanted to see you skate *naked*. That might be…dangerous."

I shrugged. "Not as much as you might think. And you'd probably be surprised to find out it wouldn't be the first time."

She shook her head, her soft laughter raising goosebumps on my skin. "I don't think anything you could say would surprise me. I have a feeling you haven't exactly been a saint."

"Now why would you think that?"

Her smile grew at the teasing tone of my voice. "Let's just say you kiss like you've had lots of practice."

I wondered if she was put off by that. She didn't seem to be, but I still hadn't mastered the art of reading a woman's mind. Probably never would.

"Is that a problem?"

She slid me a quick glance as she drove away from the arena. "Only if you don't plan on continuing to kiss me."

"You only have to ask and I'll give you whatever you want."

"Better be careful. Keep giving me whatever I want and I won't want you to stop."

At the moment, that wasn't a problem. Actually, I wasn't sure that would ever be a problem, which was ridiculous because we'd been on exactly one date. Hell, we could be awful together in bed. She might love Brussels sprouts, which would be a total turnoff. She might grow to hate the game I loved. Been there, done that, had the divorce to prove it.

"Honey, I will give you as much as you want for as long as you want it."

I thought she'd laugh again. That's what I'd been going for. Instead, she gave me another one of those looks and another one of those smiles and I had to restrain myself from kissing her.

I knew from last night we'd be at her house in a few minutes and I'd be damned if I did anything to slow us down. But, holy hell, if she didn't drive faster, I was going to put my foot on the gas pedal myself.

Turns out, I didn't have to. She gave the car a little more gas, and soon enough she was pulling to a stop in front of her house.

Conversation had died but anticipation had risen with every second.

I held myself in check as she parked the car on the street but jumped out as soon as the car stopped moving and headed for the driver's door.

She smiled up at me as I reached for her hand to help her out of the car. And she didn't let go as we walked to the door. Lacing her fingers through mine, she held on, moving close enough that I felt her breast brush against my arm.

And holy fuck, who would've thought that little bit of contact could make heat flush through my body like a flash fire?

If I wasn't careful, I'd embarrass the hell out of myself before I even got in the house.

I didn't want to give up her hand but she needed both to open the front door. I reluctantly released her but as soon as we were both inside, I took her by the shoulders, spun her around, and crowded her back against the door.

I heard her suck in a breath but I didn't hear any fear. And when I caught and held her gaze, I saw only desire.

She lifted her hands to my shoulders and settled them there, their warm weight setting a match to my already smoldering lust.

Her head dropped back against the door and she stared straight into my eyes.

"Do you want something to drink?"

I shook my head, my hands falling to her waist, caressing the flare of her hips.

Her dark blond eyebrows rose, a tease in the arch. "Not thirsty?"

"No."

"Something to eat?"

I let my mouth curve slightly and watched her cheeks redden slightly. "Not hungry…for food."

I felt her hips lift under my hands, felt the zipper of her jeans brush against my cock for a brief second before she moved away.

"Want to watch some TV?"

"Only if you're standing in front of it taking your clothes off."

She blinked and I thought maybe I'd just stuck my foot in my mouth. Then she laughed.

And hot sex against the door became a very real possibility.

She stepped into me, put her hands on my jaw and pulled me down so she could kiss me.

Surprise made me freeze for about a millisecond. Then I got with the program.

I tightened my hold on her hips and dragged her closer. She came without hesitation, plastering herself against me from chest to thighs and adding fuel to the fire already burning in my blood.

Kissing me hard, she wrapped her arms around my shoulders and opened her mouth to me.

The kiss went from blazing to inferno in the blink of an eye and my brain blanked out everything but her and my need to have her.

As my tongue slid along hers, I groaned when she returned the caress with her own.

Fuck.

My cock hardened into a painful, throbbing ache and I pulled her hips against mine, pressing my erection against her mound, trying to get some relief. She moaned into my mouth and rubbed her hips against me.

Her lips soft and open beneath me, she arched her back, pressing her breasts against my chest as she rose on her toes. Her fingers slid into my hair and tugged on the strands. My scalp stung but, damn, I liked it.

Pressing harder into the kiss, I let my hands spread on her hips then slide around to her back so I could urge her even closer. But I didn't think I'd ever be able to get her close enough. At least not with her clothes on.

And since she seemed to be totally with the program, I didn't think she'd push him away if she slipped my hand under her shirt to get to her bare skin. Because, damn, all I wanted to do right now was touch her.

Putting one hand on her ass, I let the other slip under the hem and groaned as my fingers encountered warm flesh.

So damn soft.

God damn, this was gonna get out of hand fast.

I thought about slowing down but then she scraped her nails along my scalp, shooting lightning bolts through my body and nuking any thoughts of going slow.

Tangling my tongue with hers, I put one hand on her ass and took her off her feet. She gasped but quickly wrapped her legs around my waist, never breaking the kiss.

Fuck yes.

I let our tongues tangle for several more minutes, loving the taste of her and the feel of her body against mine. She was soft in all the right places and the urge to have my hands touching every inch of her had become an overwhelming desire.

With her hands in my hair and her legs around my waist, she let me know she was right there with me.

All the frustration from tonight's game fed into my lust, made it burn hotter, until I couldn't stand to only have one hand and my mouth on her.

Pulling away, I wanted to say something but she followed me, her lips clinging and her hands pressing me back toward her. With a groan, I let her dictate terms since she seemed to be intent on kissing me and I had no trouble with that.

Her enthusiasm made my dick even harder, and I hoped like hell I didn't come in my pants. How fucking embarrassing would that be?

But damn, the woman knew exactly what to do to make me hot. Her tongue slid along mine with so much teasing eroticism, every muscle in my body clenched.

This girl might look sweet and innocent but her kisses could melt stone. Or make flesh hard as rock, which was what my cock felt like right now. A throbbing, stiff column of granite.

And now she was rolling her hips against mine, pressing her mound against my erection and making me see stars behind my closed eyelids.

Turning my head so I could talk, I caught my breath as her lips pressed against my cheek and back until she sank her teeth into my earlobe.

"*Fuck.* Aly, hold up."

"Don't want to," she whispered in my ear. "Are you getting cold feet?"

"Honey, nothing on me's cold right now. I just need to hear you say yes."

Her soft laughter in my ear made me shudder.

"I guess the fact that I'm practically getting myself off

rubbing against you right now isn't enough of a hint." As I practically swallowed my tongue, she licked my earlobe then put her lips right against my ear. "Yes."

My arms tightened around her and I had a quick second to say "Hang on" before I turned and headed for the first piece of furniture that looked sturdy. I'd broken a sofa arm once, practically ripped it off with some yoga instructor who'd been the bendiest person I'd ever met.

And there was the chair some puck bunny and I had busted in some hotel room in…oh hell, I didn't give a fuck where right now.

All I wanted was to get Aly to the couch.

Luckily, I had a clean shot straight to it, and when I finally had my ass planted on it, I had Aly right where I wanted her. With her knees spread on either side of my hips and my hands spread across her back, keeping her close.

Not that she seemed to want to go anywhere.

Her hands rose to cup my jaw and she brought our mouths back together for another one of those breath-stealing, heart-stopping kisses.

I had a brief second to wonder if I was the one being seduced instead of the other way around. Then I realized I'd be okay with that.

But only because it was Aly.

That didn't mean I was just going to sit there while she kissed her way down my jaw to my neck and made my hands tighten on her hips.

Fuck that.

Sliding my hands under her shirt, I spread my fingers across her bare skin and let the warmth of her body seep into mine.

She let out a little moan as she rose onto her knees, her hands tugging on my hair until I complied and let my head fall back. She followed, her hands releasing my hair so she could slide her fingers into the back of my shirt.

I wore a dress shirt but hadn't bothered with my tie so the first few buttons were already undone. She took full advantage by sliding her hands around my neck to the buttons I had done up and started slipping them through their holes.

When she'd gotten almost to the top of my pants, she sat back and let our gazes connect.

The half-smile on her face made it hard for me to breathe.

"I didn't realize there'd be layers." She tilted her head, silky hair sliding over her shoulder. "Good thing I'm dedicated to finishing what I started."

The husky tone of her voice sliced straight through to my gut, making my muscles clench as she pushed the shirt off my shoulders then stared at me with raised eyebrows.

I knew what she wanted and leaned forward just enough for her to push it all the way down my arms so I could push it over my hands. I left it crumpled behind me, immediately forgotten.

My lips curved in a smile as she contemplated my plain white undershirt. I figured she'd say something about how unsexy it was when the corners of her mouth tilted up and she shot me a look that made my skin sizzle.

"I'll let you in on a little secret." She trailed her fingers over the neckline, barely brushing my skin. "Women think guys who wear undershirts are hot."

Smiling at the amusement in her voice, I figured she was teasing me. "Yeah? Why's that?"

"Well, you know how guys like women in sexy lingerie? Some women think guys look just as hot in t-shirts and tight boxers. The way they cling to your muscles." She ran her fingers over my pecs and barely brushed my nipples. "It makes me want to stroke my hands along the fabric and feel what's beneath."

My mouth dried with her every word until my lungs felt heavy and tight. I sucked in air, my gaze locked on hers. She could talk all night and I didn't think I'd ever get bored. Especially not if she kept talking like this.

And kept stroking her nails along the fabric over my nipples, making them hard and sensitive. Her nails were just long enough to catch on the fabric and on my nipples, the slight sting as she caught the little piece of flesh on each upward stroke making my cock throb even harder.

"Give me a guy in tight boxers and my panties get wet."

Holy fuck. This girl might actually give better sexy talk than I did. How the hell had I gotten so damn lucky? Time to up my game.

"So I guess you wanna take my pants off now, too? 'Cause I gotta tell you, I think you're gonna like what you find."

Luckily for me, I was mainly a boxer-brief guy, though I did have a couple pairs of tighty-whiteys in my drawers.

Her smile widened as her fingers continued their way down my chest, over my stomach, stopping just short of my waistband, where my cock pressed against the zipper with ever-increasing force.

"I'm not sure I'm ready for the whole unveiling just yet."

Her fingers made that statement a lie as she moved her hand just enough that her nails brushed over the zipper of my pants.

"Then maybe you need to take a little time-out and let me help you out of a few of your clothes. Maybe I wanna see what you're hiding. Cotton? Silk? Bikinis? Granny panties?"

She laughed and the sound sparked fire along my nerve endings.

"You're out of luck if you're excited about the granny panties."

"Well, damn. Maybe next time."

Her fingers stuttered back up over my stomach. "Maybe we should concentrate on the first time for now."

"I'm a guy who likes to plan ahead."

"And what exactly are you planning now?"

"How I can get you to unzip my pants."

Her gaze flashed back up to mine and, though her smile

wasn't as wide, it was infinitely hotter and promised things I could only dream about.

"I think the magic word is 'please.'"

Lifting my hands to cup her face, I drew her closer. Our lips only a hair's breadth away, I whispered, "Please," and watched her lashes flutter before I sealed our lips together and kissed her like I needed her to breathe.

Her palms pressed to my chest as she opened her mouth and tangled her tongue with mine, licking and sucking and giving me everything I wanted and more.

I almost missed the fact that her hands were moving down my body as she rose slightly onto her knees. But when her fingers danced along my waistband, I groaned and my hands dropped to her waist and tried to pull her closer.

She resisted, probably because her hands were working at my belt. So I eased up and gave her room to work. I'd be lying if I said I wasn't enjoying the way she was taking her time.

I'd always been a fast-gratification kind of guy. I loved hockey for its speed, got a rush out of the exhilaration.

I was getting the same thrill from Aly's breathtakingly slow unbuckling of my belt. Tensed from my shoulders through my calves, I tried to loosen my muscles. But when she finally separated the two ends and her fingers pressed into my abdomen to release the button, I jerked her closer.

Her lips curved against mine and she pulled back just far enough to speak.

"I'm beginning to think you have no patience, Mr. Hatch."

"I'm beginning to think you like torturing me."

"This is torture?"

"Fuck, yeah, it's torture. The good kind."

She laughed. "Glad to hear you're enjoying it."

"I'd enjoy it a hell of a lot better if your hands found their way into my pants."

"I'm getting there. Are you always in such a rush?"

Because it's exactly what I'd been thinking about only seconds ago, I ran my hands from her hips up her sides to just under her arms, my thumbs barely brushing the sides of her breasts.

I heard her swift inhale and felt her shiver beneath my hands, making me that much hungrier for skin-on-skin contact.

"Sometimes fast is good. You can't catch your breath and your adrenaline's pumping and everything's hypersensitive."

"Are you talking about sex or hockey?"

She was definitely having trouble breathing now and my lips curved.

"Both. Hockey's much better when the pace is fast. Keeps your blood pumping and your attention focused. Fast sex can be mind-blowing. And I'm not just talking about the guy shooting off in five seconds and the girl left hanging."

Her fingers popped the button on my pants but she didn't reach for my zipper. "Glad to hear it."

"No, I'm talking about getting you so worked up in a couple of minutes that the second I get my cock inside you and start to pump, you come while I'm still getting off. You come so hard you can't breathe and your muscles don't work anymore and your brain's fuzzy."

I could barely control my own breathing right now, so fucking turned on by the woman in my arms and the images in my head. Images I planned to replace with the reality.

She sucked in a deep breath and I glanced down to find her fingers trembling over my zipper.

"Come on, baby." I leaned forward and sealed our lips together. "Let's blow our minds as fast as we can and I promise I'll take my own sweet time with you for the second round."

Her fingers hung in midair before she shook her head. "I don't know, Riley. Maybe I'm having fun tormenting you."

"Think about how much more fun you're gonna be having riding my cock."

I didn't know if it was the image I'd planted in her head or if she just took pity on me, but a second later she grabbed the tab of my zipper with deliberate fingers and began to pull it down.

Already pounding, my heart kicked into another gear as she released my cock. Her head bent, she reached into my pants and cupped my erection through my underwear.

Holy shit. Sensation shot through my erection to my balls and up my spine. If I wasn't careful, I'd come in her hands.

And that would be embarrassing as all hell.

But I didn't want her to stop as she traced her fingers around the tip of my cock, pushing at the band of my underwear.

"Lift up."

I obeyed immediately, prepared to give her anything she wanted.

Her mouth curved in another one of those smiles that made my blood run lava-hot.

"You're so agreeable."

"Sweetheart, you keep stroking me like that and I'll do whatever you want. Go ahead, ask me to rob a bank for you."

Her laughter brushed against my skin, raising more goosebumps. "Why don't you just start by taking off your shirt?"

Shifting forward, I reached one hand over my shoulders and pulled the t-shirt over my head. After I tossed it to the side, I found her staring at me intently.

"What's wrong?"

She shook her head, her gaze wandering below my chin. "Not one damn thing."

Huffing out a laugh, I leaned back into the cushions. "Glad to know you approve."

Lifting her hand, she placed her right index finger on my shoulder, her nail digging gently into my skin. "Oh, I approve. Now, I need you to lose the pants."

"That means you're going to have to move."

"I'm sure you can figure something out. Come on, Riley. Show me how you maneuver in a tight spot."

Holy fuck. When she smiled at me like that, I almost expected to see flames sparking between us.

"Your wish is my command."

A flush burned her cheeks and it was my turn to grin as I moved my hands between us. I deliberately brushed my knuckles along the zipper of her jeans and had the satisfaction of hearing her suck in a sharp breath. Her hands rose to my shoulders and gripped me tight, fingertips digging into my skin hard enough to leave marks.

They'd blend in with all the other bruises on my body, but I was having so much more fun getting them.

Going as slowly as I could, I worked my hands between our bodies, making sure I made as much contact as I could.

As I reached for my waistband, I slid my hands between her legs, pressing the seam of her jeans against her mound. Her chest rose and fell in an ever-increasing rhythm, almost matching my own.

Hooking my thumbs in the sides, I tugged at my pants. Luckily for me, they weren't that tight. If I'd had to struggle at all, I might've put just enough pressure on my rock-hard cock to trigger my orgasm.

But because of her position directly over me, I did have to lift my hips to push them down over my ass, which meant my cock rubbed right between her legs, exactly where I was going to be soon.

Making sure to drag my underwear with my pants, I worked them down just far enough to expose my cock, which was so hard, it practically pressed against my stomach.

Aly's gaze had dropped to watch, and when the tip of her tongue came out to touch her top lip, I groaned.

Leaning forward, I cupped her cheeks and brought her

forward so I could kiss her and let my tongue slide across those lips.

She caught me off guard when she drew the tip of my tongue into her mouth and sucked on it.

The sensation made me think of her sucking on my cock the exact same way.

Fuck, fuck, fuck. Concentrate, asshole, or you're gonna lose it.

I wanted to lose it inside her, not come on her stomach like a virgin.

But when she dropped one hand to wrap it around my erection, all bets were off.

Sinking my hands into her hair, I held her steady and opened my mouth over hers, eating at her with a hunger I almost couldn't control. It rose up in a rush, a tidal wave of heat, flooding my body and loosening the chains I'd been struggling not to break.

Aly appeared to have reached the same breaking point. She moaned low and deep, her hand tightening around my cock until I thought I'd have to tell her to stop. A second later, she loosened her grip. But that only made me want more.

I got to work on her jeans, getting the button undone and yanking down the zipper. But she was going to have to move if I was going to get those jeans off.

Grabbing her around the waist, I lifted her off my lap and twisted to the side, setting her on the cushion beside me.

Surprised at the sudden movement, she sprawled on her back, wide eyes blinking up at me as I shifted onto my knees to loom over her.

Her gaze locked with my own, she came up onto her elbows as I grabbed her jeans and yanked them down her legs.

Unfortunately, they were a little tighter than I'd realized and she came with them. She started to laugh a split second later, her head falling back, sending all that blonde hair spilling across the cushions.

With a growl to cover my own laughter, I yanked again and was rewarded when she lifted her ass and the denim bared a few inches of flesh.

I looked into her eyes, bright with laughter. I loved her smile but in a few seconds, I was going to make her scream. "Sweetheart, if I have to strip them off with my teeth, they're coming down."

"How about you use your teeth somewhere else and I'll get rid of the pants?"

My turn to grin. "I like the way you think. But you get rid of the pants first. I know where I want to use my teeth."

She swallowed hard and leaned back, hands working at her jeans until she had them shoved to her ankles. I took over then, pulling them away and leaving her bare from the waist down.

"Shirt too, babe. I'm gonna work my way up."

"Why not work your way down?"

"Because if I get my cock anywhere near your pussy right now, I'll revert to a thirteen-year-old and come before I get inside you."

She blinked, sucking in a short sharp breath. Shit, I needed to watch my mouth—

Her grin appeared again and a wicked light shone in her eyes. Maybe that good-girl routine really was just a front.

Time to test that theory.

Twisting, I brought my knees up onto the cushion so I knelt between her legs. I put my hands on the arm of the couch, just above her head, then leaned down. Her gaze flicked to my arms for a few seconds before she swallowed hard and looked back up.

Her grin slid away but the heat in her eyes blazed hotter.

"Condom?" she asked.

"Wallet. Back pocket."

Lifting her back slightly, she reached behind me, her hand brushing across my bare ass, accidently or not, and sparking even more heat.

I growled as she took her own sweet time pulling out my wallet while her fingers danced over my skin. Those few seconds seemed like hours and passed way too quickly as she brought the wallet between our bodies.

My breathing started to sound like a freight engine, heavy and hard. My cock felt as rigid as steel and I had to clamp down on my response if I wanted to make this last more than a minute.

Something she seemed determined not to allow.

With the condom now in one hand, she used her free hand to stroke me, lightly, with just the tips of her nails.

Holy fuck, that felt amazing. My balls drew up tight, and my cock bobbed.

"Put it on then take your shirt off. I need to feel your skin against mine."

Another smile before she reached for me and rolled the condom down my length.

Gritting my teeth, I let her linger, let her take her time, but as soon as her hands moved away, I sat back on my heels and tugged her shirt up and over her head. Thank god her sweater was loose and didn't give me a hassle. Otherwise, I would've ripped it, no lie.

But now that I had her naked in front of me, I couldn't wait.

I put my hand over her mound, sliding my fingers between her slick lips to make sure she was ready before pressing inside with one and pressing the heel of my palm against her clit.

She moaned, her hands coming up to grip my forearms.

"You want me to stop?" I had to ask.

"God, no. Don't stop."

That was all I needed to hear. I added a second finger and began to fuck her with them, keeping up the pressure on her clit and watching her intently.

Every slight shift of her body, every sound, every time her fingers dug further into my arms, I became more intent on making her come at least once before I got inside her.

"Damn, you are so fucking gorgeous."

Her bare breasts were beautiful, the nipples pale pink, and before I knew what I was doing, I leaned forward and put my lips over one, sucking the tip into my mouth and sucking on her.

Her eyes closed and her head fell back on a moan, pushing herself harder against me.

With my fingers still occupied between her legs, I switched to her neglected breast, sucking even harder this time, as if I could make her come from just my mouth on her breasts.

Next time, I'd make that a goal. Right now, I couldn't wait any longer.

Kissing my way to the center of her chest, I grabbed her knees and spread her wide. Her fingernails dug even deeper into my biceps as I guided my cock to her opening and began to press forward.

Holy fuck. She was tight. And hot. And god damn, I wanted to sink as deep into her as I could before I pulled out and shoved in again.

"Put your legs around my waist, hon. Don't let go."

She responded immediately, her legs hooking over my hips, ankles locking behind my back. Her hands lifted to clasp around my neck and she tugged, bringing my mouth back down to hers.

With my cock buried deep inside her, my tongue shot into her mouth, sliding against hers and connecting us on another level.

Mine. She's mine. Only mine.

The thought didn't sound like me. I wasn't that guy, wasn't an asshole with a Tarzan complex. But this woman made me fucking crazy.

My hips pumped harder even as I tried to slow down, to use a little finesse, not be a rutting bull.

The problem was, she seemed to have no issue. In fact, she seemed to want me to go even faster.

She lifted her hips into me harder on each thrust, pressed her lips tighter to mine, and scrambled every last working brain cell in my head.

Intense pleasure flooded my body and my hips swung faster, my cock stiff as iron and so damn sensitive I swore I'd stroke out from it.

Luckily, I didn't. I managed to hold on for another several minutes until I felt her tighten around me then moan as she came.

Mine.

Groaning, I came, wrapping my arms around her as tight as I could and holding on.

I didn't think I was letting go anytime soon.

Chapter 8

Alison

My brain still fuzzy from the amazing orgasm Riley had just given me, I sucked in air, trying to calm my racing heart.

I wasn't having much luck.

Holy hell, what'd just happened?

Okay, stupid question. I knew exactly what had happened. I just wasn't sure I'd be able to process it for a week. Or a month.

What I knew right now was that I didn't want to move, didn't want to think. I only wanted to feel.

Riley was huge and heavy, and even though he'd shifted partly to the side, he still managed to cover most of me and take up more than half the couch as well.

I liked that, too. So much so that my brain kept throwing out warning signals, but they weren't making sense because my body was still floating on a high of adrenaline and pleasure.

And every second Riley continued to breathe heavily into my ear, I grew more frantic.

This wasn't how this was supposed to work. I was supposed to be relaxed, boneless. Floating on a sea of bliss and contentment.

Instead, my brain wouldn't stop working.

I wanted him again, wanted him to kiss me like he had before, like he wanted to devour me. Wanted him to put his hands all over me, to cup my breasts and tweak my nipples then let his fingers trail down my body to between my legs and play with my clit, which still throbbed.

How could I want him again, so quickly? How—

He shifted against me and my arms automatically tightened around his shoulders, clinging. He didn't go far, just rearranged our bodies so I was lying more on top of him than beneath him and able to breathe more easily.

At least in theory. In reality, I still was having trouble catching my breath because each time I drew in air, all I smelled was him.

Clean, masculine male. The most potent aphrodisiac I'd ever encountered.

Careful now. This doesn't sound like you. You don't fall for guys like this.

It wasn't sensible. It wasn't anything like me.

But when Riley's big, rough hands began to pet my back, I could only think about the way those hands made me feel. Protected. Wanted. Desired.

Way too fast.

"Aly? You okay?"

And that voice. Oh my god, I wanted him to keep talking with that rough growl so close to my ear. Wanted to snuggle into him like he was my own personal full-size teddy bear and have him make love to me all night.

I wanted to go again in a few minutes. Wondered if he wanted the same.

God, please let him want the same.

"Aly, hon. What's—"

"I'm fine." My hands clutched at him involuntarily, as if I was afraid he'd get up and leave. "Just…trying to recover."

He huffed out a laugh and drew me closer. "Yeah, I know. That was fu— ah, amazing. Let's do it again."

Yes. Oh god, please, yes.

I almost let one hand begin a downward slide to see if I could hurry him along then stopped when I realized what I was doing.

No. No, no, no. I shouldn't be trying to get him to stay. I should be hurrying his ass out the door. Even though I wanted him to stay.

And why would you ever want him to go home? Are you crazy? This is the guy you've been waiting for.

Holy crap, I was going crazy. He'd brainwashed me, put me under a spell that made me do whatever he wanted.

"Don't you have practice tomorrow?"

He sighed. "Yeah, but one sleepless night isn't going to pull me down. Of course, after a few like this, I might not be able to move. But it sure as hell would be worth it."

Putting his strong hands against my back and drawing me even closer, he pressed a kiss against my head, making me melt even more. And my panic response kicked in again.

I wanted to ask him to stay but I knew I wasn't ready for that. Didn't know how long it would take for me to be ready for that.

Except…I really wanted him to stay.

"Hey, hon. You sure you're okay? You seem a little…quiet."

I nodded but I couldn't force myself to meet his gaze and lie to his face. "I'm fine. I'm just tired."

I held my breath and hoped he'd take the hint. For a few seconds, I wasn't sure he would. I thought I was going to have to ask him to leave and that might've sent me into a spaz attack because I didn't really want him to leave.

Get a grip, you idiot. He needs to go before you beg him to stay.

So I waited, practically holding my breath. Finally, he seemed to get the hint.

"Well then, I guess I better get going and let you sleep."

I tried not to clutch at him as he shifted us around until he was on the edge of the couch. But he'd maneuvered us so we were face-to-face. I couldn't avoid looking into his eyes, and when I did, I was fairly certain I was going to beg him to stay.

I managed, barely, to keep my mouth shut but only until he leaned forward and kissed me. And when he slid his tongue against my lips, I immediately opened for him.

He made a deep sound in his throat, a sound that made my sex clench and beg for anything he wanted to use to fill it. Fingers, tongue, cock.

Shivering, I let my arms wind around his shoulders, pressing my naked flesh to his and feeling my resolution to send him on his way sink to the soles of my feet.

I was just about to move my hands from his shoulders down his back to his ass when he released me and swung his legs off the side of the couch and planted his feet on the floor.

"I really like spending time with you." He turned to look at me, shoving long fingers into his too-long dark hair to push it out of his hazel eyes and making my chest tighten. "So, tomorrow night. Are you free?"

Blinking as he stood and his perfect ass came into view, I had to take a few seconds to think about what he'd said before I could formulate an answer.

"Yes."

When he reached to pull his pants up, I nearly swallowed my tongue. I watched him tuck his cock into his jeans but not zip them.

He looked back at me. "Bathroom?"

I had to suck in air before I could answer.

"Oh, yeah." I pointed to a small door off to the side of the room. "Just in there."

I watched the play of muscle across his back and chest as he walked to the bathroom and sat there for several seconds waiting for him to return before I realized I was naked. I'd just pulled my shirt over my head when he walked out again and returned to pick up his t-shirt and dress shirt.

As he shrugged them on, he turned to smile at me. And my heart kicked into heart-attack pace.

Not fair. And oh, so very dangerous.

"You wanna get some dinner tomorrow night after the game?"

Yes, I did. Very much. I wanted to do anything he wanted.

Which made the words stick in my throat. I wasn't that girl, the one who tossed over my entire life for a guy I'd just met. Still, I wanted to see him again.

"Sure. That's sounds… great."

How did he manage to make me feel breathless and light-headed and heavy-limbed all at the same time?

Either he ignored my slight hesitation or he just didn't hear it. His smile widened. "I'll give you a call after practice."

Leaning down, he put his hands on the back of the couch on either side of my shoulders and bent close.

I braced for another one of his mind-numbing kisses, but he put his mouth on my neck instead. He nipped at my skin, sending me into a full-body shiver. I reached for him, my hands landing on his hips, and I wasn't sure whether I wanted to pull him closer or push him away.

When he started to pull away, I almost didn't want to let him go. I actually had to force myself to release him so he could stand.

"See you after the game. Puck drops at five. Game should be over by eight."

"Okay."

Halfway to the door, he turned to look at me.

"I have a great time with you, Aly. I think…" He stopped, appeared to reconsider his words then smiled. And totally didn't say what was on his mind. "I'll see you soon."

Then he walked to the door and headed out, closing it quietly behind him.

I must have sat there for a full minute staring at the door, jeans in my hand, bare ass on the couch.

Holy shit.

I felt like I'd been run over by a steamroller.

That wasn't good, was it?

Could you actually fall in love this fast?

No. Absolutely not. That wasn't what this was.

I wasn't in love with Riley. In lust, yes. Hell, who wouldn't be? The man was worship-worthy. But he wasn't a man you fell in love with. Not if you wanted two-point-five kids and a picket fence and a house in the suburbs.

Everything I'd always wanted.

When I was a kid, my parents had always been on the move because of my dad's job in quality control for a chemical company with plants all over North America. This house was the only one we'd lived in for more than four years and only then because my dad had exhausted himself and the company owners had insisted he take a desk job.

I had hated moving every couple of years. I didn't make friends as easily as Vivi and I'd loved everything about this house, which was why I'd jumped at the chance to continue to live here when my parents moved to Florida.

Riley had the kind of life I never wanted to live again. He could be on the move next month, next week. Hell, he could be called up to play in Philly tomorrow.

Definitely not a man I wanted to get too involved with.

Chapter 9

Riley

I eased open the door to my apartment.

The landlord still hadn't fixed the squeaky hinges and I didn't want to wake Justin. It was almost two a.m. and my roommate would probably be asleep—

"Guess the date went well."

Justin grinned at me from the couch, where he held a beer in one hand and a game controller in another.

I gave him the finger before heading into the kitchen for a beer.

"Still up playing with yourself, I see." I sank into the other end of the couch.

"Hey, now. No fair picking on those of us less fortunate. I'm guessing from the grin on your face, you had a good time."

I shoved my elbow into Justin's side. "What are you, my mother?"

"No, just the guy who hasn't gotten laid in three months."

"Ashley still mad at you, huh?"

Justin grimaced at the mention of his longtime girlfriend, who still lived in their hometown of Kanata, Ottawa.

"Yeah. She keeps harping on me about taking that offer in Toronto. And I keep telling her it's the worst damn team in the league. Why the fuck would I want to go there when I can play for the damn Cup defenders? You'd think she didn't know I played fucking hockey. Fuck that. Now...tell Daddy J all about your date tonight."

Justin smirked at me and I couldn't help but laugh.

"You're a sick motherfucker, you know that, right?"

"But I know you want to spill your guts."

I took a swig of my beer and shook my head, still grinning. "No, I really don't. It'll be all over the locker room tomorrow."

"Do you actually give a shit what the other guys think? Dude, your conquests are legendary."

The beer suddenly didn't taste as good as it had as I watched the on-screen battle rage.

Justin wasn't wrong. I did have a reputation. One I hadn't been concerned about for years. Different girl every other night. No repeats.

Until this season. This season, I'd sworn off hookups, had committed myself to my career with no distractions.

After tonight... I couldn't fucking wait to see Aly again. I'd wanted to go to bed with her and wake up in the morning to see her, hair messy, skin warm and soft from sleep. I would've stayed if she'd asked. She hadn't. And that just made me want it more.

She had no idea how much of a break from the norm that was for me. And I didn't want her to know.

"Yeah, well, maybe I'm turning over a new leaf this season."

Justin went silent and I shot him a glance.

"Dude, seriously? You just met this girl and now you're all ready to reform your manwhore ways?"

I shrugged. I didn't want to get into a discussion about my dating habits at two in the morning when I should be in bed.

"Maybe I'm starting to think about what I want to do after this season. What I want to do…after hockey."

"Seriously?"

Justin's shock rang clear in his voice. I slid him another glance and found my roommate staring at me with his mouth hanging open.

Shrugging, I took another swig of beer before answering. "I've been giving it some thought."

"You're not even thirty. What the *hell*, man? Is something wrong?"

I shook my head. "Nothing's wrong. Just been thinking maybe it's time to think about what's next. You know, figure out what I'm gonna do with the rest of my life."

Justin shook his head like he hadn't heard me right. "Why? I mean seriously, why? You're only twenty-fucking-eight years old. It's not like you're forty and you can't bend your knees and your shoulder's hanging on by a ligament."

All true. "Maybe I want to get out before that happens."

Justin continued to shake his head in shock. "Dude, what *happened* tonight?"

I'd had the best damn sex of my life, that's what'd happened. And I'd met a girl I might want to live with for the rest of my life.

Even my own brain went, *"Hey, now. That's kind of a huge leap."*

But I was used to making snap decisions and changing things on the fly. And I knew myself. I wasn't some teenager just out of the draft with mad skills and no polish.

"Nothing happened." Or maybe something really big had happened. But I wasn't sharing that with Justin. "It's just something that's been on my mind."

Justin gave a full-body shake, like a dog shaking off water. "Yeah, well, get it off your damn mind or you're gonna jinx yourself. And the team. Just don't go there."

I couldn't help it. I was already there. "Don't you ever think about what you're going to do after?"

"Why should I?" Justin shrugged. "I'm gonna play 'til I can't then I'll figure it out."

It was the mantra of a lot of players. Hell, I had lived by it for years.

"Rye." The tone in Justin's voice pulled my gaze back to him. "Are you seriously thinking about giving up?"

Now there was an interesting way to put things.

I shifted on the couch to look Justin in the eyes. "Is it really giving up if you're going to find something else to do with your life?"

Justin's gaze was too damn sharp for almost two in the morning. "Is that what you want? To do something else?"

No. But I knew I wanted more. And I knew who I wanted more with.

"What I want is to get enough sleep before skate tomorrow afternoon."

"You mean this afternoon."

Shit, yeah. "Exactly. I'm going to bed. Night."

I got up and headed for my room.

"Hey, Rye."

I stopped and looked over my shoulder at Justin.

"This is your year, man."

I just shook my head and continued to my room.

Chapter 10

Aly

"Someone had a good time last night."

I gave my sister the side-eye as I made my way to the coffeemaker Sunday morning. I'd slept until nine, which was as long as my body would naturally sleep before my eyes popped open.

"Don't worry," Vivi continued. "You don't have to say anything. I can tell by the smile on your face he must've been good."

A blush heated my cheeks but I purposely ignored Vivi's sly remarks as I poured myself a mug of caffeine and headed for the cabinet for something to eat while the coffee kicked in.

"Obviously, the man knows how to move off the ice as well as on."

Yes, he certainly had. But I still wasn't giving my sister the satisfaction of responding.

Vivi sighed dramatically. "Guess I'll need to get earplugs if he's going to be sticking around. You two probably made enough noise to wake the neighbors. Maybe I should ask Tig if I can stay at her house tonight. I assume you're seeing him again tonight."

"I'm ignoring you."

Vivi huffed. "You're *trying* to ignore me. You're not doing a very good job of it. Come on, spill. You know you want to tell me all about it."

I grabbed the box of Lucky Charms out of the cabinet and poured a bowl. Every other day, I had something sensible, but on the weekends I needed my sugar. It was Sunday—and I'd probably burned enough calories last night to eat the entire box.

Which made me smile.

"Oh, now, that's just mean." Vivi threw her napkin at me as I sat across from her at the breakfast table. "If I had smoking-hot sex with a guy, I'd tell you all about it."

I gave my sister a raised eyebrow. "Whether I wanted to hear or not."

"At least admit you had a good time."

I shrugged, trying for nonchalant although I felt anything but. "I did."

"And that you want to see him again."

"I do. He's…" I struggled to find a word that wouldn't trigger all kinds of questions from her that I couldn't answer. "He's really nice."

Vivi's eyebrows rose again. "Nice? He's *nice*? Oh please. Any man who makes you look like you're still in shock from last night is not just *nice*."

"Please stop telling me how I look this morning. It's weird."

"Then maybe you should look in a mirror before you come to the table looking like you spent all night screwing your brains out."

I stuck my tongue out at my sister before I started eating, then proceeded to ignore her and read the paper.

For the first time since I'd played field hockey in high school, I looked at the sports pages. The article on the game took up about half a page but it mentioned Riley's name a few times, all favorably. The writer made special mention of Riley's work ethic, how he never gave up, even if he didn't get what he wanted the first time.

And yeah, I'd seen that part of him in action last night. Once he'd set his mind on something, he didn't stop.

When he'd said he wanted to hear me scream, he hadn't been kidding.

I swore I was still blushing when my phone rang a few minutes later.

I grabbed it…and sighed.

Not Riley.

"Hey, Mom." I exchanged a glance with Vivi, who shot out of her seat like her ass was on fire and disappeared. "What's wrong?"

"Nothing. I just forgot to remind you about the service contract yesterday. The one for the heater? You probably need to renew that this month. I remembered that when your dad complained about the heat yesterday. We've had the air running nonstop for the past six months, I swear. And we're supposed to be getting hit with that tropical storm next week…"

Stifling a sigh, I let mom ramble, answering appropriately when required, feeling guilty when I looked at the clock and rolled my eyes when I realized my mom had just spent the last twenty minutes talking about my dad's refusal to go to the doctor for his constant intestinal issues and then ran down her own health issues. All of which she'd mentioned yesterday.

I loved my parents. I did. But sometimes…

Well, sometimes I wished I wasn't the one they relied on. The one everyone relied on. Sometimes I wished I could be a little more like Vivi, born with the ability to let everything roll off my back and not feel guilty about it.

I wanted to have fun and not worry about the consequences.

I wanted to have hot sex with Riley and not think about the

fact that one day he'd move on to another team, another city. Another girl.

I wished I didn't feel like the two nights we'd spent together had been the start of something amazing.

Riley

"If that kid skates by me again with that smirk on his face, I'm gonna lay him out on his ass." I glared at CJ. "I get it, he's young. But he's a twig and I'm gonna snap him."

"You can't hurt our best scorer." Justin laughed. "We need him. You know, you'd think you'd be in a better mood, considering you got laid last night."

Justin and I skated together Sunday afternoon. Almost the entire team was here, even though today's practice was optional. We'd had a good game last night and Coach had given us the morning off before the game this afternoon.

I hadn't considered skipping. Apparently most of the guys felt the same.

"Keep your damn mouth shut about that." I slashed my stick across Justin's shins, almost hard enough to hurt. "The whole damn team doesn't need to know."

"Umm, the whole damn team already knows."

I shot him a glare. "What the fuck?"

Justin grinned, completely unrepentant. "Come on, you know hockey players gossip worse than old ladies."

Yeah, unfortunately I did.

Shaking my head, I sighed and pivoted to skate backward. "Christ almighty. I don't want Aly to think I'm a douche who told my entire team we slept together."

"So you gonna see her again?"

"I'm gonna text her after practice to see if she's coming to the game tonight."

"Wow, three nights in a row. Must be true love."

I grimaced. "How fucking old are you? Seriously, like, twelve?"

Justin laughed maniacally and skated away, leaving me to skate by myself for a few blissfully quiet seconds, thinking about those two little, four-letter words.

True love.

Yes, I believed in love, enough to know I'd loved my ex but not in the way I'd needed to make our marriage work. I also knew what I felt for Aly, even after such a short time, might be something worth fighting for.

And I had the feeling I was going to have to fight for it, if her unwillingness to let me stay the night was anything to go by.

Our personalities were in direct opposition. She was quiet and calm, reserved. I wasn't. Maybe that was what drew me to her.

Out of the corner of my eye, I saw CJ coming up on me again.

Christ, this kid was gonna step on my last nerve today.

Just keep skating, kid. You don't wanna mess with me today.

Apparently, CJ couldn't read minds. He slowed until we were skating together.

"Uh, hey. Hi."

I barely kept myself from rolling my eyes. "What's up, CJ?"

"Um, yeah, so I was wondering if I could work with you a little today?"

I took a longer look at the twenty-one-year-old, surprised and waiting for the punchline. When it didn't come, I said, "What's up?"

CJ shrugged. "Just wanna work on a few things. I know I need to get better in the corners and you're damn good at that. So maybe we could work together for a while."

"No problem."

The kid broke out in a huge smile. Midwestern farm boy from his gold hair to his broad shoulders and his powerful legs, CJ used those legs to propel him to blazing-fast speeds. He had one hell of a natural talent, but he was still young and still growing into that body. He also had a stutter that only appeared off the ice.

"Great. Thanks! So, how'd your date go last night? She was really pretty."

And the kid had no filter whatsoever around his teammates.

"Oh, for fuck's sake." I reached out and smacked the kid on the back of the helmet. "Do a couple more laps before I kick your ass."

CJ turned and back-skated, grinning all the way down the ice. "Only if you can catch me."

I didn't bother to chase CJ. The kid would come back to me, like a huge, gangly puppy, ready to play.

I had much prettier prey to pursue.

Chapter 11

"Hey, Aly. I had a great time last night and I really want to see you again tonight. Game's at five tonight if you want to come. I'll leave tickets at will-call. Then maybe we can get some food." He paused and, when he spoke again, his voice had dropped a few octaves and I had to listen closely to hear him. "Or maybe we can just find a bed and I can make you come a few times before we get to the really good stuff. Up to you. Let me know about the tickets."

Standing in my kitchen by myself, I blushed even though no one could hear the message Riley had left on my phone.

But that blush wasn't embarrassment. No, his words ignited a firestorm of heat in my body. My thighs clenched, my nipples peaked, and my hand curled into fists.

It was my own fault. I'd told him last night I wanted everything he had to give me and to be as dirty as he wanted. He'd taken me at my word, which I loved.

Riley hadn't known me all my life. He didn't know that I was such a goody-two-shoes that most people who knew me were shocked when I said "damn."

They'd probably think I'd been possessed by the devil if they found out what I'd done with Riley last night. And what I planned to do with Riley tonight.

I wanted to be bad.

Shaking my head, I forced myself to put the groceries away instead of listening to that message again.

Vivi was at the tattoo studio, where she'd be most of the day before she and her friends headed out to the bars, where they'd be before hitting the after-hours clubs until four or five in the morning.

I had never understood the appeal of getting so drunk you couldn't remember what you did the night before, but Vivi seemed to enjoy the hell out of it. Mostly because our mom absolutely *hated* that she did it.

But tonight it meant that Vivi would probably crash on a friend's couch for the night and Riley and I could make as much noise as we wanted and I wouldn't have to hear about it from my sister tomorrow morning.

But it also meant I'd probably be going to the game by myself tonight. Hopefully I'd be able to sit with Lori and Bliss.

Finally, after every last can had been stowed, I pressed the call button on my phone and was a little disappointed when it went straight to voice mail.

"You've reached Riley. Leave me a message."

Holy crap. How amazing was it that just the sound of his voice made me want to pant?

"Hi. It's me. Aly." I rolled my eyes. "I'd love to come to the game tonight so thanks. And," I paused and sucked in a fortifying breath, "why don't we come back to my place for drinks afterward? See you soon."

I hung up, hoping I hadn't sounded like a rabid nympho whose only goal in life was to get laid. Or worse, like a pathetic twenty-eight-year-old who hadn't gotten laid for months before last night.

"Well, you got laid last night. And you can't complain about that."

With a smile, I looked at the clock and sighed, wondering if I'd be able to breathe by the time the puck dropped.

* * *

Riley

"You look like the cat who ate the pussy. You obviously had a good time last night. She is very nice, yes, to put that smile on your face."

The noise level in the locker room was high as the team dressed for warm-ups, but Jake had made sure everyone could hear him.

I stifled a groan as the rest of the team threw things at Jake for his deliberate mangling of the English language. Everyone knew he'd done it deliberately. His English was perfect when it had to be.

I even managed to suppress my instinct to flip Jake off because that would just make him worse and draw attention I didn't want.

If the team didn't need the little prick so badly, I would lay Jake out on the ice. I'd ring his bell hard and then I'd do it once more for good measure. And the rest of the team would laugh because the guy fucking deserved it.

But the guy was too damn good on the ice.

"Dude, you fucking score more than Ovechkin." Winger Tyler Richardson shook his head, shit-eating grin on his face as he pulled up his shorts. "I wanna be you when I grow up."

On the other hand, Tyler would probably ride the bench

most of the season. I could take him out with no hassle. Except then I would be riding the bench.

"Maybe you could give me some pointers," Tyler continued to needle me. "Like how you managed those twins last year. Your reputation precedes you, man. I bow down to your expertise."

And then the little shit actually got down on his knees and laid himself out.

"Dickardson, get your ass off the floor." Lad Marchenko put his foot on Tyler's ass and shoved him just hard enough for Tyler to feel it. And then roll over onto his back and act like he'd been shot.

I shook my head and gave Tyler the finger I'd been going to give Jake.

As the conversation thankfully moved on to something else as we got ready for warm-ups before the game, I shrugged off comments.

For fuck's sake, Tyler's reputation was almost as bad as my own, although he was five years younger. Then again, I hadn't gained my reputation overnight. I'd built it up over the past ten years. And it'd be a hard thing to live down in just a few short weeks.

I hoped like hell Aly never got wind of it.

"Just ignore him. He's being a dick." Shane sat on the bench across from me, strapping on his leg pads. "Bliss likes her. Said Aly's really smart. Like brainy smart. And maybe a little shy."

That made my eyebrows rise. "Shy? Really?"

That certainly hadn't been my impression.

"Yeah. She also said she was really nice." Now Shane looked up at me with raised eyebrows. "So you seeing her again tonight?"

Since it was Shane asking, and not one of the kids, I answered. "Yeah."

I didn't say anything else and Shane's eyebrows rose higher. "That's kind of unusual for you, isn't it?"

The words "fuck" and "you" were on the tip of my tongue, but Shane didn't have a shit-eating grin on his face and he wasn't looking to bust my ass. He actually sounded curious.

"Actually, no, it's not." I tugged my sweater over my head and grabbed my helmet. "At least, not lately."

"Turning over a new leaf?"

"Don't you have a pre-game routine to go through?"

Like almost every goalie I had ever met, Shane had a specific ritual he performed before each game.

Shane grinned now. "Yes, I do. Talk to you later, Rye."

"Not if we're gonna talk about our feelings."

Now Shane laughed, drawing the interest of the rest of the team for the simple reason that the goalie was always so intensely focused before a game. This season, though, he'd been loosening up a little. And playing better than he'd ever played. Yes, we were only a couple months into the season, but everyone had noticed his playing had elevated to another level.

He wouldn't be in this league long.

I was thrilled for the guy. Shane worked hard and was talented as all hell.

And I should take that to heart and concentrate on the game tonight and not a certain woman who'd be waiting for me after the game.

Chapter 12

Aly

"…older than most of the guys…fuckable…gorgeous…a real manwhore…love to get in those pants…shouldn't have much trouble…Riley…never last…"

The two women holding the conversation behind me hadn't registered until I heard Riley's name. The noise level in the arena this afternoon was higher than it'd been last night. Bigger crowd, too.

Every seat around me was taken, a few by other girlfriends introduced to me by Bliss and Lori.

Most were friendly. But there'd been a couple who'd taken one look at me and immediately dismissed me, going back to their whispered conversation. I shrugged it off and dropped back into conversation with Bliss and Lori.

But now they were talking about Riley. *My* Riley. I hadn't heard everything they'd said but I'd heard enough. Riley had a reputation, at least according to the girls behind me. He slept around. A lot.

Somewhere beyond the buzzing in my ears, I heard the horn announcing the end of the first period.

"Hey, Aly. You okay?"

I glanced up at Bliss's voice, forcing a smile I didn't feel.

"I'm fine." I stood to let Lori get by her. "It's really loud in here today. Hard to hold a conversation."

"Yeah, the team's been on a marketing push to get people in the seats. Seems to be working."

Bliss's gaze shot over my shoulder to the younger women who were still chatting away, although now it was harder to hear them, what with the throbbing music and the announcer talking about season tickets.

"There are definitely more people here today than last night." She raised her brows at me. "Some of them really don't need to be. Guess you heard the idiot twins spouting off?"

"No, not really. Sounds like they know Riley, though."

Bliss rolled her eyes. "They don't know shit. Ignore them."

Shrugging, I sighed. "I don't know him either. I only met the man two days ago. How can you get to know someone in such a short time?"

Especially when some of that time had been spent scrambling my brain cells with amazing sex.

Which just meant he'd had a lot of practice.

"Well, I'm glad you're here again today." Bliss smiled. "And that you're enjoying the game. I'd never really been to a Redtails game before I started dating Shane. Now I can't even think about summer and the off season. It's like being punished."

I laughed, shaking my head. "You've become a true convert."

"I have. It doesn't hurt that my guy is a damn good player."

Behind us, the younger girls who'd been talking about Riley exploded into laughter, though now they'd lowered their voices enough that I couldn't hear them.

Bliss rolled her eyes again and leaned over to whisper into my ear. "The puck bunnies are just jealous because they haven't been able to snag a player yet this season. Most of the older guys are beyond screwing every girl who gives them a look. And a lot of this year's team seem a little more…grounded, if you know what I mean. Don't get me wrong, there are still a few looking to get laid every night, but they're not all horndogs."

"But Riley has a reputation, doesn't he?"

Sighing, Bliss's nose wrinkled. "I'm really not trying to deflect and I'm not making excuses but…yeah, he has a reputation. Although I can honestly say, since he's been here, he hasn't dated anyone but you. I think, after his divorce, he—"

"His divorce?"

Bliss's eyes went wide. "Shit, he didn't tell you?" She groaned. "Me and my big mouth. Damn it, I thought you knew. I don't think it's a state secret or anything because he mentioned it in passing when we'd met. I think it's been years since it was finalized. She was his high school sweetheart but she couldn't deal with him being on the road all the time. Or something. I really don't know details. You need to ask him." She grimaced. "And then tell him I'm sorry for opening my big mouth."

I shook my head, feeling sorry for making Bliss feel bad. "No harm, no foul. I mean, we've all got a past."

"You're absolutely right. My past involved an emotionally abusive ex who almost made me give up Shane. Luckily I pulled my shit together and now I can't imagine my life without him. Stuff works out. And now I need a drink so I don't continue to run at the mouth."

I laughed and followed Bliss to the beer stand, but throughout the rest of the game, my mind continued to come back to the fact that Riley had been married.

I didn't know why it bothered me. Hell, we'd just met. It wasn't like we'd shared every aspect of our lives and he'd hidden that fact from me. It just hadn't come up yet.

And so what if he'd slept with a few girls, or maybe more

than a few? I'd slept with other guys. Okay, maybe I could count on one hand the number of guys I'd slept with. That only made me picky. Nothing wrong with that.

Riley hadn't been picky. I couldn't exactly hold that against him. We didn't have an exclusive relationship. We'd had two dates and spent one absolutely amazing hour fucking each other's brains out.

It just meant there was no way I would get attached. Yes, the sex had been great. And I hoped there'd be more tonight. And if our affair continued for a week or a month…great. Eventually it would end. I'd keep my emotions out of the equation and enjoy the hell out of the orgasms.

As I waited for Riley, I saw Shane wrap his arms around Bliss and kiss her, smiling when Shane grabbed her tight and lifted her off her feet.

The expression on his face…no one could doubt how he felt about Bliss.

The guy loved her.

I wanted that kind of love. Where all you had to do was look at the person and you knew. And that didn't happen over a weekend. That took months. Sometimes it took years.

Riley emerged from the locker room at that moment. He spared a quick grin for Bliss and Shane then turned that grin on me. And that grin did weird and wonderful things to my body.

Easy, girl.

I smiled back, unable to do anything else.

And then he reached for me and pulled me against him. I had a quick second to appreciate how much bigger he was than me. And then he bent and kissed me and it was almost as intensely passionate as the kiss Shane had laid on Bliss.

"Get a room."

The taunt filtered through the open hall and I heard laughter. Maybe I should be embarrassed by the PDA, especially because

Riley held nothing back. He kissed me like we'd been dating for years, not just since two nights ago.

But I couldn't be angry at him. I didn't want him to stop.

And he didn't, not for a good minute, while he fried my brain with his lips and his tongue. Hell, he only had to put his hand low on my back and I was ready to slide my hands down his pants and cup his ass.

Good thing I had some common sense left.

A second later, Riley pulled back, gave me another smile then hustled me toward the exit.

"Glad you could make it tonight. I'm starving. You mind if we get a drink somewhere that has decent food?"

"Of course not. You—"

"Hey, Riley. Good game tonight."

A woman I didn't recognize smiled at Riley as we made our way through the hall. He nodded at her but kept moving.

"Thanks a lot."

But she wasn't giving up that easy. "Will I see you at the Spruce?"

"Not tonight."

This time he didn't even bother to look at the woman, just gave a vague wave as he spoke over his shoulder. Dismissed her as if he hadn't even seen her. And maybe he hadn't.

Had he slept with her? Is that how he'd treat me one day?

Jesus, when did you become such a whiny, needy bitch?

"So where should we go?" Riley steered me around the maze of cars in the small parking lot next to the rink where the team parked. "I haven't been around long enough to figure out more than a few decent places."

"Are you sure you don't want to go out with the rest of the team? I wouldn't have a problem with that."

"I'd rather spend the time with you." His frank answer drew my gaze up to his, and I found him staring intently down at me. "If that's okay?"

I couldn't help but smile back at him. "I'm fine with that. What are you hungry for?"

"Red meat." His grin made a reappearance and he leaned a little closer. "And later, some a little more…pink."

I couldn't help it. I blushed. "Riley."

He looked so damn innocent. "What? What'd I say?"

Shaking my head, I kept walking. "Are you always like this?"

"Like what? Hey, where'd you park? Do we need to drop your car off at home before we head out?"

Another blush because my sister had insisted on driving me into the game tonight so Riley would have to take me home. "No, I don't have my car. I, ah, caught a ride with my sister. She works a few blocks away at a tattoo shop."

Riley's smile grew impossibly wider and hotter. "I like your sister."

He stopped at his truck, threw his bag in the back then opened the passenger door for me before getting in the other side.

"I'm sure you would. She's amazing."

"Then she's probably a lot like you."

I'd never dated a guy who was so comfortable dishing out compliments. It was a little unnerving. And completely endearing.

"Actually we're pretty different."

He just smiled. "So, where are we going?"

I thought about it for a few seconds as he started the truck. I wanted to have him to herself.

"There's a place in Exeter that does great burgers. The kitchen's open until midnight. It's kind of quiet—"

"Sounds perfect. Just point me in the right direction."

I thought about my response for a second. "You didn't seem to have trouble finding your way around last night."

His laughter filled the car, making me want to close the space between us and snuggle up to his side. "There you go, hon. You do have a little naughty in you."

Shaking my head, I rolled my eyes. "You're the only one who seems to bring it out in me."

His grin got impossibly hotter. "Glad to hear it. Now let's go eat so I can corrupt you a little more."

Riley

I had had a great fucking game.

My line had actually had a better plus-minus than the first line tonight and I'd scored and had an assist.

Now, I had only one goal in mind: Get her in bed.

Before the game, I'd only been able to think about her. During the game, I'd compartmentalized that lust. But now it burned like lava in my veins.

It might have blinded me to the fact that I didn't realize Aly had something on her mind until we were on our way back to her place.

I hadn't noticed anything wrong during dinner. We'd talked and laughed and I'd flirted and she'd smiled. And my dick had gotten harder every time she looked at me and shook her head at something I told her.

But I'd noticed a hesitancy about her, like she had something on the tip of her tongue but every time she thought about speaking, she held back.

I'd thought maybe it was just because we didn't know each other that well and I was hyped from the game.

But now, sitting alone together in the quiet cab, I knew something was up.

I didn't want to get into it while we were driving, so I'd waited until I'd parked in front of her house.

As I watched, she glanced at her home then looked back at me. "Do you want to come in?"

"Yeah, I do, but… Are you sure you want me to? Is something wrong?"

She tried to hide her grimace but I caught it before she could.

I moved a little closer. "Did something happen at the game?"

"No, no. Nothing happened. I just…" Her nose wrinkled. "I heard about your divorce."

I blinked. "Oh. It's not recent. I mean, I've been divorced for almost five years. Sorry, I guess I should've said something but it never even occurred to me—"

"No, wait." She held up one hand. "I'm sorry. It doesn't matter to me that you're divorced. I just…you never said anything. And I know how stupid that sounds considering we only met Friday."

Grimacing, I shook my head. "How bad am I gonna sound if I say I barely ever think about being married anymore? It was years ago and I kinda…forget."

Damn, that sounded really lame or really self-absorbed. *Fuck.*

"Really, I don't mean to pry—"

"Whoa, no. You're not prying. Seriously. What do you want to know? Just ask. I'm an open book."

Her lips curved. "Okay but why don't we go inside where it's not so cold?"

I jumped out of the car and hustled around to take her hand and help her out. Then I put my arm around her shoulders and tucked her into my side. She didn't stiffen or try to pull away. If she had, I would've released her. Instead, her arm went around my waist and she pulled me even closer.

Now I wanted to run for the house and nail her against the front door.

I refrained, but just barely.

"Do you want something to drink?" She took off her coat and hung it on the hook by the door.

"Yeah, I'd love some water."

She smiled over her shoulder as she headed toward the back of the house. "I'll be right back."

Shedding my coat, I sat on the couch, grinning when I had a flashback to last night. I couldn't wait to repeat but first…

Aly returned with a bottle of water for both of us then sat next to me.

"I really didn't mean to pry," she said. "If you don't want to talk about your marriage, we don't have to. It just kind of took me off guard."

"It's not a big secret." I shrugged. "It's just been a while since I was married. Kind of seems like another life, if that makes sense."

Drawing her legs up underneath her, she propped her arm on the back of the couch and rested her head on her hand. "How long were you married?"

"Two years. The first year was good." I grimaced. "Mostly. We were high school sweethearts and the plan was to get married after I finished college. But…my second year of college didn't go so well." Total understatement. "I partied too much, didn't study enough. The only thing I had going for me was hockey but I… Well, I flunked out."

I could still remember the look on my dad's face when my parents had come to get me at the end of the semester. So damn disappointed.

"I'd planned to enter the draft that following summer, but my parents convinced me to take the year off, move back home and work, then go back to school for my degree and get drafted between junior and senior year."

"Sounds like you had it all planned out."

"What's the saying? Best laid plans?" I shook my head. "The only job I could find was working night shift in the local mill.

And I fucking hated it. Then I got picked up by the Great Lakes Hockey league. It's a full-contact amateur league and it filled that hole."

That hole had been a gaping wound. I'd never told anyone, not even my parents, just how much *not* playing hockey had hurt.

"I think Ann figured since I was home, that's where I was gonna stay."

"Did you want to go back to college?"

Aly watched me with intent blue eyes. Those eyes mesmerized. I wanted the light to be on tonight when I made love to her so I could see those eyes.

"Yeah, I did. I wanted my degree. Even back then, I knew I couldn't play hockey all my life. I needed something for after. With a degree in sports management, I figure I can stay involved with the game even after I can't play anymore.

"I played amateur for a season and got married because I loved her and I figured there wasn't much difference between marrying her then and waiting a couple of years until I graduated. But Ann didn't count on me going back to school. We had a huge fight the night before I left to go back. That was pretty much the beginning of the end. I wanted her to come with me. She didn't want to leave our hometown. And I realized it was never going to work. I don't think she ever really believed I was going to make hockey my career."

"I'm sorry. That must've sucked."

It had. It'd sucked big time because it'd been my second failure. "I was divorced by the time I was twenty-one. Wow. Seven years ago. Seems like forever."

"But you finished college and you're playing professionally. That's a great achievement."

I nodded, her smile making me want to close the distance between us and kiss her. But I didn't want to push her. If she wanted to talk, I'd talk. I got almost as much satisfaction from that as I did from kissing her. Almost.

"Thanks."

Yes, it was an achievement but I still hadn't made the leap I wanted to make. The one to the NHL. And I was starting to realize it might be out of my reach.

"But?" she prompted.

I shook my head, amazed she'd read me so easily.

"But I still haven't made it to the NHL. A lot of the guys I started out with have been playing up for years. My parents have always been supportive but they're starting to ask when I'm going to come home and get a real job."

Her nose wrinkled. "Ouch."

I huffed out a laugh. "Yeah. They've always been my biggest supporters but my dad's a pragmatist. If I haven't reached my goal in ten years, it's time for a new goal."

"Is twenty-eight old for a player?"

"Not really, no. A lot of guys play until they're in their late thirties but," I sighed, "I guess I'm a lot like my dad. I told myself I'd play until I'd made it to the NHL or I turned twenty-eight. At the time, twenty-eight seemed like a lifetime away. Now…"

I shook my head.

"Now you're twenty-eight and you still enjoy playing." She tilted her head, blonde hair spilling over her shoulder and making me want to run my fingers through it. "So why are you even thinking about giving it up? Goals change all the time. Do your parents expect you to come home?"

"Probably, yeah. We've always been close and that's kind of what I figured I'd do. I'm their only and I think they're counting on me to be around when they get older."

She nodded. "My parents are the same. They keep telling me how much I'd love living in Florida and that I should come to visit more often and, oh yeah, Millie across the street, her son just moved down from Milwaukee and he's wonderful and they want to introduce me to him."

A surge of jealousy ripped through me and I had a moment

to think "What the fuck?" before I got it under control. The feeling was still there but I reined in the urge to tell her to forget it.

This whole caveman act was not my deal but there was something about Aly that made me want to beat my chest and lock her in my cave.

"Do you *want* to move to Florida?"

She shrugged, her gaze sliding away. "I've thought about it. But…I'm settled here. I like my job. I like my house. We moved around a lot when I was a kid and I hated it. Every year or two, we'd end up in some new town where I didn't know anyone."

A pit opened in my stomach. There'd been seasons where I'd moved three or four times, sometimes across the country. Sounded like Aly would hate that.

"Guess you're used to it," she said. "Moving all the time?"

"Yeah. But I'm realizing there might be a good reason for me to stay in one place."

"And what would that be?"

Did I imagine the breathlessness in her voice? No, I didn't think so. Not combined with the look in her eyes.

Sitting here listening to her, I realized how much I'd miss her if I couldn't see her tomorrow. Or the next day. Or the day after that.

I also knew that if I blurted out exactly what I wanted to say, she would think I was crazy.

If there was one thing I'd learned about Aly, it was that she was nothing if not logical. And declaring my ever-lasting devotion after only three days wouldn't fit into her neat, logical life. And my life was anything but neat and logical.

So what the fuck should I say?

The truth, asshole. Anything else'll just get you in trouble.

I smiled, attempting to be both charming and disarming. Hopefully not failing at both.

"Well, you see, I met this woman…"

Her lips curved in a sweet smile, one I was fast becoming addicted to.

"And you're saying you'd stay for her? Even though you haven't known her that long?"

"Haven't you ever had that feeling that you know what you're doing is right? It's kind of like when you've got a good team. There's a feeling in the air in the locker room. An excitement you can almost touch."

Her smile dimmed a little. "And you'd stay just because you think she might be…important to you?"

I leaned forward, getting in her space now because I couldn't resist her anymore. "I'm saying I might be persuaded to give up everything for the right girl."

She opened her mouth to speak again but I'd waited too long to kiss her. I sealed my mouth over hers for a deep, intensely sensual taste of her.

Her hands had fallen to my shoulders as if to hold me off, but as soon as my tongue slid against hers, she gripped me and tugged me closer. I came willingly, breathing a sigh of relief that she'd initiated the kiss after I'd laid that bombshell on her.

And now that she had, all bets were off.

But tonight, I was taking my time. Last night had been frantic. Fantastic but over way too fucking fast. And she hadn't asked me to stay the night.

Tonight, I was hoping for an invitation into her bed.

But first, I was content to just kiss her. Because, holy fucking hell, I loved the way she kissed. Like she couldn't get enough of me.

I certainly couldn't get enough of her. And she definitely wasn't close enough. No way.

Reaching for her hips, I grabbed her and lifted her onto my lap, wrapping my arms around her and crushing her against me. She didn't seem to mind.

Her arms went around my shoulders, her hands sliding into my hair and fingers raking against my scalp.

Christ, that felt amazing. I really wanted to feel those nails elsewhere on my body. Like, lower. Along my thighs. On the inside of my thighs. On my cock.

Hell, I'd take her hands on my body anywhere I could get them.

I'd take her any way I could get her.

Chapter 13

Aly

My heart pounded against my ribs, lungs working overtime as my desire for Riley consumed me.

Yes, I'd felt out of control last night, but I was beginning to believe I'd never be in control when it came to Riley. Right now, that didn't bother me. Tomorrow morning, it was going to bother the hell out of me.

But it wasn't tomorrow yet.

It was tonight and tonight was going to be amazing.

Tilting my head to the side so he could deepen the kiss, I let myself sink into him, let him hold me tight against him like he couldn't bear to release me. Soaking in the heat of his body, I let myself disconnect from reality.

And Riley became my world. I could only see him, only smell him. Only taste him. Every muscle in my body relaxed and I gave myself over to him. I had no idea why or how. It just happened.

Apparently, Riley was so attuned to me, he noticed immediately, took the reins, and ran with it.

Dragging his mouth away from mine, he kissed his way down to my neck as his hands spread across my back and held me close to his chest.

He was so big, I almost felt small against him. But not lost. Riley held me too tightly for me to feel lost.

And his mouth… Oh my god, his tongue traced decadent patterns on my skin that made me shiver, my body moving against his until I'd begun to rub my mound against his erection, which I felt through his dress pants.

"Fuck, sweetheart. Keep that up. I'm loving that."

His voice fired my libido, my muscles tightening as his hands continued to pet me. Down my back then up again, several times, until my skin felt so sensitized, my clothing was a nuisance.

"I want your clothes off." I drew my hands down from his shoulders to his shirt, pushing buttons through their holes as fast as my hands would go. "You need to be naked."

I could feel his mouth curve in a smile against the sensitive skin where my neck met my shoulder.

"I agree. But you need to lose the clothes, too. You have the most amazingly soft skin I've ever felt. I want to rub my cock between your thighs then I'm going to flip you over and rub it between your ass cheeks. Do you know how soft you are there? Like silk, baby."

His hands landed on my ass and scooped me closer, making me shudder.

"And holy fuck, when I get my hands between your legs, it's like butter. So soft. I can't wait to put my mouth on you."

My breath caught in my throat as he spoke, my brain unable to process the heat coursing through my body.

My first instinct was to give him whatever he wanted. And since he wanted what I wanted, there was no decision to make.

I gave in.

Turning my face into his neck, I bit him, hard enough to make him flinch. And groan.

His hands clutched at my ass for a second before moving to my front, where he snapped the button on my black jeans and began to work them down my hips.

My hands had already begun to work at his shirt but our actions kept getting in the way of each other.

Frustration began to make my fingers more frantic until finally I moaned.

And he grabbed my hands, forcing me to look up at him. "Aly. Hon. Wait."

I raised my eyebrows, barely able to breathe. "You want to wait?"

His smile made my thighs clench. It was playful and wicked and sweet all at the same time.

"No, I really don't. I want you naked and riding me right now, but I'd also like to do that on a bed. Because first, I'm gonna lay you out naked and put my face between your legs and make you come."

My lips parted at the carnality in his tone and my lungs contracted. And, holy hell, I soaked my panties.

"That mouth of yours is dangerous."

That mouth curved into another one of his wicked grins.

"So I've been told. But usually only by people who want to punch it."

Scrambling to my feet, I held out my hand, which he grabbed as he stood.

"Well, I definitely don't want to punch it. I have much better uses for it."

"Lead the way, sweetheart. I'm all yours."

I continued to stare into his beautiful eyes for a few more seconds and the triumph I felt at his statement took the rest of my breath away.

With a grin of my own, I turned and pulled him along behind me. By the time we reached the stairs to the second floor, we were practically running.

And when he swung me into his arms and took the stairs two at a time, I very nearly lost my ability to function.

No man had ever made me feel like he couldn't wait to get me in a bed because he wanted to make *me* feel good.

Riley did.

"Which way?"

"Right then last door on the left."

"Damn, that's far away."

I laughed and he looked down, smiling like making me laugh was his main goal in life.

"Christ, you're gorgeous when you smile. You're fucking hot all the damn time but when you smile like that, I forget how to breathe."

"Riley, that's…"

I didn't know what to say to that but he'd reached the door to my room by then. In the next second, I was airborne for a split second before my ass hit the bed and I sprawled on top of my quilt.

A second later, Riley came down on top of me, covering me better than any quilt ever could. The heat of him seared through my clothing and the second his lips pressed against mine, all thoughts of taking this slow blew apart like fireworks exploding.

I had my hands on his shirt, ready to rip it open, when he rose to his knees over me, trapping me with his knees on either side of my thighs.

"I'll take mine off if you take yours off." He already had his hands on his belt buckle. "Don't wanna rip your clothes but I'm so hot for you, I might tear them off with my teeth."

The image that flashed through my head at what else he could do with his teeth made me gasp.

And he groaned. "God damn, hon. Look at me like that again and I'm not giving any guarantees."

I got to work.

"I'm going to need to get heavier clothes so I can wear less of them to the game."

His deep laughter did wild and wonderful things to my insides. "I'm all for less clothing. And skirts. I think you should wear skirts every damn day. They come off easy and your legs look fucking amazing in them."

I wanted to agree with him. I'd stripped off my top layers easily but my damn jeans were tight on my hips and a struggle to push down my legs. Especially with two-hundred-plus pounds of fucking hot man looming over me.

He'd stripped his pants and underwear down to his knees and his cock stood straight out from his body, ruddy and ready and tempting me to reach for it.

But I needed him to move if I was going to get my jeans off.

About to open my mouth and tell him to strip me, I let out a squeak when he backed off the bed and stood at the side, shoving his pants down then grabbing my jeans and yanking them off. It took him a few tugs but he finally got them down. I wanted to laugh because he had the same intense look on his face that I'd seen when he played. But I couldn't quite manage because I was way too excited.

And horny. Definitely horny.

When he put his hands on my knees and spread my legs then knelt between them, I was practically panting.

Even more so when he dragged his hands, palms down, up my thighs to rest right at the juncture of my hips. His thumbs brushed against my mound and I wanted to clench my thighs together but his knees held me open. Wet and aching, I held my hand out to him. But he just smiled and moved his thumbs closer to my clit.

My stomach contracted and I sucked in a sharp breath.

"Something hurt, sweetheart?" His rough chuckle made my muscles tighten even more. "Do you need me to do something?"

"Yes, I need you to stop teasing me."

His grin widened. "Aw, that's half the fun." His thumbs moved infinitesimally closer to my clit, which was throbbing and tingling and dying for him to touch me. "I don't want to rush things this time. Last time, you made me lose my control. And it usually takes a hell of a long time to get me to break. So, this time, I'm determined."

"Determined to do what?"

"Well, how about I start with 'lick you until you scream'?"

Before I'd finished drawing in much needed air, he'd slid his hands between my thighs to spread me even more and bent to put his mouth over my sex.

I arched as his tongue flicked over my clit just before he sucked the little nub between his lips. My eyes rolled back in my head before they closed completely and I sank my fingers into his hair so he wouldn't get away. At least not without a battle.

Because...*oh my god*, the man knew how to use his mouth. And not just to talk. His lips and tongue worked together to make my body do what he wanted. Which was to writhe in ecstasy, apparently.

Every flick of his tongue made my back arch off the bed. Every time he sucked on my clit, I pressed my mound even harder against his mouth.

I moved so much, he finally put his hands on my hips and held me down on the bed so he could make good on his promise to make me scream.

I resisted as long as I could. I wasn't a screamer. It just wasn't in my nature. But when he bared his teeth and nibbled at me, I couldn't help myself.

The sensation was too much for me to process and the sound that came out of my mouth was probably pretty close to a scream. My body shuddered, sensation zipping through me, and I almost ripped his hair out by the roots before I relaxed my fingers.

I tried to catch my breath but he wouldn't let me. As his lips moved up my body, pressing open-mouth kisses along my belly, one hand slipped between my legs to play with my labia, already slick and full.

As he moved up my body, stopping to suck on each of my nipples before moving to nibble my neck, I got a quick chance to catch my breath before his fingers slipped into my channel and began to fuck me.

My hands slipped from his hair and onto his shoulders, pulling him closer, that big body covering me like a heavy blanket, his heat searing my skin and driving my desire for him to a fever pitch.

But he still wasn't close enough. My hands slid lower as his fingers spread me wide and stroked high inside me. If I lifted my hips, I might be able to rub my mound against his erection. And if I got my hands on his ass, I could pull him in even closer.

With my few remaining brain cells, I slid my hands to his ass and pulled him closer. He barely budged but it was enough to feel his cock brush against the trimmed curls on my mound.

I felt his groan rumble through his body, making me shiver.

"You want me closer, sweetheart? If I get any closer, I'm gonna be nailing you to the bed in a second and I'm not done playing yet."

My fingers scraped over the sleek muscles of his ass and down to his thighs, my nails dragging along his skin. A shudder rippled through him and he bit me at the tender junction of my neck and shoulder.

"If you play any more," I gasped as he licked at his bite, "I'm going to come before you get inside."

"That's okay. I'll just make you come again." His fingers twisted inside me, making me arch as my hands clenched around his thighs. "And again. And again."

His fingers thrust in an ever-increasing rhythm that had my body moving along.

Kissing his way back to my mouth, he sealed our lips together and drew his hand from between my legs as he dropped over me.

He was so heavy, I almost couldn't breathe but I wrapped my arms around him so he couldn't get away. My legs followed, draping over his hips as I arched into him, trapping his cock between us.

That made him groan again and he moved just enough so his cock was between my thighs, the tip nudging at my sensitive labia.

He rubbed there for a few long seconds, teasing me, before he punched his hands into the mattress on either side of me and pushed up so he could stare down at me.

Hazel eyes blazing, he leaned down to rub his nose against mine in a tender motion that made my heart melt.

Oh, wow. So not fair.

It made me want…so much more.

"Condom?"

I blinked and amazingly my brain figured out what he'd said. "Top drawer, bedside table."

"Can you reach it?" His lips curved. "I don't want to move."

Neither did I but I did want him to make love to me. Right now.

So I stretched my arm out and caught the drawer with my fingertips, grabbing the box and digging inside while he dipped his head and tugged on my left earlobe with his teeth.

I nearly dropped the condom when he flexed his hips and rubbed his cock head against my clit, making me moan at the sharp burst of pleasure. His tongue drew patterns along my throat, making my heart skip beats like a scratched CD. And making me frantic to have him fill the aching void inside me.

"What's wrong, hon?" Riley whispered directly into my ear before rubbing his bristly cheek against my temple…and rubbing the head of his erection against my labia in a motion guaranteed to make me crazy. "Something you need? Ask me for anything."

"I want you."

He pulled back until I could see his lips curved in a grin I'd seen him give opposing players. Usually just before those players attempted to take his head off.

"Really? I don't know about that. I think you're gonna have to be a little more convincing."

Her gaze narrowed as my thighs clenched at the teasing tone of his voice. "And how exactly do you think I should do that?"

His turn to groan. "Damn, I love when you talk like that, all prim and proper like we're not lying here naked and I've got my cock between your legs."

Jesus, if he kept talking, I might actually come without penetration. My body tingled from head to toe.

Shoving the condom against his chest with one hand, I used the other to weave through his hair and tug, hard.

"Use the damn condom and fuck me, Riley."

His grin faded but the lust in his eyes tripled. "And then you talk like that and, holy shit, babe, I might just come now."

"Don't you dare."

"Then put it on me."

He rose back up on his knees and I realized the light in the hall was still lit and I could see every ripple of muscle in his abs as he breathed and the flex of his thighs as he moved his knees farther apart. Opening my legs even more.

Still holding the condom, I ripped it open with my teeth then reached for him, rolling it down his hard, thick shaft, barely able to breathe.

As soon as I was done, he dropped back over me, hands planted on either side of my shoulders. And still not where I needed him.

"Riley…"

"Guide me in. I fucking love having your hands on me."

Tilting my hips up, I reached for his cock with one hand and put my other hand on his jaw to guide him down to kiss me as he slid home.

My eyes closed as our lips meshed and I groaned at the thickness of him. He stretched me tight, filled me completely and was almost too much to bear.

But I knew from the night before just how much pleasure it would bring me when he started to move. The man had a gift.

Moving my free hand to his ass, I gripped him hard and pulled.

And felt his lips curve against me.

But he refused to move. Instead, he tilted his head to get a better angle and then slid his tongue into my mouth, doing exactly what I wanted him to be doing with his cock.

For at least a minute, he tormented me with his tongue, the rest of him perfectly still.

So I moved, arched my back to push him farther inside then sank down so he slipped out just the tiniest bit.

It was enough to give me some satisfaction but it was also enough to taunt Riley.

After a few moments, I heard Riley groan and his kiss became more frantic, his tongue sinking deeper and deeper until finally I felt him start to move.

Every time he pulled out, I followed him, tried to get him to come back. And every time, he pushed forward, I tried to take him deeper.

It almost seemed like we were working at odds but nothing could've been further from the truth.

Our bodies synced in seconds and then Riley loosened the chains.

Lowering himself, he wrapped one arm around my shoulders and the other behind the small of my back, lifting my hips into him so he rubbed against my clit every time he slammed into me.

I'd never been to bed with a guy as strong as Riley. Every

thrust forced him deeper until I thought he couldn't go any further. And still I wanted more.

But he was so much bigger than me, he practically enveloped me. I didn't mind but he did, apparently.

Without warning, he rolled until I was on top. But he kept me wrapped so tightly against him, I could barely move. At least now I could breathe. Until he lifted his head and started to kiss me again.

I wanted to move with him, but his hand on my ass kept me where he wanted me. Not that it was a bad place to be.

It was an awesome place to be, actually.

With Riley's mouth on mine and his cock moving inside me and his hands spread on my back and my ass, I felt taken.

I loved it.

And when I felt all that tension inside me reach its breaking point, I moaned into his mouth as I came, feeling him freeze as I clenched around him before he pumped his own release into me with a groan.

Chapter 14

Riley

An annoying beep woke me out of a deep sleep.

I frowned, ready to chew Justin's ass for not turning off his alarm, especially since this was our morning off.

Then I realized this wasn't my bed. And Justin was nowhere to be found.

Beside me, Aly was a sleek mass of warm, naked flesh and silky hair. I'd curled around her so her back was nestled against my chest and her ass snuggled against my groin. Of course, I had stiff morning wood pressed right between her cheeks and damn, if that didn't feel great.

Her head lay on my bicep and I was pretty sure my arm was asleep and would hurt like a bitch when she moved, but I could lie here all fucking day and never get up, if I got to keep her naked and warm beside me.

Turning my head, I rubbed my chin against her hair and curled my arm even more tightly around her waist.

I breathed in her scent, something warm and floral and sexy as hell.

Fuck.

She was going to have to get up soon, but I wondered if she'd have enough time for a quickie before she needed to get ready for work.

I was bending forward to nuzzle my nose into her neck before I bit her and slid my hand from her stomach to her mound when she sighed and shot straight up in bed.

"Oh *shit.*"

Flopping onto my back, I laughed so hard my stomach hurt but it was worth it when she turned to glare at me.

Jesus, she was gorgeous. Her hair was all messy and it looked good on her, falling over those beautiful tits and making me want to get my mouth on them again.

Scrambling onto her knees, she put her hands on her naked hips and glared even harder. Which just made my cock stiffer. "How long have you been awake?"

"Long enough to want to get back inside you before you have to go to work."

She blinked at me a few times, her lips parted like she was going to say something, but she never did. Finally, she shook her head and huffed out a laugh.

"I really wish I had time for that. But I have to be there in an hour and I need a shower."

Crunching up, I grabbed her around the waist before she could move away, loving the little squeak she made when I lifted her into the air so I could move her over me. Her knees landed on either side of my hips and her hands slapped down on my shoulders.

"I could make that shower worth your while."

Laughing, she bent to kiss me, her hair hanging down around my face, a silky curtain I wanted to feel on my chest, my stomach. My thighs.

I wanted her to bend down and kiss me, but she stayed where she was, staring in my eyes. "And then I would definitely be late for work. Don't you have practice this morning?"

"Not until eleven because of the back-to-back-to-back games."

Shaking her head, her lips were curved in a smile I wanted to taste. "Well, *I* can't be late. We have a staff meeting every Monday at ten."

"Then take the day off. I'll take you to breakfast and we can buy lunch and we can eat it in bed where we'll spend the rest of the day until I have to go to practice."

"Oh, so you go to practice but I can't go to work?" She lifted her eyebrows at me and my cock jerked in response.

She must have felt it move against her leg because she glanced down before looking back into my eyes. But she was still grinning.

"Okay, Plan B. Quickie now then you go to work and I go to practice. Then we'll meet up for dinner and we can get to bed a little earlier so we don't have this same problem tomorrow morning."

She sucked in her bottom lip and bit on it for a few seconds before she answered. "So you want to be here again tomorrow morning?"

"Of course." I shrugged like it was no big deal, but I could see by her expression that she was going to be a harder nut to crack than a pro with twenty years under my belt. "But we've got a road trip to Springfield Wednesday and we've got practice daily until then so maybe I should get some sleep, at least a few nights."

She smiled, but I could tell she still was trying to figure out what to do with me.

Besides the obvious.

And since it went against every fiber of my being to keep my mouth shut, I added, "But I'm willing to give up my beauty rest if you are. Not that you need much because, sweetheart, you're the most beautiful girl I've ever seen at seven in the morning."

The flush on her cheeks deepened but I knew it wasn't embarrassment. It was heat.

Just when I thought she might take me up on my offer, her lips twisted and she shook her head, silky strands catching in my scruff until I wove my fingers through her hair and pulled it back behind her neck. I fucking loved the feel of it in my hands.

She bent and pressed her lips against mine, kissing me so sweetly, I panicked for a second. Fuck, what'd I say? Was she going to shove me out the door and I'd never see her again? I already knew I wouldn't let that happen. I knew this girl was something special and I wasn't about to let her go.

I was all ready to open my mouth and say whatever I could to get her to agree to see me again tonight when she said, "Can we take a rain check until tonight? I really need to get in the shower, and if I don't have at least two cups of coffee before work, I will rip someone's head off."

Her perfectly deadpan delivery amused the hell out of me, and I laughed before I lifted her off my body and to the side of the bed, where she put her feet on the floor.

But before she could get away, I shot up to my knees, grabbed her head in my hands, and kissed her hard, pressing her lips open and sliding my tongue into her mouth to tangle with hers. She responded immediately, her hands gripping my hips... but not pulling me closer. Which was where my cock wanted to be.

Down, boy.

Then again, I loved kissing her so I could deal. I'd see her again tonight and we'd figure out the rest of their lives when I got back from my road trip. Hopefully while we were naked in bed.

After several long seconds, she sighed and pulled away. I let her go, but not without one last, hard kiss. And a sweep of my hand down her sleek ass.

The look she gave me made me want to put both hands on her.

"You're dangerous." She stuck on finger in my chest when I made a move forward. "And I need to get in the shower."

"Want some company?"

She sighed and shook her head, but her expression was amused. "Like I said…you're dangerous. And I have to leave in less than an hour."

"Then I guess the least I can do is make you coffee."

Teeth in her lips again. Why the hell did I find that so sexy?

"Sure. But I really do have to go to work."

I held my hand up and tried to look like the Boy Scout I'd never had time to be. "Promise I won't distract you again."

Now her brows rose and she shook her head as she turned to the bathroom. "Like you can help it."

I barely heard her as she grabbed a robe from the hook on the back of her door then opened it as quietly as she could. But I couldn't help smiling as she turned to look at me just before disappearing down the hall and shaking her head, a grin flirting with her mouth.

Damn, I wanted this. Every morning. Wanted to wake up next to her and have her give me that smile before she left for work.

Wanted to crawl into bed next to her after a great game, after a shitty game… Hell, after any game. Wanted to come home to her after a two-week road trip and kiss the hell out of her before I tossed her into bed, tore off her clothes, and got inside her.

Tomorrow, the next day, most of the mornings after that.

But she wouldn't want to hear that. Not my Little Miss Cautious.

So how the hell was I supposed to let her know I was serious about her when I'd be gone for the next two weeks?

Usually I was good at talking. I could convince a rational man to drop his gloves by the end of the first period simply by talking shit. Hell, I was an expert at it. But I'd fucked up one relationship before. I didn't want to fuck this up.

But first…I'd promised her coffee.

Grabbing my clothes, I pulled them on then headed for the stairs, passing the bathroom, where I could hear the water running. Damn, I wanted to push the door open and join her but that wouldn't get her to trust me.

In the kitchen, I found the coffeemaker—a huge, twelve-pot monstrosity—on the counter, located the filters in the cabinet above it and the coffee in the freezer.

I'd finished my first cup by the time I heard the click of heels on the stairs.

I automatically looked toward the sound—and nearly swallowed my tongue.

Holy fuck, I was in so much goddamn trouble.

Her skirt was black and thin and reached her knees, her shirt was gray and tight and unbuttoned just enough that I could imagine I saw cleavage and her heels were black and red.

She'd pulled her hair into some twist on the back of her head that made my fingers itch to release it and she was wearing pearls. A double string that lay over her breasts and made me imagine how she'd look wearing only those damn pearls.

Jesus. I'd finally managed to will my erection away but now I was pretty sure I'd spend the rest of the day thinking about those pearls and getting a hard-on.

"You know, I never understood the whole librarian fixation." I grinned as she gave me a bemused look and headed for the coffee. "I totally get it now."

She rolled her eyes at me but I caught her smiling before she put the mug to her mouth.

And groaned.

"Oh. My. God. Where did you learn to make coffee this good?" Her eyes widened as she took another sip. "My sister's always tastes like sludge and is so damn strong, I feel like I'm on speed all day. Mine never tastes this good. I think I'm going to keep you locked in my house as my personal coffee slave."

"Not your sex slave, huh? Well, damn, I guess I'll have to up my game in bed."

Her eyebrows rose. "What time is practice?"

"Eleven. We go until one then refuel and hit the gym for a few hours. Refuel again." A thought occurred to me. "Shit. Forgot I've got a thing this afternoon. An after-school program. Don't know how long that'll go but I should be done by six. Let's get some dinner after that. Or we could cook. Which I can do, by the way. If you don't mind someone in your kitchen. I'd have you over to the apartment but my roommate's kind of a slob so…"

She didn't say anything right away, just watched me with those steady blue eyes. I couldn't tell what she was thinking and I was about to open my mouth and keep going when she nodded.

"Sure, we can cook here, if you don't mind having my sister around."

I shrugged. "Course not. Her house, too, right?"

"Should I—"

"I'll pick up everything after the event and be here around seven. That work for you?"

"That's fine."

"Anything you don't like?"

Her lips quirked. "I'm assuming you mean food?"

"I did but if you wanna talk about something else, I'm all ears."

Her head tilted to the side, as if she were thinking about it, but then she shook her head. "I really do need to get to work. And you're dangerous to my concentration."

I didn't bother to hide my smile and she shook her head and walked to the sink to dump her mug.

Standing, I did the same then wrapped an arm around her waist to bring her in against me for a quick kiss.

"I'll see you tonight, hon."

Then I walked out before she changed her mind.

Chapter 15

Riley

"Dude, you look like you had a good night's sleep, which is weird because I could swear you didn't make it home last night." Justin's shit-eating grin spread. "Whose couch did you sleep on? Must've been comfortable."

I had been the last one into the locker room by only a minute. But it was late enough for Justin to jump on my ass about it.

In response, I gave him the finger, which made Justin laugh maniacally.

"And where did you sleep last night, jackass?" Jake smacked Justin on the back of the head as I started to strip. "All by yourself in your own bed. I think maybe you are a little jealous."

Stripping as fast as I could, I pulled on my base layers then began strapping on my pads. For the first time in god knew how long, I had no desire to talk shit with my teammates. Especially not about Aly.

"And when was the last time a girl let you in her bed? I think it was never, yes?"

Lad directed the dig at Jake. The two defensemen were tight as brothers and trash-talked each other like mortal enemies. It worked for them.

They were the best defensive line in the league and they came to play every day. And if they occasionally acted like douchebag teenagers… Well, nobody was perfect.

"Says the man who still does not know what a rim shot is."

"Rim *job*," shouted CJ as the rest of the team either groaned or laughed hysterically. "It's rim *job*."

Lad and Jake exchanged a look, said a few words in Russian then Jake focused his famed Russian glare at CJ. "This from the child who still hordes his cherries."

Now the entire team busted into laughter and CJ turned the same color as the fruit Jake had just mentioned.

I shook my head, my brain working on a smart-ass response, but when CJ sat next to me on the bench, my mouth snapped shut.

CJ's downbent head and bright red neck brought out my protective instincts. Same as if we'd been on the ice and someone went after the kid, I jumped to CJ's defense.

"Considering you two need each other to get laid, I figure you have a few cherries you haven't popped yet."

With an almost imperceptible glance at CJ, Lad took the hint. "I have no cherries. Jake, however, has entire bush."

Holding his gut, he was laughing so hard, Derek turned to Jake. "Son, if you have a bush instead of a tree, maybe that's the problem you been having hooking up."

"Hey, something up?" I asked CJ as he pulled his sweater over his head, just as Coach walked in the room.

Before CJ could answer, Coach said, "Listen up," and launched into his game plan for the week. Twenty minutes later, right before the team was ready to hit the ice, Coach looked at me and inclined his chin.

"Hatch. Young. Stick here. Everyone else, on the ice."

Not expecting anything other than Coach Scott wanting us to work together on technique or drills, I nearly fell off the bench when Coach started to talk.

"The big club had a couple of injuries last night and you two are headed to the Colonials. They get back from a road trip today and Coach Angstadt wants you two at the practice barn for morning skate tomorrow. Today, you skate with us but they want you down to talk to the assistant coach tonight."

Coach turned to grab a piece of paper from his desk, detailing where we needed to be and when and the hotel we'd be staying at. CJ and I would be bunking together for the duration, could be an extended stay, but we would probably see ice time.

Beside me, CJ vibrated like a fucking puppy, running at the mouth with questions Coach answered with a grin. I just sat there.

Holy shit. Finally. Fucking finally.

And on the heels of that...

I can't fucking wait to tell Aly.

Yeah, I couldn't wait to tell my parents. But Aly was different. I wanted to share everything with her. Wanted her to be happy for me. Wanted her to come to the game and be waiting for me afterward.

Philly wasn't that far away. If I stayed with the Colonials for any length of time, Aly and I would make it work—

"Riley, you have any questions?"

Coach's question knocked me out of my thoughts and I smiled, shaking my head. "Nah. I think I'm good."

"All right then. Get out on the ice. You can text your parents after practice."

CJ bounced up, grinning from ear to ear, and headed out. I got up slower, watching the kid disappear down the hall to the ice.

I took a few seconds to make sure my laces were tight and found Coach watching me, arms crossed over his chest.

"Sure you don't have any questions?"

"Honestly," I shook my head, "I've got a shit-ton of them but I don't think you can answer any of them."

Coach grinned and slapped me on the shoulder. "Keep your head in the game. Just like you've been doing for the past eight years. You made it this far. Just keep pushing. You've got the skills, Riley. You've proved it. I have no doubt you can make this happen. Don't let anything get in your way."

I had no intention of letting anything get in my way. But I had no intention of giving anything up either.

Aly

I had gone to work with a smile on my face that faded about fifteen minutes after I walked in the door.

The billing system had gone down and the techs weren't sure why. Which meant my department was hamstrung. Which meant the people who called in to get their bills straightened out had something else to complain about.

And they did. All morning.

It left me very little time to daydream about Riley and last night, but when I did, holy crap, I couldn't stop.

So when his number popped up on my phone after lunch, I shut myself in my office and sank into my chair.

"Hey," I said. "I was hoping you'd call."

"And I've been dying to talk to you. I got called up. I'll probably be on the ice tomorrow night with the Colonials in Philly."

It took me a second to process what he'd said then I started to smile. "Riley! That's amazing! Oh my god, that's so wonderful. We can celebrate tonight at dinner."

"Yeah, about dinner. I need to cancel. I hate to do it but CJ and I have to be in Philly tonight. They're putting us up in a hotel for the night so we're ready for morning skate tomorrow. I'm really sorry—"

"Are you kidding? Don't you dare apologize for getting what you've been working for for so long. I'm so happy for you."

"Happy enough to want to drive to Philly tomorrow night? Game starts at seven and I know it's short notice but I can get you a ticket."

He wanted me at the game? My heart began to pound and I wanted to say yes.

But I also had to be practical. I worked until five-thirty and then had an evaluation with my boss that I couldn't miss. Even if I didn't go home to change and left straight from the office, I wouldn't be on the road until six-thirty and it'd take me at least two hours to navigate the Schuylkill Expressway at that time of night.

"Aly?"

But he wanted me there. Just the thought made my heart pound against my ribs and my thighs clench like he'd told me he wanted to strip me naked and do me against a wall.

It made no sense whatsoever because we'd met four days ago. *Four days.* People didn't become this invested in another person's life that fast.

And if they did, it wouldn't last.

"I would really love to go," I said. "I just…I'm afraid I wouldn't make it in time."

He paused and my throat dried. Anxiety made my stomach ache.

But realistically, I'd probably get stuck in traffic and would probably miss the entire game.

And maybe he was only asking to be nice. Maybe he felt obligated to ask me because we'd slept together.

Maybe—

"Yeah, okay, no problem. Seriously, I get it. I'll give you a call after the game, okay?"

And maybe he really hadn't wanted me there to begin with. "Of course."

"Great. Okay, I really gotta get moving. CJ and I need to be on the road in a few. We have to check in with the assistant coach…"

"Oh, that's—"

"…before six. And yeah, traffic's gonna be a bitch."

Feeling sick to my stomach and fighting the urge to hyperventilate, I sucked in a deep breath. "Riley…you're going to be amazing tomorrow."

"Thanks, hon." He huffed out a little laugh. "I hope like hell you're right. You can probably catch the game on TV. Let me know how I look."

A lump formed in my throat.

"Of course. Riley…I'm really happy for you."

"Thanks. Appreciate it. Look, I hate to cut this short—"

"No, I totally understand. You have to go. Just…have a great game. I have no doubt you'll be wonderful."

"Let's hope. I'll talk to you tomorrow night."

"That's great. Good luck, Riley."

"Thanks, hon."

He didn't say good-bye, just disconnected.

And by the time I put my phone down on my desk, I had to suck in air because it was getting tougher and tougher to breathe.

My eyes burned and I blinked fast, willing back the tears that had popped up for no reason.

It wasn't like I'd never see him again. And if I didn't, well…

It would suck. Go ahead, at least you can admit it to yourself.

My desk phone rang, startling me so badly, I flinched and gasped, my hand flattening over my heart.

After another three rings, I grabbed it and tried to go back to work.

Knowing I'd made the totally wrong decision and still unable to do anything to change it.

———

Riley

CJ ran at the mouth the entire drive to Philly.

I was driving, partly because I was worried the kid would be overly excited and run us into a wall. And partly because it would keep my mind off my conversation with Aly.

While CJ catalogued every player on the Colonials—their strengths, their weaknesses, their freaking PIMs, for chrissakes—I answered when I needed to and kept my eyes on the road because, holy fuck, was there a shit-ton of traffic.

Logically, I knew Aly had been right. She never would've made the game for puck drop.

So why the hell are you so fucking frustrated?

Because I'd wanted her there. I wanted to share this with her, wanted her to be there after the game to celebrate. Hell, I didn't care if I got five minutes of ice time or twenty.

I'd finally fucking made it.

And I found the girl I wanted to share this milestone with.

But the girl had turned me down.

Yeah, I knew it wasn't that simple. She had a job, a demanding job. She couldn't just take off at a moment's notice and follow me wherever.

Except…

"Oh, and hey, I got a heads-up from Ian MacDonald that

Duchene isn't really hurt. Mac says Duchene and the coach got into it over something and that the team wants to trade him. I heard some of the stories about Duchene. Do you think it's true?"

Hell, everyone had heard the stories about the Colonials' third-line right winger. He partied hard, played a physical game, and led the team in penalty minutes. A loose cannon who'd been a scoring machine. But he was thirty-five now and didn't score as much as he used to.

I had heard the talk that the team had considered not picking up his contract last year and he'd been a late addition on a one-year contract.

Sucked for Duchene, but it opened up a spot if they actually decided to get rid of the guy. Still, I knew I was a long shot for the position. More likely the club would go with CJ. He'd been a first-round draft pick and the kid improved every day. And even though I had better numbers this season, the Philly coach would probably go with the rookie if he kept one of them up.

And for a split second, I thought that would be okay.

Are you fucking crazy?

I must be. Because I was seriously thinking that if I got sent back to Reading, I'd be closer to Aly.

How fucked was that? I should be doing everything I could to grab a spot with the Colonials, not hope to be sent back to the Redtails.

"Riley?"

"Yeah, sorry. Got a lot on my mind. Do I think it's true? Probably. Does it mean they'll trade him? Hell if I know. They've got some money invested in him so they'll wanna make that back, and with his record, I don't know that anyone'll want to take a chance on him."

Same could've been said about me last year. But Coach Scott had taken a chance on me and I thought I'd proven myself this year.

"So how long do you think we'll be up? I heard Vanderske's injury won't have him out long…and I'm bugging the shit out of you, aren't I?"

I glanced over to see CJ shaking his head and grimacing.

"Sorry, man. I don't know how to shut up sometimes. I'm—"

"CJ, you're not bugging me. Everything's good. Just got stuff on my mind."

"Like the girl you're seeing?"

I shot the kid another glance and now the little shit wore a smart-ass grin. "Why the fuck do you think that?"

"Everybody knows you didn't go home last night and Justin said you can't stop talking about her and—"

"All right, all right. Forget I asked. And…" he sighed. "Yeah. She's part of it. But I'm not sure she's as…invested as I am."

"What do you mean?"

Damn, was I really going to do this? Spill my guts to this kid?

Well, I had no one else to talk to for the next two hours, did I?

"I mean I don't think she likes me as much as I like her."

CJ shrugged. "Did you ask her if she likes you?"

I laughed. The kid really was young.

"I'm pretty sure she likes me. I'm just not sure she likes me enough to keep me."

"Why? What'd you do?"

"Good question."

"Did you piss her off?"

"Not exactly. I asked her to come to the game tonight. She said she had to work."

"Well, she's got a job, right? My parents can't get to the game tonight either." CJ shrugged. "It sucks but I know they'll be watching. There'll be another game. I know I just need to focus tonight. Probably better if they're not here."

I huffed out a laugh then shook my head. "Damn, kid. Maybe you're smarter than you look."

"Hey, what do you mean maybe? I'm way smarter than I look."

And maybe I needed to take a page out of the kid's book and just focus on tomorrow.

And when I'd made my mark in Philly, I'd be back to make my mark on Aly.

Chapter 16

Aly

I had too much work to do Tuesday to let myself be distracted.

That didn't mean Riley didn't creep into my thoughts at all.

He did. More than I would've liked. Or would admit to. Especially to my sister.

"He's gone already." Vivi snorted at the dinner table Monday night. "That didn't take long."

Taking a bite of the corn bread Vivi had made to go with her homemade chili gave me a few seconds to formulate a response. The sharp edge in Vivi's voice made me want to jump to Riley's defense. Which was ridiculous. He didn't need to be defended.

"I'm really happy for him." I nodded, deciding to ignore Vivi's snark. "It's what he's been working toward for so many years. I hope they keep him. I can't wait to watch the game tomorrow night. It'll be amazing to see him on TV. I really hope he gets to play."

Vivi gave me a sidelong glance. "Huh. Guess he wasn't that

good in bed. You don't sound all that broken up over him leaving."

I shrugged and spooned up chili, trying for nonchalant and probably ending up somewhere around pained wince. "We've known each other for four days. No one falls in love in four days."

Vivi went quiet and we ate in silence for at least a minute. I thought my sister would let it go. I should've known better.

"No, *you* don't. You're too smart for that."

I put my spoon down. "What does that mean?"

Vivi grimaced. "Sorry. I didn't mean that to sound…so bitchy. It's just…I did. Fall in love in four days. Actually, it only took me one. And we both know how much disaster *that* ended in."

Yeah, that had been a disaster. "But none of that was your fault, Viv. He was the asshole. Riley's not an asshole."

Vivi shrugged, her mouth twisting. "Maybe not. But athletes have this special power. They blind you to everything except what they want you to see. They draw you in and make you think you're the most important thing in their world, when, really, it's just all about how important they are to you. They see you as a reflection of themselves. And when they don't see themselves being reflected back enough, they're not interested anymore."

I heard so much bitterness in my sister's voice, I had to blink away the tears that popped into my eyes.

"Viv…"

Damn, I didn't know what to say to that, wasn't sure I could say anything to make her feel better.

If I ever saw Jamie Dunbar again, he better have his running shoes on because I would beat him to a pulp for making my sister hurt like this.

But of course that would never happen because the guy was now the star running back of the Dallas NFL franchise, who would probably sue me to hell and back if I dared lay a finger on the man. Which didn't mean I hadn't considered multiple ways to exact revenge.

Vivi rolled her eyes and shrugged, as if it didn't matter anymore.

"At least the guy didn't publicly humiliate you in front of his team when he dumped you. He gets points for that."

No, Riley hadn't dumped me at the first sign of stardom.

"He wanted me to be there."

Vivi frowned. "What?"

"He offered to get me tickets for the game. But Wednesday's my busy day. Meetings all day and I've got an evaluation after work and…"

"And?" Vivi looked at me with raised eyebrows.

"And I can't imagine that he'd want some girl he just met there for the biggest night of his life."

Vivi sat and blinked at me for several long seconds. "He actually said he wanted you there?"

I nodded. "I think he was disappointed when I said I couldn't go."

"Do you *want* to go?"

Yes. "I'm not sure."

Vivi's eyebrows rose again. "What was your first response?"

I bit my tongue because I'd wanted to say yes. Then I shook my head and dropped my spoon back into my bowl. "Of course I want to be at the game. But I have a job that I need. I can't just drop everything and drive to Philly because some hot guy wants me to go to his game."

Vivi's lips curved in a surprisingly bittersweet smile. "You've always been so much more grown-up than everyone else. Even our parents. When Mom and Dad used to have their shouting matches and they'd throw things at each other and slam doors, you'd be the one to go talk to them and get them to calm down. Some days, I still think you're the only adult in the family."

My back stiffened. "That's not a bad thing."

Shaking her head, Vivi sighed. "No, it's not. I didn't mean to sound like it was. I'm just saying…you don't always have to be the grown-up. You don't always have to be rational and sane and fair. Sometimes you need to cut loose."

"I did." *And see where it's gotten you.* "I slept with him. I didn't even wait for the third date. Or until I had a background check done." At my sister's startled face, I rolled my eyes. "I'm kidding. Jeez, do you really think I'm that anal?"

Vivi shrugged. "Sometimes, yeah, because you are. And that's not always bad. You and I wouldn't be able to live here if you weren't because you're the one that makes sure we have enough money to pay the bills."

"And that makes me the most boring person on earth."

"Oh please." It was Vivi's turn to roll her eyes. "Obviously you're not or Riley wouldn't want you at his game. And…I think you should go."

"No." I shook my head. "I already told him I couldn't."

Besides, I'd checked for tickets. The game was sold out and resales were way beyond my means.

"Anyway, it's better this way. He needs to concentrate and I don't want to be a distraction. And I don't even know if I could see him after the game. He'll probably want to go out with the team and I don't want to get in the way of that."

Vivi stared at me with a bemused expression. "You have it all figured out, don't you?"

"I have to. I'm an adult."

"And what if you're wrong?"

"What do you mean?"

Vivi leaned forward, her expression intent. "I mean…what if he's the one?"

My breath caught in my throat and I had to swallow before I could speak. "Then I guess if it doesn't work out, I'll have to be rational and move on."

"Or maybe it's your time to do something just for you."

"No—"

"Aly. Go to the game."

Smiling, I shook my head. "I wish it was that simple."

"Are you sure it's not?"

Yeah, I was. Because nothing in life was.

Riley

"Good practice, boys. Hit the showers, get some food then rest up for the game. New York's a tough defensive team, but I've got confidence in our offense. Doesn't mean I don't want our defense to slack. I'm expecting you all to play hard and smart. Special teams are going to be crucial tonight and we're down two of our regular penalty killers so everyone's expected to pick up the slack. See you tonight."

As Coach Angstadt left the room, the team stood and most began to file out. A few hung back and two headed toward me.

"Hey, man. Haven't seen you for…what? Like a year?" Holding out his hand to me, center Colin Williams grinned. "It's great to see you. Congrats on the call-up."

I smiled back as we shook. The blond Canadian stood an inch or so shorter but was built like a bulldog. Powerful body and a face that looked like it'd taken a few too many beatings, the scar from a horrific skate-to-the-face injury from years ago fading but still visible.

"Been at least a year," I said. "Heard the Crush traded you after I left. Glad to know it's working out."

"Aw, yeah, it's been great. Suki loves the area and at least we're on the same coast as her parents now. With the new baby, that's been a real help."

"I heard. That's great, man. Congrats."

Colin's grin grew even wider. "Thanks. You wanna see her picture?"

The man beside Colin groaned, but the smile on his face was amused. "At least tell me you got new ones. The last ones I saw were at least two days old."

Colin flipped Travis Walker the finger as he dug out his phone, which made Travis bray like a donkey.

I took Travis's hand when he stuck it out.

"Welcome up, bud." Travis shook my hand with a punishing grip but I had been ready for it. "Good to see you again."

"Good to see you, too." The defenseman and I had been teammates years ago in Grand Rapids, where we'd played in the ECHL right after I had graduated from college. Travis had been a hotshot with a huge talent until he'd taken a devastating hit to the boards that'd nearly ended his career. But the guy had bounced back to become one of the league's steadiest defensemen.

For a few weeks three seasons ago, the three of us had played for the same AHL team before being traded to different franchises.

We caught up for a few minutes while Colin swiped through his phone for pictures of his adorable baby girl. I smiled at pictures of the hulking Colin holding a tiny human with his arm around his college sweetheart-now-wife.

I had met Suki several times when we'd been on the same team and I'd liked her. She had that no-nonsense Canadian humor I'd grown accustomed to playing hockey. And she could swear like a man. Better than her husband, actually.

It wasn't until a few minutes later that I saw Travis glance over his shoulder and grimace.

"Hey, man. Looks like your kid's gonna need a watchdog. He's...what? Twenty-one, right? He does not want to get messed up with the Strakas. Looks a little green to be messing in their shit."

Looking over my shoulder, I saw CJ nodding at something Hubert Straka had said. CJ didn't look like he was in trouble but he didn't exactly look comfortable either.

Hubert and Christian Straka, Russian machines straight out of central casting, were tall, blond, and almost identical, from their intimidating faces to their wicked right-hand slapshots. They were great defensive wingers and racked up serious points every season, but they had a reputation for partying hard and had occasionally dragged some of the younger players down with them.

I stuck my fingers in my mouth and whistled, catching CJ's and the Strakas' attention. "Kid, let's haul."

Relief crossed CJ's face but he covered it by turning his head to check his locker then grabbing his bag and nodding at the brothers before hustling over to my side.

After I introduced CJ to Travis and Colin, we all walked out together. While Colin went home, Travis offered to take me and CJ to lunch before we went back to the hotel before the game.

The hostess at the restaurant knew Travis by name, and the smile they exchanged made it clear she knew a lot more than that.

I shook my head. Some things never changed. Travis and I had slept our way through half the population of women under thirty in Rapid City during our time there.

When we were seated and had ordered, Travis motioned with his head toward the hostess.

"She's got a sister." Travis smiled at me. "Dude, we could relive Wilkes-Barre."

CJ's eyes rounded and he glanced between Travis and I but kept his mouth shut, shoveling bread like they wouldn't bring more.

With a soft huff, I shook my head. "Nah, man. I'm turning over a new leaf."

Travis looked stunned before he started to smile.

"Yeah, right," Travis scoffed. "You're too young to be tied down. And when you lock down your slot on the team, you're gonna want your freedom. Dude, women will be crawling all over you. And I'm not just talking small-town sweethearts. I'm talking Victoria's Secret models and fucking porn stars. You will think you've died and gone to heaven. The sheer amount of ass and the quality available for the taking will be overwhelming at first but you'll learn to weed out the ones who want to land a husband fast."

Actually, that sounded…like hell.

I shook my head. "Maybe I'm actually looking for a wife."

Travis blinked, like his brain was trying to process input and couldn't. I started to laugh, which actually made CJ pause with a piece of bread halfway to his mouth.

"Just keep eating, kid." I grinned at CJ. "You're gonna need the calories for tonight. And Travis, more power to you but if I stay, I think you're gonna be chasing women without me."

With a bemused smile, Travis started on the second basket of bread the server had brought. Apparently, Travis was a regular here. "Well, damn, I can't wait to meet the woman who brought you to heel. Is she coming to the game tonight?"

I shook my head, the subject still tender. And one he'd have to shelve until later. "No, she has to work. Besides, I need all my concentration focused on the game tonight."

"You're absolutely right. Try not to overthink it. This is your time. You're gonna nail it."

Travis looked so damn confident, I had to smile even as I shook my head. "Let's hope I'm not the one getting nailed to the boards."

"Nah, that's your specialty, man. You're a grinder. Go out there and fucking grind them into submission. And if that doesn't work, you do some of your best work with your mouth. Mind-fuck 'em. New York won't know what hit them. And if you really want the girl, same thing applies. Talk until she agrees just to shut you up." Travis shrugged. "Or punches you in the mouth. With you, it can go either way."

Chapter 17

Aly

I glanced at the clock, my heart pounding a mile a minute.

Six-fifty. If I left now, I'd still get to see the start of the game.

But as my boss droned on about performance issues to one of the men in my office, I knew I wasn't going to make it home for puck drop.

Yes, I was recording the game and the pre-game show but I'd wanted to be home to see if Riley made the lineup.

I hadn't heard from him overnight but he had texted me earlier today. He must have sent it before he left for the arena this afternoon.

Getting ready for the game. Hoping like hell I don't forget anything. Hope you get to watch the game. Let me know. Talk to you soon.

Since then…nothing.

So why do you feel slighted?

Because I was a bitch who couldn't be bothered to drive two hours to his first NHL game.

Grr.

Hell, even I knew that wasn't fair. This, my job, was important to me and so were the people I worked with. Which was why
I was in this evaluation. Because my job mattered.

But when my boss finally wrapped up the meeting after we'd
managed to resolve at least a few of my coworker's concerns, I
excused myself and took off as fast as my heels would let me.

I was tempted to take off my pumps and run but figured
that'd be a little too out of character.

Grabbing my stuff from my office, I swapped out my pumps
for sneakers and now I took off at a restrained run. Okay, more
like a hurried shuffle because my damn skirt was so tight, but I
cleared the building in two minutes and was home in ten.

"Vivi! Do you have—"

"Don't worry." My sister called back from the TV room.
"The game's on. You didn't miss anything."

"Is he on the bench?"

Breathless from my sprint from the car to the house, I fell
onto the couch next to Vivi and started to scan the players on the
ice. The game was in motion so I couldn't tell who any of the
players were. I could barely see their numbers much less their
names on their jerseys.

"Did you watch the pre-game show? Did they mention him?
Did they—"

"I just got home, too. So, no, I didn't see any of it. And I
already ordered pizza so we don't have to worry about dinner."

Without taking my eyes off the TV, I hugged Vivi. "Keep
your eyes peeled. I know he's going to play tonight. I just
know it."

"You know if he plays well, he might not come back, right?"

"I know that."

"And you're okay with that?"

No, I wasn't. I just didn't know how to fix it. Couldn't fix it.
"Maybe I'd be willing to find a way to make it work."

Vivi didn't say anything right away and I snuck a glance away from the TV.

"What?"

My sister smiled. "It's kind of nice to see you want something enough to mess with your schedule."

I held Vivi's gaze. "Am I really that rigid?"

Vivi grimaced. Then she nodded. "Yeah. Sometimes. You know I love you, sis, but sometimes I think you're never going to bust out of your shell and have a real life. And you're gonna miss so much."

"And now Hatch takes the puck for the Colonials. The twenty-eight-year-old is making his NHL debut tonight…"

The rest was lost as Vivi and I squealed and locked hands, bouncing up and down on the couch.

Tears actually popped into my eyes as I watched Riley race down the ice with the puck before passing to another player and getting checked into the boards.

For the next two hours, as we watched the game and ate dinner between periods, I watched Riley's every move. I held my breath every time he was on the ice and only breathed when he headed for the bench.

Even with my extremely limited knowledge of the game, I could tell he was doing well. He seemed to be on the ice often, CJ always with him. They played well together, and by the end of the night, although neither of them had scored, the announcers had mentioned Riley as a good addition to the third line.

I had no idea what that meant other than that he'd done well. He'd had an assist on one of the team's goals, which helped because it'd been a tie game until then.

The Colonials had gone on to score again and won the game.

Vivi and I had high-fived then she had said she was heading out to meet up with friends.

And left me alone.

I reached for my phone without thinking, even though I knew there was no way he'd call or text now.

But I still sat there with my phone in my hand until I went to bed an hour later.

Riley

"We want you to take practice with the team tomorrow and Thursday, and we'll make a determination about Friday then. You had a great game tonight, Riley. We're all pleased with your play and looking forward to seeing what else you can do. See you tomorrow."

"Thanks, Coach. I appreciate this opportunity."

Coach Angstadt smiled and clapped me on the shoulder in his office. He'd called me in as soon as I'd been showered and dressed after the game.

Because of the cellphone-blackout in the locker room, I had been counting down the minutes until I could call Aly. And my parents, of course.

But first, I wanted to hear her voice. Couldn't fucking wait to hear her voice.

"Just keep doing what you're doing and I think you'll be pleased with the results."

I left with a nod and headed out of the office, not surprised to see CJ waiting in the hall, looking nervous as hell.

I grabbed his shoulder and gave him a little shake. "Breathe, CJ. You played a great game."

That made the kid smile. "You, too, man. All right. You gonna wait for me?"

"Won't leave without you."

Another smile and the kid headed into the office and I headed back to the locker room.

I wanted to grab my coat and my bag and head out so I could call Aly, but Travis met me at my locker.

"You ready to get out of here?" Travis smacked me on the back as I pulled on my jacket. "Time to celebrate."

I grinned at him and nodded. "Sounds good. I just need to make a call. Told CJ I'd wait for him, too."

I had to raise my voice to be heard over the rest of the team. They'd been on a three-game losing streak before tonight and were psyched about the win.

"Well, hurry up. There's alcohol to drink and women to hit on."

Colin joined us, nudging me with his shoulder. "What'd Coach say? You staying?"

"At least until Thursday. I'm gonna take practice with the team then I guess he'll make a decision."

I was cautiously optimistic but wasn't getting my hopes up

"You don't have anything to worry about." Travis clapped me on the back again. "Come on. Let's get the hell out of here."

"Sure. CJ should be out in a— wait, there he is."

Colin twisted to look over his shoulder. "You two had a great night."

CJ was grinning like a loon as he practically ran over to us. Apparently, he was staying, too. Good. The kid had played an amazing game.

"Coach said you're staying, too. That's awesome."

Laughing, I put my arm around CJ's shoulders and steered him toward the door.

"Yeah, it is. Come on, kid. Let's go celebrate. I just gotta make a call first."

CJ's grin turned sly. "Gonna call Aly?"

Now I smacked the kid on the back of the head. "You're just jealous. You gonna call your parents?"

"Shit." CJ shook his head. "We better leave now."

I was still laughing when I finally found a quiet spot in the hall to make my call.

She answered on the second ring.

"Riley?"

"Hey."

"Hi. We saw the game. You looked great!"

Damn, it was good to hear her voice. "Thanks. We had a great game."

"I'm so happy for you. Are you going out to celebrate?'

"CJ and I and a couple of the guys are heading to a bar."

She paused for a second. Or maybe I just imagined it. "I'm really happy for you, Riley. So…are you staying in Philly?"

"Yeah, at least until Thursday. Coach said they'd decide whether or not to keep me or send me down."

"I have no doubt they're going to keep you."

Well, hell. She didn't have to sound so damn happy about it. Which was stupid to even think about.

"Thanks. I'm happy with the way I played."

"You should be."

"If I'm still here Friday, do you want to come to the game?"

Another quick pause. "I… Can I let you know that morning? I'd really love to come but—"

"Yeah, no problem. I guess I'll wait to hear from you."

"Oh, wait. Do you—oh, I forgot. You're going out."

"Yeah. And I still need to give my parents a call."

Another pause.

"I'm so glad you called, Riley. I don't want to keep you from your parents. I just… I'll talk to you soon."

"Sure. Night."

I hung up before she could respond and the second the call disconnected, I wanted to throw my phone against the wall.

Goddammit.

That was not how I'd wanted that conversation to go.

I felt like I'd just blown playoff game seven with a turnover in the defensive end. My heart pounding, I took a couple of deep breaths. Getting pissed wasn't going to help. Besides, if I stayed in Philly, I might never see her again.

Which would totally suck.

Shit.

And there wasn't a damn thing I could do about it now. Now, it was time to celebrate finally achieving my goal.

Tomorrow, I needed to make sure I held on to my spot on this team.

And maybe to start getting over this damn crush I had on a girl who obviously didn't care enough about me.

Chapter 18

Aly

"You look like shit."

I gave my sister a death glare as I headed for the coffeepot. "Gee, thanks. And what are you doing up this early, anyway?"

Vivi shrugged. "Haven't been to bed yet. And I wanted to know if he called last night."

Pouring myself coffee, I didn't answer until I'd taken my first sip.

"Yes, he called."

And I'd been an ass.

"That's it? He called." Vivi sighed. "What'd he *say?*"

"That he'll be staying in Philly at least until Friday."

"Ah."

Yeah, ah. That kind of summed up my feelings this morning.

I'd told myself last night that I was happy for him. And I was. I really was. But I was also practical and I knew that if he stayed with the Colonials, our relationship was doomed.

What relationship? You spent two nights together. What the hell did you expect? A proposal?

Of course not.

"Aly? You're thinking way too hard this early. You're making *my* brain hurt."

"You're right. It's too early for this."

Vivi tipped her head to look at me. "Why do I get the feeling we're not talking about the same thing?"

Because we weren't and my sister was no fool. "I need to break it off. Tell him it was nice while it lasted and cut ties."

"Uh-huh."

I shot her another glare. "And what does that mean?"

"Doesn't mean a thing." Vivi shrugged, pissing me off even more. "I think you're totally right."

Of course, I was right.

Then why is it so hard to breathe?

"It would never work out." I took another sip of coffee and watched my sister nod.

"Uh-huh."

"I just need to let this go."

Vivi nodded sagely. "Yep."

"You're totally mocking me, aren't you?"

Vivi shrugged but her lips twitched. "Maybe a little." Then she rolled her eyes. "Jesus, Aly. A blind person could see how much you like the guy. So you won't be able to jump his bones every night. If he likes you as much as he seems to, he won't be a prick and cheat on you. He'll wait for you and you can send disgustingly sweet texts every day, and when he's on a road trip, you can send him tit pics."

About to open my mouth and protest, I snapped it shut when Vivi started to laugh.

"Okay, maybe no titty pictures. But, Aly…live a little. Life doesn't only happen in this little bubble of our house and the hospital. Hell, even Mom and Dad figured that out. And now,

I'm going to bed. I have used up all my brain power and need to recharge."

With a wry grin, Vivi headed out of the kitchen.

And I sipped my coffee, wondering how to break a two-decade habit of being a stick in the mud.

Riley

"Hatch, come in and close the door and take a seat."

Stone-faced, I followed Coach's orders Thursday morning and slipped into the chair in front of the desk. Still angry with myself for a shitty practice this morning, I figured I was headed back to Reading and the Redtails.

The guys would probably be glad to see me. At least I had that to look forward to.

"Tough morning. You struggled to hit the net, had some trouble making passes."

"Yes, sir." My jaw locked against the need to make excuses. I didn't have any. I'd sucked. Maybe self-sabotage. Maybe nothing more than a bad morning. I only knew one thing. I—

"Well, hopefully you'll play better tonight." Coach smiled. "We're adding you and CJ to the third line. We like what you add to the team. Your grit and determination and his speed, combined with your ability to work together, are exactly what we need right now."

Coach went on to say more and I heard and responded to everything, but half of my brain was doing somersaults in victory.

I'd made it. I'd fucking made it.

"Get yourself fed and rested and back here ready to play tonight. And send CJ in if he's out there."

As Coach stood, he held out his hand. I jumped to my feet and shook, my face actually hurt from smiling.

"Yes, sir. And thank you."

I walked out into the hall, still grinning, and caught sight of CJ, slumped against the wall waiting. The kid shoved away from the wall, eyes wide like a deer in the headlights.

I nodded toward the coach's office. "You're up." I reached for CJ's shoulder. "Breathe. Seriously. Try not to pass out."

"What'd he say?"

"We'll talk when you get out, okay? I'll wait for you."

CJ looked ridiculously relieved. "Okay, yeah. Sounds good."

Then he disappeared behind the door and I started to grin again. I needed to call my parents. My dad had mentioned flying in for a game. I didn't think they'd be able to get in by tonight, but we had another game Saturday night and one Tuesday. Maybe they'd be able to get here for one of those.

And what about Aly?

Should I call? Text? Hell, did she even want to hear from me? Or had she already written me off? We'd exchanged a few texts over the past two days but I'd been busy so there hadn't been many.

Fuck, maybe I needed to face facts. She just wasn't that into me. Maybe she never had been. Or maybe she'd only wanted me when it'd been convenient.

Either way, she fucked with my head, and I didn't need that right now.

So I pulled out my phone and called my parents.

And tried not to think about a certain blonde.

Chapter 19

I paused Friday afternoon, teeth lodged in my upper lip, thumbs poised over my phone.

Bliss's text enticed like the promise of a strong margarita at Third and Spruce after work.

Come over to our place tonight to watch the Colonials game. Lori and Cary will be here and a few other guys from the team. We can't wait to watch Riley and CJ again!!!

I *so* wanted to go. The desire was a gnawing ache in my gut.

I'd been moping most of the afternoon, figuring I'd be home watching the game by myself tonight because Vivi had to work.

For the past day, I'd thought about contacting Bliss but had talked myself out of it. The Redtails probably had a game or, if they didn't, why would they even think to invite me along with them? I really didn't know anyone on the team.

But Bliss hadn't forgotten me. And I wanted to go.

But…Riley hadn't called or texted.

Not since yesterday morning. And even though I'd picked up the phone a thousand times to contact him, I hadn't. I hadn't known what to say. That wasn't right either.

I'd known exactly what I should've said.

"I miss you. I'm so happy for you. I can't wait to see you."

But I also knew this was the biggest break of his career and I wanted him to succeed so I didn't want to distract him.

If you'd even be a distraction.

Maybe he'd moved on. Maybe he'd spent the last two nights picking up women.

But I knew that wasn't right, either. I knew there was no way Riley would screw up this chance.

Fuck it.

I would love to! Thanks for asking. What can I bring?

Glancing at the clock, I sighed when I realized I still had two hours before I could leave. And another two before the game started.

Damn, how much did that suck?

About as much as waking up this morning and wishing he was lying next to me, smiling that grin of his. The one I'd seen Monday morning. The one that made my toes curl. And the one that usually made opposing players want to punch him.

God, I was so stupid. I wanted Riley any way I could get him.

And you probably lost him for good.

No. Just…no.

I'd figure something out, even if I had to go to Philly and bang on the glass at the next home game to get his attention.

But for that, I was gonna need help.

Good thing I knew a few guys who would know exactly what to do.

Riley

"Riley, my friend. How are you?"

"Jake." I grinned, my mood immediately lifted as I held my phone to my ear. "Hey, man. How's it going?"

"That is a question I will be asking you. You looked good last night. You and CJ. Tonight you will be even better."

Last night's game had been a hard-fought battle for sixty long minutes. The Colonials had been on top of the game the entire night until the final minutes when the Hawks had scored twice, winning the game.

"Thanks, man. So you got to watch?"

"Yes, most of the team was at Shane's place last night to watch. Some people who weren't with the team, too."

If I'd been a dog, my ears would've pointed. "Oh yeah? Like who?"

"Like Aly. Very pretty. Confused as to what she saw in you but seems like a smart lady otherwise."

Sitting in my car in the arena's underground parking lot, I shook my head, ignoring the sharp pain in my chest at the mention of her name. I'd arrived early for tonight's game, but once I entered the arena, I'd have to turn his phone off. The team banned cell phone use once the guys got to the arena before a game and until we were on their way home afterward.

"And fuck you twice, my Russian friend. Don't you have a game tonight that you need to be getting ready for?"

Jake laughed. "That is all you have to say? I am disappointed. What happened to Chickie? Seems your new team might need a guy like you tonight. Get people fired up. And your geography skills remain sadly lacking. Okay, I only want to call and give you hard time. And tell you good luck tonight."

By the time Jake had shut up, I was grinning.

"Hey, Jake. Thanks. I appreciate the love."

"I have much love to spread today so is no problem. Just remember the little people you came up with, yes? Talk to you soon."

I nodded though I knew Jake couldn't see me. "Keep in touch. Seriously."

"You too. Kick ass tonight, Hatch."

Jake didn't say good-bye. The call simply disconnected, leaving me with one burning question.

Why had Aly watched the game with my team?

Only because she and Bliss had become friends? Or was I right to think maybe—

Fuck. I shook my head. Now wasn't the time to think about this. I didn't want it to fuck with my head before the game. Last night had sucked, to be ahead for all of the game and to lose it in the last seconds. Coach hadn't been happy last night and a few of the guys, me included, had gone out to drown our sorrows.

Probably not something I'd do again. I'd gone only because I had nothing else to do. No one to go home to, no one I wanted to call to talk to.

No Aly.

But she'd been at Shane's last night.

So what? That only proved she liked Bliss.

She hadn't called or texted me the entire day.

And there's your answer, asshole.

Time to move on.

I got out of my car and headed into the arena.

Aly

"So? Are you ready?"

I rolled my eyes and sighed. "I don't know. Maybe this wasn't such a great idea, Viv. What if he doesn't want to see me? What if he's already dating someone else? What if he just doesn't care that I'm here? I don't want to make him uncomfortable. This is his job."

"He'll feel the same way you would if he showed up at the hospital with a sign proclaiming his feelings for you. You'd melt into a little puddle of goo and promise him sexual favors when you get him alone."

Sitting in my seat in the Colonials offensive end of the arena, I pulled a face at my sister and reached inside my purse to tap the sign I'd made in a moment of sheer stupidity.

It'd seemed like a good idea last night after a couple of beers and a profane discussion with Riley's friends, who'd been more than eager to help me figure out what my sign should say.

But now that I was actually here, common sense was trying to kick in. Or maybe it was fear.

Hell, maybe he wouldn't remember what the sign meant.

"Oh, I know that look. Don't wimp out now, Aly. Come on, we braved the Schuylkill Expressway. Don't let a little performance anxiety get in your way."

Yes, the Schuylkill had been a mess today. We'd passed two accidents, had crawled at five miles an hour for long stretches, and got lost twice in Center City on the way to the arena.

Now here I was, waiting to get my first live glimpse of Riley in his uniform during the pre-game warm-up. Trying to work up the courage to walk over to the other side of the arena, walk down the stairs to the glass at the ice, and wait for Riley to notice me standing there with my little sign that was meant only for him.

Could I do it?

Hell, yes, I could.

I checked the clock. Only three minutes until the teams made it out to the ice for warm-ups.

Standing, I took a deep breath. "If this doesn't work, we're leaving. Immediately."

Vivi grinned and settled deeper into her seat. "You forget. I drove. Besides, I figure I'm driving home alone tonight."

I could only hope.

———

Chapter 20

Riley

"Okay, boys. Work out the kinks, get loose, and get ready to play."

Assistant Coach Domenic Mann slapped each man on the back as we passed through the hall for warm-ups and I nodded before hitting the ice.

The music was nothing more than a throbbing beat in my ears, the crowd noise barely a consideration at this point. It'd get louder when the game started but I'd learned how to put it aside and concentrate on the game.

Tonight, it was merely noise.

Just like the people gathered at the glass, banging and cheering. None of them were there for me. No one knew me yet. Hopefully that would change and soon. But for now, I was okay with anonymity.

It wasn't until me and CJ and a few other guys were flipping the last pucks into the ice before the buzzer rang that CJ skated up next to me.

"Uh, Riley."

"Yeah, what's up?"

"Uh—"

"Dude." Travis flanked me. "There's some girl here with your jersey on. Don't know how the fuck you got puck bunnies already but if you throw this one back, put in a good word for me. I got a thing for blondes."

I nearly tripped myself as my head shot up.

"Seriously? Where?"

Travis laughed and shook his head. "Right corner. She's a few rows up and she looks way too civilized for you. She needs a guy like me."

My head shot around to the direction Travis pointed and I sucked in air.

Christ, how the hell had I missed her?

Aly stood perfectly still, five rows back from the ice. She was wearing a Colonials sweater and damn if Travis wasn't right. She was wearing my number. I could just make out the seven on her arm when she lifted her hand to wave. Her wary expression made me smile.

I was so fucking happy to see her, my heart literally felt like it could pound out of my chest.

She was here. Holy *fuck*, she was *actually* here.

All the bullshit I'd told myself about how I was over her and how it didn't matter if she didn't like me… Yeah, that was all shit. I knew that now.

The only thing that mattered was that she was here. She'd taken that huge first step and showed up. And I wasn't about to let her hang.

Skating over to the ice, ignoring the catcalls from the few guys still there, I put my hand on the glass and waited.

The fans on the other side high-fived me but soon realized that I wasn't looking at them.

I only had eyes for Aly.

I watched her make her way down the stairs, trying to wade through the sea of blue-and-white-clad fans to the glass, where the usher, a guy wearing a huge, shit-eating grin, made a space for her.

She didn't say anything. I wasn't sure I would've heard her anyway. But the smile on her face was all I needed to see.

And then she looked down and pulled something out of her purse.

A piece of paper that she held up on the glass next to my hand.

She'd only written one word in perfect block letters.

Please

Then she put her hand on the glass to mirror mine and I smiled until my face hurt.

"Stay."

I wasn't sure she'd heard me, but she nodded and her smile widened.

And I knew, no matter how the game ended, I'd already won.

The guys were pumped after tonight's win and the locker room sounded like a frat house on homecoming weekend.

"So, Riley. Guess you're not coming out to celebrate tonight, huh?"

Ignoring Travis's sly dig was easy, considering I had somewhere infinitely more interesting to be tonight.

I'd been able to keep my attention focused squarely on the game, but the second the final buzzer rang, I'd started to grin. And not because my team had won. Well, not only that.

"Hell, I wouldn't be going out with you tonight if I had someone who looked like that waiting for me tonight," Colin responded. "Damn, Riley, how'd you snag her, anyway? Seriously, man, she looks way too smart for you."

I didn't bother to look up as I shoved my legs into my pants then shrugged into my shirt. I was on a mission and wasn't about to be deterred. But I did manage to shoot Colin and Travis the finger over my shoulder.

While the two of them laughed, I rolled my tie and stuffed it in the pocket of my jacket. I didn't want to take the time to knot it. Coach had already done his post-game talk, which meant I was free to go as soon as I was ready.

And I was pretty much ready to go now…when I remembered I'd driven in with CJ. Because I was sharing a hotel room with him.

Shit.

I stopped, totally stymied.

"Uh, Riley?" Sitting next to me on the bench, CJ looked up, frowning. "You okay?"

"Yeah, but I need you to find somewhere to crash tonight. I'll make it up to you, I swe—"

CJ's laughter cut me off.

"Dude, I'm not stupid. As soon as I saw Aly at the game, I checked around. I'm gonna crash at Malone's place tonight. He's got an extra bed since O'Neill's still in the hospital—"

I grabbed CJ by the nape and yanked him forward to kiss his head. "I love you, kid."

CJ pushed me away with a laugh. "Yeah, yeah. You owe me, Rye. Just don't fuck it up."

"Don't plan to."

Seconds later, I was out of the locker room and into the hall. Pulling out my phone, I breathed a sigh of relief to see a text from Aly.

Not sure where I should meet you so I'll wait outside until I hear from you. If something changes, I'll go home with Vivi and you can text me.

Hell, nothing was going to change my mind. She'd made the

next step and I was going to make sure the only way we kept moving was forward.

I'm done. Where are you?

Already on my way out of the building, I stopped and looked around. There were still a crowd of fans milling around, waiting for the crush at the train station to ease. I didn't think I'd be recognized. I wore a beanie that hid my hair but had forgotten to factor in the suit. Dead giveaway.

"Riley! Will you sign my program?"

A little girl in pigtails and a Colonials sweater asked me to sign her souvenir stick, the smile on her face adorable. Of course, I said yes. Five seconds later, I had a crowd of people around me.

And the vague remembrance of a conversation with the team PR woman to be polite at all times and not to open my mouth too much. Which was a virtual impossibility for me.

I spoke to everyone who stuck something in my hands. Mostly they were kids who wanted me to sign their sweaters or their programs. I'd done it thousands of times before but never on an NHL sweater.

My face hurt by the time I'd signed every piece, I'd smiled and talked and took photos.

And when I looked up after the last person walked away, I found Aly, smiling at me from a bench lining the walk to the entrance.

She had her hands stuffed in the pockets of her coat and she looked cold. Standing when she saw I'd noticed her, she walked toward me. I met her halfway, trying to find the perfect thing to say. She looked like she was doing the same thing, her smile a little strained, like she didn't have a clue what I was going to say.

When she stood right in front of me, I realized I didn't need to say anything. Wrapping my arms around her, I pressed my lips against hers and kissed the hell out of her.

I kissed her like a parched man gulped water after three days in the desert.

Her lips softened under mine and her arms went around my waist to hold me almost as tightly as I held her. I lost myself in her taste and her touch. Not even the catcalls from the security guards and the few lingering fans made me want to stop.

Hell, if I could continue to kiss her and still get to my hotel room, I would've considered it.

I didn't know how long we stood there, kissing each other like we hadn't seen each other in weeks. I couldn't get enough of her, probably would never get enough of her. This… She was exactly what I wanted to come home to every night.

But when Aly pulled away, I let her go. Reluctantly. And not far. I kept my arms around her shoulders and her body tucked against mine.

"I fucking missed you." I spoke before she could say anything and probably should've taken time to think of something better. But the truth was, I meant every word. "I don't want to miss you again. I want you to be the first person I see when I get back from a road trip. I want to be the first person you want to talk to in the morning and the last person you want to talk to before you go to sleep. And I want to be inside you as often as I can. Starting in the next half hour."

Laughing, she slipped one hand under my beanie, into my still-wet hair, and tugged me down for another kiss that made every part of my body hot and ready. Some more than others. "I missed you too, Riley."

My cock hardened even more than it already was. The walk to the car would be interesting. "You have no idea how damn glad I am to hear that."

Her smiled softened a little. "I'm not sure how we're going to figure out the distance, but," she pressed her fingers to my lips when I opened my mouth to respond, "I want to make this work. I will try my damnedest to make it work. I would rather have you some of the time than not at all."

My heart practically hurt at the sweet tone of her voice and the look in her eyes. "And I will take you any way I can get you. Every way. All ways." I waggled my eyebrows at her. "Some ways we haven't tried yet."

She laughed again and settled her hands on my shoulders, staring up into my eyes and making me wish for a dark corner. "Then take me to your hotel and let me do bad things to you."

"Honey, you can do anything you want to me. As long as I get to return the favor. I will make it my mission in life to please you in ways you never imagined."

Pulling my head down, she rubbed her cold nose against mine. "I think I'll be the one owing you favors. And I'll love every minute of it."

My grin grew even wider. "Then let me show you some of my moves, hon."

"I'm all yours, Riley."

I wrapped my arm around her shoulders and pointed us in the direction of the parking garage. "Damn right, babe. Damn right."

Falling for the Enforcer

He's used to making an impression...

Will

It can be tough coming into a team mid-season, but I'm a veteran, and it comes with the territory. I'm not afraid to drop my gloves in defense of my teammates, and I've never met a woman who's made my heart pound as hard as a good fight. Until a chance collision with a curvy brunette makes me want more than Jess is willing to give.

She's not used to being distracted by a hot hockey hunk...

Jess

I've been around hockey all my life. My dad taught me everything he knows about the game as an NHL scout, and I believes Will is just what the young Redtails team needs. He brings grit and determination and stability. He's just not what I need in my life, even if he is huge, hot and hard-bodied.

Will is used to fighting for what he wants but winning Jess's heart might be the toughest battle of his life.

Chapter 1

Jess

Head down as I glanced over the contracts for the new promotional opportunities, I grinned at my own handiwork as I hurried through the hall.

I had no doubt I'd get approval from the Redtails' front office to go after sponsors. I knew exactly who I'd approach first—

"Oh!"

A huge, immoveable object suddenly appeared in front of me, and in the next second, my ass hit the floor and the papers in my hands went flying.

"Holy shit. Damn, I'm sorry. Here, give me your hand. Let me help you up."

As pain started to radiate up my back, a large hand appeared in front of my face. Stunned, I stared at it for several seconds.

"Hey, hon. You okay?"

Hon?

I looked up…and up…into eyes so dark, I wasn't sure if they were black or brown. Or possibly navy.

A face I didn't know but that looked familiar.

Scowling up at him, I shook my head. "Who are you?"

His lips quirked into a grin that made his eyes narrow down to slits. "Will MacDonald. And you're still on the floor. Come on, take my hand. You're gonna get that skirt all dirty."

My lips parted in surprise. Well, damn. That's why he looked familiar. Coach had taken my recommendation seriously.

I started to grin and noticed MacDonald's eyes widen.

"Uh, you sure you're okay, miss? How hard did you hit?"

For a split second, I wondered what the hell he was talking about. And then I remembered I was sprawled on the floor.

Looking down at myself, I realized my skirt had ridden up almost to my hips and was damn close to revealing what color underwear I'd picked out this morning. My legs were spread wide, and the few strands of hair falling in my eyes meant I'd lost a few of the pins holding it up in an already messy bun.

Grimacing, I reached for his outstretched hand, knowing it'd be easier to accept his help than try to scramble up on my own.

"Well, my skirt wouldn't be dirty if you hadn't body-checked me—"

I gave a totally girly squeal as he ignored my hand, grabbed me under my arms, and lifted me off the floor.

Holy crap. The guy had some serious muscle to have dead-lifted me off the floor like I was a kid and not a full-grown woman.

Duh, you work for a hockey team.

And this was definitely a hockey player.

Unkempt dark brown hair, curly and way too long to be civilized. At least a week's worth of stubble on his chin. Broad shoulders and chest that filled my vision when I stared straight ahead. Even in four-inch heels, I knew the top of my head didn't reach his chin.

He wore a suit but no tie, but I could tell, even in dress pants, he had powerful legs. Again, not surprising considering what he did for a living.

"Sorry, but I'm pretty sure you walked straight into my back. And since I don't have eyes in the back of my head…"

Okay, maybe I hadn't been looking where I was going, but I was the one who'd ended up on my ass on the floor. He could be a little more sympathetic.

Then again, he was a hockey player. As much as I loved the game, I'd been around the sport all my life. Most players were interested in only two things—hockey and sex.

If it didn't directly affect their game or getting laid, it didn't register.

And since I didn't mix business with pleasure… Probably best to just keep walking.

With a sigh, I decided to ignore him and turned to pick up the papers still scattered all over the floor.

"Let me give you a hand with that."

Amazingly, he brushed by me to gather up my contracts scattered all over the floor.

Okay, maybe he wasn't a total prick.

Bending over to reach the papers at my feet, I winced as pain shot up my hip.

Sucking in a sharp breath, I rubbed one hand on my abused hip and shook my head. Yeah, that was gonna hurt. Maybe I'd go down to see the trainer about an ice pack.

"You sure you're okay? You must've gone down a little harder than I thought. Do you need a hand getting wherever you're going? Where *are* you going anyway?"

"I'm fine. Really." *Just need to get away from you before you accidentally put me in a full body cast.* "I'll take those."

I held out my hand and refrained from rolling my eyes when he didn't immediately hand over my papers.

Great. One of those.

With a barely repressed sigh, I reached for calm and took another look at the man standing in front of her.

If anyone asked, I might admit that I found him attractive. Okay, hot. The guy was totally hot. But I'd been around professional athletes all my life. I was used to handsome faces and ripped bodies. And huge egos.

I had to admit that even the less…attractive players still had that certain something that made them irresistible to most women.

Most women being *other* women. I had made the mistake of dating a few hockey players in my time. But I'd learned my lesson by the time I was twenty, when the last one had packed up his bags and moved to a team in Europe without so much as a good-bye.

That had been eight years ago.

This one…

Going through the files of hockey stats in my brain, I searched for Will's. I knew he was older than most of the guys on the Redtails. Close to mid-thirties. Somewhat unusual for the AHL, but he still had several good years in him. At least that's what I'd told Coach at the staff meeting last month.

Coach Scott always listened when I spoke up about players. I didn't do it often, but when Coach had been talking about possible replacement players at the monthly staff meeting a few weeks ago, I'd piped in with my two cents on MacDonald.

The guy's stats spoke for themselves, but for some reason, the Colonials talent scout had put MacDonald low on the list of potentials, far below players I wouldn't have given a second glance. Okay, yeah, the NHL scout had a few decades of experience on me, but I knew my team.

And MacDonald was the perfect fit.

But I didn't have to personally like the guy.

"Do you think I can have my contracts back now?"

He blinked and looked down at his hands, as if he hadn't realized he still held them.

"Oh, yeah. Sorry about that. And about knocking you on your ass."

Then his gaze slid down my body and my eyes rolled again.

What did you expect? Hockey player.

The voice in my head was my mom's and I had to grit my teeth against the urge to growl. Like, seriously, I wanted to growl.

Then again, my mom wasn't wrong. Which just pissed me off even more.

Forcing a smile, I held my hand out. "Not a problem. I just need those."

"Sure." He held them out with another smile.

Okay, maybe he had a nice smile. Maybe better than nice. He didn't look so…arrogant when he grinned like that. It also made him look younger than he was.

No. Nope. Not a chance in hell.

Taking the papers, I nodded and started to walk past him.

And damn if the man didn't start to walk along with me.

"So, any chance you're heading to the main office? Just got here and not exactly sure where I need to be."

Looking up, I found him grinning down at me, that smile getting more attractive by the moment.

And, oh, that was *so* not good.

I stifled a sigh. "Sure. I'm headed there anyway."

"Great. Thanks, Miss…"

"Gardiner. Jess Gardiner."

Out of the corner of my eye, I saw him shoot me another glance, and when I looked up, his eyes were narrowed, as if he was thinking really hard.

"Any relation to Doug Gardiner? The NHL scout?"

So he did know my dad. "Yep, that's my dad."

"Ah."

I snuck another glance his way and noticed his easy grin had been replaced with a bit of a scowl.

Okay, *not* a fan of my dad's. Well, he wasn't the only one.

"So, what do you do for the Redtails?"

Small talk. *Lovely.* Luckily, the office was just down the hall.

"I'm the marketing and promotions manager."

"Nice. I guess."

Now an awkward silence fell, and I almost wished he'd continue to talk. He had a nice voice, deep and rough, like he had gravel in his throat.

And what the hell does that matter?

Shit.

"So, Jess the marketing and promotions manager, do you like working here?"

Because answering was easier than an awkward silence, I said, "I do." It just wasn't where I wanted to spend the rest of my career, but he didn't need to know that. "The organization's great, we're drawing well, and the team's playing well. You're coming in at a good time."

"So I've been told."

Something in his tone caught my ear and I looked up again to find him grimacing, though his expression quickly cleared.

Curiosity made me ask, "I haven't heard of any trades lately so how did you get here?"

I wanted to take the words back when he looked at me with another one of those smiles. That smile said, *Hey, I know you want me.*

Though it took some effort on my part, I refrained from rolling my eyes.

"Picked up off waivers yesterday from the Roadies." He shrugged. "Been riding the bench for a month there so hopefully I'll see some ice time here. Heard good things about Coach Scott. Looking forward to playing for him."

My smile was genuine now. "Coach is wonderful. The team's

having a great year, even though we recently lost two of our best players to call-ups."

"Not a bad way to lose them."

"It's great for them. CJ will probably be back at some point, but I don't think Riley will. CJ's offensive game is tight, but his defense needs some work to play at the NHL level. Riley's a damn good grinder and the Colonials need a player like him to get them going."

"Sounds like your dad rubbed off."

Now why didn't that sound like a compliment?

Slowing to a stop outside the door to the front office, I turned to look up at Will. He'd stopped beside me, watching me with raised eyebrows. Kind of seemed to me that he was daring me to say something.

Or maybe I was totally reading something into his expression that wasn't there.

Either way, I didn't have time for this. I had several businesses to contact about future events, needed to get started on the design for next season's Ugly Christmas sweaters and giveaways, and had several phone calls to return about an upcoming affiliation night program. We had two well-known Colonial alumni coming to sign autographs at next Friday's game and I needed to smooth some ruffled feathers over billing.

Ugh.

I loved the game of hockey. Always had, always would. It was in my DNA. And growing up, I'd idolized the players. They'd been my heroes, my idols. My first crushes.

But I'd learned quickly that those heroes didn't always measure up to the public image.

"Here we are. Welcome to the Redtails, Will."

He nodded, watching me with sharp eyes. "Thanks. Nice to meet you, Jess. I guess I'll see you around."

I nodded. "I guess you will."

Will

I opened the door for Jess and watched her walk through.

And yes, my gaze might have fallen to her ass. The girl had some curves, even though she couldn't weigh more than a hundred pounds soaking wet and she probably only stood about five-two, more than a foot shorter than me.

Not my typical type. I usually liked them tall, stacked, and exotic. Blonde, brunette, redhead, didn't matter. What did matter was that they were beautiful.

I'd never been attracted to the girl next door. Not even in high school. College had been a blur of hockey, classes, and parties. And a whole lot of girls.

And even if certain parts of my body wanted me to lick her up like ice cream, I certainly didn't have time for Doug Gardiner's daughter now.

Damn, that name always managed to make me want to punch something. Jaw tightening, I took a deep breath and followed Jess through the door.

She'd stopped in the office to the right of the door, glancing over her shoulder at me before nodding and walking farther into the office.

Looking at the sign on the open door, I realized this was the office I needed.

"Will! It's great to have you here. Come on in." The former player behind the desk stood and held out his hand. "I'm Greg Bell, VP of hockey ops. Welcome to Reading."

I took Greg's hand and shook. "Thanks. I'm happy to be here."

"Well, we can certainly use a guy with your skill. We've got a great team, but they're young and they need a leader. We're hoping you're the man to step into that role."

I had heard all of this from the coach when I'd talked to him last week so it wasn't a surprise. So I nodded and smiled.

"I'll do my best. Just glad to be playing."

"I know you weren't getting a lot of ice time before but that shouldn't be a problem here."

"I'm looking forward to it."

"Good, good. I'm sure you're tired from your trip so why don't we head downstairs and you can meet Coach Scott then get to your apartment and rest up for tomorrow."

As I followed the GM through the empty arena, I took a cursory look around, but if you'd played in one arena, the others were pretty much the same.

And I'd played in hundreds since starting hockey when I was five and traveling for the game since I was ten. I'd grown up in Saskatchewan, where hockey was a religion, not a sport. And my parents had been more than eager to help me achieve my goals.

That'd been when I'd been young, bigger, and better than every kid in my small town and on the path for stardom. And when that fame didn't pan out…

Shoving those old, damaging thoughts out of my head, I tuned back into the GM's talk about the team and the area and how great the fans were. I'd heard this spiel before from the previous GM, who'd wanted to sign me a few years ago. That deal hadn't worked out, and not much had changed apparently.

The Redtails had been around for more than four decades, had a long streak of winning years and Calder Cup trophies, and were coming off a Calder Cup win last year. They still had more than half the team intact from last year, but a few call-ups had hurt their roster.

Yes, I was happy to be here. But secretly, I was surprised as shit that I'd gotten the call. At thirty-three, I was almost a decade older than most of the Redtails players. So yeah, it made sense that Coach Scott would want someone with a few years under his belt to help anchor his young guys.

But I had been starting to wonder if I'd be stuck in a downward spiral until I finally decided to retire. I was sure I'd been on my way down to the ECHL when I'd gotten the call from Coach Scott. It'd been unexpected and exactly what I'd needed.

"Will, good to see you. Welcome to Reading. Hope you had a good trip from Minnesota."

Smiling, I reached for the hand of the man I'd only met a few times but had heard great things about. Coach Scott was a league legend. A former player with a couple NHL seasons as an assistant coach under his belt. No Stanley Cups, but he'd been a member of the Redtails' Calder Cup-winning team in the mid-90s and had been the coach here for more than ten years. Rumor had it he was in line for the Colonials head job when Angstadt retired. And that Cary Lenville was in line for Scott's job.

Which was another reason I had been surprised to get the call.

"Good to be here. Thank you for the opportunity. I'm really looking forward to playing."

While it was something I'd say to any new coach, I had to admit that the words meant more this time.

"That's good to hear because we're going to be expecting a lot of you."

Waving me into a seat on the other side of his desk, Scott nodded to Bell, who excused himself and shut the door behind him.

"You probably haven't heard because we haven't made an announcement yet but Coach Novak is leaving for another position and we're pulling Lenville up to take his place."

My face must have shown my surprise because Scott nodded.

"I understand you and Cary have some history."

Well, shit. I made sure I didn't look away and I didn't falter. "We do. But that won't be a problem."

"Glad to hear it. I'm sure you'll find some time to talk privately but let me just tell you, he agreed that you were the guy we needed after your name was floated."

Now that was interesting. "Do you mind if I ask who that was?"

Coach's smile spread. "You can thank our promotions manager. She put your name out at a staff meeting. She's Doug Gardiner's daughter and sometimes I think she knows the game better than I do. She's done great things for our marketing department but there are times I think she missed her calling. She'd make a damn good scout."

Well, hell. How about that?

"I actually, uh, ran into her upstairs. She seems…nice."

Coach nodded. "She is. And smart. She won't be around long. Some NHL club'll snap her up soon enough. Be a huge loss for the Redtails. Anyway, you're bunking with Justin, right? Have you two met before?"

"Yes, but only briefly."

Coach's grin appeared again. "He's a character. Great guy and a damn good player. Needs some polish, and I'm hoping you can help with that. I'm putting you and Justin together on the second line. He's got skill but he's not big and we need a big guy in front of the net."

Being put on the second line was another shock. I knew the top defensive line of Marchenko and Mozik was white-hot at the moment but I'd been expecting third line because of my recent record. Which consisted of not a lot of ice time. And yeah, that had sucked. And made me doubt myself, which made me not play as well as I could.

The rest wasn't anything I hadn't heard before. I was a big guy and I knew how to use my body. But with the changes in the game in recent years, my style of play was falling out of favor.

Nodding, I waited for the rest of the speech. There was always more.

Coach lost his grin and his expression turned serious. "We're looking for a leader on the ice, Will. That means controlling penalty minutes. You've had a problem with that in the past."

I held the coach's gaze steadily. "I have but it's something I've been actively working on."

"I know, which is why you're here. You and I have a lot more in common than you probably know, Will. Play hard but play smart. That's what I need from you."

Then Coach stood and held out his hand and I rose to shake. "You'll get it. I appreciate the opportunity."

"And we're glad to have you. Welcome to the Redtails."

Jess

"Honey, I'm home."

With a sigh, I dropped my bags on the chair by the front door then kicked off my shoes into the pile under the chair.

Saturday morning, like I did every week, I'd take that pile and put them back in my closet and start the process over again Monday morning.

A meow from the kitchen made me smile and change direction for the back of my town house.

"There you are. Sorry I'm late. I know it's past your feeding time but if you want Mommy to continue to buy you food, then I'm going to be late occasionally."

As I entered the kitchen, I saw Honey, my huge, battle-scarred former stray orange tabby, sitting on the counter. Where he was most definitely not allowed to sit. Picking him up, I rubbed his head and snuggled my nose into his fur for as long as he let me. Then he leaped from my arms back onto the counter and stared at me.

Smiling at his regal glare, not at all ruined by his battered left ear and scarred nose, I dished his food and had just set the bowl on the floor when I heard my phone ring.

My smiled widened when I saw the name on the screen.

"Hey, Dad. How's it going?"

"Hi, sweetheart. It's going. Got a game tonight in Nashville. Cold as hell here. Thought Nashville was supposed to be warm. Next week, Vancouver. I'll need to wear three layers and I won't even step outside the whole time. Hell, I'm going to request the Florida loop next time and screw Bill and his arthritis."

Laughing, I started putting together my own dinner.

"So, I heard the Redtails signed MacDonald. You have anything to do with that?"

Suppressing a sigh, I rolled my eyes instead. "I guess you already know the answer to that."

"Yeah, I guess I do. And you know I think you're wrong. If he doesn't work out, you can kiss any plans you have to be a scout good-bye."

"You know that's not gonna happen, Dad." Now I did sigh. "And it's not what I want. I love my job. You know that."

"I know you're good at it. But, sweetheart, we both know where your true passion lies."

Well, shit. This was an old battle that I would never win. Mainly because there was no way any team would hire me to scout. I hadn't played the game and I wasn't the right sex.

And while my dad, of all people, believed I could be the one to break that wall, I knew it'd never happen. So I didn't allow myself to even think about the possibility.

"So, Dad. Find any good new prospects?"

With a barely concealed sigh, my dad allowed me to change the subject.

And maybe I let myself silently consider a dream I'd never achieve.

Chapter 2

Will

I knocked on the door to my new apartment. Yeah, I had a key, but I didn't know my new roommate well, so…

From the other side of the door, I heard a couple of thumps that grew increasingly louder until the door finally flew open. The guy standing on the other side had a towel around his waist and not much else. And he was dripping wet, shoulder-length brown hair streaming water down a broad chest covered with one spectacular black-and-blue bruise.

"Damn, thought you were the cable guy. Hey, I'm Justin." He stuck out his wet hand. "You're Will."

"That's me."

"Come on in." Justin stepped back, slid on the wood floor, probably because of the trail of water, and righted himself just before falling. "Sorry, thought I'd be out of the shower before you got here but got tied up at the gym."

"No problem."

I walked through the open door, lugging two huge duffel bags full of my belongings, shaking my head when Justin turned and headed toward the back of the apartment, grabbing for his towel as it started to slip off his hips.

"Your room's back here on the left," Justin yelled as he closed the bathroom door behind him. "Riley was kind of a neat freak so you should be good."

As opposed to Justin, apparently. The common areas of the apartment didn't look too bad but when I glanced into the room across from mine, I shook my head.

Holy hell. Justin's closet must have exploded. Only explanation for the piles of clothes on every available surface.

With a shrug, I walked into my room. Place was spotless. Guess Justin wasn't wrong about Riley being a neat freak. Tossing my duffels on the floor, I sighed and fell on my back onto the queen bed. Home sweet home for the next however long.

Hopefully, I'd be here until the end of the season at least. Be nice if I lasted more than a season. I was getting too old to be moving all the hell over the country.

"Hey, a couple of the guys are getting together tonight for dinner at Jake and Lad's place," Justin yelled from the bathroom. "We're hoping you'll show."

And there went my plans to spend the night doing absolutely nothing except sleeping. But I recalled what Coach had said about me being a leader, and I knew I couldn't say no. No better time than the present to get started on that.

Which is how I found myself surrounded by seven twenty-somethings, laughing my ass off with a beer in my hand a couple of hours later.

"So I told him, 'You need to check cooler. I think your dick is there.' He was so drunk, he looked. I shit you not."

Jake Mozik put his hand over his heart, his expression a study in absolute sincerity. But there was a gleam in his eyes that made me laugh even harder. The guy was seriously yanking his best buddy's chain to the amusement of the other guys in the room.

Jake's linemate and butt of the joke, Lad Marchenko, just sat there, shaking his head, waiting for the laughter to die down so he could defend himself.

The two defensemen were tighter than knotted skate strings and played like psychic twins on the ice. Off ice, they acted like bickering teenagers forced to share a bedroom.

I had gotten the rundown on the players from Justin on the way over. Jake, cocky but hilarious. Lad, Jake's straight man with a dry, intelligent wit. Derek Flaherty, Boston Irishman and resident smart-ass. Ian Clark, youngest guy on the team with the most skill, voted most likely to be a virgin. Robbie Lindback, amazing puck handler with very few social skills and a stutter that made him almost silent, unless he was on the ice.

Dirk Bennett, stable and laid-back, and Tony Dellafranco, the excitable Italian, were both a little older than the other guys, but still eight years younger than me. The age difference didn't matter, though, because the language of hockey was universal among players, no matter where they were from. The guys had made me feel at home, first by welcoming me and second by proceeding to rag the shit out of me. Mostly about my age, which didn't bother me because I could give as good as I got. My ex-girlfriend would've turned up her nose and told me it was because I was the mental age of these kids.

Which was part of the reason she was the ex. There'd been other problems, like the fact that she was a cheating bitch who'd traded up for a career NHL player who'd been snowed under by her stunning beauty. By the time she'd left, I'd been damn glad to be rid of her toxicity. And I actually pitied the guy who'd ended up with her because I knew, sure as shit, she'd cheat on him, too.

While most of these guys were too young to be married, I wasn't surprised when the conversation turned to women. Or rather, the lack of sex among all of them.

Apparently, since none of them had been getting laid, super-stition had set in. And hockey players were insanely superstitious. Everybody knew you didn't mess with a streak. If you weren't getting laid and your team was winning, well, then, you did without until you started to lose.

"The only one of us who gets any is Franco, the bastard." Jake motioned toward Tony with his water bottle. "He has regular girlfriend and gets laid before every game. The rest of us only love ourselves."

As the rest of the guys cracked up around me and threw chips at Jake, I shook my head and grinned. I'd already figured out that Jake deliberately butchered the English language for dramatic effect. But I couldn't deny the guy was funny as hell.

But since Jake had brought up the subject…

"So I ran into Jess Gardiner today in the hall—"

A chorus of groans went up around the table.

"Dude, don't even." Justin shook his head. "You're totally not gonna score there. Not ever. She's really nice but you are *so* not gonna get anywhere with Miss Jess."

I frowned. "*Miss* Jess?"

Derek huffed out a sarcastic laugh, dark red hair falling over into his eyes as he shook his head.

"Man, she's hockey royalty. You know that, right? The legendary Doug Gardiner's daughter. Seems nice but she *never* gives players a second look off the ice. Probably thinks she's too good for us."

"She does not appear stuck up." Lad leaned back into his chair as they all crowded around a table made for four. "But no one has cracked her case yet."

"Or figured out how to get in her pants— Ow!" Derek rubbed the back of his head where Tony had smacked him. "What the hell, dude?"

"I'm not your dude and no wonder you can't get a girl to go

out on a second date with you. Your fuckin' mouth is a disgrace. Grow the fuck up."

"I've heard some of the other guys say she scouts for Coach."

Everyone turned to Robbie like he'd returned from the dead.

"Holy crap." Dirk huffed out a laugh. "Don't use up all your words for the month at one shot. There's still another three weeks."

Robbie rolled his eyes and shot Dirk the finger, though Robbie's cheeks turned bright red.

"No, no, he is absolutely right." Jake smacked Robbie on the back, hard enough to make the guy pitch forward. "I hear same thing. She has good eye, they say. Knows more about hockey than most men in front office. I think she is very hot but lesser men could be threatened. I would not be threatened."

"And you, my friend, have tried and failed." Lad raised his beer at Jake.

"She mistakenly believes I am too young for her." Jake shrugged. "Not a bad problem."

"So how old is she?" I asked.

"Probably too young for you, old man."

Justin's wide grin made me laugh along with the table, but I had to wonder if Justin wasn't right.

Jess

I had my head bent over my desk, my entire attention focused on the sketch I was working on Wednesday morning.

The team had a game tonight and I should be running down my checklist but I'd started this sketch and couldn't seem to stop.

So when I heard a man say, "Apparently, I have you to thank

for my job," I gave a short, sharp scream and embarrassed the hell out of myself.

My head shot up to find six-plus-feet of amused player standing in my doorway.

And when I caught sight of Will's grin, I wanted to take the pencil in my hand and poke him with it. Nowhere that'd injure him, of course. The team needed him.

"Oh my god, are you seriously going to sneak up on me every time? I'm going to get you a little bell to wear around your neck."

The damn man's smile grew even wider and I had to admit it was a pretty nice smile. Totally transformed his face. I'd watched enough film to know Will's game face was intense. When he was on the ice, he was all business.

I'd expected him to be as serious and intense off the ice as well so I was taken off guard by his easy smiles.

And, if I was honest with myself, I had to admit the damn man was sweetly adorable when he smiled. Maybe someday I'd tell him that.

Today was not that day.

"Blue's my favorite color."

I shook my head, trying to figure out what the hell his favorite color had to do with anything.

"And why do I need to know that?"

"In case you want to buy me that bell. I don't want to make you mad at me every time you see me. And it goes with my eyes."

Of course, that made me look even more closely at his eyes. Damn him, he had beautiful eyes.

Which meant absolutely nothing.

"Can I do something for you, Mr. MacDonald?"

Leaning a shoulder against the doorframe, he looked so at ease, I couldn't imagine that this was a guy who had a reputation for being an enforcer.

Yeah, he was big but he wasn't huge. He wouldn't be out of place in a goalie uniform these days. Years ago, when my dad had first started scouting, goalies didn't need to be the massive walls they were today. But back when I'd first started going to games with my dad, every team had a guy they called an enforcer. The guy you put on the ice when you needed to retaliate for a bad hit or you needed to rile up your team.

Will had been that guy for several teams, but in the past few years, the game had changed, at least at the NHL level, which had trickled down to the AHL. The fighters had gone by the wayside for the most part and the skill guys, the ones whose highlights you saw on SportsCenter, were more in demand than ever.

But you still needed guys like Will, the guys who the team knew they could rely on to stand up for guys like Robbie and Ian, who skated like the hot shots they were but didn't know how to land a punch to save their soul.

"Just wanted to say thanks."

I frowned, confused. "For what?"

"For recommending me to Coach Scott."

I blinked. *Oh shit.* "I'm not sure I know what you mean."

He watched me so intently, I had a few seconds to wonder if Coach had actually told Will I'd recommended him.

"Yeah, I'm pretty sure you do know what I mean. What I find interesting is that you don't want anyone to know."

Shaking my head, I raised my eyebrows and tried to look… well, innocent. "Still not sure what you're talking about but I've got to get this sketch finished—"

"So you do it but no one's supposed to know about it." Walking into the room, Will shut the door behind him and draped himself into the chair across from my desk. "Damn, that must suck."

Refusing to give him the upper hand, I sighed and made a production out of dropping my pencil and leaning back in my chair. Apparently, he wasn't going to be a good boy and leave.

And I had to admit, the view wasn't bad. Like most players, he came to the arena for practice dressed in sweats and a t-shirt.

But even in shapeless nylon and worn cotton, there was something about him that made me want to put my hands on his chest and pet him like a cat.

A little ping of regret hit me low in my gut because that just was *not* going to happen. Because no, he wasn't wrong. It did kind of suck. But I wasn't going to tell him that.

"Is there something I can help you with, Mr. MacDonald? Otherwise—"

"Well, first off, you can call me Will. We're both adults. And I'm not *that* much older than you."

The slight emphasis in his sentence made me look a little more closely at him. Was he actually asking how old I was?

Does he think I'm too young?

Shit, not what I should be thinking about.

"Okay, Will. Is that all?"

"Actually, no, it's not. Come out with me after the game tomorrow."

My mouth dropped open before I could stop it. Stunned, my brain spun for several seconds before I blinked and got it to stop.

"I… That's not a good idea."

His head cocked to the side. "Why?"

"Because I don't date players."

"Why not?"

My eyebrows rose. "Seriously? How old are you?"

"Thirty-three. But you know that already." He pointed his chin at me. "How old are you?"

My eyes widened even more. "Don't you know you're not supposed to ask a woman her age?"

Now he shrugged, looking completely unconcerned. "Why? You know pretty much everything about me, apparently, except which side I adjust to. Or maybe you know that, too."

My lips parted but I couldn't think of a damn thing to say. And now I was thinking about things I shouldn't be thinking about.

I had to struggle to keep my gaze from dipping to his crotch but I managed. Barely. Which was probably exactly what he wanted.

Will wasn't known for instigating most fights, but the damn man was a menace just the same.

I was tempted to take the high road and tell him his crude mouth wasn't appreciated. But that would be pretty hypocritical considering I'd grown up around hockey players and only just managed to keep my own dirty mouth in check when I was in public.

So, I was going to have to be straightforward.

"Look, Mr. MacDonald. You're a good player. You're going to make a great addition to the team. I wish you luck. But I'm not going to go out with you. I don't date players."

He didn't look surprised, and he didn't get out of his chair and leave like I'd hoped he would. "Who do you date?"

No one.

I stopped my grimace mid-formation. "None of your damn business."

His lips quirked into a grin that made my thighs clench and my girly parts get hot.

Oh no. No, no, no. That wasn't happening. I'd given up lusting after hockey players a long, long time ago. Either they broke your damn heart when they left you behind or you found out they were engaged to their high school sweetheart back home but they had an "arrangement" and no, screwing around was not cheating.

Okay, maybe I had a few issues but that just meant I was absolutely right not to say yes.

Even though you want to.

No, I didn't. I really didn't.

Liar.

As if he could read my mind, Will's smile got even wider. "So there's no one steaming up your sheets right now?"

Damn him. Why the hell was I now imagining him naked on my bed?

Fuck.

With an effort, I smiled, making sure he knew it was fake. "I am not going to dignify your question with an answer. I think you'd probably better leave because if you don't, Coach is going to wonder why you're limping."

"And I think he'd laugh his ass off when he found out I pissed you off so bad, you kicked me in the balls."

A laugh bubbled up along with the knowledge that this man had no filter and absolutely no idea how to take no for an answer.

"Mr. MacDo—"

"Will." He shrugged like he didn't have a care in the world. "Call me Will and I'll leave."

I opened my mouth to call him a few other choice words, but out of the corner of my eye, I saw the organization's event manager walk into the main office. Judi hadn't noticed that I had someone in my office, but that wouldn't last long. Judi prided herself on knowing exactly what everyone in the entire organization was up to. It wouldn't take long for her to put one and one together and make a complete mess of my life.

Women didn't get far in the business side of this sport if they slept with the players. It wasn't professional, especially if you wanted to climb the ladder and work for an NHL team.

I didn't want a reputation like that. And I didn't want to sleep with this damn man.

Liar, liar, pants on fire.

Okay, now who's acting like the twelve-year-old?

Smiling a smile that held a very sharp edge, I leaned back into my chair.

It might take Will a few times to get the hint because apparently he was dense, but he would understand eventually.

"Mr. MacDonald. I have work to do. And if you don't leave, you're going to be late for practice. And I'm pretty sure you don't want to be late for your first day of practice with your new team."

His slow smile made certain parts of me flutter. And I didn't mean my heart.

"Okay, Miss Jess. I can take a hint."

Relief made me suck in a breath. It had absolutely nothing to do with that smile. Nothing at all.

But I couldn't help but watch his every move as he stood and turned toward the door. And if my gaze happened to land on that perfect ass… Well, no one would know.

"But just to be clear." He stopped in the door, turned to look over his shoulder and grinned at me a little more. "I'll be back to ask again."

And now my heart did give a traitorous little thump. "The answer will be the same."

"Well, I'm nothing if not persistent." He knocked on the doorjamb. "Talk to you later, Miss Jess."

Only when I sucked in air did I realize I'd been holding my breath.

"Hey, Will. How's it going?"

I hadn't exactly been dreading this meeting but I had to admit I hadn't been looking forward to it.

Rising from the bench, I held my hand out to Cary Lenville. "Going well. Glad to be here."

"And we're glad to have you here."

I was aware that everyone else in the room was paying attention while trying not to make it obvious. The rest of the team were in various stages of dress for practice. Cary was ready to go, of course. The guy always had been an over-achiever.

"Lori's looking forward to seeing you again. We're hosting the team dinner next week so you'll get to see her there if you don't catch her at the games this weekend."

Surprised Cary had mentioned Lori, considering their history, I nodded. "It'll be nice to see her again."

Cary's expression didn't change a bit when he nodded. "See you on the ice."

Then he walked off and I went back to getting dressed.

Well, that had gone better than I'd expected. Honestly, I hadn't known what to expect but I should've realized Cary would never do anything in front of his team. Because the guy really wasn't a dick. They just didn't see eye to eye on almost everything.

"So, you and Cary. There's history there, right?"

I glanced over at Tony, watching him with steady dark eyes. He'd kept his voice low so only I could hear him.

Pulling my sweater over my head, I shook my hair out of my eyes. "We played together in California for part of a season. We weren't the best of friends but that was a long time ago. I've grown up since then."

Tony grinned. "Yeah, right. So, hey. I saw you coming down the stairs earlier. Did you need to make a stop in the front office before practice for something?"

I grabbed my helmet, shoved my hair out of my face, and jammed the helmet on my head. "I don't know what you're talking about."

"Uh-huh." Tony's smirk made me want to pop him in the nose. "I'm rooting for you, buddy, but you're not gonna get anywhere with her."

Fucking hockey players. Worse gossips than old ladies.

I ignored Tony's smartass comment and headed out to the ice. Though the thought that maybe Tony was right niggled at the back of my brain all through practice.

First day with a new team was always a learning experience but this wasn't my first rodeo. Hell, it wasn't even my tenth. Probably more like eighteenth, if I had to guess. But who was counting. I was still getting calls to play and I still got excited to answer those calls.

I'd play until the thrill was gone or the calls didn't come.

Today, I had a little more speed in my stride and maybe a little more enthusiasm. A lot of the guys here were young and I didn't just mean under twenty-five. Nearly a third of the team was twenty-two or younger. Skill players who'd been playing for a decade and more but were still learning to handle the professional side of the game.

Cary and I, at thirty-six, were the oldest players and I watched how the younger forwards took their cues from Cary.

When the team broke into offensive and defensive squads about a half hour into practice, I took a look at my fellow defensemen.

Justin was twenty-four, and though he looked like a huge puppy learning to walk off the ice, the guy flew on skates, like he'd been born with them strapped to his feet.

Derek looked to be a good all-around guy, the class clown who'd never met a swear word he couldn't use in even the most innocent sentence, but determined and focused on ice.

Jake and Lad were all business, more in sync than even the Fransechetti twins, who at nineteen were the team's second-youngest players. Luckily, the identical twins grew their hair different lengths, or I would've never been able to tell them apart.

The only defenseman I hadn't met yet was Joey Constantino, on the IR for concussion and not allowed to skate. With Joey out, we were down a defenseman but apparently Coach would be calling one up from the ECHL affiliate later today.

Practice was practically over when I caught sight of the figure in the arena entrance near the handicapped section.

Jess stood far enough back that I wasn't sure at first it was her. But as I took a few more laps around the ice, I realized I was right. And she was watching me.

Yeah, she was standing there talking to someone, but every now and then her head would move and I could tell she was looking toward the ice.

How long had she been standing there? I'd been rightfully focused on practice and hadn't noticed when she'd shown up, but now I was curious as hell.

Which didn't mean a damn thing because we had a game tonight and I needed to head back to the apartment and eat lunch before I took a nap and headed back to the arena for the team dinner.

"So you, my friend, are probably wondering why I am waiting here for you, yes?"

Jake stood just outside the boards, leaning on his stick wearing a shit-eating grin, no one else around.

Suppressing a grin, I ignored him, heading for the locker room.

Jake easily caught up and matched my stride. "Well, I will tell you. You will need my help with this one."

"Don't know what you're talking about, Jake."

"Yes, you do." Jake tapped me on the arm with the butt end of his stick for emphasis. "I can be an asset in this. I know much about women."

I had to laugh, stopping just outside the door. "And what is it you think you can help me with?"

"She is always here on game nights."

I looked over my shoulder at Jake. "Most of the front office staff is. Not exactly earth-shattering news."

"What you probably do not know is, after the game, she always goes back to her office for ten or fifteen minutes."

My gaze narrowed. "And you know this how?"

"Because I am an observant guy. And because one night I had to drop off something in the office and saw her there."

"What's she doing?"

Jake shrugged. "I do not know. Writing report or something.

What does it matter? You can have a few minutes alone with her. Ask her out for a drink. Maybe she will like you better after a few beers."

The glint in Jake's pale blue eyes made me want to smack the guy. But he had given me a decent tip so I'd give the guy a pass. This time.

"Thanks."

Jake gave a little bow. "Is no problem. I have a feeling you will have more luck than I did. Bastard."

Chapter 3

Jess

"Hey, Jess, how are you?"

"Oh, hey, Lori. Sorry, didn't see you. Busy as always."

Cary's wife laughed and squeezed my arm. "You work way harder than you should. We need to do a girls' night out. The guys are on the road this coming week; we should plan to meet one night."

"That sounds awesome." I nodded earnestly. "Absolutely. But right now, I've got to run. I've got a group of fifty senior citizens complete with walkers, canes, and enough alcohol to sedate an entire team in two suites and their food is delayed. I'm having visions of rowdy little old ladies tossing their bras at the ice."

Lori's laughter rang out again and I smiled, even though my stress level was high enough to make my heart race.

I had several large groups tonight, including the seniors, who were funny as hell and probably going to run out of alcohol before the end of the second period. I hadn't expected them to drink more than the suite full of businessmen on the other side of the arena.

I also had two children's birthday parties, each with almost twenty people, and a school group of nearly a hundred kids and adults.

"You definitely have your hands full tonight," Lori waved as she started to move away, "so I won't hold you up any longer. But I *am* going to hold you to our date."

"I'll text, I promise. Gotta go!"

Hustling away, I got to the senior center's box just as the team was taking the ice for the start of the game.

It was just another game, one of seventy-six times the team would skate out onto the ice this season. No big deal.

I'd seen this scene happen more times than I could count.

Still, I stopped to watch. And to tell myself I wasn't watching for one infuriating player.

And now you're lying to yourself.

I didn't even need to see his number to realize I'd already spotted him.

Will was a big guy, one of the biggest on the team. It made him easier to pick out, but I realized I would've known him if he'd been in a crowd of guys with the exact same build. It was the way he skated, so deliberately.

Damn. *Damn, damn, damn.* This was not good.

I refused to fall for a hockey player. No way in hell.

Tearing my gaze away from the ice, I put on my game face and waded into the fray.

Tonight was going to be one of those nights when my face would hurt from smiling. And that wasn't a bad thing.

The seniors in this party were freaking hilarious. Smiling, funny, happy to be out and about.

"Wow, what I wouldn't give to work around those men all day." A tiny white-haired woman smiled at me as I headed for the exit on my way to the next suite. "Men didn't look like that when I was your age. Lucky girl to work around that eye candy all day."

"They are definitely nice to look at," I agreed. "But you don't want to be anywhere near the locker room after practice. You'd change your mind about getting up close and personal."

"My sense of smell doesn't work as well it did fifty years ago, babe." Another woman who had to be at least ninety stepped up beside the other. "So that definitely wouldn't be a problem. I'm sure I could show those boys a few new tricks. The young don't have a monopoly on sex."

"These young people forget where they came from sometimes, Edie."

"Sex certainly isn't everything in life, but damn, I do like a good tumble every now and then. Thank god for little blue pills."

Swallowing my own burst of laughter, I headed to the next suite to check on that group of seniors.

"I don't have a clue what you're talking about, John. There's three quarters in hockey, not four."

"How can there be only three quarters? And when's halftime?"

On my next stop, the businessmen weren't even paying attention to the game, all of them wrapped in private discussions, a few of them stopping to smile at me as I walked through to check with the organizer to see if they needed anything.

One guy deliberately caught my eye and smiled. Nice-looking. Maybe thirty, short brown hair, nice blue eyes, sincere smile. I smiled in return as I made my way out the door.

I'd be back later. Maybe I'd say hi.

He's not your type. Way too clean-cut.

Ignoring that little voice in my head, I made my rounds to the rest of the groups then stopped to talk to the catering manager to see if there were any problems. Then, since everything was running smoothly at the moment and there were ten minutes before the end of the period, I made my way back up to the private box where the injured and scratched players sat. Tonight, three guys sat hunched over the wall, completely focused on the game.

They barely noticed as I took a seat at the other end of the row to watch a few minutes of the game. They all knew me, were used to seeing me around, so they never really took notice of what I was doing.

The Syracuse team had several young players I'd been watching this season, and since Syracuse was in the same division as the Redtails, I'd already seen them a couple of times.

But there was one guy who stood out even more than the kids.

At twenty-eight, T.J. Delauria hadn't yet had his shot at the NHL and that baffled the hell out of me. Everything I'd heard about him had been positive. Steady right winger with good plus-minus numbers. Fast skater, not flashy, but something had changed with his game this year. Something good. Kind of like he'd hit another gear. He'd played overseas last season and since his return, he'd been even more focused.

I'd talked to dad about him and he'd told me to keep my eye on the guy.

And I was. He'd already scored a goal off a juicy rebound that would make the Redtails goalie, Shane, obsess for hours after the game. And he'd had another couple of good chances.

But even as I tried to keep my focus on Delauria, my gaze kept wandering to a certain Redtails sweater with a fourteen on the back.

Will didn't have any points yet but it wasn't for lack of trying. In fact, he and Justin played like they'd been on the same line for months instead of days.

He was a skilled skater, though not as fast as some, and moved the puck well. He cleared the crease and blocked shots but he wasn't afraid to shoot and when he did, most were on net.

In the past couple of years, he'd become much more of an offensive defenseman, something a lot of people overlooked when they talked about him. They mentioned how he took stupid penalties and was fast to drop his gloves. But that shift in his playing was exactly why he'd caught my eye.

It was almost like he'd changed his mind-set, something that was really hard to do, especially for guys who'd had a certain style of play ingrained in them since they were ten.

For the next few minutes, I allowed myself to simply watch the game, something I didn't get to do much. Usually I was working, whether I was taking care of my groups or doing my other, off-the-books work. Which couldn't really be counted as work. It was a hobby.

Hobby.

I huffed so loudly one of the players turned to look at me. Luckily, something happened on the ice and his attention shifted back. I didn't want to deal with questions right now. I had too many of my own.

Like, what the hell was it about a certain defenseman who made me want to throw out years of caution to find out what it'd be like to be bad? Just for one night.

It had been so damn long since I'd gone on a date and liked a guy enough to bring him home for sex. During the season, I sometimes worked twelve and thirteen hours a day so that didn't leave a lot of time for dating anyway. But even during the summer, when I had a little extra time, I'd maybe hooked up twice.

Had it really been that long since I'd gotten laid?

Maybe I didn't want to think about that too closely. Besides, it wasn't like I didn't have toys so I wasn't a frustrated, needy bitch.

And maybe you need to find someone more suitable to scratch this itch before you do something you'll regret.

Like let Will seduce me.

Not gonna happen, girl.

Didn't mean I could stop thinking about it, though.

Will

Frustration ate at me. The game wasn't going our way and that fucking little Syracuse dipshit prick Mason had been in my face all night, gunning for a fight.

Mason was young, probably all of twenty-three, and looking to get a notch on his belt with the name MacDonald beside it.

And if the kid wasn't careful, he was going to get exactly what he wanted. And maybe sooner rather than later.

The Redtails needed a kick in the ass. We were down two to nothing near the end of the second and we needed to make something happen.

The buzzer sounded for the last in-arena timeout and the players skated to the bench, frustration on all five faces, as well as every face on the bench.

As the coach laid out the strategy for the next play, he made specific eye contact with me.

"I want to see movement out there," Coach Scott said. "I want to see spark. Shoot the puck. Nothing bad comes from shooting the puck. Too many passes, too many turnovers."

When the ref blew his whistle, Coach and I shared another quick glance, and when my shift came, I jumped the boards and charged the puck in their defensive end.

Mason was at my back seconds later, battling me for the puck. I had gotten it tied up in my skates in the corner and Mason was digging. And shoving the butt end of his stick in my ribs whenever he could. I heard the roar of the crowd, heard my team-mates yelling.

Then Mason got in one more hard jab and the crowd started to bang on the glass as I caught sight of Mason's smirk.

So I kicked the puck to my nearest teammate and shoved Mason away with a little more force than before. Mason retaliated with an elbow in my side before skating toward the puck and hitting my teammate Robbie into the boards with a cheap shot.

As Robbie went down on one knee, I shoved Mason away.

"Come on, old man." Mason skated backward as the ref blew his whistle to stop play when Shane covered the puck at the net. "Let's go. Or are you afraid of breaking a hip at your advanced age?"

I had heard that and much worse for the past three years. It had no effect on me, didn't piss me off, but this wasn't about being pissed off.

My team watched intently as Mason circled behind me.

"Come back in a few years when you can grow a beard, kid." Then I deliberately turned my back on him and laughed, shaking my head.

Justin's eyes widened and that was the only warning I needed. I was ready when Mason cross-checked me from behind. I pitched forward, mainly for show, then spun around, landing my fist squarely on Mason's jaw.

Mason's head snapped back and his feet shifted. For a second, I thought the guy was gonna go down, which wouldn't have been a bad thing. But Mason recovered quickly and got in a few quick jabs. Pain sizzled as Mason connected with my right cheekbone then got in a few body shots. But while the younger guy had strength, he let his anger get away from him.

I wasn't pissed. I'd done this dance enough to have calculated out every move ahead of time.

So I was able to let the guy get in a few good blows before I hit him with a bone-rattling body shot then took him to the ice.

I didn't want to hurt the guy. I never fought with that end in mind. And I'd gotten even more aware of the consequences as I'd gotten older.

Getting Mason's head under my arm, I kept him locked down as the linesmen came in to separate us.

And when we both got back to our feet, I nodded at Mason as we made our way back to the bench. We were both getting five-minute penalties for fighting so we were being sent back to the locker room because there was less than four minutes on the clock.

As I passed through the bench, I got a nod and a pat on the back from Coach Scott.

Maybe now we'd score some goddamn goals.

The crowd erupted with a roar and, since the horn hadn't sounded, I knew something other than a goal was going on.

Looking out over the arena from the suite level, I wasn't surprised to find Will squared off with Syracuse's enforcer, Mason.

It should've been a fair fight. Looking at them, you'd think they were evenly matched. Both about the same size and height. But I knew better.

Will would kick the guy's ass.

Wincing as Mason landed the first punch, I bit my tongue against the urge to yell along with the crowd. The sound rose to ear-splitting levels as Will shook off the hit. And then he smiled and the crowd went crazy.

Cocking back his arm, Will threw one solid hit to Mason's jaw and the guy went to the ice. Where he stayed.

Another player would've gloated or taunted. Will simply skated to the bench and headed back to the locker room as there was less than five minute to play in the period.

A minute later, the Redtails got a power-play goal because Mason also got a minor penalty for instigation.

I had been *so* right. The Redtails needed Will. He was the right fit at the right time.

If I was keeping track—

Okay, not if. I *was* keeping track, damn it. I was keeping track of every time I'd been right about a guy and the team who needed him.

As I stood in the hallway outside the suites on the arena's second level, I allowed myself to gloat.

My dad was going to have to pay up on their bet. First, because he hadn't thought Coach Scott would go for Will. And second, because he'd been convinced Will couldn't add anything to a team as stacked with talent as the Redtails.

My dad was one hell of a scout but sometimes he forgot that on paper, things were a lot different than on the ice. Of course, I could count on one finger how many times I'd had a coach take my direct advice. Unlike my dad, who got paid for it. Something I never would.

"Well, damn, I'd hate to be the man who put that look on your face. Everything okay?"

My head shot up and my gaze locked with the businessman I'd noticed earlier. I smiled automatically, my default setting at work.

"Of course. Can I help you, Mr. ..."

"Mike. Mike Northwick." He held out his hand as he came forward and I took it out of habit.

"Jess Gardiner. Nice to meet you."

He held onto my hand when I would've released him and it gave me time to notice how soft his palm was.

Will's had been rough with calluses and cuts, his grip strong but not tight.

Why the hell are you comparing them?

Damn it.

"Nice to meet you, too." Finally, he released my hand. "You look a little flushed. Everything okay?"

"I'm fine. Are you having a good time tonight, Mr. Northwick?"

"Well, the home team could be putting out a little more effort but yeah, I'm enjoying myself."

I had to bite her tongue not to defend my guys, but in my line of work, the customer was always right. I just didn't have to agree with him.

And, just like that, Mike Northwick became a little less attractive.

"Can I do anything for you? Does your group need anything?"

I saw him think about his response and controlled the urge to roll my eyes. If I could read his mind, I was pretty sure he'd be thinking something dirty. And stupid.

And how is that any different than Will?

Nope. Not going there.

"I think we're good, thank you."

Keeping my smile light, I excused myself. I really did have to check in on the rest of the groups before the end of the game.

It took a while to finish my rounds and there were only a few minutes left in the game when I headed for ice level and the Zamboni gate.

The Redtails were still losing, but they'd pulled the goalie and were pressing hard in the offensive end. My gaze unerringly found Will at the blue line, his big, solid body poised and ready to take a shot or crash the net.

His intense focus was no different than anyone else's on the ice but there was something about him that made me stare only at him.

Maybe it was the way he held so still. He didn't shuffle his feet or move his stick or twist his head. He was utterly intent on the game when the puck was in play.

Maybe you're becoming just a little obsessed.

And that really would be a problem because I couldn't even say what it was about Will that made me unable to look away.

Okay, that's total bullshit. You know exactly why.

And there wasn't a damn thing I was going to do about it.

Except stand here and stare at him for these last few minutes of the game.

When the final buzzer sounded, the Redtails had lost by one point, which sucked. This was the second game in a row they'd lost. Definitely not a streak but not something they'd want to continue either.

I was almost ready to turn and head back to my office when I saw Will stand and start to smile as he spoke to Justin, who shook his head and reluctantly grinned as well. Then Will went over to Robbie and bumped his shoulder before skating to center ice to knock helmets with Shane as he headed to the bench.

He exchanged a fist bump and a nod with Cary, standing on the ice at the gate to the bench, before he disappeared down the hall to the locker room.

Trying to ignore the butterflies in my stomach, which were definitely *not* from Will's smile, I made my way back to my office. Had the team won, I'd have heard whoops and cheers but now it was quiet.

And so was my office when I finally sat down at my desk.

I didn't bother to turn on the overhead light. I could find my way around blindfolded and the small lamp I kept on my desk provided more than enough light. Besides, if I turned on the ceiling light, someone would feel compelled to check in on me, and I really only wanted a few minutes of peace and quiet to get my thoughts written down.

Yes, I could do this at home, but I'd learned that if I waited, I lost that sense of urgency I still had here in the arena. My dad had the luxury of being able to write his thoughts out as they happened. I didn't.

For the next fifteen minutes, I typed furiously. And when I was finished, I read back through them and smiled.

Damn, I *was* good at this. Too damn bad I'd never get a job doing what I was so damn good at.

My smile quickly faded.

I'd told myself, when I'd finally settled on a sports marketing major at Penn State University almost ten years ago, that I'd never regret my choice. And there was nothing to regret. I'd graduated with honors and had had my choice of jobs at graduation. I'd taken the job with the Elmira ECHL team and had never looked back.

And if I occasionally longed for something I'd never have… Well, that was just human nature, right?

"No rest for the wicked, huh? Shouldn't you be gone by now?"

I sucked in a sharp breath but my brain had already identified that deep voice and my body had responded. Thankfully, the man in the doorway couldn't see how my nipples had peaked, both because of the dark and because I wore a padded bra. One of the first lessons a woman learned when I worked in an ice arena in a male-dominated sport.

"I was just getting ready to leave. I could ask you the same thing. Is there something you need, Mr. MacDonald?"

As he moved away from the door, the light from my lamp began to illuminate his body but hadn't reached his face. But I still heard the smile in his voice when he said, "I guess you could say that."

The teasing tone of his voice made my thighs clench, damn him.

"Well, then you better tell me what it is so I can get it for you. Then we can both go home. I'm sure you need to rest up after tonight's game."

He stopped right at the edge of the other side of my desk and now he was close enough for me to see that smile on his lips.

Damn, damn, damn. He had a beautiful mouth. A mouth that made me wonder how it'd feel on my skin.

Which wasn't going to happen. Like, ever.

"Are you trying to politely tell me I need to get to bed because I'm old?"

I rolled my eyes, made sure he could see it. "I'm not the one who keeps bringing up your age. Maybe you're the one with the problem."

With another soft laugh, he dropped into the chair across from my desk. I bit my lip against the urge to return his smile, but it was hard to keep a straight face. His smile taunted and made him that much more handsome. Such a different man than the one on the ice.

But I knew that intensity was still there, lurking under the surface.

He must be amazing in bed.

Totally the wrong thought to have at this minute. Luckily, it was probably too dark for him to see the flush on my cheeks.

But, of course, his eyes narrowed and I had to wonder if he knew exactly what I was thinking.

"Oh, I've got a lot of problems, but right now, I'm not so worried about my age. I've got a few other things on my mind."

Don't do it. Don't— "Like what?"

His smile widened. "Well, my face hurts like a sonuvabitch right now. Fucking Mason has one hell of a right hook." He raised his hand to rub at his jaw, and I now saw the bruise that would probably be a spectacular color tomorrow. "Guess I should be glad he didn't go after Robbie. The kid probably would've broken his hand on Mason's jaw."

My heart gave a seriously unnecessary flutter at the fact that he'd stuck up for his teammate. When had I become such a girl about things like that?

"And how is your hand? It's not like you don't need it."

"I can take a hell of a lot more damage than some of these

kids. They're fucking twigs. I'm surprised Colin doesn't break a bone every time he gets checked into the boards."

Shaking my head, I had to work to hold back a smile. "You make them sound like they're fragile. Hockey players are the least fragile athletes I've ever met."

"But our hearts get broken just like everyone else, hon."

I laughed, couldn't help myself. He looked so sincere but that twinkle in his eyes… It was killer.

"Did you want something in particular, Mr. MacDonald, or are you just here to delay my departure for some reason?"

"What would you say if I asked you out for drinks one night?"

I had to bite my tongue against the urge to say yes. The thought didn't even surprise me. "I'd say I don't date hockey players."

He didn't look surprised by my answer. "Because you work with them or because you don't like them?"

"I love the game and I like hockey players. I just don't think I should date men I work with. It can create…problems."

His gaze narrowed. "Have some experience with those problems, do you?"

"Not for many years, no. Because I don't date hockey players."

"So that's a hard-and-fast rule?"

"Pretty much so, yes."

"And I guess sex is out of the question?"

I blinked and my mouth dropped open. I wanted to laugh because I could still see that glint in his eyes, the one that wanted to rile me up, see how far he could push me. But I could see that intensity lurking there as well, the patient predator stalking his prey. My heart gave a little flip to realize I was the prey.

And since I now had an image of me and Will in bed, I swallowed hard and took a breath before leaning back in my chair, never breaking his gaze.

"Sex is never out of the question, but I definitely don't have sex with hockey players, especially not hockey players on my team."

Mirroring my movement, he leaned back in his chair, putting his right ankle on his left knee and resting his left hand on his ankle. The casual position made my breath catch in my throat and that made not one damn bit of sense.

He wore a suit, as all the players did on game day. His was blue, his shirt white, the first couple of buttons undone. I could just see a hint of skin in that vee and I had the insane urge to crawl onto my desk, lean forward, and lick him right there.

I wondered what he'd do if I said exactly what was on my mind. Not that I would. I loved my job and would do nothing to jeopardize it. But still…

"I guess I can understand your position." He shrugged. "Lot of these guys are kids. Too unstable, don't really know what to do with a woman. You need an older guy, one who knows what he wants."

My lips twitched and I had to work hard to keep a straight face. I didn't want to encourage him. Couldn't encourage him because even though I might want to play with this man, I couldn't allow myself to. I had to remind myself that I wasn't charmed by the whole alpha-male thing.

"So you think I have daddy issues?"

His face screwed up in a grimace. "Jesus, I hope not. I've met your dad." For a second, I thought he might add something, but whatever he was thinking, he kept to himself. "No, hon. I mean you need a guy who knows how to make you scream his name while he's going down on you."

Oh my god.

I blinked and my lips parted but I had no idea what would come out so I quickly snapped them shut. I should be offended. Should tell him I didn't appreciate his lewd comments.

Instead, my thighs clenched again and my gut hollowed as heat exploded through me.

It took me several long seconds before I could get my brain to reset. Hopefully, he'd think I was pissed off and not turned on.

I was still trying to think of what to say when he continued.

"You sure you don't want to get that drink?"

No, I wasn't sure, damn him. My resolution was fading fast.

His steady gaze caught and held mine until I felt like I couldn't breathe.

Swallowing hard, I deliberately looked down at my keyboard, filed my notes and shut down my computer. I'd finish at home tonight. Or tomorrow morning. My dad would wait.

Right now, I needed to get out of my office before I did or said something I couldn't take back.

"I need to get going, Mr. MacDonald. If you have nothing else to say..."

I was proud of the way my voice held steady, even if nothing else was. My hands had a slight tremble and my thighs quivered. And I was trying my damnedest to ignore what was going on internally.

He shrugged, as if he hadn't just made my panties wet. "I guess not. At least not now. Come on, I'll walk you to your car."

I wanted to tell him no but he'd probably get the idea that he'd had an effect on me.

He had. He just didn't need to know it.

I gave him a small smile. "Sure. Just let me get my things together."

Standing, I grabbed my coat off the hook behind my desk and swiped my tote off the floor. I'd already switched out my low heels for boots. It was January in Pennsylvania and there'd been snow on the ground for the past week.

And unlike most of the other women who worked here, I wore a skirt. I didn't go out on the ice so there was no danger of slipping and embarrassing the hell out of myself, and it presented

a more professional image, something I was very careful to culti-
vate. I had an endgame and I did everything I could to ensure I
got there.

Will stood by the door, tall and imposing, watching me with
that slight grin.

I couldn't help myself. I stopped beside him, my gaze caught
on the bruise already darkening on his chin. He also had a slight
cut above his eye, and his forehead still bore the marks from his
helmet.

I was used to seeing the guys like this, battered and bruised.
Will's chin would be all sorts of different colors tomorrow and he
probably had a few on his body I couldn't see.

My free hand clenched into a fist in an attempt to keep from
touching him.

I lost that battle.

His gaze locked with mine as I raised my hand and ran my
index finger along his jaw, just below the bruise. The muscles in
his jaw clenched but he didn't flinch away, and that glint in his
eye got hotter until I thought I might have to look away.

"Does it hurt?"

He didn't answer right away. When he did, I swore his voice
had dropped at least an octave. "It hurts. Just not there."

I raised my brows, trying to corral a smile. "You took a
couple of hard hits to the boards tonight. I'm sure at your age, it
takes you a little longer to recover."

I knew exactly what I was saying and wondered how he'd
take it. Would he play or take offense?

His mouth spread in a wide grin and I had my answer.

"Now you're just being mean." Raising one hand, he caught
mine before I could draw away, bringing my index finger closer
to his mouth. "And you should know I'm not one to let a slight go
unchallenged."

Before I could say anything else, he tugged my hand even
closer and bit the tip of my finger.

It didn't hurt. It stung a little but it did worse damage internally. My sex clenched against a wave of desire so fierce, I had to bite my tongue against a gasp.

And when he sucked on the tip of my finger and flicked at it with his tongue, I had to swallow hard because, oh my god, my mouth was watering.

Damn, damn, damn. How could you be so stupid?

This was exactly where I shouldn't be. Not this close to him, with my damn finger in his mouth and his tongue making me want him to use it somewhere other than my finger.

Thank god he couldn't read my mind because if he could…

In the next second, my hand was free but his lips had covered my mouth.

My breath froze in my lungs, my body poised for…what?

I had no idea because the heat of his kiss had seeped through my lips and into my bloodstream, making me sizzle from the inside out.

Damn him.

His mouth moved over mine with a burning passion that shot through my blood. My hands itched to grab his shoulders and pull him closer but I knew I shouldn't. I should push him away.

Then his hands landed on my shoulders and I shivered, sensation rushing through me like electricity. Combined with his lips moving over mine, playing with me, he coaxed me into a response I knew I shouldn't give.

And yet…

My lips softened under his, parted slightly, and my traitorous tongue slipped by to flick at his lips.

A deep rumble sounded in his chest and his hands slid from my shoulders to my back, where he only had to apply a little pressure to bring me closer.

I took that first step and he took the opening and ran with it. His hands spread across my back, pressing me tight against his broad chest. I tilted my head up at a sharper angle, giving him more access to my mouth. Which he took immediately.

He kissed me harder now, his tongue slipping between my lips to tangle with mine. His taste, warm and masculine, exploded in my mouth and I sucked him in, giddy with triumph when he groaned and his hands spread across my back to pull me even closer.

My tote fell to the floor. I didn't remember releasing it but now I had both hands free to grab his shoulders and hold tight.

Which was apparently exactly what he wanted.

As soon as my fingers curled into firm muscle, he shifted the kiss into overdrive, twisting his head to get an even better angle.

He attacked my mouth with such deliberate intent, I wanted to urge him to let loose. But the still-sane part of my brain telling me this was crazy held me back.

Instead, I let him explore my mouth at his own pace and tried not to enjoy the hell out of it. Which I did anyway.

Because, oh my god, the man could kiss. He didn't let me up for air except for small hurried breaths that left me only half-satisfied, my fingers digging into his shoulders until I was afraid I might actually hurt him.

He didn't seem to mind, just shifted the angle of his mouth so he could take even more.

My breathing came even heavier now, as the ache in my gut began to spread lower. I wanted to rub my breasts against him, wanted to press my hips against his and feel just how much he wanted me.

Because according to this kiss, he did. I wanted to lean back and look down, see just how much of that old saying was true about a guy and the size of his feet. Because I'd seen Will's skates and they were huge.

And it had been a damn long time since I'd kissed a guy who made me want to stick my hands down his pants on the first date.

Hell, this wasn't even a date.

We were kissing. In my office. In the arena where we both worked.

My eyes snapped open and I broke away. To his credit, he let me. He released me immediately but he didn't back off. All I could hear was our heavy breathing and the sound of the heating system as it kicked in.

Blinking up at him, I carefully removed my hands from his shoulders and took a step back.

"I need to get home."

"Yeah, it's getting late and I've got to be up for practice tomorrow."

Blinking at his immediate acquiescence, I watched with wide eyes as he bent. My heart sped up as I thought he was going to kiss me again but he kept going until he'd snagged my coat off the floor.

My cheeks heated but I told myself he wouldn't notice. I should've known I'd be wrong. His gaze narrowed when he towered over me again, staring down at me.

"Jess—"

"Could you give me a hand with that?"

I turned, giving him my back, then glanced over my shoulder at him. When he didn't immediately help me into my coat, I raised my eyebrows.

That put the slight grin back on his face and he made a show of shaking out my coat and sliding it up my outstretched arms.

The thick woolen material immediately made me too warm but I'd be out in the cold soon enough.

Then maybe I'd stick my head in a snowbank just to point out how stupid I'd been.

"Thank you."

Without waiting for him to respond, I grabbed my tote off the floor and headed for the exit. He followed at my heels, his long legs eating up way more real estate than mine did with each step.

Since we were the only ones left on this floor as far as I should tell, I dug my keys out of my tote and locked the office before heading for the stairwell down to the entrance into the side parking lot.

Will followed at my back, silently stalking me.

My brain continued to buzz with white noise. Sleep would probably be a no-show tonight. Jesus, I'd been so stupid.

Okay, maybe not stupid. Just… No, stupid was definitely the right word.

Christ, I'd have to fix this.

Tomorrow.

Tonight, my brain kept skipping back to that kiss.

Luckily, we ran into no one, the only sound in the building the compressors firing up and rumbling. The evening security guard was probably making rounds so there was no one at the door when we reached it.

Stopping with my hand on the door, I straightened my back and stared up at him.

"This can't happen again. It was a mistake."

His eyebrows rose and that glint was back in his eyes. "By 'this,' I assume you mean that kiss."

I swallowed a sigh. "You know that's exactly what I mean."

He shrugged like it hadn't meant a damn thing to him. "Sure, if that's how you want to play it."

My brows lifted. Seriously? He wasn't going to give me a hassle? He'd just kissed me like he'd wanted to strip me naked and lay me out on my desk and it hadn't meant a damn thing to him?

Oh god. I was losing it. I should be happy I'd gotten off so easily, not pissed that he wasn't going to fight for me.

Taking a deep breath, I nodded, even though I wanted to stick my finger in his side and jab him.

"Fine. Good night, Mr. MacDonald."

His grin was back. "See you tomorrow, Miss Jess."

My teeth gritted at his tone. A little mocking, a whole lot of teasing. "Not if I see you first" was on the tip of my tongue but I managed to bite it back. How juvenile would that have been?

I was at my car when I heard him say, "But that was no damn mistake. And you won't be able to hide from me forever."

I turned to gape at him but he was already hauling himself into his Jeep Cherokee. He started the engine then waited until I got into my Subaru and drove away before he followed me out of the parking lot.

Chapter 4

Will

"Damn, that looks nasty, even worse than yesterday. Hope you aren't planning to get laid tonight after the game. Women'll take one look at you and run in the other direction. We'll have to put a bag over your head if you come out with us after the game."

I gave Justin the finger as I headed for the freezer to grab one of the many icepacks all hockey players kept there.

"Does it hurt as bad as it looks?"

Yeah, it still hurt like a bitch and I'd already downed three ibuprofen. "Nah, it's fine."

Justin shrugged and went back to shoveling scrambled eggs into his mouth. It was eight a.m. Friday morning and we had to be at the arena by nine-thirty to get ready for practice at ten.

"Man, practice was rough yesterday but considering the last two games, I thought Coach would be a lot tougher." Justin sounded like he still had a mouth full of eggs. "He seems to like you, though. Didn't give you much shit for that fight with Mason Wednesday night."

Sitting at the table holding the ice pack to my jaw, I let Justin ramble. And Jesus, the guy could talk. Stream of consciousness had nothing on him. But while Justin allowed his brain to unwind, it gave me a little time to think about Jess.

I hadn't seen her at all yesterday. After practice, I'd made up some excuse to go to her office, hoping to catch her alone for a few minutes.

I'd been looking forward to it, almost as much as I'd been looking forward to getting back on the ice and working out the kinks from the game the night before.

But she hadn't been there. Her intern had been happy to tell her she wasn't going to be in until later that afternoon because of sponsorship meetings.

The crushing sense of loss I'd felt when I'd realized I wasn't going to see her had stopped me in my tracks for several seconds.

I'd talked to her twice, for Christ's sake.

Yeah, and you already know she's one-of-a-kind.

"So the game's probably gonna get chippy tonight." Justin stood, snapping my attention back to the conversation. "I think Mason's gonna be in your face most of the game. Gotta get my stuff together. You wanna drive in together?"

With a sigh, I tossed the ice pack back into the freezer and started to make my own breakfast. "Sounds good."

At least that would stop me from doing anything stupid. Like asking Jess out to lunch and getting shot down.

But even as I ate breakfast and drove Justin to practice, I couldn't stop thinking about that damn kiss.

I wondered if I'd thought about it as much as I had the past day.

Had I come on too strong?

Yeah, probably. I was like a bull in a china shop most of the time, but I'd never seen much point in pretending you didn't want something or someone when, really, they were all you could think about.

And she hadn't said no. If she had, I would've backed the hell away immediately. Instead, she'd kissed me back.

Had I misread her response?

I didn't think so but I wasn't the sharpest tool in the shed when it came to women so anything was possible.

But… No, she'd kissed me back. I hadn't been wrong about that.

Christ almighty, I didn't need this. Not now. Didn't need to be attracted to a woman at the exact moment I got to a new team, one with as many expectations as this one held.

Then again, I wasn't getting any younger and why the hell should I deny myself a woman I wanted? Was I destined to be alone for the rest of this life?

And why the fuck was I even thinking about this anyway?

I had to get ready for practice.

An hour later, I was about to skate out onto the ice when Coach called my name from the hall outside the locker room.

Will stopped, waiting for Coach to catch up to me.

"How's the face?"

I shrugged. "Doesn't hurt."

Coach's mouth moved in a slight grin. "Glad to hear it. Don't get a matching one tonight. No stupid penalties. I need you to play smart. Stay out of the box. You and Justin played well together Wednesday and I expect the same from you tonight. But I want more leadership out there. I want more effort."

"You'll get it."

A few guys passed us on the way to the ice, keeping their gazes trained straight ahead. Only Cary made eye contact as he passed. No smirk but definitely some kind of message there.

I was going to have to deal with Cary soon.

"I know I will." Coach smacked me on the shoulder. "See you on the ice."

Coach didn't wait for a response. He headed out through the gate and I sucked in a deep breath before I followed.

Time to get my head in the game. And a certain woman out of my head.

Jess

I found myself in the box that night, watching the end of the third period.

Watching one certain player, in particular. After I'd spent all of yesterday telling myself I needed to stay away from Will MacDonald. Far away.

Damn him.

There was something about him that made every single female hormone in my body sit up and take notice.

What I couldn't figure out was why. Yes, he was older than most of the other guys and yeah, that was appealing. He had a maturity that was sexy as hell.

And when I watched him skate… I couldn't help but imagine watching all those muscles work while he was naked.

I wanted to run my hands over that broad chest and down those strong thighs and over that tight ass—

Shit. I had to stop or the guys sitting here with me would think I was about to spontaneously combust. My cheeks felt like they were on fire and if anyone looked over at me right now, they'd want to know what was wrong.

I couldn't exactly say, "Oh, I want to jump our new defenseman. Don't mind me."

Dammit, I should head back down to the suites to make sure my groups were happy but Will was on the ice and the Redtails were rushing the puck into their offensive zone to the cheers of the crowd.

Neither team had scored, though it'd been one hell of a game so far. The cheering crowd chanted, "Let's go, Redtails," as the offense set up their shot, looking for an open lane.

But the Milwaukee defense was tough and the Redtails couldn't get a shot. And when Robbie finally took one, Milwaukee slapped it out of the way easily.

The opposing team could've had a breakaway but Will made an incredible move to block the pass and then made a shot on net that had the crowd on their feet. While it didn't go in, the Milwaukee goalie gave up a rebound that Robbie snagged and slapped into the back of the net with less than a minute to play.

As the crowd jumped to its feet and roared, the team celebrated with them. Robbie skated straight for Will, grabbing him for a bear hug as the other guys crowded around them.

In the box, I jumped to my feet and hollered and clapped with the crowd then watched the guys circle around to the bench to knock gloves with the rest of the team.

And just before he turned to skate over to Shane, Will looked up at the box and straight at me.

I froze, my lungs stuttering for several seconds before I started breathing again.

Damn it all to hell. This shouldn't be happening. This couldn't be happening. This wasn't *supposed* to be happening.

And yet, when he grinned up at me—and I knew he was looking at me and not anyone else—I smiled back.

I knew I shouldn't encourage him but, in that split-second connection, I realized I wanted more of him. No, that kiss last night should've never happened.

But now that it had…

Dammit, I had a plan and that plan did *not* include falling for a veteran hockey player.

A former player? Maybe. Someone who shared my love of the game but wouldn't be subject to the whim of a coach's trade or an injury that laid him up for months.

"Ya know, I wasn't too sure about Mac when I heard they'd

signed him." Joey Constantino had to raise his voice to be heard over the noise of the crowd. "Couldn't figure out why they'd want some over-the-hill goon for a team with as much skill as we have."

Biting my tongue, I sat back in my seat and focused on the puck drop at center ice. The other team was going to pull their goalie as soon as they could get the puck in the Redtails' defensive zone and would put on a hard press for the last fifty seconds of the game.

But I kept my ears peeled for Milan Hanzel's response.

"Yes, I wondered that, too. But I believe the man will surprise us."

"The guy can skate, no doubt. He's a solid defenseman but he's too slow and he's not getting any younger."

My damn tongue was gonna need stitches but I kept my mouth shut. This wasn't my conversation.

And damn it, he didn't need me to be his champion. Will's playing spoke for itself.

Still, it was tough not to point out his record over the past year, how his game had been evolving. Was I really the only one who'd noticed?

No, I wasn't. Coach never would've signed him if he hadn't seen the same. He'd just needed a nudge to look in the right direction.

And when the final horn sounded to mark the end of the game and the Redtails gathered at center ice to raise their sticks for the fans, I said a silent "Fuck you" to Joey for his "goon" comment.

Slipping out of the box before I did something stupid, like point out how Will had had the assist on the game-winning goal, I headed back to my office to write up my notes.

And tried not to think about him. Or wonder if he'd show up again.

As if I'd conjured him with my thoughts, I heard the door to the outer office open then footsteps walking toward my office.

Sure, it could be any number of other people, but my heart kicked up a heavy beat and my lungs tightened until I could barely suck in air.

And when Will stopped in my doorway and caught my gaze, I had to make a concerted effort not to fidget in my chair. Luckily, he couldn't see my thighs clench under my desk.

"Working late again."

His deep voice raised all the tiny hairs on my arms and I had to clench my hands against the urge to rub them. Instead, I leaned back in my chair and met his gaze.

"There's never enough time in the day. Good game tonight."

He nodded. "Thanks. Want to get a drink?"

I knew my answer should be no but I couldn't get the word to come out of my mouth.

In his suit with his shirt unbuttoned at the neck, hands in his pockets and his hair still wet from a shower, he made me pant just by standing in front of me.

A traitorous little voice in the back of my head urged me to say yes. We could go somewhere I knew we wouldn't be recognized. Somewhere dark we could be alone and I could stare into his eyes and let myself flirt.

It'd been so long since I'd flirted with a guy, I wondered if I still knew how. I knew how to charm clients without going over a line, but I was totally out of practice in this situation.

When I didn't answer his question after several seconds, I saw his lips quirk up at one corner.

"That was a simple yes-or-no question. Tell me no and I'll walk away." He looked so sincere, I had the sudden fear that he'd do just that. He'd walk away and I'd never see him again except on the ice or passing by in the hall.

And I knew that's not what I wanted.

"Yes. There's a bar in West Reading, it's quiet and we can talk. Unless you want to go——"

"Sounds great." He straightened away from the door. "Are you ready?"

My lips twitched at his immediate agreement but when I caught a glimpse of his smile flirting with the corners of his mouth, I suddenly found it hard to breathe.

How did he get more handsome every time I was in the same room with him? No, it didn't make any sense at all but, dammit, that's how it seemed. From his wet, too-long hair to his scruffy square jaw to the dark navy of his eyes and the constant glint of humor I saw there, he made me want...him.

I shouldn't give in to my attraction. The front office frowned on relationships with players. We weren't explicitly forbidden but you pretty much knew it shouldn't happen.

And I still couldn't help myself.

"I just need to close this file and we can get out of here."

"Is this a habit for you?"

Glancing over my file, I made a few more notes then closed it out. I'd look over it again at home tomorrow morning.

"Is what a habit?"

"Staying this late after a game? I assume you don't have a boyfriend to go home to since you just agreed to go out with me, but don't you get burned out?"

I shrugged, though it was something my mom had picked at me about the last time we'd spoken. I had brushed off my mom's comment about having no life outside of work. It was the middle of the season. Of course I had no life other than work right now. That's how this job worked.

Looking at Will with raised eyebrows, I said, "Don't you think you should've asked about a boyfriend *before* you asked me out?"

"I figured you'd tell me to go pound sand if you did." He shrugged and his grin made a slight appearance. "Besides, I might've decided to fight him for you."

Damn him, that should sound cheesy as all hell. So why was my heart fluttering like a stupid teenager on a date with my first real crush?

"Luckily, you won't have to do that. Not sure your jaw could take any more abuse."

"My jaw's fine but it's probably better I don't throw any punches anyway."

I heard something in his voice as I shut down my computer and stood to put on my coat.

"Did Coach call you out for that fight Wednesday night? You didn't have any penalty minutes tonight. And you got a point. That would seem like a good thing."

He straightened away from the doorjamb as I rounded my desk and I couldn't help the hitch in my breath at the sheer size of him.

Sue me, I had a thing for big guys. Broad shoulders, muscular chests, thick thighs. Rock-hard abs.

If I ever got the chance to see Will naked, I'd have to be sure I didn't swallow my tongue. Or drool. I didn't know which would be more embarrassing.

"Points are always a good thing." He shrugged. "And sometimes you need to stick up for your teammates."

I couldn't argue with that so I grabbed my coat off the hook by the door and went to get my tote…and found he already had it in his hand.

"Jesus, what the hell do you have in here? I swear this weighs more than my gear bag."

Grabbing it out of his hand while rolling my eyes, I slung it on my shoulder and walked by him out the door.

"Too heavy for you, big guy? I know it weighs a little more than your stick but I'm sure you can handle it."

I didn't look over my shoulder to see if he followed. He was. I could feel him behind me.

"I don't know, Miss Jess. I may need some help with that

stick. It can get damn heavy."

I was pretty sure he wasn't talking about his hockey stick at the moment. And I should probably pretend to be offended at his crass humor. But I wasn't a prude and I'd been around professional athletes all my life. I'd learned to hold my own in a battle of words.

"Or maybe your stick is just a twig and not all that much to handle."

Silence from behind me. Oh hell. Had I offended—

His laughter rang out in the empty halls as I looked over my shoulder.

Bad move. Really bad move.

Because when he smiled, he was irresistible. And when he laughed… Hell, I wanted to climb him like a tree, wrap myself around him and kiss him until neither of us could breathe.

And maybe I'd lick my way back down his body until I—

Shit. That was definitely enough of that.

"I have a feeling you and I are going to get along pretty damn well, Miss Jess."

Unfortunately, that's what I was afraid of.

Scrambling for something nonthreatening to say, I settled on innocuous. "So, how are you and Justin getting along? You're staying with him, aren't you?"

He paused and I wondered if he was going to let me off the hook so easily. "Yeah, I am. He's a character but he's a great guy and a damn good partner on the ice. You wouldn't think the guy could skate like he does when you watch him walk. I swear he trips over his own feet every couple of steps."

Smiling, I nodded. "He's a really nice guy."

"Close to your age, isn't he?"

Justin happened to be only three years younger than my twenty-eight. I knew Will was five years older than me.

"I guess." I shot him a glance over my shoulder, curious. "Does that bother you?"

"What? That you're younger than me?" He shot me another one of those cocky grins. "Nah. Women mature faster than men. I figure in a few years, I'll have caught up to you."

My smile widened. "Well, at least you're honest about it."

"So tell me, Miss Jess. Why's a smart, beautiful woman like you dateless on a Friday night?"

I slid him a glance over my shoulder. "Maybe because I haven't found one I'm willing to put up with."

"Are you warning me away? Because I gotta tell you, I love a challenge."

I didn't answer as he held open the door for me and waved for me to precede him out into the parking lot. Only four cars remained and I recognized Coach's as one of them.

Damn, I hoped we got away before he saw us. I wasn't embarrassed to be seen with Will, but I didn't want Coach worrying about Will splitting his focus.

And that isn't your call to make, is it?

"If I was warning you away, I wouldn't be taking you out for a drink."

He laughed again; this time I swore it was even rougher and impossibly sexier than before.

"You're absolutely right. And I have a feeling I'll be saying that a hell of a lot with you."

I rolled my eyes, though he couldn't see. But I had to admit I liked the way he flirted.

And he was definitely flirting.

"In case we get separated, the bar's right on the corner of Penn Avenue and Eighth. It's not hard to find."

We'd stopped at my car and I clicked open the door. He had his hand on the door handle and opened it for me.

"I'll try to keep up. You can't shake me off your tail that easily, Miss Jess."

This time I was facing him as he spoke so he could see me roll my eyes. His answering grin and low chuckle made it hard for me to keep my composure.

"See you at the bar, Mr. MacDonald."

"Yes, you will, Miss Jess."

Five minutes later, I was overthinking my decision as I parked across the street from the bar.

As I shut off the car, I gave myself a few seconds to breathe.

This is a really bad idea. You should know better.

Except Will wasn't like the other hockey players I'd dated. He was older, more stable. He didn't boast and brag and talk shit like a lot of the younger guys.

Headlights flashed in my rearview and my heart kicked into another gear.

Fuck it. If I was going to be bad, I was going to do it with a man who made me wet with only his voice.

I remembered to check for traffic a second before I pushed open my door. Would've been embarrassing as hell to have it ripped off by a passing car.

As soon as I stepped out, Will was by my side. He didn't touch me as we walked across the street, but he was close enough that I felt the heat coming off his body. I wanted to rub up against him, like Honey did whenever I walked into my apartment.

He opened the door for me and I gave a quick wave to Sophie, behind the bar as usual and staring at me like I'd grown another head. Instead of stopping to say hi, I led Will past the bar to my left to a table in the back. Luckily, Will didn't seem to notice that Sophie watched us the whole way but he would if I did what I wanted to do and stuck my tongue out at my friend.

"Nice place." Will glanced around after we were seated at a table near the back. "Do you live around here?"

"No, I have an apartment in Reading. Shane's girlfriend, Bliss, introduced me to this place and the bartender's become a friend. Sophie's dad owns the place and he works in the kitchen but Sophie runs the bar. She's the youngest of five girls. Her sisters are all married and her dad and her are always fighting about something, so don't be surprised to hear them shouting in the kitchen. But unless you speak Greek, you won't be able to understand them."

When I stopped to draw in much-needed air, I found Will smiling at me with that grin that probably got women to drop their panties in seconds. At least, my panties were ready to drop.

"You spend a lot of time here?"

I shrugged. "The food's good, the alcohol's not expensive, and the company's great. And I don't feel like I'm at a meat market. When I moved here to take this job, I didn't really know anyone and I didn't really go out much until Lori introduced herself. She's Cary's wife. Have you met her?"

Nodding, he picked up the menu lying on the table and looked it over. "Yeah, I have. Cary and I played together a few years ago, before they were married. Where'd you move from?"

Something about his too-casual tone caught my attention, especially when he immediately changed the subject. I almost pressed him on it. Instead, I shrugged it off.

"Lancaster. I came over from the Redtails' ECHL affiliate. Before that I was with Elmira."

"I played in Elmira for a few months a year or so ago." He shook his head, his grin resurfacing. "Crazy-ass fans."

"Dedicated fans. Tough market, though."

Before I could answer, the waitress stopped at the table to take our order. I ordered wine and he ordered beer, along with a burger and fries.

"You don't want anything to eat?"

I shook my head. "No, thanks. I didn't just play sixty minutes of hockey."

He frowned. "No dessert? Come on, you like chocolate, right? If I get cake, you'll help me eat it?"

Since I knew Sophie's mom made all the baked goods for the

menu and I also knew Sophie's mom was an awesome baker, I rolled my eyes but nodded. "Sure."

His smile made another appearance, the one that made me feel like he'd trailed his fingers along my skin. Somewhere usually covered by clothing.

And if I kept thinking like that, I was going to flush bright red and he'd know exactly what I was thinking. Will turned that smile on the waitress, who gave him an appreciative grin in return. And when she turned to head back to the bar, the girl arched her brows and gave me a thumbs-up which Will couldn't see.

I had to restrain myself from rolling my eyes but I totally understood the response. Especially when he leaned back in his chair, legs stretched out in front of him while he gave me his full attention.

"So how long have you been with the Redtails?"

"A little over two years. Eventually I plan to work for an NHL team."

He huffed out a laugh. "Don't we all? Sometimes it's just not in the cards."

Was that bitterness in his voice? Probably a little. "I know. And sometimes it's not fair. Some players have the skill but not the drive. Some have the drive but not the skill. And sometimes, they have both and still don't get their break. It sucks, especially when you know someone's been passed over who shouldn't have been. The system's not perfect and I think scouts and coaches focus too much on skills instead of overall performance. The game has changed so much in the past ten years that there are a lot of guys who get overlooked."

His laser-sharp gaze never left mine. "Sounds like you spent a lot of time with your dad at games growing up. Did you play at all?"

I shook my head. "Not really. I can skate and I can hold a stick and shoot, but don't expect me to fly up and down a sheet of ice chasing after a puck. I'm not delusional."

His laughter made it hard for me to swallow. "And that's all I've ever wanted to do. But you spent a lot of time at games, didn't you?"

I nodded. "When I could, yes. I love the sport, even though I know the system's flawed and corporate interference is rampant. When the guys are out on the ice and they're playing as hard as they can, there's nothing I'd rather be doing than watching a game."

"And I can't imagine doing anything else."

The longing in his voice made me wonder if he'd been thinking about retirement lately but I wasn't sure I wanted to mention it. "You've been playing for a long time."

"Since I was five. But you know that's not unusual."

"No, it's not. But I also know you were a damn good baseball player in junior high."

His brows rose. "Now how the hell did you find that out?"

Damn. Probably should've kept my mouth shut. When I started to talk hockey with someone who knew the game, I couldn't help myself. All kinds of random facts fell out of my mouth.

I shrugged, tried to blow it off. "You know who my dad is. He's thorough."

Will didn't look like he was buying my explanation. "So your dad went through his notes with you?"

"All the time. I spent most of my childhood at hockey games with him. I loved it. My mom..." I grimaced. "Not so much."

"You and your mom don't get along?"

"Oh no. We do. She just doesn't share my love of hockey. She and my dad weren't married very long and they got divorced when I was three so I don't remember a time when they were living together. Probably for the best because they can't agree on anything."

"Sounds like a tough way to grow up."

I had a few seconds to think about my answer when the waitress returned with our drinks and I took a sip before speaking.

"I didn't know any different. And they both loved me. My mom got remarried and my stepdad is good guy. I actually had a pretty great childhood. When I was a teenager and my mom and I couldn't be in the same room together for more than two minutes without fighting, I'd stay with my dad for a while. He bought a house a few blocks away from my mom's after the divorce so he'd be close. During the week, I'd go to school like a regular kid. On weekends, I got to travel all over North America to watch hockey. Whatever city we were in, my dad always made time to show me around, even if it was only his favorite place to eat."

"Learned a lot about the game, huh?"

Nodding, I watched as he took a swallow of his beer, watched the muscles of his jaw work, and wondered how badly I would embarrass herself by drooling.

What the hell was it about this man that made me want to throw years of careful avoidance of relationships with hockey players out the window?

Tearing my gaze away from his throat before he caught me staring like a madwoman, I said, "As much as anyone who doesn't play the sport can."

Then he set his mug on the table and I ended up watching his hands. The man had big hands, all nicked up. Oh hell, even his hands were turning me on.

"So why marketing?"

"Honestly? It's the only avenue open to a woman in the field. And there was no way in hell I was going to be an ice girl." I shuddered at the thought. "And there are no female scouts in the sport."

The slight narrowing of his eyes was the only hint that I'd piqued his interest. But his next question was directly to the point.

"So you wanted to be a scout?"

Damn, he had no idea how much of a loaded question that was.

I played off his comment with a shrug. "I love my job. It's challenging."

"But it's not really what you want to be doing."

I bit my tongue, so tempted to tell him the truth. To spill out such a closely held secret to a man I'd only known for days. What was it about Will that made me want to throw away years of restraint and do something so foolish as to give in to my reckless side and jump this man's bones?

Would it really be that disastrous?

"It *is* what I want to do."

When he raised an eyebrow at me, I rolled my eyes and huffed. Damn him, I didn't owe him anything but I still wanted to spill my guts to him.

"Maybe I considered *possibly* pursuing scouting when I was younger. But I knew it would never happen and, even if it did, it would only happen because of my dad. It wouldn't be because I was so good at it that the fact I'm a woman wouldn't matter. Instead, I focused on what I knew I could actually do. And I'm damn good at my job, by the way."

He raised his hands in surrender. "Hey, no argument from me. But it's kind of frustrating, isn't it? Having only so much control over your own life."

Well, hell. Of course, he understood exactly what I was saying.

I shook my head. "Sorry, I didn't mean to jump down your throat."

"No problem. Touched a nerve, huh?"

Shrugging, I glanced away for a second. "Maybe a little one. What about you, Mr. MacDonald? Do you like your new team?"

He nodded decisively. "I do. Great bunch of guys even if sometimes I wanna punch Flaherty."

Laughing, I reached for my drink. "You'd have to get in line. He's a sweetheart but the guy just doesn't know when to shut up."

His eyebrows rose. "A sweetheart, huh? What does it take for you to call a guy a sweetheart?"

Did I hear jealousy in his voice? Or was that my imagination? "Well, he can't be a dick. And he has to have a sense of humor and a great smile and be nice to kittens and puppies and little old ladies."

Will's laugh rang out and my breath caught in my throat. Of course, my thighs clenched, too, but I wasn't going to think about that.

"Aw, hell, I guess I'm out of the running then. I haven't met a little old lady yet that I haven't wanted to run over."

And there was that humor again. Just slightly on the edge of being over the line into ridiculous.

"Are you ever serious?"

"Yeah. When I take a woman to bed, I'm deadly serious about treating her right. And when I'm on the ice, I'm there to do my job, protect my teammates and score goals."

My breath caught in my throat and an image of Will, naked and stretched out on my bed, planted itself in my mind.

My bed had never looked more inviting.

Blinking those thoughts out of my mind, I took another sip of my wine and hoped he didn't notice the flush creeping onto my cheeks.

Hell, I'd fan my face if I thought he wouldn't look at me like I was nuts.

Right now, he watched me so intently, he probably knew exactly what I was thinking, damn him.

"That's why you're a good fit for the team." I totally ignored the first part of his statement. Way too many landmines. "We didn't have anyone with your specific strengths and experience. If all we'd needed were an enforcer, we could've picked up any number of guys from the WHL. But you had exactly what we needed."

His gaze narrowed "So it is true."

"What's true?"

"You recommended me, didn't you?"

My nose wrinkled as I considered my answer, which was a dead giveaway.

"I may have said something to Coach Scott about you a couple of weeks ago."

I was saved from saying anything else when the waitress returned with his food. I'd be sure to slip Sophie's young cousin a little something extra for the inadvertent interruption.

Will turned his smile on the girl and I watched her light up.

Ugh. He wasn't even trying. I wanted to shake my head and throw my hands in the air in disgust.

He was *not* that damn attractive.

Except when he smiled. Then, yeah, he was.

Shit.

"Hey, could you bring the chocolate cake awhile. Jess might wanna start on that."

"Oh sure. No problem." The girl's smile widened. "Be right back."

Then she turned her back to Will and mimed, "Oh, my god" at me before she hurried off to the kitchen to do the man's bidding.

I wanted to kick said man under the table just for being exactly what I didn't need in my life right now.

Handsome, nice, decent, funny, and he'd graduated in the top twenty percent of his class at UMass with a degree in math. Full scholarship for hockey and academics. Yes, he was that smart.

And how did I know that? Because I was damn thorough, that's why.

Stifling a sigh, I shifted in my chair, tucking back the strands of hair that had fallen into my face.

"Why are you staring at the table like you want to stab it?"

Busted. Lifting my gaze back to his, I saw that glint in his eyes was gone. He watched me with complete seriousness.

"I don't want to stab the table."

"Then I'm assuming you want to take a stab at me."

Was he being a smart-ass with the double entendre? I couldn't tell.

With a slight shrug, I sniffed. "I wouldn't want to hurt you. The team needs you."

His lips quirked. "Oh, there are more than a couple of ways you can take a stab at me that won't affect the way I play."

Yes, there were. And the more he spoke, the more I wanted to take him up on every unspoken thing he wasn't saying.

"I think…this was a mistake."

Will

I settled more easily into my chair, watching Jess try to hide her confusion.

If she thought I'd back down after her last statement, she had another think coming. If she knew me as well as she thought she did, she should know I didn't give up easily.

And I'd already made up my mind.

I wanted her.

And since I planned to be here in Reading at least until the end of the season, I had some time to bring her around.

But I'd have to lay the groundwork.

"Having chocolate cake is a mistake?"

She gave me that look I was beginning to find irresistible. The smile that said she wasn't swayed by my charm. That's okay. I could work with the fact that she'd agreed to come out with me.

"You know that's not what I meant."

I shrugged but didn't answer right away because the waitress was back with the cake. When she'd left again, I leaned forward and picked up my burger. My stomach had been growling for a half hour.

But I also knew she'd be frustrated by my silence and that was okay, too. Because she hadn't gotten up and walked out yet.

I heard her huff but she picked up her fork and took a swipe at the cake. While I chewed, I watched her lips part as she slipped the fork between them.

Holy fuck. Electricity zinged through me like I'd grabbed a live wire.

I wanted to lick those lips then smash my mouth against hers. She'd taste like chocolate and, damn, I loved chocolate.

After I swallowed, I set my burger down. "We're eating, talking. How is that a mistake?"

Her adorable jaw set and I knew she was getting ready to tell me she didn't want to see me again, at least not like this. Alone. Together. On a date.

Which was exactly what I did want.

I wanted more time with her. She intrigued me like no other woman I'd ever met. And I'd met many. Women who had no idea what a blue line was and women who knew what two-one-two meant in hockey terms.

This woman probably knew more about hockey than any other woman I'd ever met and that turned me on. The fact that she'd had something to do with me being signed by the Redtails turned me on even more.

"What exactly *do* you mean? Come on, Jess. Was there something in my contract I missed? Is there a clause in there about dating front office staff?"

She looked straight at me and held my gaze. "No, there isn't. But it's not a good idea and you know it."

"So it's not a good idea to want to date someone who knows

the game and knows what a player's life is like during the season? It's not like you control the team in any way, right? You're not the one making decisions on how much ice time I get or how much money I make, right?"

She rolled her eyes and my dick hardened even more. "Of course not."

"And you're not going to, right?"

Shaking her head, she leaned forward in her chair a little. "Look, I see where you're going with this and you're not wrong, okay? I don't have that kind of influence. It just…doesn't feel right."

"Are you saying being here with me feels wrong?"

She opened her mouth to say something but quickly closed it again.

Stifling a smile, I didn't wait for her to get her thoughts together. "Because I gotta tell you, it feels pretty damn good to me."

"Will—"

"I like you, Jess. No bullshit. You're smart, you know your hockey, and you're beautiful." Her eyes widened at that but I didn't stop to push the point. I wanted to keep her off balance. "I'm new here. Don't know many people but I want to get to know you. You don't want anything to jeopardize your job. I get that. But I don't think being friends with me will put your job in danger. You don't want to jump my bones, I'll respect that. But don't shut me down because you think sex is all I want. We've got a lot in more in common than you want to admit and it's nice to have someone close to my own age to talk to."

That last one hit a nerve. I saw it register, saw her consider it and turn it over in her mind. I had a second to wonder if bringing up her age had been the wrong move, but when her nose wrinkled, I realized I might have found the right button to push.

Letting her think about that, I picked up my burger again and we ate in silence for a while.

Finally, the cake half eaten, she stopped and put her fork down.

"So, you want us to be friends? And that's all?"

"I'd love to count you as a friend, Jess."

Her teeth lodged into her bottom lip, which I found sexy as all hell. It took most of my self- control to keep my mouth shut and not tell her that I also really wanted to take her to bed. But, hey, I'd managed to mold myself into a different player at my age. I could handle this.

"Of course, you can consider me a friend. I'd… That's great. I just don't want you to…to expect anything."

No, I didn't expect anything. But I sure as hell hoped for something more. "I'm enjoying the company. And the only thing I'll expect is unbiased hockey analysis. Sound good?"

She didn't answer right away, just continued to stare at me like she was trying to read my mind. Good thing she couldn't, because she'd be marching her cute little ass out the door.

I'd meant every word out of my mouth but that didn't mean I was going to give up on getting her in bed. It just meant I'd have to bide my time.

Most people assumed that because I had a reputation as an enforcer, I had a quick trigger. Totally not true. I had one hell of a long fuse. And I could be patient.

That trait made me dangerous, which most people only realized after I'd drawn them in and pounced.

Finally, she nodded slowly, holding my gaze. "Sure. I can do that."

"Good. So what'd you think of the game tonight?"

It took her a couple of seconds to respond, as if she were searching for hidden meaning in my words. And when she did, her response was almost tentative.

"The third d-line still needs some tweaking."

I settled back into my chair. "Yeah, I noticed that. Not intuitive."

Picking up my burger, I started to eat again as she warmed up to the conversation. I didn't have to nudge her very hard. I knew she loved the game but I hadn't known exactly how knowledgeable she was until she started to talk statistics.

I'd been a math major in college but I'd hated statistics.

Jess apparently loved them. She could recite stats off the top of her head like she was reciting the national anthem. Hell, she knew some of my stats that even I would've had trouble pulling up.

I would've listened to her talk all night but she wouldn't let me slack on my end of the conversation. She'd prod and needle me until I spoke. Sometimes we agreed, sometimes we didn't. We got into a fifteen-minute argument about shootouts that shouldn't have made my dick even harder for her but damn if I could help myself.

She got so passionate about her subject, I couldn't help but want to keep her talking.

I didn't realize until I'd finished two beers, she'd had another glass of wine, and I'd ordered a second piece of cake because she'd finished the first by herself, that it was close to one a.m. I looked at the bar to see the bartender wiping down as he glanced at our table.

Shit. He really didn't want to say good night yet because I wasn't sure when I'd see her again.

We had a rare Saturday night off tomorrow, then another home game Sunday afternoon, practice Monday and Tuesday then we left for a five-day road trip. When we got back, we had games Wednesday, Friday, and Saturday. I should be thinking more about the upcoming games than her but it was late and I was in full-blown lust.

I wanted to spend the rest of the night with her, and if she were anyone else, I'd be putting on a full-court press to get into her bed.

Not going to happen. At least not tonight.

She must have noticed the bartender as well because she glanced at the band on her wrist and sighed.

"We should probably clear out." Her smile looked rueful. "I didn't realize it was so late."

I almost asked if she wanted to go for coffee at the all-night diner I'd noticed down the street but figured I'd be pushing my luck. Instead, I nodded and stood.

"Guess I should get some sleep before practice tomorrow morning. Then I need to get to the store for food. I swear Justin exists solely on eggs and bread."

She stood, slipping on her coat and grabbing her purse from her chair, then hesitated, her teeth lodging in her lip. She looked like she was going to say something then thought better of it.

I really wanted to know what she'd been going to say but kept my mouth shut. So I followed her out of the bar after slipping the bartender another ten and walked her to her car in silence.

There wasn't much traffic along Penn Avenue at one in the morning so we stopped by her car. Looking up at me with a smile that made my breath catch in my lungs, she jangled her keys in her hand.

"Thanks for the cake and the wine. Much better than anything I had at home. And for the discussion. I love to talk hockey but I guess you could tell."

"Hey, I owe you for keeping me company tonight. So I guess I'll see you at the arena Sunday."

I wanted to ask her what she was doing tomorrow, wanted to ask her out to lunch, dinner, drinks, whatever. But I knew I'd be pushing her so I didn't.

"I'll be there. I usually work on setting up player appearances on Mondays." Her eyes widened and she grabbed my forearm and gave me a little shake. "Oh! Which reminds me. Are you willing to do a children's ward visit Tuesday? Several of the guys are on board but I didn't have a chance to ask you yet. And I know it's short notice but I'd really love to have as many guys there as we can."

Hell, I'd agree to anything so long as she touched my arm and stared into my eyes while she asked.

"Sure. But that means I have to do wash tomorrow or I won't have any clothes to wear."

She blinked and I wished like hell that I could read her mind because whatever she'd just thought must have been fascinating. I swore she blushed but with the light from the streetlamp, I couldn't be sure.

Was she thinking about me without clothes? Or was I just delusional?

Probably the last.

Then she smiled. "Great! That's great. Thanks. I'll put you down and text you the details." She snatched her hand back like she'd been burned. Or like she'd remembered she was touching me. "Good night, Will."

"Night, Jess."

Her smile stayed with me while she drove away.

Jess

"Yes, of course, Mrs. Lease. I'll make sure you can get into the suite earlier in the day so you can decorate. And the mascot will be there to deliver your grandson's cake. I just need the bakery's number so I can talk to them about delivery."

I ended the call Saturday morning with Dylan Lease's grandmother with a promise that everything would be perfect. The entire Lease clan of fifty would be gathering to celebrate the youngest grandson's birthday tomorrow and Angela Lease had spared no expense to make sure it would be memorable.

The little boy had had one hell of a year between his eighth and ninth birthdays, including being treated for spinal meningitis and spending five months in the hospital after complications.

While he was in the hospital, he'd met a few of the players from the team, who'd promised him an awesome game when he was well enough to attend. Jake Mozik had become especially close with the little boy and had invited Dylan onto the bench for warm-ups and set up a visit to the locker room after the game, as well.

This was the part of my job I loved more than anything and it was the number one reason why I'd hate to make a move up the chain. Of course, I wanted a better position. But with that move came other considerations. Like the fact that I wouldn't be helping to plan children's birthday parties.

No, I'd spend more time dealing with crowds of rowdy salesmen who drank too much and corporate businessmen who also drank too much and expected much more in return for their money than a visit to the locker room and a cake.

I'd heard stories from the female office staff at the NHL level. Not about their bosses but about the increased hassle from corporate sponsors. Still, it hadn't stopped me from applying for a recent opening in the Colonials marketing department.

No one at the Redtails knew I'd applied for the position. My secret wouldn't keep for long and I was dreading the moment my boss found out, but it wouldn't come as a surprise to anyone who knew me. I had a plan.

With a sigh, I pushed out of my chair and headed for the concourse. I'd been sitting for the past two hours and needed to stretch my legs.

And yes, if that meant I could catch the last few minutes of practice, all the better. I needed to head down to the locker room anyway to talk to Jake about tomorrow before he left for the day.

And if I ran into Will… Well, that'd be okay too.

I'd spent most of this morning thinking about him. And spent the rest of the time telling myself I shouldn't be thinking about him.

After a lap around the concourse, I couldn't help myself. I stopped at an entrance and walked out into the seats.

The sound of blades cutting through the ice and the yells of the guys as they worked on a passing drill were familiar, almost soothing. Then I heard Coach Scott call the guys in to talk.

I caught sight of Will immediately. He'd taken off his helmet and that hair was unmistakable. Wet as it was with sweat and the water he'd dumped over his head, it hung around his face in wavy strands until he shoved his fingers through it and pushed it away from his face with one hand.

The bruise on his jaw did nothing at all to detract from his handsome face. My gaze traced all the sharp angles and curves as muscles low in my body clenched and ached.

Sighing, I crossed my arms over breasts that also ached.

Okay, this was getting out of hand. I should head back to my office and make a few final checks before I left for the rest of the day. Since we had no game tonight, I really didn't need to be here today but this job was not a nine-to-five position and I'd known that when I took it.

My conversation with Will from last night popped into my head, all that talk about me enjoying my job. I hadn't been lying.

But wouldn't it be amazing to follow in Dad's footsteps? To become the first female scout in professional men's hockey?

Never going to happen.

Sighing heavily, I shook my head and was about to turn when Will looked up and caught my eye. Had he known I was there all this time? Or had he happened to look up at the right time?

I couldn't help myself. I smiled back and was rewarded with another one of those amazing, stomach-clenching, all-out grins.

Would it *really* be that bad to have a fling with the hot new player? A man who intrigued the hell out of me and made every nerve ending in my body tingle with excitement just by looking at me?

That kind of man was dangerous to a girl with plans, especially a player like Will, who'd bounced all over the league for his entire career. An affair with him would be doomed to failure because we'd always be going in different directions.

But damn, it'd be fun while it lasted.

He continued to smile at me until the team started to head off the ice and Jake elbowed him, drawing his attention away from me to give Jake a shove. I left before he could mesmerize me again.

I had work to do and it wasn't getting done like this.

Will

"You work fast, my new friend."

I pulled on my t-shirt and ignored Jake. Probably best not to give in to temptation and tell the younger guy to back the hell off. If I did, I'd have the entire team on my ass, wanting to know what was up. And I knew Jess wouldn't want that.

"Not that I disapprove. I have a feeling you will not be joining us for lunch today."

Zipping up my jeans, I sat on the bench to pull on my boots. "Didn't know there was lunch."

"Yes, most of the team gets together for lunch after practice on Tuesday to discuss upcoming week but because we are going to hospital Tuesday, we moved lunch to Saturday. Mostly we bullshit but we do discuss some team business so we want to make sure you knew."

Well, fuck. That threw a wrench in my plans. I'd been about

to head up to the main level so I could talk to Jess and convince her to go out to lunch with me. I figured that was less threatening than asking her to dinner, which would feel a hell of a lot more like a date.

Which is exactly what it would be.

But that wasn't going to happen now because I needed to go to this lunch. Coach wanted me to be a leader so that meant spending time with the troops. Besides, I liked these guys.

But, dammit, I wanted to talk to Jess. I had a good practice and I was pumped. And then I'd caught her watching and now I wanted to talk to her, even if it was only for a few minutes.

"Where's lunch? I'll meet you there in a few minutes"

Jake's grin widened and I gave him a look that should've wiped it off his face. Instead, the guy had a death wish and winked at me.

"We go to the restaurant down the street, the one on the corner. You can meet us there. Unless you get better offer, of course."

I stood, smacked Jake on the back of the head then grabbed my coat. "I'll see you there."

"We will order without you."

I shot Jake the finger behind my back and took the stairs two at a time. Everyone else was either heading out the doors on the lower level or still in the locker room so no one questioned me.

I swallowed a smile as I hit the concourse, my stomach tight with anticipation. Totally ridiculous but I'd spent most of last night trying to figure out an excuse to talk to her today, so, yeah, I was excited.

And yeah, my excuse was flimsy as hell but I didn't give a fuck. I only hoped she hadn't left already and that no one else was in the office.

I didn't quite get my wish.

"Oh, hey, Will. Can I help you with something?"

One of the interns, whose name I couldn't remember, smiled

at me with so many teeth showing, I thought he was in a toothpaste commercial.

"No. I just need to talk to Miss Gardiner for a minute."

"Sure. No problem." An even bigger smile now. "She's in her office."

I refrained from rolling my eyes because I couldn't help thinking this kid looked to be about twelve. Damn, I was getting old.

"Thanks, Damien. You can take off for the day. I'll see you tomorrow."

"Okay. Thanks, Jess."

And off I bounded, like a big puppy, straight out of the office.

I turned back to Jess, letting my smile loose now.

"Are the interns getting younger or am I just that old?"

Her answering grin made that pit in my stomach expand. But now I realized that it wasn't a pit. It was anticipation. And a shit-ton of desire.

"Maybe a little of both. That one's only twenty. He's a junior at Albright. He's a great kid. He's just…" she shrugged, "young. So, what can I do for you, Mr. MacDonald?"

Oh, there were so many things I could think of when she called me Mr. MacDonald in that tone but none of them I could say aloud. "Just checking in about Tuesday's hospital visit. I hate leaving things 'til the last minute."

"I was going to text you the details." She glanced away for a second like she was embarrassed and I had a second to frown before she caught my gaze again. "I was waiting to see if you'd stop by after practice."

My frown immediately became a grin as I leaned against the door jamb. "And here I am. So what else can I do for you?"

"Oh, I'm sure I'll have more appearances for you to make. You've become pretty popular on our social media sites and you haven't even been here a week. You've made a good impression on our fans."

"Nice to hear. I've got Twitter but I never use the damn thing. Too much trouble."

Damn, when she laughed, I wanted to kiss her. I figured that really wouldn't go over well.

But I was getting close to the point where I wouldn't care. Still, I knew she would, so I'd wait.

"It's nice to keep in touch with the fans." Her nose scrunched in the way that made me hot and hard. "When you're winning. I don't suggest you check it much when you're losing or having a bad week. They can be pretty brutal."

I shrugged. "I've got a thick skin and broad shoulders. I think I can take it."

Her gaze slipped to my shoulders for a second before flipping back to my face. "I'm sure you can."

Silence fell, not awkward but not exactly easy, either. Too much sexual tension for it to be easy.

If I didn't get out of here now, I wasn't going to make lunch with the team. And they should come first.

I pushed away from the frame. "So I'm meeting the team for lunch down the street. I better get going."

Her smile widened. "They really must like you. It took the guys at least two weeks to invite Derek to the team lunch. Then again, it was *Derek*."

As she rolled her eyes, I knew I wasn't going to wait any more.

"Hey, let me buy you dinner tonight. You pick the place then you can show me where I should shop for food and stuff. I haven't had a chance to stock up yet and I think Justin might shop at the closest convenience store."

Okay, that was a total lie. Justin had given me the rundown on the closest places to get food. But one little white lie wasn't going to damn me to hell. Besides, it was for a good cause.

Sucking in her bottom lip, I saw her teeth sink into the plump flesh, her indecision clear. I was about to press a little harder when she nodded with a smile.

"Sure. I can help with that. What time?"

I controlled the urge to do a victory fist pump. "Great. Justin and I are going to work out this afternoon after lunch so is six okay?"

"That's fine. There's a pizza place in the shopping complex that makes good pizza."

I'd been thinking somewhere more intimate than a pizza joint but I could make do with baby steps. I had a foot in the door and that was more than I'd expected.

"Then I'll pick you up at six. Text me your address along with the stuff for Tuesday." I had to force myself to back out the door. "See you tonight."

I turned before she saw the shit-eating grin on my face.

Chapter 5

Will

"Best pizza I ever had was at a dive in Wilkes-Barre. They had this shifty-looking brick oven that looked like a twelve-year-old put it together—"

"Vito's! Oh my god, yes! Dad took me there when I was in high school. I can't believe it's still there."

As we stopped at a red light, I glanced over at Jess as she continued to talk about some out-of-the-way pizza joint, grinning at the wide smile on her face. I should've known she'd have heard about Vito's.

Just proved we were meant to be together, I'd decided.

We'd spent the past three hours in ongoing discussion while we ate dinner then shopped. And if I had my way, I wouldn't be going back to my apartment. I'd be staying in her bed tonight and every other night I wasn't traveling with the team.

Okay, I knew that wasn't feasible and I also knew that spending a few amazing hours with her didn't mean we'd be compatible for the rest of our lives. But damn, so far I hadn't been able to find a single thing that was a deal breaker for me. This girl just did it for me.

"I can't remember…have you ever played in Alaska?" She was still turned in her seat, facing me. "I was there once with Dad. Not as cold as I thought it was going to be and there's this place that makes the best hamburger I've ever had in my life…"

Hell, I even liked how much she talked. She could go on all night and I'd sit here and let her voice wash over me, making me hard. Good thing we had a few miles to go. We'd already been to Target and the grocery store and now we were headed back to her place so I could drop her off.

I was hoping to get an invite inside. And if all she wanted to do was talk, I'd sit on her couch and let her choose the subject. Then I'd figure out a way to get invited back tomorrow after the game. And the day after that.

Of course, if I didn't come home tonight, Justin would be in my face tomorrow. My teammate had grilled me before leaving the apartment.

"So, you really aren't going to tell me where you're going? Because, dude, you look like you're going on a date. You've been here less than a week. What the fuck? Can you tell me your secret?"

At least Justin hadn't come right out and asked who I was seeing, which either meant I'd managed to hide my attraction to Jess or everyone already knew. When I'd walked into the restaurant, Jake had given me a shit-eating grin but I had given him a death stare and he'd wiped it away.

Good to know I could still control the kids with a glare. Otherwise, they'd walk all over me.

"So how was lunch today? I mean, I don't want to pry. I get the whole guy-code thing but I'm curious. The younger guys seem to really like you."

I smiled as I pulled onto her street. Her building wasn't far from the arena, in what looked like a nice area. Her apartment was the second floor of an old Victorian-looking building that had once been a single-family home.

I'd only gotten a quick glance at the place when I'd picked her up earlier. She'd been ready to leave as soon as I'd knocked but now I was hoping to get an invitation inside. I planned to carry her bags like a true gentleman. My mom would be proud. Of course, my dad would completely understand my ulterior motives.

My dad understood that sometimes you had to play a little dirty to get the job done. Nice guys sometimes wound up in the penalty box. And sometimes you got away with a few infractions.

"And I like them. It's a great group of guys, even Derek, who can't keep his mouth shut to save his soul. I swear even his mother's embarrassed by him."

Her laugh made me want more, made me want to hear her laughing as I tumbled her onto a bed and kissed my way down her body until she wasn't laughing anymore but was sighing my name.

"Yeah, he can be a bit of a loose cannon but he means well. I don't think the guy has a mean bone in his body. He just... doesn't know when to stop. He's still young."

I wasn't. And I was more than old enough to know exactly what I wanted.

Parking the car along the street, I jumped out before she could say anything and got her bags out of the back. I wondered if she'd discourage me from coming up and figured I wouldn't give her the time say anything.

But she only smiled when I followed her to the front door and up the stairs.

"Come on in." She widened the door so I could follow her and led me into the kitchen. I took a quick second look around, noting the distinctly feminine decorations and bright colors.

Definitely a girly room and I liked that, too. Hell, even her kitchen was girly, with pink curtains and dish towels and a pink mixer on her counter.

It shouldn't have been a shock. I'd seen her dressed for work…sexy skirts and sleek blouses that hugged her curves and made me lust after her freaking calves and want to lick the hollow between her breasts.

Tonight, she wore tight jeans and a tight white v-neck sweater that dipped low enough that I could see the swells of her breasts and that made me salivate.

"Thanks for bringing the bags up for me."

"No problem. Gotta get my steps in for the day."

Her laugh was magical. "I thought you worked out this afternoon."

"I did but it was mostly weights. Monday I'll work on cardio."

I happened to turn at that moment and caught her staring at my ass.

She tried to cover by reaching for the bags I'd set on the counter, but I knew I hadn't imagined it.

"Would you like a beer?"

Her question came out in a rush and I wasn't about to turn her down. Groceries in my truck be damned. It was cold out. We'd be fine.

"Sure."

"I'm not sure what I have." She turned toward the fridge behind her to open the door and I took the opportunity to get closer. Glancing up at me, she smiled before grabbing a bottle from the back. "I don't drink it much but I always keep some in the fridge for the guys upstairs."

Say what? "The guys upstairs?"

As she handed me a bottle of dark porter from a company I'd never heard of, I took the opportunity to stare into her eyes. So pretty, the color of the dark chocolate I loved.

She blinked but didn't move away and I could've closed the distance between us in a flash and pressed my mouth against hers, we were that close.

I heard her suck in a short, sharp breath and her lips parted in anticipation but I managed to control myself and pulled back to twist off the cap.

So I might end up with blue balls tonight but it'd be worth it if she invited me back. And I wanted to be invited back.

Putting some space between us, I leaned back against the counter as she put away her few groceries.

"You can go sit down if you want. You don't have to stand here."

"I'm good. Nice place. I wasn't expecting you to like pink so much."

She straightened from putting a box in one of the lower cabinets and, when she headed back to the fridge to pour herself a glass of wine, she had a lopsided little grin on her face. So damn cute. And sexy. How the hell did she manage that?

"The wallpaper and paint were already here so the pink matches that." Then her nose scrunched up. "Okay, I like pink. Not a big deal. Besides, it fits with the house. I fell in love with this place when I was looking at apartments in the area. All the buildings I'd seen were industrial and I hated them. Then the real estate agent showed me this and I fell in love. I've always had a thing for these old Victorians. Wasn't sure I wanted to live in the city but this is a good neighborhood, close to the arena, and it was in my price range."

"Hey, I'm not dissing your house. This place has a lot of character."

Shooing me out of the kitchen now, she pointed toward the couch. I went but waited until she'd sat on the couch before lowering myself next to her. Not too close. Didn't want to make her nervous.

"It does. And after I met the upstairs and downstairs neighbors, I knew this was it."

Pulling her legs up onto the couch, she leaned back and began to tell me about her neighbors. The male couple upstairs who were planning their wedding after being together for twenty-five years. The seventy-something woman downstairs. The young couple next door expecting their first baby and the older couple on the other side whose son had drug problems and had been in and out of rehab.

"Sounds like you're pretty involved with your neighborhood. How long have you lived here?"

"About two years. I'll really miss them when I leave."

"Are you planning to leave?"

She glanced down at the glass in her hand before taking a sip. Covering her expression.

Shit, she was.

"Jess? Are you looking for another job?"

She raised her head and her lips twisted. "There's an opening in Philly in the marketing department. Not exactly what I'm doing here but it's where I want to be, an NHL club with a good reputation, and they know my work. It'd be a good move."

It'd be a great move. *Fuck.* "Then why don't you sound more enthusiastic?"

Her eyes widened. "I am. I mean, it'd be a *big* step but I've been working toward it for years. I like what I'm doing here I like the people I work with. And there's more I can do here. There's room to grow and a lot more latitude to do things my way."

"There're always trade-offs. Bigger club, bigger headaches."

"True, but it's too good an opportunity to pass up."

I got that. I did. But... Shit, I didn't want her to leave. Not now.

And wouldn't that make you a total prick.

"Yeah, I guess it would be."

Shrugging, she took another sip of wine. "I don't think it'll matter anyway. I don't think I'll get it. I'm not sure I have enough experience for what they're looking for."

"Why do you think that?"

"Because the person they're replacing has about twenty years more experience than I do and they'll probably promote from within. There are a couple of qualified people already on staff, but if they hire one of those to fill the spot, they'll be looking for someone to fill *that* spot, so that's why I applied."

"Sounds like you're always thinking one step ahead."

"You have to be thinking at least three or four steps ahead. That's what my dad always said."

Her dad. I'd almost forgotten. I tried to smother my instantaneous reaction but she must have seen something on my face because her gaze narrowed.

"You don't like my dad, do you?"

"I don't really know your dad." Which was the absolute truth.

Her eyebrows rose. "But something happened, didn't it? He did something or said something—"

"It was a long time ago."

And I probably should've left it there. Talking about it now, with her, wasn't going to do me any good and might put a wedge between us. And that was definitely not what I wanted.

What I wanted was to close the space between us, her body plastered against mine while I kissed her hard and took her breath away.

But she continued to stare at me, expecting an answer, and I figured it wouldn't help my cause to lie. All she had to do was ask her dad. Who might not even remember an offhand comment he'd made more than a decade ago.

Maybe it's time to let this go.

"I was young, probably twenty-one, twenty-two, just getting my feet under me. I'd graduated from college and had some interest from a couple of AHL teams. Back then, you still had a decent shot at getting picked up by an AHL team even if you weren't drafted. Today, it's harder—" I shook my head. "Never mind, off topic. Basically, your dad told a former coach of mine that I had more of a chance of having a career as a brain surgeon than I did a career in the NHL and that I should seriously consider taking my degree and getting a job where I might actually make a difference."

Her nose wrinkled again and she shook her head, looking pained.

"Yeah, that sounds like my dad. He can be a real ballbuster. I can't believe he said it in front of you, though. Usually he's not quite so much of an…asshole."

Smiling, I shook my head. "He didn't know I was there." Or he had and hadn't cared. "I guess you could say he motivated me to work harder. And hey, I'm still here."

I had wondered about that, occasionally, if Gardiner's words had had any effect on my game, at least inadvertently.

Her smile had softened as I'd spoken, and by the time I was finished, she was nodding. "You are. And you've had two of the best seasons of any other player in the league. Your stats were amazing. I don't know why you didn't get the press some of the other players got. I mean, I know why you didn't and it sucks because you're not a flashy player like some of the kids out there, but still… It's why I talked you up to Coach. I knew this team needed someone like you."

I couldn't hide my grin because she'd just admitted she'd been the one to recommend me. Made me feel like I was king of the world.

But she obviously didn't feel the same. Her gaze dropped and her teeth sank into her bottom lip.

Putting my beer on the coffee table, I reached for her glass, setting it next to mine. Then I grabbed her hands in both of mine and laced our fingers together. Her eyes widened slightly but she didn't pull away, which made me wonder, if I pulled her even closer and kissed her, would she slap me? Or would she lean in and kiss me back?

I didn't want to do anything to jeopardize our relationship but I also didn't want to pass up an opportunity.

And I wanted to get a hell of a lot closer.

"And I can't thank you enough for that. Seriously. The team's great. There's a lot of talent and the guys are awesome. But the main reason I'm fucking thrilled to be here is because I met you."

Her eyes widened even farther and I wondered if I'd pushed too hard, too fast. But she didn't pull away.

"I don't know what to say to that."

I shook my head. "You don't need to say anything now. I'm just giving you fair warning."

Her gaze narrowed but she still didn't pull her hands away from mine. "Fair warning for what?"

"For this."

Wrapping one hand around her neck, I leaned in and did what I'd been dying to do.

I kissed her. Flat-out, full-on, pressed our lips together and kissed the hell out of her. And when she didn't move away, I let my tongue slide against her lips and demand entrance.

She froze at the first lick but I didn't give up easily. Turning my head, I got a better angle and flicked at the seam of her lips.

Damn, she was soft and I wanted to taste her, wanted to lick into her mouth and tangle with her tongue. But if she didn't let me in, I was going to have to pull back—

With a quiet sigh, she wrapped her arms around my shoulders and practically crawled onto my lap.

Oh hell *yes*.

With her knees on either side of mine, her lips parted and gave me what I wanted. All access.

My tongue slid into her mouth and I tasted the slightly sweet wine she'd just had but I also tasted *her*. And that was so much more intoxicating than any liquor.

My lungs began to labor almost immediately, as if I'd done wind sprints for the past hour, and my muscles tensed. I tried not to crush her against me but it was a battle, one I was going to lose pretty damn quickly because every time I breathed in, her scent invaded my lungs and made my blood rush south.

Christ, my cock had already been pressing against the zipper of my jeans but now it began to throb as her lips moved over mine. Every time she shifted or put the slightest bit of air between us, I pulled her back and sealed our mouths together more tightly.

I'd gladly suffocate as long as she stayed glued to me. I had her right where I wanted her and I wasn't going to give up the ground I'd won so easily.

Even though she kneeled over me, I couldn't help that I still managed to loom over her. Compared to me, she was tiny. Curvy and rounded and totally female but small enough that she had to feel a little overwhelmed by me.

Of course, she didn't show it. And maybe she really didn't notice because I let her have all the control. Her hands gripped my neck tight, as if she thought I might try to get away. Like that was really gonna happen.

No fucking way was I leaving this exact spot until she told me to get the hell out.

And that didn't seem like it was going to happen anytime soon because she tightened her arms around my shoulders and drew me in even closer.

When I took a deep breath, my chest brushed against her breasts, making me hypersensitive to every slight move she made. And she made a lot of them.

As her knees sank even deeper into the cushions, she shifted her hips closer and the heat of her body increased exponentially. Excitement chugged through my veins like lava.

Her fingers clenched then spread on my shoulders then clenched again, like a cat kneading its paws. Every time she dug her fingertips into my muscles, I wanted to groan with pleasure. I wished she'd slide her fingers into my shirt collar and knead my bare skin. I wanted to tell her to do it, to touch me, but I didn't want to stop kissing her.

Because she was the best damn kisser I'd ever met. Her mouth fit perfectly against me, her tongue playful and so damn sensuous against mine. I drew back several times just so I could dive back in and slide my tongue against hers again.

With each second that passed, my control grew more frayed. The hand at her nape tightened until I realized she was pushing back against me. I released her neck immediately but let my hand slide down her back in a slow caress, landing on her hip to mirror my other hand. Which I didn't remember putting there.

Since she didn't seem to mind, I gripped her tighter and began to draw her closer, letting our kiss ramp up in intensity. I found it harder to breathe with every passing second, my heart pounding against my ribs, my cock throbbing in my jeans.

I had the almost overwhelming urge to tug on her hips and bring her down farther, press her against my erection and let her rub against me. I wanted her to be crazy for me, as crazy as I was for her.

Yes, she'd initiated the kiss. And yes, she was currently attacking my mouth like she couldn't get enough of me. I knew exactly what that felt like because I couldn't get enough of her.

Her scent, something light and spicy, made me want to move my mouth along her jaw and down her neck so I could lick at the hollow. From there, I'd move to her breasts…

My hands began to creep up her sides as I thought about her breasts. The girl had curves—

Jess pulled back with a little gasp, beautiful dark eyes wide as she stared into mine.

Shit. I didn't want her to stop. I wanted a hell of a lot more than just a kiss and now that I'd had a taste, I was willing to push a little to get more.

Blinking up at me, she swallowed hard then sucked in air. "I'm still not sure this is a good idea."

I knew it was one *hell* of a good idea. "We're the only people here right now. No one else needs to know what happens. It's just us. Right here, right now. Take what you want."

I saw her considering, saw her head tilt to the side, and saw the exact moment she made up her mind.

Chapter 6

Jess

I couldn't get enough of Will.

Even though I knew I shouldn't be indulging my lust for him, I hadn't been able to deny myself a taste.

But now that I'd had a taste, I wanted so much more.

And why not? There was no reason to deny myself except for the fact that he played for my team. And I knew better than to get involved with a player.

But in the time I'd spent with Will, I'd realized he wasn't like other players I'd known.

"Jess?"

He stared at me with steady eyes, pinning me in place. Demanding a response without making me feel like he was forcing one.

Will had a commanding presence, on ice and off. Maybe it was his age and experience. Maybe it was the fact that he wasn't an arrogant douche, like many other professional athletes.

Maybe it was the fact that when he smiled, my stomach did a

stupid little flip-flop. That smile was a little goofy, a little cocky, and more than a little hot.

But he wasn't smiling right now.

The look in his eyes made my heart beat even faster and I sucked in a deep, steadying breath. Which made his gaze drop to my lips.

Holy shit. How did he manage to make me want him even more by simply staring at my mouth?

"This isn't a good idea."

The words coming out of my mouth meant absolutely nothing because my body had disconnected from my brain. My body thought it was a fucking awesome idea and that he should get back over here and let me kiss him again.

I'd been the one to initiate. This situation was entirely my fault. The fact that he hadn't kept me at arms' length wasn't a surprise. The fact that he was waiting for me to make the next move was.

Had I really expected him to simply take over? To take the decision out of my hands and relieve me of responsibility?

Damn, that totally made me sound like a coward.

Own it, babe. Always own your mistakes and *your triumphs.*

My dad's mantra, drilled into my head over two decades.

Well, damn. Mistake or triumph, I wasn't ready to stop.

"I think it's a damn fine idea but if you want me to walk," Will shrugged, "I'm out the door. I'll probably look over my shoulder, maybe whimper like a puppy and hope you invite me back, but if you want me to stop…"

My mouth dropped open for a second before I started to laugh and that grin of his made a reappearance. And I was a goner. I had no defenses against how that smile made me feel. Or the fact that I was so turned on yet couldn't stop laughing.

"So, does this mean you still think this is a bad idea or—"

"Shut up and kiss me."

"Yes, ma'am."

He raised his hands to cup my cheeks and I had a second to breathe before he plastered his lips over mine again and took me straight into a deep kiss that curled my toes.

When he tilted my head to the side so he could get a better angle, I gave him what he wanted. And when his hands slid from my face to my shoulders to my arms, I scooted closer so my breasts finally pressed tight against his chest.

Yes. God, yes, finally.

Will's chest was everything a man's chest should be, hard and broad and, damn, I wished he'd take off his shirt. But he seemed more intent on kissing me than on taking off his clothes. And my hands were busy at the moment, sinking deep into that unruly mop of hair that fascinated me.

I shouldn't like it as much as I did, shouldn't be so damn turned on by it. I usually went for guys with razor-sharp short hair who looked like they got a trim every two weeks.

I was pretty sure Will's hair hadn't seen scissors in months. Again, not uncommon for hockey players. And probably why I—

With a quick move that made me squeak into his mouth and tug on his hair, he twisted us until he had his back propped against the couch arm and my body stretched out over top of him.

Amazingly, he never stopped kissing me. And now I was pressed from breast to thighs and everywhere in between against his body.

That broad chest was a solid wall beneath my soft breasts. Hard thighs bunched and flexed against mine. And his thick erection pressed against my mound and stomach.

Holy hell, the man was hung.

My sex gave an enthusiastic clench as I moaned into his mouth and practically melted into him.

Christ, where did I start?

Since he was handling the kiss so well, maybe I'd start at the opposite end. Releasing his hair, I slid my hands to his shoulders so I could get a little leverage to get my knees on either side of his hips.

It took a little maneuvering because I wasn't giving up his mouth but I finally got them set. Sitting back on his thighs, I sucked on his tongue and put my hands flat on his chest.

And, oh, holy fuck, did he feel amazing. So firm. So warm. So…delicious. I wanted to take a bite out of him.

Instead, I kneaded at those flat, taut muscles before I found his pointed nipples and plucked them between my fingertips.

I heard him growl low in his throat and his hands clamped onto my hips, not dragging me closer but holding me tight enough that I wanted to lean forward. Okay, maybe I'd already wanted to lean forward so I could rub against that firm ridge in his jeans, but now I wanted it even more.

But if I rubbed against him, I wouldn't be able to get my hands on him. And I really wanted to put my hands around his cock. And probably my mouth, too. If I was lucky, he'd return the favor and put his mouth on me. All over me.

He made a move to break our kiss but I followed him, making him give me more of what I wanted. And I wanted it all.

Every tiny movement of his lips against mine made my blood pound harder in my veins. Every slide of his tongue made my pussy wetter.

When he pulled away this time, I let him go.

"So, just to be clear." He raised his eyebrows. "We're gonna do this?"

"If by 'this' you mean make out some more? Absolutely."

"And if I mean have sex? Does making out mean having sex? You're several years younger than me so the terminology might be different."

My smile widened as he spoke. "You're not *that* much older. Unless…there's some issues I need to know about?"

Now, his lips curved in a grin that made me want magical

powers so I could wish away our clothes and then, yes, there would be sex. Lots of sex.

And I would be breaking my most important rule. Well, technically, I'd already broken my rules by going out with him tonight. So I might as well say to hell with everything and indulge myself.

And Will was one big freaking indulgence I planned to devour all night. Might as well not bother to get cute about it. Might as well own it because now that I had him here, I wasn't stopping.

"Hon, I have no issues. Unless you count the massive hard-on I wish to hell you'd give some attention."

"Oh, I'm paying attention, big guy. You just need to learn a little patience."

"Patience is overrated."

And yet, he hadn't moved. His hands remained exactly where he'd put them several minutes ago, which was on my hips.

"No, it's not."

Now that I'd made up my mind to have him, a little of my urgency faded. I didn't want him any less. But I was no longer in a hurry.

Until—

"Wait, I totally forgot. You play Binghamton tomorrow." Jesus, how could I forget? "Shit, you need to get home and get some sleep. That's a big game. Their offense has been on fire—"

He laughed so loudly, I was pretty sure my neighbors could hear him.

"Hey! This is no laughing matter. The team needs you to be on your game—Will!"

Suddenly, I found myself on my back on the couch beneath him, staring up at him. His hands pressed into the cushions on either side of my shoulders as he leaned down. All those messy waves of hair curtained his face and I bit my lip against the urge to sink my fingers in it again. Damn, I really had a thing for his hair.

"Sweetheart, I'm pretty sure if I leave now, I wouldn't be able to sleep anyway. Trust me. You'll be doing me a favor if you keep me up a few more hours taking care of my…issues."

I swallowed as he lowered his hips and pressed his erection firmly into my mound. If he rolled just the tiniest bit, he'd press against my clit and that would simply be the best thing in the world right now.

"So can I stay or must I go home to my own, cold little bed?"

He attempted a pitiful expression that only managed to make me laugh. "You were a menace as a kid, weren't you?"

"I haven't been a kid in a long time. But my mom will tell you yes. And so will almost every team I've ever played against."

I gave in to the overwhelming urge to touch him and ran my fingers through that silky mess of hair. Pulling it away from his face, I let it fall seconds later so I could cup his jaw and rub my palms against the stubble. And imagine how it was going to feel against my breasts, my stomach, my thighs.

Swallowing hard, I sucked in a deep breath. "This…can't leave my apartment. My job—"

"If that's what you want, I'm fine with it." He stared at me steadily. "My feelings won't be hurt. As long as I can have you here and now, I'll pretend I'm not looking at you like I want to strip your clothes off at the arena. No one will know."

When he said it like that, I felt like a total bitch. A horny, achy, sex-starved, arrogant bitch. And that sucked.

"I just don't want people to get the wrong idea."

He raised his eyebrows and I knew exactly what he was thinking.

The idea being that we're screwing around.

Damn it, I was a hypocritical bitch, too.

Still, I wasn't going to turn into a goody-two-shoes and send him away now. I wasn't a tease. Besides, I wanted him too much to let him leave.

We'd figure out the rest of the shit later.

"Can I stop talking now?" I shook my head. "I'm not making any sense. Can we just go back to kissing?"

"I think that's probably a good plan."

Dropping his head, he kissed me again, and this time he put a little more force behind it, a little more demand.

And oh, holy hell, did I like it. With him looming over me, every single one of my long-buried fantasies about hockey players surged into my head.

The fantasies I'd pushed aside years ago to make room for all those clean-cut, safe boys who pushed pencils instead of the men who slapped pucks and smashed other men into wooden boards.

Will completely surrounded me, shutting out everything else. Settling more heavily over me, the heat of his body combined with the more-demanding kiss made me melt beneath him and I gave a girly little moan that should've embarrassed the hell out of me.

Instead, I wrapped my arms around his broad shoulders and pulled him even closer.

But it still wasn't close enough.

Wiggling my hips a little, I managed to get him positioned more squarely between my legs. Which meant I had an even better impression of his erection. The man felt huge. And hard. And, oh my god, I wanted to get in his pants. Wanted to wrap my hands around him and pump him until he groaned like I had.

But the guy was now an immoveable force. He barely allowed me enough room to breathe much less get my hands down his pants. And I really wanted to get my hands down his pants. It'd been a damn long time since I'd been as turned on as I was now. So horny I could barely function except to react to his touch, his kiss, his every move.

Oh my god, when did I become that girl? The one who went all gooey over a guy?

And why the hell shouldn't you? Isn't that how attraction is supposed to work?

Breaking the seal of our lips, he pressed a line of biting kisses along my jaw to my left ear and bit the lobe, hard enough to sting.

"Your attention is drifting." His husky voice made my skin shiver with goosebumps. "Obviously, I'm not distracting enough."

My hands moved of their own volition to sink into his hair again, tugging until he lifted his head to look me in the eyes.

"I think we both know exactly how distracting you are. You're here, aren't you?"

His mouth quirked into one of those smiles I found irresistible.

"Yes, I am and I'm not leaving unless you throw me the hell out."

"Don't commit any penalties and you won't be asked to leave."

His smile deepened and my stomach flipped at the glint in his eyes. "What penalties do I need to avoid? Checking?" He pressed his hips down until his erection ground against my mound until I thought his cock had to hurt. "Unsportsmanlike conduct?" He leaned closer and bit me on the jaw then licked away the slight hurt. "Delay of game?"

He pulled himself upright onto his knees so that he loomed over me, crossing his arms over his chest. I had to bite my lip to protest his retreat even as I fought a grin.

Propping myself up on my elbows, I rolled my eyes at him and shrugged. "If you're not careful, you're going to get a bench minor for continuing to chirp at the referee."

He threw back his head and laughed, the sound huge in my

quiet apartment. "I can't fucking wait to get you naked and in bed."

Before I could formulate a response, he hopped off the couch then bent and grabbed me around the waist, deadlifting me off the couch. Automatically, I put my legs around his waist and my arms around his shoulders.

"Bed's that way." I nodded my head in the direction of the loft. "Up the stairs." Raising my eyebrows, I couldn't help but challenge him. "Sure you can make it? Wouldn't want you to put your back out."

He started walking, the shift and play of his muscles against my body causing my sex to clench and making sensation shimmer through me.

"Hon, I've been dragging two-hundred-pound men around the ice and out of dive bars for the past fifteen years. I think I can haul your skinny butt up a flight of stairs."

It was on the tip of my tongue to say something disparaging about my ass but then he petted one hand over it and I wanted to melt like ice cream on a hot day. All over him.

"It's a nice ass, by the way." He shifted me closer as he headed up the stairs. "I gotta admit I like watching you walk away from me. You do a lot of that, by the way. Walk away from me. Don't be surprised when I flip you on your stomach so I can fuck you from behind and pet that ass."

My mouth dropped open before I could catch it and I blinked up at him.

Holy crap, how the hell did that make me even hotter for him? I'd never had anyone speak to me like that before. Not one of the other desk jockeys I'd dated had ever made me want to shove my hands down his pants, pull out his cock, and ride him right here on the steps, within about ten feet of my bed.

No one but this shaggy behemoth with a foul mouth and a reputation for being a tough guy. Who I was discovering had a soft, sweet center.

"Jess." He stopped halfway up the stairs, eyes narrowed as he stared at me. "Shit. Did I—"

Jamming my mouth over his, I cupped his jaw in my hands and kissed him, forgetting for the moment that we were standing on the stairs. Turns out he was just as steady on stairs as he was on ice.

But I must have taken him by surprise because he hesitated for a millisecond before he opened to me and let me handle the heavy lifting on this kiss. Probably so he could concentrate on getting us up the stairs.

Which was a good thing. I wanted to be spread out on my bed with him naked on top of me.

He got us moving again as I moved my mouth to his neck, where I bit him. And had the satisfaction of feeling him shudder.

The arm around my hips tightened and the hand he had on my back pressed me even closer. A groan rumbled in his chest, and I smiled against his skin and nuzzled my nose against the stubble on his jaw.

"Walk faster." I tugged at his hair. "And when you get to the bed, you need to get your clothes off."

"Fuck."

His voice had dropped another octave but he took the rest of the stairs two at a time without hesitation.

I'd already begun to move my hands down his back, grabbing his shirt and tugging it upward, so by the time I felt him stop, I had his shirt halfway up his back.

"Take this off."

"Sure, hon."

The next thing I knew, I was falling. Hell, he'd practically thrown me at the bed and had his shirt over his head in a flash. I had a second to gape at the chiseled perfection of his chest before he reached for my jeans.

"Fair play." He popped the button with one hand as the other went to his own. "Shirt off now."

The next few seconds were a scramble as we fought to get out of our clothes, tossing them on the floor in a heap.

Our arms tangled as we "helped" each other with our jeans. He tugged mine off while I pushed his down, taking his underwear with them and leaving him naked.

I paused to let out a totally embarrassing little squeak at the sight of his erection. Thick, not as long as I'd imagined but longer than anything I'd ever seen in person. Porn didn't count. Actually, he put some of the guys I'd seen in porn to shame.

I reached for him—

And found myself flat on my back as he lifted my legs so he could pull off my jeans and panties.

But they were tight and he had to tug at them, which pulled me closer to the edge of the bed.

"What the fuck, Jess? Did you glue them to your legs? Not that I don't appreciate the way they make your legs look, but next time, wear a damn skirt, okay? Your ass looks just as good if not better in one of those."

I'd started to laugh the second time he tugged me so hard, my ass was hanging off the edge of the bed. I had to brace my feet against his bare thighs so I didn't wind up on the floor.

By the time he had them down around my ankles, yanked off my short boots then pulled my pants off, I was gasping.

"Don't wear yourself out." He kicked off his sneakers and dropped to his knees, like he was blocking a shot. "You're gonna need some air."

Then he put his mouth over my pussy and nearly made me scream. My body had no time to process the sensations as his tongue licked along my labia and up to my clit. My back arched and I reached above my head to grab at the other side of the mattress, trying to anchor myself.

The man had a wicked tongue that he used to drive me crazy. Swirling over my clit, he flicked at the little nub before sucking on it and making me moan.

As I writhed, he grabbed my hips to hold me steady. Who would've thought the man would be so methodical as he devoured me? I'd expected a fast, almost frantic fuck followed by something a little more leisurely.

Instead, I found myself being pushed, slowly and steadily and maddeningly, toward an orgasm that promised to be epic. Spreading my legs even wider, I reached down with one hand to grab at his hair. Not that he seemed to be going anywhere, but a girl could never be too careful. As he licked and sucked with dedication, my blood chugged through my veins.

With my eyes closed, I gave in to the drugging desire and allowed myself to merely feel.

His tongue worked my clit until I was sure I wouldn't be able to take the sensations anymore. And just when I was ready to beg him to stop, he speared his tongue into my channel and teased me with the hint of what was to come.

By the time he pulled away, my bones felt like they'd melted and my lungs struggled for air.

Forcing my eyes open, I watched as he stood, all traces of his smirk gone. He looked deadly serious and I shivered with anticipation.

His gaze burned as he swept it up my body. My belly quivered, my breasts ached, and I could barely swallow.

I wanted more, so much more, but even though I wanted to make him rush, I wanted to savor the building heat.

"You look fucking amazing."

His voice triggered tiny explosions all over my body, particularly in my sex, which clenched and begged for his cock.

"Shouldn't that be amazingly fuckable?"

The words popped out of my mouth before I really thought about them but when he grinned, the slight hint of teeth showing in the dim light in the room, I knew it was the right thing to say.

"All of the above, hon. Condoms?"

"Top drawer. Wait. Do condoms expire?" His grin widened

and I scowled at him. "Don't you *even* smile about that. You have no idea why those condoms might have been there for…well, too long."

He chuckled and my sex clenched and I wanted to throw something at the damn man. And I wanted him to hurry the fuck up and fuck me already.

"Not laughing at you. I'm wondering how the hell I got so lucky."

My mouth opened and closed as he turned to the table.

Then I remembered. I'd actually bought new ones the last time I'd made a Target run a few weeks ago. I'd thrown them in my cart almost as a plea to the gods of sex that maybe I'd actually get some if I bought them.

Apparently, it'd worked because I now had a hockey god grabbing those condoms out of my bedside table.

As he turned, I let my gaze fall down his back, where a huge bruise colored his right side above his hip. It looked nasty and I'd be careful and try not to hit it with my heels when I wrapped them around his waist.

Then my gaze slipped even farther, to his ass. And oh holy hell, did the man have one fine ass. I wanted to take a bite out of it. I wanted to pet it.

And then he turned around and I knew I wanted something else much, much more.

Sitting upright, I reached for his cock, wrapping my hands around the hot, hard shaft and squeezing. Not too tight, just tight enough to make him groan.

"Oh hell." His head fell back as I pumped him from root to tip, my heart racing at the feel of his smooth skin sliding against me. "You keep doing that and I can't guarantee I won't come in your hand."

"Maybe that's something I'd like to see."

I looked up to find him staring intently down at me. "And

maybe someday you'll get to but tonight I want to come inside you."

"First, you're going to need to show some of that restraint you've been practicing on the ice."

That was all the warning I gave him. Leaning forward, I put my mouth over the fat tip, swirling my tongue over the slit then sliding my hand down so my mouth could follow.

Hot, hard, and silky smooth, his cock slid against my tongue, drawing a groan from him as his fingers wove through my hair. He didn't pull but he did tug, and the slight sting on my scalp sent a thrill through me as the taste of him on my tongue made me want to test his limits.

He was big enough that I couldn't take him all the way in without feeling overwhelmed. He didn't force the issue but let me work him at my own pace.

And I savored every long, slow slide down his shaft and every hard suck at the tip. With my legs still spread on either side of his knees, I felt sexy and achy and if I weren't using both hands on him right now, I'd put one between my own legs to relieve some of that ache. But as my body tightened and pulsed with building need, I knew that would only make what was going to happen even better.

I moaned around his cock on my next downward swoop and heard his answering groan. Now his hands cupped my head and as I drew back, he pulled me away.

"Enough." His voice sounded like five miles of gravel road, and when I looked up at him through my lashes, I sucked in a quick breath. His face was all hard lines and sharp edges that thrilled me.

"Lie back." He ripped open the condom and my gaze followed his hands as he rolled it down his erection. I had a second to regret the fact that he had to use it but then he grabbed my thighs with those big, rough hands and tugged me closer. My naked ass slid across the comforter, startling a laugh out of me that quickly died when he wrapped one hand around his cock and angled it down. The tip brushed against my labia, cutting off my laughter as I gasped at the sensation.

Red-hot heat shot through my body from the point of contact, making my legs wrap around his thighs. As if I thought he'd try to get away.

"That's right. That's exactly where I want you. Hold on tight and don't let go, hon."

I was about to tell him to hurry when he shoved forward, stretching me wide and filling me until I wasn't sure I could take any more.

Moaning, I levered my hips up and wriggled even closer, loving the burn.

"Fuck, Jess. You are so fucking sexy. Go ahead. Work yourself on my dick."

I opened my eyes and stared straight into his. "Come on, Will. You need to move."

"I'd rather watch you fuck me. I love the way you move."

His gaze had slipped down to where we were joined and my sex clenched around him in response.

"But I need you. Now."

His gaze shot back to me and his hands tightened on my hips. "Then hold on."

I reached for his wrists as he started to pound into me. He was almost too much to take. Everything about him overwhelmed me. The way he stared at me as he moved in and out of my body. The feel of his cock stretching me. The pinch of his fingers against my skin.

Sucking in air, I tried not to hyperventilate but, oh my god, he made me light-headed. I'd never experienced anything like this before. Had never felt so emotionally connected to another person.

I'd worry about that tomorrow. Tonight, I only wanted to let myself go.

Will's deliberate pace didn't allow me to completely lose myself. If he'd merely pounded into me to get off, I would've been able to simply feel.

Will kept me engaged every second. He watched me, those dark eyes glittering. That connection created an intensely intimate sensation that I couldn't shake. Didn't want to shake.

Moving with him, I fell into a deeper state of excitement that felt like lethargy, even as my body tingled with energy.

"There you go, hon. Let go."

If I let go, I was afraid I'd fall hard. And I couldn't.

But I couldn't help myself as Will thrust again and again, pressing against my clit and building another orgasm.

I tried to stave it off, to hold on to my sanity for just a little while longer. But the more I tried to hold back, the harder Will fucked me.

And I liked it. I liked it a lot. Liked the way he made every thrust feel like a homecoming and every retreat a fucking Greek tragedy.

He held me so tight, I couldn't move. Not that I wanted to but I couldn't help the instinct to writhe against him, to try to take him deeper, even if I knew I couldn't.

On his next retreat, I lifted my upper body so I could put my hand on his abs. "Come closer."

His breath audible in my bedroom, he shook his head. "I'll crush you."

I shook my head from side to side as he pushed inside me again, this time more slowly. "I don't care."

"You will when you can't breathe."

"I can't breathe now. Come here, Will."

For a second, I thought he wasn't going to listen and I was going to have to get demanding.

Then he pulled out and released me completely.

I had a second to mourn the loss as my sex clenched almost painfully around nothing. And then he threw himself down on the bed next to me on his back before reaching for me and pulling me over him.

I had a few moments to marvel at the hardness of his body beneath me before he smacked my ass lightly. "On your knees, hon."

I was already on my way by the time he finished speaking and had my hand on his cock, aiming it back into the aching emptiness between my thighs.

Letting my head fall back as I sank onto him, I moaned as he stretched me wide once again.

"Goddamn, you feel amazing."

My eyes opened and I looked down at him, another wave of excitement flowing through me at the blazing heat in his eyes.

"But you're still kind of far away," he continued. "Come down here and kiss me."

Putting his hands on my hips, he smoothed them up my sides to just below my breasts, which ached for his touch. As I waited, breathing even more heavily than I had been, his gaze slipped down and he watched his hands continue up to cup my breasts.

My breasts weren't tiny but they weren't huge either and his hands completely covered them. Molding them to his palms, he caressed me with a firm hold, his thumbs and forefingers pinching my nipples into tight points.

With a moan, I fell forward onto his chest, my hands braced on his shoulders as his hips began to move again. Slowly at first then picking up the pace.

My mouth dropped onto his, surprising him with a demanding kiss.

As our rhythm began to get out of control, he curved one arm around my hips to keep me pinned to him, while his other hand laced through my hair to hold me steady while he kissed me.

Our tongues dueling and my pussy squeezing around his cock, I came, crying into his mouth as he continued to fuck me through it.

And as I shuddered around him, he gave one last thrust and groaned as his cock pulsed.

Damn.

Just…damn.

Chapter 7

Jess

I woke when the bed moved.

My eyes flew open with shock a split second before I remembered what'd happened last night.

"Will?"

"Shit, sorry. Didn't mean to wake you. It's still pretty early. Go back to sleep."

"Are you leaving?"

He'd made it around to my side of the bed and looked down at me. "Wasn't sure how you wanted to handle the morning after so I figured I'd make it easy on you and leave."

Trust Will to want to make it easy on me by saying the one thing guaranteed to make me feel guilty. Even though I didn't feel guilty about last night. Not at all.

I held out my hand. "Stay."

He looked from my hand back to my face. "Don't have to ask me twice."

Dropping his pants back onto the floor, he grabbed the covers and yanked them down, causing me to yelp in surprise then laugh as he crowded against me until I scooted over just enough for him to fit on the bed.

Without missing a beat, he curled his arm around me and rolled me onto my other side so he could pull me back into the curve of his body. Where I quickly realized morning sex was *not* out of the picture.

"Were you really going to leave?"

I felt him shrug. "Didn't want to but I would've if you hadn't woken up. And yeah, I might've made a little more noise than I should have."

Chuckling under my breath, I snuggled back into him, marveling at the amount of heat coming off this man's body. "I don't want you to go. You're like my own personal furnace."

"Hon, I'll be your own personal whatever-you-want. But I gotta tell you, I'm probably gonna eat you out of house and home this morning."

"Then you're lucky I just went to the grocery store."

Mentally, I took stock. Eggs, pancake mix, milk, fruit, bread. More than enough to feed a man who probably ate a thousand calories at breakfast, especially on a game day.

"What time is it?"

"Close to seven."

Stifling a yawn with one hand, I pressed my ass against his crotch and grinned when he clamped his hand on my hip to hold me still then leaned close and bit my neck.

"Play nice or you're gonna find yourself riding my cock again."

My pussy clenched and my lungs seized. "And why do you think I'd have a problem with that?"

His lips quirked. "Glad to hear it. But I don't want you to get the idea that I'm easy."

God, I loved how he made me laugh. I didn't think I'd ever

laughed with a man as much as I did with Will. Especially not in bed.

Dangerous. Oh so dangerous.

"And now you're laughing at me. If I wasn't so secure in my masculinity, I might have a problem with loss of critical mass."

The glint in his eyes made it clear he wasn't serious. And I couldn't help myself.

I reached behind me to pet his hip, felt his heart beating hard and strong against my back. "I think I need to check that for myself."

Then I wiggled around until I was on my side facing him. My fingers landed on his chest then started a slow slide down, trailing over his nipples, tight and pointed, to his washboard abs.

My breath caught in my lungs as his muscles shifted and hardened. I had the almost overwhelming urge to follow my hands with my tongue. And why shouldn't I? I'd already crossed the line by having him in my bed. What's a little blowjob after the night we'd had?

Just thinking about making him come with my mouth made every muscle in my body tense with anticipation.

"Jess."

My hands continued their downward track as I stared into his eyes, narrowed with lust. Holding his gaze, I brushed the backs of my hands along his shaft, feeling it jerk in response. My fingers, however, continued lower, between his legs to cup his balls. Heavy and warm, they filled my palms and I fondled them carefully. His breathing deepened and he swallowed hard, but he didn't move.

Emboldened, I kept one hand on his balls and moved the other to his cock. My fingers curved around him, my grip tightening before I began to pump him.

His eyelids flickered closed for several seconds, his lips parting as he audibly sucked in air. I went wet with lust and ached to feel his hands on me.

I got my wish a second later when one hand landed on my hip and slid back to cup my ass. His other hand slid beneath me to land in the middle of my back. I wouldn't have been able to move unless he allowed it.

I wasn't going anywhere except closer.

Increasing my pace, I tightened my hold and leaned in for a kiss. He obliged immediately, his mouth devouring mine as if he were starved. Pulling me closer, he trapped my hands between us until I was practically jerking myself off as I did him.

My knuckles brushed against my clit every time I stroked his cock, winding me even tighter.

And the way he kissed me, like he wanted to inhale me, made me press my hips even more firmly against his. I couldn't ever remember wanting someone so much I burned for him. All it had taken was one confident hockey player and I was sunk.

Now I just needed to get him on his back—

He shifted away from me without warning and my eyes flew open. He'd moved so fast, I'd barely gasped out my distress when he flipped me onto my stomach.

"On your knees." He didn't wait for me to comply. He picked me up by the hips and set me on my knees. "God damn— Hold that thought."

Face pressed against the mattress, ass in the air, I started to laugh. Beneath me, the bed jiggled as he hopped off to get a condom from the drawer. I wanted to tell him it was okay not to use it, that I'd been cleared and I knew he had been, too, or he wouldn't be allowed to play.

But it felt too intimate, which was ridiculous considering.

"I guess it takes a little while for your brain to get moving in the morning."

"Hon, you scrambled my brain last night and I'm in no hurry to get it back together."

My bare thighs barely had time to chill before he was back, working his knees between mine and spreading my legs apart.

I groaned as he rubbed his cock between my cheeks, his hair-roughened thighs pressed against me, teasing and tormenting.

"You have the cutest fucking ass I have ever seen." His hands punctuated his statement by cupping my cheeks and kneading them, then spreading them apart. "Open your legs. I want back in."

Which was exactly where I wanted him, filling that empty space inside me that ached for him.

But even as I was complying, he slipped one hand between my thighs to test my readiness. Fingers sliding through my slick lower lips, he groaned as he played with me. Flicking my clit then dipping his fingers inside me. At first, it was only one and I needed more. But he seemed determined to tease.

"Will, please."

He worked another finger in beside the first and stroked high inside, setting off tiny quakes throughout my body.

"So tight. So fucking hot. I want to feel you come around my fingers. Do it, hon. Come around my fingers and then I'll give you what you want."

Just the sound of his voice pushed me over the edge and I cried out into the mattress as I orgasmed.

"Fuck, yes."

When he pulled his fingers out seconds later, I pounded my fists in frustration, bereft and aching.

A millisecond later, I felt him fit his cock at my entrance and thrust forward. He didn't go slow. He barreled his way inside and it was exactly what I wanted. Filled hot and hard and so stretched, it almost hurt.

Wiggling my ass back at him, I tried to get him even deeper, even though I felt the slap of his balls against my thighs and knew he was in all the way.

Without waiting for him, I began to move, grinding on him as I became increasingly frantic and my orgasm continued to roll through me.

"Jesus, Jess. That's— Holy fuck, you're gonna make me— *Fuck.*"

On my next push back, he shoved forward, getting impossibly deeper and spreading me even wider.

Crying out, I grabbed at the sheets to hold myself steady as he fucked me hard. He didn't hold back and I let him have me as I wound down from my climax.

He seemed in no hurry to come, slowing his pace slightly, as if he were drawing out the moment.

"Jesus, you feel amazing. I wanna stay here all fucking day, making you come."

In a sexual haze, I knew I'd agree to anything right now so I bit my tongue, afraid to reveal too much.

Instead, I tightened my muscles around him and had the satisfaction of hearing him groan. One hand slid around my waist and before I knew what he was doing, he'd lifted my upper body off the bed until we were both upright.

It changed the angle of penetration, hitting different sensory spots inside that had me groaning and clutching at his arms to steady myself.

Now he slowed even more, each thrust seeming to take forever and each retreat an eternity until he came back inside.

My head fell back on his shoulder as my body gave itself over to him and let him have anything and everything he wanted.

On his next thrust, he held himself inside as we both breathed so heavily I was sure the neighbors could hear us.

"You were made for me, I swear. Perfect." His words brushed against my neck as he pulled my hair to one side so he could sink his teeth into me. "Fucking perfect."

Shuddering as he bit me again, I dug my fingernails into his arms. "Move, dammit."

"Maybe I don't want to." He licked at my earlobe then bit it, hard enough for me to wince. "Maybe I want to keep you here all fucking day, coming around my dick."

Every passing second made the ache in my pussy stronger. I hadn't thought I'd be able to come again but he was proving me wrong and now I wanted it. Now.

"Then you need to actually fuck me."

"I'm going to. I just need to—"

He lifted me, just enough to get my knees off the bed but still keeping his cock inside me. Then he moved us closer to the headboard.

"Hands on top. Hold tight. Don't wanna hurt you but now I'm going to fuck you like I need to."

I had a split second to suck in much-needed air before I did exactly what he wanted.

Gripping the top of my sleigh bed's frame, I braced just in time for his first thrust. Strong enough to move me forward, even as I held myself away.

God, yes.

Now he gave me exactly what I wanted and what he needed.

A hard, rough fuck that wrung us both dry.

Will

"Morning skate is optional today, yes? So you don't have to be to the arena until three for the game."

I gathered up the dishes and walked to the counter to put them in the dishwasher. Jess had made pancakes and eggs and sausage, enough to feed an army. Which was a good thing because I was hungry enough to eat a horse. After the sex last night and more sex this morning, I needed the calories.

"Yeah, but I told Justin and a few of the other guys I'd meet them this morning. Justin and I want to run a few drills before tonight's game. But after the game, I don't have any plans."

I hoped to hell to be back here after the game but I didn't want to push. I had a feeling if I did, I wouldn't get far. It had to be her decision.

She remained silent so I continued. "You gonna be busy tonight?"

Leaning back against the counter in her open kitchen, I let my gaze travel over her.

Wearing yoga pants and an oversized shirt that fell off her shoulders and was buttery soft to the touch, her hair loose and wavy around her shoulders, she looked sexy as fuck. Like she'd spent the night in bed getting wild, which was pretty much what had happened.

Sitting at the small breakfast bar dividing the kitchen area from the rest of the living space, she had her chin propped on her hand as she watched me with those soft brown eyes. I couldn't read her expression, couldn't tell how she felt about me.

Which sucked, because I knew how I felt about her.

Last night had been the best night of my life not spent on the ice. The sex had been amazing but my feelings for her were about more than sex. It'd gone way past sex and into an emotion I'd never experienced, not even with my former fiancé. An emotion that had taken root from the first moment I'd met her.

I wasn't ready to put a label on it yet but I knew myself well enough to know I wanted to pursue whatever it was we had.

Shaking her head and breaking the connection between us, she reached for her mug of hot chocolate and took a sip before answering. "Three groups of fifteen or more and a couple of birthday parties. Nothing huge. Should be an easy day. But you guys'll have your hands full tonight."

"Binghamton's been on a winning streak and their offense is red hot."

"Yeah, their defense has been on fire, too."

The conversation that followed was totally unique in my morning-after experience as Jess broke down Binghamton's stats in a way not even Coach had. It made me adjust my growing erection in my shorts.

A woman who could talk hockey wasn't unusual. I'd met several. But a woman who could quote meaningful stats off the top of her head made me want to pledge my undying adoration.

Fuck it. "Can I see you after the game?"

She didn't say anything right away but she didn't look surprised, either. She looked like she was considering her choices, and I had a few seconds to wonder if maybe I needed to get on my knees and do a little begging. Or maybe I'd pull those pants off her, set her on the counter, and lick her pussy like I had last night. She'd liked that. And it wouldn't be a bad way to continue the morning.

As the silence dragged on, I noticed a faint blush start to paint her cheeks. Maybe she could read my mind. Or maybe she was having the same dirty thoughts I was.

Finally, she drew in a deep breath. "Yes. I'll meet you here." Her smile made a quick appearance. "I'll even feed you."

"You do that and I'll make you come at least twice before I have to leave."

I added that last bit so she didn't think I'd expect to stay the night. Besides, the team had practice Monday and I needed to get enough sleep to keep up with the kids. If I stayed with her, which was what I wanted to do, I'd be awake most of the night making her cry out my name.

Her smile made my heart beat like a Metallica drum line. Christ, I felt like a teenager with a hard-on for the cheerleader. Although I'd never really had a thing for cheerleaders. Too perky, too much work, too high maintenance.

Which probably explained why I was still single at thirty-three. I hadn't met a woman yet who wasn't high maintenance.

But this one…

Her head cocked to the side, a smile flirting at the corners of her mouth. "Are you going to bring dessert?"

She wanted to play. I could do that. "Depends on what you have in mind. I know you like chocolate, but what's your opinion on strawberries? Bananas? Chocolate-covered strawberries and bananas?"

Her smile grew. "Why don't you just bring a jar of hot fudge and whatever…fruit you like and we can find out what we want to dip in the fudge."

By the time she'd finished, I was grinning and she had a gleam in her eyes that promised so much more than dinner later tonight.

Chapter 8

Will

"Will, hang on a minute."

Turning just before I reached the door to the arena parking lot after the optional practice, I saw Cary striding up the hall behind me and resisted the urge to grimace.

"Hey, what's up?"

"Can you and I talk for a few minutes?"

"Sure."

Truthfully, I didn't really want to talk to Cary, at least not right now. I wanted to get back to the apartment and take a nap before the game tonight. I'd had a good practice but I'd mentally switched gears and was in game mode. Like all players, I had a system for game days and hated to be thrown off. Of course, staying with Jess last night had been a huge disruption. But a good one.

Justin had given me a shit-eating grin when I'd walked into the apartment this morning but I'd been surprisingly silent and hadn't asked where I'd been. As if he'd already known.

Which probably should've concerned me but really, the only thing I was thinking about was Jess.

Cary looked me straight in the eyes. "Novak's leaving earlier than expected. I'm stepping behind the bench Wednesday night."

Well, shit.

I held out my hand with a sincere smile. "Congrats, man. Well deserved."

Cary took my hand, his expression wry, as if he wasn't quite sure how to take my compliment. "Thanks. Appreciate it. It's a little more sudden than I thought it was going to be but…I'm ready. Have been for a little while."

I took a closer look at Cary. I'd noticed the guy had seemed a little quieter than normal during practice, but I'd put that down to Cary being Cary. I'd known the guy for years, knew he internalized everything, sometimes to a fault.

Cary thought I didn't internalize enough. Just one of the differences between us.

"I know you and I haven't exactly seen eye to eye before so I want us to be on the same page here."

That didn't sound promising and my expression must have shown my thoughts because Cary grimaced.

"Do we have a problem I don't know about?" Will asked.

Cary rubbed a hand through his hair. "No, actually, we don't. We have some history and I want to put that behind us. You and I are really different players, and years ago I may have been a little, ah, less than flexible about certain things."

I couldn't help myself. "Are you trying to say you had a stick up your ass about the kind of game I played?

Cary's smile was a surprise. "Maybe a little. But you've got to admit you played a different game back then. Your game has changed and so have you."

I shrugged, conceding the point. "Maybe we've both gained a little experience over the years."

"I like to think so. I just wanted you to know we aren't going to have a problem now that I'm behind the bench. You've been a good addition to the team. I admit I wasn't too sure before you got here, but in just three games, you've managed to stabilize these kids a little. That fight Friday… You stuck up for our guys. That's why Coach brought you in. He recognized a hole in our lineup and he knew how to fill it."

Which gave me an opening I hadn't expected. "About that… Is it true Jess Gardiner had a hand in bringing me in?"

Cary's brows raised. "Where'd you hear that?"

"Does it matter?"

"No, actually, it doesn't. Yeah, she did. But you know she's Doug Gardiner's daughter, right?"

I nodded.

"Then you know she's been around the game all her life. She's like a hockey statistics database. When she threw out your name, my immediate response was, 'Hell no.'" Cary held up his hands with a grimace. "But then she threw out your stats and surprised everyone. She was absolutely right."

"Does she scout for the team?"

"Not in any official capacity. She's never come out and said she wanted to be considered for a position as a scout."

"Would she be? Considered, I mean."

Cary's gaze narrowed with speculation. "Why are you so interested?"

I had never believed in blowing smoke, but I knew Jess didn't want our relationship to be common knowledge. "Just curious, I guess. If she was smart enough to look at me," he grinned to let Cary know he wasn't being a completely self-centered dick, "she must be good at what she does."

"She's amazing at her job but she's a natural scout. Too bad it's not what she wants to do or I'd ask the club to hire her in a heartbeat."

"Have you ever told her that?"

Cary nodded. "As a matter of fact, I have."

"Out of still more curiosity, what'd she say?"

Pausing for a moment, Cary gave me another searching glance before his mouth curved into a slight grin. "So there is something going on between the two of you. Damn, I owe Lori money."

Okay, maybe keeping our secret was going to be a hell of a lot harder than I'd thought. "I don't know what you're talking about."

"Uh-huh." Shaking his head, Cary's grin faded. "She laughed and said something like the good-ol'-boys club wasn't something she wanted to join and then shut me down. She's smart as hell and she's not wrong about a lot of things, but if you have any sway with her, please feel free to repeat my offer. Not sure the big club would agree but I trust her judgment implicitly."

I felt the exact same way.

Jess

Because I only had a few groups to take care of today, I was pretty much finished by the end of the second intermission.

Which meant I could sit and watch the entire third period unless something came up.

I'd already realized Lori and Bliss weren't in our usual row, where the wives and girlfriends usually sat. Which meant...

Yep, there they were. In the ADA section with Bliss's friend Faith, who used a wheelchair.

"Hey, Jess. How've you been? Haven't seen you for a while."

"Hi, Faith. Good to see you."

"Hey, there." Lori patted the seat beside her. "Are you done for the day?"

"Pretty much. The guys look good today."

From the other side of Faith, Bliss leaned over and smiled but I saw the nerves in her eyes. "I'm trying to watch but, oh my god, I cringe every time Binghamton has the puck. And sometimes, I actually have to close my eyes. Don't tell Shane. I'm such a wuss."

While everyone laughed, no one mentioned the "S" word. The score was two-nothing with seventeen minutes to play. If that stayed the same, Shane would have a shutout. But hockey superstition was strong and everyone knew you didn't even whisper that word until the game was over.

"Shane already knows you're a wuss." Faith paused as the crowd shouted at the referee for a missed call on Lad, who looked like he was having trouble getting to the bench. "But the man still loves you. If *I* didn't love you, I'd be all over that hot bod of his."

"Shane is a—"

I gasped as Will skated onto the ice and immediately got checked hard into the boards as he went after the puck.

The crowd started to yell and berate the refs but I couldn't take my eyes off Will. He was slow to respond, slightly bent at the waist as if he'd had the wind knocked out of him.

I wasn't aware I was on her feet until Will finally started to move again and I sank back into my seat.

And found three women staring at me with knowing grins on their faces.

Busted.

"So…" Lori smirked. "Someone's been keeping secrets."

I bit my tongue, thought about my response, and settled for, "I don't know what you're talking about."

Which I knew wouldn't fly.

"Uh-huh. You know you're not fooling anyone, right?"

I slid Lori a quick glance, fighting the urge to stick out my tongue, which would prove exactly what Lori thought she knew.

"I don't know why you think you need to keep it a secret."

Lori leaned over and knocked her shoulder against mine. "It's not like you're breaking any laws."

"I still don't know what you're talking about." Then, because I couldn't help myself, I asked, "But out of curiosity, what, exactly, did you hear?"

Lori's smile spread. "You know exactly what I'm talking about. Hockey players gossip like little old ladies. Cary came home this afternoon and told me. Said Justin mentioned that Will hadn't come home last night and that the guy had been here less than a week and was already dating the untouchable Miss Jess. They're all in awe, by the way. Most of the kids already think he's the next best thing to replaceable blades."

"Come on, Jess. Spill." Faith leaned over, wrapping her arm around Lori's shoulder. "Some of us haven't seen a naked male body in longer than we care to admit. And that one looks like he's all sorts of fine."

Dammit, what the hell did I say to that? On one hand, I wanted to spill everything, tell them just how fine he was. On the other... Fuck it.

Leaning over so I didn't have to raise my voice, I said, "He's amazing. He's quiet but he's funny and, oh my god, he's just so..."

I shook my head.

"Hot?" Faith said.

"Sweet?" Bliss.

"Fuckable?"

That last was from Lori, who waggled her eyebrows and grinned as Faith and Bliss laughed and I closed my eyes and shook my head.

"Oh, come on." Lori knocked her shoulder against mine. "We're happy for you. I've been worried that you've been all work and no play lately. I know it's tough during the season because you're always busy but you need to make time for yourself."

I heard the genuine affection in Lori's voice and flashed my friend a quick smile. "It's just new."

Which it was. But…it didn't feel new. It felt right. More right than any other relationship. And as much as I didn't want to get involved with a hockey player, I wanted Will. I wanted to *try* with Will.

"And…" Lori prompted.

I opened my mouth to speak but the crowd began to cheer and my gaze immediately sought out Will. Who was in the middle of an unruly gathering in the Redtails' defensive zone.

A Redtails player lay on the ice behind him as he shoved bodies out of the way. Lad knelt on the ice over their downed man.

"Oh, no." Lori leaned forward in her seat, almost as if she was going to rush out on to the ice. "That's Jake."

My heart gave a painful lurch. I hated to see any player laid out on the ice, but Jake was one of those guys who was a favorite of the team and the fans.

Several long seconds passed as the Binghamton players retreated to their bench and the Redtails trainer shuffled out onto the ice. Kneeling down next to Jake, he leaned over and spoke in Jake's ear. Jake hadn't moved since going down and I knew the trainer was asking how bad it was.

And when the trainer looked up into the stands to where the team doctor usually sat, I knew it might be really bad.

"Dammit, that was a bad hit." The anger in Lori's voice didn't surprise me. I would've said the same. "And no penalty. That guy better watch his back next shift. Someone's gonna take him out."

My gaze automatically went to Will, as he and Lad helped Jake off the ice to the crowd's applause. Between them, Jake used only his right leg to skate to the bench, then slung his arm around the trainers' shoulders as they helped him down the hall to the locker room.

As the team gathered at the bench before play resumed, I saw Will stare directly at the opposing team's bench before taking a seat and waiting for his next shift.

"Your guy just marked that player for a world of hurt," Lori said. "And I don't blame him one bit. That was a cheap shot."

"I hope Will lays the bastard out."

Will

"Pucks deep, guys. Make smart passes. Two minutes to go. No stupid penalties. Mac, you're double-shifting with Lad."

I nodded as the ref blew his whistle, calling the team back onto the ice for the face-off. Jake had looked scared as they'd taken him off the ice. I could tell there was definitely something wrong with the kid's leg that wasn't just a sprain. I'd seen him go down, his leg twisted at a weird angle. If he hadn't broken it, then he was lucky as shit. And if he had…

We'd be without him for weeks. Possibly the rest of the season.

Fuck.

I wanted to flatten the sonuvabitch who'd hurt Jake but I'd heard Coach. No stupid penalties. Which meant I had to keep my shit together, even when my first instinct was to lay out the other player hard.

But if I did, I was afraid the entire team would devolve around me. They were pissed off and worried, and that made for a toxic mix.

Cary was on the ice taking the faceoff, stoic as always. The other four guys—Flaherty, Lindback, Johnson, and Perry—looked tense but determined.

The puck dropped and I watched Cary battle for control and win, giving the Redtails the opportunity for a shot on net.

They kept up the pressure, managing to keep the puck in the offensive end, and after another four shots, the goalie finally covered the puck and the next shift took the ice.

As Lad and I went over the boards, Lad caught my eye and I saw fury.

I skated over to him. "Ninety seconds. We keep the puck in their zone. We don't let them shift us off our game."

Lad growled, his Russian accent so thick I could barely understand. "I will knock that asshole into next week."

"No, you won't." I stared into Lad's eyes. "We stay focused. We get outta this game up three and then we take names. Got it?"

Lad drew in a deep breath, his jaw clenched, then drew in another breath and nodded.

Now we worked.

Relentlessly, we kept the puck in Binghamton's end. And even when Binghamton took a few more cheap shots, everyone stayed focused.

And when the final buzzer sounded and the team skated back to congratulate Shane on the shutout, I made sure I locked eyes with the player who'd hit Jake. The guy smirked and headed off, but I had his name and number.

We had a game in Binghamton in two weeks. And I had a long memory.

But first...I had a date tonight.

Chapter 9

Will

"Come on, hon. Let go."

With Jess's body draped over mine, my hands on her hips holding her steady, I pumped inside her warm body at a pace guaranteed to give me heart failure.

But what a hell of a way to go.

"Not yet." Her voice whispered in my ear just before she licked at it. "Don't want you to stop."

I could barely hear her over the sound of my own labored breathing, but I definitely felt her latch her sharp little teeth onto my earlobe and bite down. Jerking beneath her, I jammed my cock even higher inside her, wanting to consume her completely.

"I'm not going anywhere. But you have to come first. I want to feel you milking my cock. I want you to scream so loud your neighbors hear. And then I'm gonna roll you over and I'm going to fuck you until you pass out."

I groaned when she clenched around me, my hands tightening on her hips as she worked her clit against the base of my cock.

"That's right, hon." I petted one hand down her flank, cupping her ass and pressing her down even harder. "Take what you want. I'll give you anything."

She could have it all. Everything and anything she wanted from me.

And I hoped to hell she wanted everything because I certainly did.

She'd left the light on when we'd come upstairs not long after I'd arrived. I hadn't expected her to grab my hand and tug me up the stairs after her. Hadn't expected her to strip me with quick hands, making me even harder and hornier than I'd been when I walked through her door.

But when she'd gotten my pants halfway down my legs, cupped my balls in one hand, and wrapped the other around my cock, raw need for her consumed me. Nothing had mattered except getting inside her.

I'd *missed* her today, had literally ached for her. The game had been tough and Jake's injury had set everyone on edge.

Now, here with her, all of that faded until all I knew, every conscious thought was about her.

Her warm naked body pressed against mine and kept my cock hard and my blood pumping furiously. Every sound she made deepened the connection I felt to her as my body strained toward release.

When she angled her body up with her hands on my chest and let her head drop back, I watched her ride me. She looked transported, her lips parted slightly, plump and wet from my kisses.

Her body moved so sinuously, I couldn't resist running my hands up her sides to mold over her breasts. As I caressed her, she sank even lower on my cock, wriggling her hips until I had to bite my tongue against the urge to come.

"So fucking beautiful."

My guttural statement made her eyes flutter open.

"I could say the same about you." Deliberately slowing her pace, she smiled down at me, so beautiful she took my breath away. "So strong. So tough. So hard."

She clenched around my cock, making my eyes roll back in my head at the rush of heat.

"Come on, Will. Lose it. I want you to—"

The rest was lost in a moan as I thrust my hips off the bed to meet her next downward stroke, setting off her orgasm.

She fell forward, draping over me again as she climaxed, her body squeezing me, milking my response.

Wrapping my arms around her, I made good on my earlier promise and flipped us without losing a stroke.

And then I fucked her hard and fast, my hips pistoning as I lost myself in her.

When my cock finally began to soften, I sighed and shifted off her, rolling us both onto our sides then drawing her in tight against my still-heaving chest.

She was just as out of breath as I was as she tucked her head under my chin and went boneless against me.

Soft, warm, and scented like sex and a hint of something floral, she made me think of nights spent making love and days spent together. All day. Every day. I liked the sound of that.

When she yawned and snuggled even closer, I figured she was about to fall asleep. Since I was beat, that wouldn't be a bad thing but I needed to know if I could stay. I wanted to stay. Hell, I'd even packed extra clothes in my bag just in case. But I had to ask.

"Jess?"

"Mm-hmm."

"Can I stay?"

She didn't answer right away and several long seconds

passed. Then she pulled back and looked up at me with drowsy, beautiful eyes.

"Yes. Please." Then she snuggled back into me. "God, you're warm. Like a huge furnace."

I chuckled. "Glad to know I'm good for something."

"I think you know just how good you are. I didn't get to ask when you got here—"

"Because you were ripping my clothes off, by the—ow!"

She bit my pec, hard enough to make me flinch. Then she licked at it before she stared up at me with a grin.

"Hey, now." I wove my fingers through her hair and held her steady so she couldn't look away. "What was that for?"

Her eyebrows rose in a superior little arch. Adorable. "You know exactly what that was for." Then her expression sobered. "But seriously, did you hear anything about Jake?"

I shook my head, my expression darkening. "All I know is he was still being evaluated. We need Jake whole if we're gonna make another push for the Cup. If he's out six weeks, that's a serious blow to our defense."

"I know. He and Lad were playing like a well-oiled machine. That's really going to throw a wrench in the lines."

The conversation I'd had with Cary earlier today popped into my head. "Who would you bring in to fill the hole?"

She took a bare second to think about her response. "Abbot. He's been on fire for Lancaster— Why are you smiling at me like that?"

"Because when you talk hockey, you make me hard."

She rolled her eyes but her lips curved in a smile I wanted to lick off her lips.

"Then I guess we'd better stop. Wouldn't want to sap all your strength for practice."

Tightening my arms around her, I repositioned her so she was eye-to-eye.

"I'll be sure to carbo load before we spend time together. I plan to do a hell of a lot of carbo loading."

Her smile faded. "Will—"

"Hey, it's okay. I'm not trying to pressure you, okay? You don't want anyone to know we're involved. I get it. And I'm okay with it."

Jess

Tilting my head to the side, I narrowed my gaze at Will.

What the hell? Had he read my mind?

Ridiculous, considering I wasn't sure what I'd been going to say.

But now that he'd brought up the subject, I should be grateful. Right?

Then why did I have an ache dead center in my chest? Did he not want anyone to know we were dating?

"And you're okay with that? Seriously?"

He shrugged, looking as if he didn't really care one way or the other. "I guess I can understand your reasoning. And I'm willing to go along with it."

Really? This was *not* what I'd expected. I'd expected him to give me a hassle.

And now...I didn't know what to think.

This is what you wanted, right?

Wasn't it?

Lying here naked with him, his hair messy and sticking up all over the place and his scruff even more pronounced than it had been earlier, I couldn't honestly care if anyone else knew we were together.

Because he was still here. And I wanted him to be here for as long as I could have him. And that thought did not include hiding our relationship.

"And if I said that's not what *I* wanted?"

His gaze never wavered, but I saw a glint of humor spark. "Then I guess I'd ask if you were going to start sitting with the WAGs."

My mouth curved in a smile. "I was tonight. Lori and Bliss and Bliss's friend, Faith. But I can't do that every night. I do have a job."

"A job you're good at. Cary praised you to high heaven today. Although…"

He paused, and I could tell he was trying to decide if he wanted to finish that sentence.

"Although…what?"

His hand ran up and down my spine, as if soothing my ruffled feelings. "It's nothing bad. He just said he'd put your name in as a scout in an instant if you expressed an interest."

What the hell? "Did you *say* something to him? About me being a scout? Because he's never said a word to me."

"Maybe because you've never said anything to him. I mean, how would he know you were interested? Except for the fact that you talk hockey like a pro and the coach takes your advice on players. But hey, I guess he got the wrong idea."

I thought about that for a second. "Did he say anything else?"

"Nope. Hear anything about that new job?"

I shook my head, my brain still working over Cary's comments. "No, and I don't really expect to, at least not this soon. Like I said, I'm not sure I'm really the right person for it."

And I'd been having serious second thoughts. All because of this man.

He'd barreled into my life and blown up my steady world like a Mentos in soda in less than a week.

"You're thinking too hard for just having mind-blowing sex." Rolling over onto his back, he drew me along until I was draped over his chest, his heart beating strong under my ear. "A guy could get a complex. Get some sleep. Got practice in the morning and I'm hoping to get a workout in before that. And I don't mean in the gym."

His hand smoothed down my back to pet my ass and I snuggled closer, my body already thinking about more sex. But I felt Will slipping into sleep and knew he needed it.

It took me quite a while longer to shut down my brain enough to sleep.

***

Will

"I'll meet you in the lot. I just need to make a quick stop upstairs."

Justin rolled his eyes at me as his smile widened. "Dude, you're gonna see her in, like, an hour at the hospital. You're pathetic."

I didn't bother to respond but shot Justin the finger over my shoulder as I headed out of the locker room Tuesday after practice. Jess had texted me while I was on the ice, asking me to stop up before I headed out to lunch.

Justin was right, I'd see her at the hospital. She accompanied the players whenever they made promotional visits.

But when the woman I'd decided I wanted to keep, probably forever, texted me to stop by before I left for lunch, I went.

I had no idea what she wanted, but when I walked into her office, her expression made me close the door behind me, everyone else be damned. "Hey, what's wrong?"

Her smile was forced and I closed the distance between us in seconds.

"Jess—"

"I have an interview in Philly tomorrow for that job I told you about."

I stopped cold. "What?"

"Tori Roman, head of the marketing department, called me right after I got to the office. She said they've had their eye on me and were glad I'd applied."

My brain spinning, I grappled for something to say. "Damn, that was fast."

"I know. Tori said they'd just found out they were losing someone else in the office for health reasons and they had to move up their timetable."

She ran a hand through her hair, pushing it back over her shoulders. She'd worn it down today and it made me want to twist it around my fingers and tug her closer for a kiss. But I knew that was definitely out of the question.

"What'd you say?"

She rolled her eyes like I'd asked a stupid question, which I probably had. "That I'd be there around ten."

I took a deep, steadying breath, knowing I couldn't say what was on the tip of my tongue. Which was *Don't go.*

Then I took a closer look at her.

"So why don't you look happy?"

"I am." Her brow furrowed. "I *am.* It's just…happening quicker than I thought it would. And I kind of had myself talked into thinking I wouldn't get a call."

Time to suck it up and be the supportive boyfriend even though I wanted to be the asshole who told her not to go. Christ, I'd just found her and I didn't want to lose her, period, end of story.

And that was the perfect way to get kicked out of her bed forever.

"Of course they want you. You're brilliant, dedicated, and know hockey inside and out. But is it really what you want to do?"

She hesitated a split second too long. "Yes. Of course it is.

I've been working toward this for six years."

"Then what do you need from me?"

She shook her head. "I don't need anything from you. I don't need your validation if that's what you're asking."

Shit, I was going to fuck this up completely. "That's not what I mean. But you don't look excited."

She huffed out a sigh. "I am. It's just…" She looked up at me, shaking her head. "You complicate things."

Since I knew exactly what she meant, she didn't get offended. But I was getting angry and I couldn't help it. She was torn, I got that. But dammit, it wasn't like I didn't have options.

"Jess, do you want to leave?"

"This is a huge opportunity for me."

"You didn't answer the question."

She grimaced. "I can't because I'm not sure."

"Then I guess you have to make a choice. But I think you should talk to Cary and Coach before you make up your mind."

Her gaze dropped as she shook her head. "That's not going to change anything."

My jaw set against the urge to say something I really might regret. "Jess—"

"You should probably get going. You need to eat before the hospital visit and I have a call I need to make." She smiled up at me, but it didn't reach her eyes, and the pit in the stomach opened just a little deeper. "I'll see you at the hospital."

"Jess, dammit, let me—"

"Will, it's fine. Everything's fine." She smiled again and this time it was a little more natural. But it didn't do anything to fix the feeling of dread starting to creep over me. "It was just a shock and I needed to talk it out with someone so thank you. We can talk about it more tonight."

"In bed?"

Her smile widened. "Yes, in bed, if that's really what you want to spend our time there doing. You have to get to bed early tonight because you leave early tomorrow for your road trip."

I had the almost overwhelming desire to kiss her right now but knew I couldn't. The entire front of her office was glass. Anyone could see in.

Frustrated, I shook my head but knew I couldn't do anything but leave. "We'll make it a short conversation."

"I'm sure we will. Now go. I'll see you at the hospital."

I went but I definitely wasn't happy about it.

Chapter 10

Jess

"Hey, sweetheart. I'm so glad you could meet me."

Giving my dad a tight hug and a kiss on the cheek, I grinned at his happy smile Thursday night.

"Me too. With the team on the road, it was perfect timing."

"I'm just glad to have my baby by my side again at a game."

Sliding his arm around my shoulders, my dad ushered me through security at the team entrance to the Mohegan Sun arena, introducing me to an older man at the door who greeted my dad with a big grin and a hearty handshake.

Everyone knew Doug Gardiner and my dad knew everyone. I'd learned that early on but was reminded as I walked with him through the bowels of the arena a few minutes before the game between Wilkes-Barre and Providence.

I'd been thrilled to get his call Wednesday morning, asking me to meet him here tonight. I'd just said good-bye to Will, as the Redtails headed out on a five-day road trip, and I'd been missing him already.

If you take that job in Philly, you're going to be even lonelier.

Now, as my dad introduced me to everyone from security guards to concession workers to a few season ticket holders he knew by name, I couldn't stop thinking about my very short conversation in bed Tuesday night with Will before he rolled me onto my belly and spread himself over top of me to make love to me with a passion that exhausted me.

Will had only said I should talk to Cary before I made my decision.

What he hadn't known was that I had. When I'd gotten back to the office after the hospital visit, I'd been able to catch both Cary and Coach in Coach's office before they'd left the arena for the day.

Neither of them had been surprised by my request to talk. But I'd left more confused than before.

Will had sensed that something was wrong, but he'd had to leave early the next morning to catch the bus for their road trip and I'd still been asleep.

Wednesday night, I'd gone to Lori's to watch the Redtails game with her, Bliss, Faith, and Tony Dellafranco's fiancé, Mia Wachowski, a shy twenty-two-year-old from a small town in rural Maine where she and Tony had been high school sweethearts.

I had spent much of last night talking to Mia, who was very sweet but very lonely. Mia had said something last night that had rolled around my head all day.

"Being apart is hell. And even though I know he's out there and I can see him on the computer during games or talk to him, it's still like I'm missing a limb. But the worst part is that you get used to it. I've gotten used to being lonely and sad."

The thought depressed the hell out of me.

And then the interview this morning—

"Jess? Are you sure you're okay? You've been awfully quiet all night."

Turning to my dad, I saw concern in his eyes. "I had an interview with the Colonials marketing team this morning."

His expression cleared immediately. "You had me worried there for a minute. I thought it was something dire."

"How do you know it's not?"

"Because you're too good for them not to want to bring you up."

His praise made grateful tears spring to my eyes but I blinked them away. "What if it's not what I want?"

Why didn't he look surprised by that? "Then what do you want?"

"What if…I had the chance to scout?"

He didn't look surprised at that either. "Has the PWHL come calling finally?"

I shook my head. "What if Coach Scott pitched my name to the Colonials as a developmental player scout for the ECHL and AHL? What would you tell me?"

His gaze narrowed but he didn't look surprised. "I'd tell you what I've always told you. If you want something, go after it and don't do it half-assed. You're going to face a hell of a lot of opposition but, honey, I trust your judgment more than a few of the men who've been scouting for decades. Yes, I may be biased but I know what you can do."

"What if they give me a shot and I suck? Then I've turned down a major career opportunity and burned that bridge. Hell, the Colonials office might laugh themselves sick at the thought of having the only female scout in the NHL."

"Then they'd be bigoted idiots." His voice had a rough edge but then he shook his head. "Sweetheart, I know Angstadt and Miller. Angstadt is a fairly young coach, and he's more open-minded than most. And Miller's one of the most liberal general managers I've ever met. Word is he's training his daughter to take his place one day."

"But she's played and she's coached at the college level. I don't have that experience."

"No, but what you do have is twenty years of experience by my side and that's more than most scouts can say about their scouting experience." Dad paused, his eyes narrowed thoughtfully. "I can't make this decision for you, but I don't want you to make it based on what you think others might say about you. Do what *you* want to do and don't let anyone tell you you can't."

Sighing, I nodded. "I know. I guess... I just need a little guidance."

My dad patted my cheek, making me feel like I was ten again. "Sweetheart, do what makes you happiest. And don't apologize or be afraid to fail. We all fail sometimes. If we didn't, we wouldn't learn anything. But if you don't even try, well, then you're a coward. And *you* are not a coward."

Will

The team bus hadn't pulled into the arena until after two a.m. Sunday night. Monday morning. Whatever.

I had been too damn tired to do anything other than drive back to my apartment with Justin and drop into bed. Coach had called off practice for the morning, but most of the team had made plans to meet for lunch then to work out in the afternoon.

By the time I woke Monday morning, it was almost ten a. m. and Jess had texted several times. I'd called and we'd made plans for me to come over for dinner tonight.

And hopefully stay the night. Our next games were Wednesday and Friday and I had practice every day. I'd had a couple of great games while we'd been away and I planned to keep it up. Which meant being focused. And not letting my head get screwed up with this stuff with Jess.

If she took the job in Philly, she took the job. We'd figure it out. And if we didn't...

I shook off the thought, preferring instead to look forward to tonight.

By the time I knocked on her door, I had half a hard-on just thinking about seeing her again. I didn't want to fall on her like a starving animal, but lust burned through my veins, making my muscles tighten and my lungs labor.

When she opened the door, all my good intentions fled. Her soft smile hit me hard in the gut, my cock pulsing in my jeans. I crossed the threshold as she took a step back but before she could move even farther, I dropped my bag and reached for her waist, lifted her off her feet, and brought her mouth level with mine so I could kiss her.

I heard her gasp before her lips met me with heat and passion, her hands sinking into my hair to grip me tight and her legs wrapping around my waist.

When her tongue clashed with mine, I won the battle and plunged into the warm depths of her mouth. Moaning, she wriggled her hips against the hard ridge of my erection, inflaming my need.

A split second later, I turned and plastered her back to the door. She wore another pair of those stretchy yoga pants that made her ass look pettable and a soft, flowy top that draped over her curves and gave me immediate access to her bare skin beneath.

Our mouths locked together, my hands slid beneath that top and swept up to cup her bare breasts. With their warm weight filling my palms, I groaned into her mouth, grinding my cock into the softness of her belly.

Arching her back, she softened against me even more, her hands releasing my hair to wrap her arms around my shoulders.

Tilting her head to the side, she gave me a little more access to her mouth and I took it hungrily.

That same hunger led me to let my hands drop to her pants and shove them over her hips to bare her ass.

As soon as she dropped her legs for me, I dragged them down to her knees where they then fell to the floor.

As her hands stroked over my shoulders, I wrapped one arm around her waist and used the other to rip open my jeans. I managed to get the condom out of my wallet and pulled back to hold it between us.

"Put it on, hon."

Her lips curved in a quick smile but her hands shook slightly as she ripped it open then rolled it down my shaft.

Her fingers danced along my cock, her gaze burning into me. Her lips, swollen from my kiss, drew me back but only for a second. I wanted to watch her as I lowered her onto me.

It only took a slight adjustment to slip inside her, my cock immediately enveloped in heat. The need to thrust hard and fast threatened to steal my control, but I reined in the raging desire and eased in, centimeter by centimeter.

Leaning forward, I pressed my lips to her forehead then pressed mine against hers. "I missed you."

Her labored breathing filled my ears as she stretched around me. "I missed you, too. God, Will, you need to move."

A few more centimeters and sweat beaded my forehead. "No fucking way. This feels too damn good."

"Too fucking slow."

I huffed out a laugh at the frustration in her voice. "There's the classy lady who makes me so fucking hot I can't think."

"I think you need to stop thinking so damn much and move."

She arched her back, sinking down until she almost had me completely engulfed.

"Yes, ma'am. Whatever you want."

Before she had time to draw in another breath, I pulled out

and thrust back in. Dirty and hard, my hips nailed hers to the door. Her arms clung to my shoulders and her legs tightened around my waist.

Her every gasping breath brushed against my cheek, making me shudder and thrust faster. I could feel my orgasm building, felt her pussy clenching around me with increased pressure.

"Are you—"

"Harder." Her fingers dug into my back. "Will. Harder. Make me—"

Her cry as she came pierced me to the core and I hammered home several more times before I finally came.

I stood, trying to catch my breath as she went limp against me.

As my cock finally started to soften, I pressed my lips against her cheek.

"Missed you, hon."

"Missed you, too."

Half an hour later, we sat at her dining table, finishing dinner.

She'd had lasagna in the oven so we'd been able to eat as soon as we'd cleaned up.

I hadn't realized something was wrong until just a few minutes ago when I looked at her plate and realized she'd been pushing food around for the past five minutes.

Setting down my fork, I leaned back in my chair. "Jess? What's wrong?"

It took her a second but she finally lifted her gaze to mine.

"I talked to Cary and Coach Tuesday before you left."

I put my fork down, curiosity making me jumpy. "Oh?"

"I asked them about scouting."

Fierce triumph flooded through me, and I wanted to cheer but I could tell she wasn't done.

"And?"

"They told me if I wanted them to put my name in for consideration, they would. And if the Colonials agreed to give me a trial run, they'd request that the Redtails hire a marketing assistant to help me."

Fuck yeah! That was great news. So why the hell didn't she look happier?

"That sounds great."

She took a deep breath as she shook her head. "I'm going to take the job in Philly."

My heart started to pound and I took a couple of deep breaths. "Why?"

"I have to think long-term. Scouting gives me no options for advancement. Marketing does. I'm going to give them my answer Friday. They want me to start in three weeks."

"You don't know that. Jesus, you'd just be starting—"

"I know I will never get the chance to go farther than the AHL level as a scout." Shaking her head, she looked determined. "I'll always be a *curiosity*. I won't be taken seriously—"

"I take you as seriously as a fucking heart attack. *Coach* takes you seriously. *Cary* takes you seriously. They wouldn't have agreed to float your name if they didn't think you could do it."

She shook her head, her gaze slipping away from mine. "But to everyone else I'll just be Doug Gardiner's daughter playing at her dad's job."

"And what everyone else thinks of you is going to stop you from doing what you love?"

Her gaze dropped for a second. "I love my marketing career. I can go so much farther—"

"So all that bullshit about living out your dreams is just that…bullshit. Patting me on the head and telling me how playing at this level is fulfilling my dreams. Of course my dream was to play in the NHL. And I've never stopped playing my best—"

"No, Will, that's not—"

"—to get where I want to be. And if that shot comes, you know I'm damn well going to take it. I'm not going throw up my hands and say 'oh well, I think I'll just stay here because it's safe.'"

Her mouth set in a flat line and I knew I should probably just shut the fuck up.

"That's not fair. Jesus, Will. Why are you sabotaging me on this? I've been working toward this for years, working my way up the chain to an NHL club, and now you're telling me I'm selling out? That's not fair."

"I'm not saying you're selling out. I'm saying you're selling yourself short."

"And I'm leaving you behind and you're pissed."

I could see from her expression that she wanted to take back her words immediately. But they'd already done their damage.

"I'm sorry." Her face crinkled in an angry frown. "Dammit, I'm sorry. I shouldn't have—"

"No." I stood, my chest so tight I could barely breathe. "You're absolutely right. I am pissed but not for the reasons you think. You're right. You should take the job in Philly. You'll be fantastic. I'm not pissed at you. I'm fucking furious at myself for not seeing how this was going to go."

Then I walked to the door and left myself out, closing it behind me with barely a snick.

Chapter 11

"Jess? Can I come in?"

The voice was familiar but unexpected Wednesday noon.

"Lori. Hey, what are you doing here?"

The smile Cary's wife gave me was sweet and serene and way too calm. "I stopped by to take Cary to lunch since I have the afternoon off, but he's busy for another few minutes so I figured I'd say hi."

I leaned back in my chair as Lori walked through the door and closed it behind her.

Honestly, I didn't really want to talk to anyone. Since my fight with Will two nights ago, I hadn't seen or spoken to him. And when I knew he was in the building, I found it hard to breathe, even though I knew he wouldn't stop to see me.

Just thinking about him made my heart hurt. But I hadn't sought him out and I wasn't going to. Better this way. A clean break. Less heartbreak.

Not that clean and damn, my heart hurts.

Forcing a smile, I watched Lori fall into the seat opposite me.

"So Cary told me you turned him down for the scouting position because you've been offered a job with the Colonials. Congrats on that. That'll be a big promotion for you."

Nothing stayed secret in this business. I should've known. "Thanks, though it's not a done deal yet."

"Want to tell me why you look like you're dreading it?"

I grimaced, shaking my head. "Did Cary send you in here to talk to me?"

Lori's smile softened. "No, but he's worried about you. He said you've seemed…not yourself the last couple of days. Are you okay?"

"I'm fine."

Lori's eyebrows rose, and I huffed.

"I'm *fine*. Honestly. Of course, I'm nervous about a new job. I've got a lot to do here before I leave but I'm excited, too. I'm just…"

"Just what?"

I considered my next words carefully, thought about not saying anything at all, but I'd been heartsick since Monday night and I'd had no one to talk to.

"Will and I are done."

Lori didn't look surprised by that. "What happened?"

He broke my heart. "He thinks I'm selling myself short. How can I be selling myself short when I'm taking this huge step in my career? I'm so pissed at him."

"And what do *you* think?"

I shook my head. "About what?"

Lori's eyebrows rose. "Do *you* think you're selling yourself short?"

My first instinct was to deny. But I found I couldn't because I wasn't exactly sure. "Am I? I don't even know anymore."

Lori shrugged. "I can't answer that for you. That's something you need to figure out yourself."

Sighing, I felt all the frustration I'd been trying to ignore begin to crush down on me. "You're not helping."

Laughing softly, Lori rose and walked behind the desk to give me a hug. "I'm sorry, but I have to say I'm with Cary. I don't want to lose you. Yes, I know this job is a great opportunity. But, Jess, maybe you do need to think about what you're potentially giving up. Maybe it's more than you think."

Will

"Dude, you are like cold rain over ice. What the fuck is up with you?"

I shot Jake a glance as I dressed for Wednesday night's game. Jake was sitting in his spot on the bench, looking like he'd just walked off a GQ photo shoot. The kid had style. Too bad he also had a mild concussion and a "lower body injury," which in Jake's case was a hamstring tear.

Jake would be on the injured reserve for the next four to six weeks, possibly longer. The kid appeared to be taking it in stride, popping off digs at Lad and the other players and generally being his smart-ass normal self.

But I sensed a deeper feeling of loss that Jake covered really well.

Or maybe that was me projecting. Since Monday night, I'd pretty much felt lost, like I'd had a chunk of myself cut out.

And what'd you expect? That she was going to give up a great opportunity to stay here with your sorry ass as you wind down your second-rate career?

Yeah, right.

Shaking my head, I brought my focus back to where it should be—on Coach and my pre-game speech. Important game tonight. We needed these two points to get into second place in the division. Middle of the season and every point began to matter just a little bit more.

No stupid penalties, especially with Bakersfield. I had some history with the team. I had been traded there three seasons ago, and the coach and I had butted heads almost immediately. It had been one of the most insanely frustrating times of my life. Coach Lamarche knew exactly which strings to pull to make me lose my shit, and the bastard held a grudge.

But tonight, I couldn't afford to let anything get to me. Had to prove, if only to myself, that I could be more than people expected.

As Coach wrapped up his speech and the team rose to grab our sticks and helmets before heading down the hall to the ice, Jake stopped next to me, staring at me with a question in his eyes.

"What's up, Jake?"

"You look…not yourself."

I pretty much didn't feel like myself either, but apparently no one but Jake had noticed. Or they hadn't wanted to take their lives in their hands and ask outright.

But Jake got away with a lot of shit no one else could because the guy genuinely cared.

"I'm good. Big game. How're you feeling?"

"I will heal. Eventually."

A slight scowl crossed his face but Jake wiped it away fast. If I hadn't been watching closely, I might've missed it. Now wasn't the time to call Jake on it but I filed it away for later.

"You," Jake continued, "have problem. But this conversation will keep. Tonight," he leaned close and lowered his voice, "you need to keep Lad in check. He can sometimes have wild streak. And Robbie sometimes needs good kick in the ass to get motivated after he makes bad play. And Tyler can be total dick when he is pissed off and will need to be put in his place."

By the time Jake finished, I had a grin on my face, my first since Monday night when I'd had my heart ripped out of my chest.

"You got it, Mom."

Jake gave me the finger as I made my way out onto the ice.

Take care of my teammates. That's what an enforcer did. Too bad I couldn't do the same for my heart.

***

Jess

Another slow Wednesday night for attendance meant another slow night for me. Tonight, I only had one group and, after the first period, they didn't have much need for me so I chose a relatively crowded section and found a seat.

I told myself I could just sit and watch the game. Neither Lori nor Bliss were there tonight and Mia was chatting away with a couple of players' girlfriends who were closer to her own age.

Which just made me feel even more lonely.

You're pathetic. It's not like you got a divorce, for chrissake.

And yet I still felt like part of me had been ripped away.

What are you giving up?

Lori's question kept circling around my head. Drawing in a deep breath, I let my gaze find Will again. I didn't have to work hard. I only had to glance at the ice and my gaze went right to him. Already, the first period had been chippy and a couple of players had gone after Will specifically.

So far, he'd managed to stay out of the penalty box but I could tell he was getting pissed.

By the middle of the second period, the score was still tied at zero and both teams had started to show cracks from frustration.

Stupid penalties on both sides, a lot of shoving and shouting, and a few dirty hits from Bakersfield, one of which left Will on the ice on his knees for a few seconds as he caught his breath and had the audience on its feet, shouting at the ref.

In front of me, a season ticket holder I recognized by face shouted, "Did you swallow your damn whistle or are you just blind?"

Then he turned to me and shook his head. "Christ, it's like they've been paid off or something. They're letting Bakersfield get away with murder. Someone's gonna get hurt out there."

Though I knew I shouldn't bad-mouth the referees, especially not as a known member of the front office staff, I couldn't help myself. "He's calling an awful game tonight."

"I'm just waiting for Mac to take care of that little bastard, Branson," the man's wife chimed in. "He needs to step up here."

As play continued, I silently agreed. So far, Will had been steady as a rock. But he played without the spark I'd seen in him at the past few games. Was that my fault? Was our breakup, or whatever you wanted to call it, to blame?

Or maybe he was just having a bad night and I was giving myself too much credit.

But as the game wore on, and the game got uglier, I began to wonder if I hadn't totally screwed us both.

Chapter 12

Will

At the end of the second intermission, as the team lined up to head back onto the ice, I glanced up to find Cary stopped next to me.

In his first game as an assistant coach, Cary had proved to be just as steady behind the bench as he'd been on it. And I had forced myself to play the kind of game I thought Cary wanted, even though Bakersfield was taunting the shit out of me, trying to get me to retaliate.

But now Cary looked at me with a question in his eyes.

"You've been pretty quiet the first two periods. We need you to shake things up."

My eyebrows rose. That almost sounded like Cary wanted me to go out there and crack open some heads. But I had been wrong before. Recently, I'd been pretty fucking wrong about a certain woman and that still stung. I didn't need to get my wires crossed with Cary either.

"You're gonna need to spell it out, man. I don't wanna get this wrong."

Cary didn't blink as he leaned in a little closer. "Go out there and make Bakersfield regret their actions. It's time to show them exactly how our enforcer takes care of things."

Well, would you look at that? Vindication of my skills should've been sweet. And maybe someday it would be.

My mouth curved in the ghost of a grin. "I think I can manage that."

"Good." Cary nodded. "Just do it without getting hurt. Team needs you healthy."

"Do my best, Coach."

Cary's grin was wider than mine. "Be still my heart."

Now I rolled my eyes. "Don't press your luck."

Cary clapped me on the shoulder. "Be smart, Mac. Be persistent but be ready to go when you get the chance. Don't play into their expectations, because if you do, they'll control the situation. And don't break your damn hand on Branson's hard head."

With a nod, I headed out onto the ice for the third period.

My first two shifts, I took a couple hard hits against the boards, but Cary's words stuck with me.

Don't play into their expectations.

On my third shift, as Branson charged the Redtails goal from the blue line, I saw my chance. Branson had his head down, something every player learned not to do in peewees. Sure, sometimes you forgot. And sometimes you paid for it.

I skated at him full out as the crowd cheered. They could see the collision coming in the two seconds it took for me to cross the ice.

And right before I leveled Branson, I slowed just enough so I didn't completely wreck the guy. I wasn't out for blood, but it was time for payback.

Branson went down hard, the crowd erupted in cheers, and I

snagged the puck as the guy sat on his ass on the ice, shaking his head and probably seeing stars.

Another Bakersfield player immediately tried to knock me off the puck, but the guy was no match, not in size or determination. Skating toward the Redtails' offensive end, I passed to Tyler, whose line set up for a play on goal.

The next few seconds were especially satisfying as the Bakersfield players scrambled to prevent the Redtails from scoring.

And failed.

Tyler passed to Robbie, who one-timed it straight to the back of the net.

The crowd roared and jumped to its feet as us players on the ice jumped Robbie and knocked helmets before skating back to the bench for fist bumps before taking our seats on the bench as the lines changed.

As soon as my ass hit the bench, I felt a fist tap on my shoulder pads.

"Nice work." Cary leaned down to speak near my ear. "Expectations, Mac. Sometimes you gotta defy them."

Jess

I sat on the edge of my seat as the seconds ticked away on the clock.

The Redtails had the only goal of the game and less than two minutes remained on the clock.

And after that hit Will had laid on Branson, he'd become a marked man. Any time he was on the ice, the Bakersfield players were all over him.

I had no idea how he managed to maintain his cool. Another

player would've gone off by now, drawing a stupid penalty. But Will hung tough. He took the abuse like he was oblivious to everything and kept his eyes on the prize.

Bakersfield battled hard but their frustration was no match for the Redtails' determination. And when the final buzzer sounded, I finally released the breath I swore I'd been holding for the last minute.

As the opposing team made a quick exit from the ice, the Redtails gathered at center ice to salute the crowd.

I saw only Will. He smiled as he knocked helmets with Shane then put his arm around Lad's shoulders as they skated toward the hall to the locker rooms. He stopped just inside the boards, knocking gloves with his teammates as they stepped off the ice.

And just before he left the ice himself, he looked up, his gaze circling the arena. Was I imagining things or was he looking for me?

My heart pounded so hard, it hurt. Damn it.

"Good game tonight. Your dad was right. I'm glad I came."

Startled by the voice from behind me, I turned in my seat. And found Victor Galiev in the row behind me.

A genuine smile curving my lips, I held my hand out to the NHL scout. "Mr. Galiev, it's nice to see you. It's been a while."

"Yes, it has been." His mouth curved in a wry grin. "And please, call me Vic. You make me feel old when you call me Mister. I'm forty, not eighty."

I nodded, knowing it'd be a hard habit to break. I'd known Vic for years. A former player who'd become my father's protégé after retiring because of injuries, he'd moved on to scout for Washington a few years ago.

"What are you doing in Reading? I had no idea you'd be here or I would've made a point to find you earlier."

"Oh, I've got my eyes on a couple of guys on both teams so figured I'd kill two birds with one stone. And I only remembered your dad telling me you worked here when I saw you sitting there. Your dad loves to brag about his brilliant daughter."

I rolled my eyes. "My dad's a little biased, obviously."

"Of course he is. Doesn't mean he's wrong, though. You're in marketing, right?"

"Yes."

"More power to you. That stuff hurts my brain. But I guess it's stable, huh? None of this traveling all over the country every other day, watching five, six games a week."

"Actually, that sounds pretty good to me."

Vic laughed. "Forgot who I was talking to. Should've known Doug Gardiner's daughter would have hockey in her blood. A little surprised you haven't been snapped up as a scout for the PWHL yet."

His comment made my smile freeze in place but he didn't notice as he continued.

"You've got a playoff team here again this year. They should get far. Hopefully Mozik's injury won't put him out for the season. Your D's gonna miss him. Wasn't expecting to see such control from MacDonald. That was a shocker. He's getting a little old to be learning new tricks."

And now I had to bite my tongue against the urge to tell Vic to go fuck himself.

Mac wasn't old and he damn well had more control than anyone gave him credit for.

Don't let it get to you. He's fishing.

Holy shit. The realization hit me like a puck in the gut. He was absolutely fishing for information. From me.

There was no way I was going to give him any. Not to use against my team.

And dammit, it was *my* team.

Not for long.

Forcing a smile, I stood, holding my hand out to Vic. "It was so nice to see you again but I've gotta get going. I'll tell Dad you said hi."

Vic nodded and shook. "Nice to see you, too, Jess. I'll be sure to stop and say hi next time I'm in town."

Walking back to my office, I sat behind my desk for several long minutes as the arena cleared. Staring out into the empty office, I let the anger build.

I didn't even know why I felt so pissed off but it'd been building all night, making me feel like a soda that'd been shaken for hours.

At least it's better than feeling like you had your heart ripped out of your chest and then stomped on by some chauvinist pig.

Which was totally unfair. Vic hadn't meant anything derogatory with that comment about the NWHL. I was female. It was an easy assumption to make, that the NWHL might be interested in my skills. And yet...

With a growl, I picked up my phone.

"Hi, sweetheart, what's going on? Everything okay?"

"Hi, Daddy, nothing's wrong. I'm just..." She sighed. "I saw Vic Galiev tonight."

"Oh? How's he doing?"

"Fine. He said to say hi."

My dad paused. "That's nice. But that's not the only reason you called, is it?"

I thought about my response for several long seconds. "No. I'm just...out of sorts. I haven't told anyone yet," except Will, of course, "but Philly offered me that job."

"Hey, honey, that's great." The pride in his voice didn't ease my mood at all. "Seriously. I know you've been busting your ass for that move for a while."

"What if I don't want it?"

My dad didn't miss a beat. "Then don't take it."

I snorted. Of course, that's what he'd say. "What if this is my big break and I pass it up?"

"Then I'd tell you there will be other opportunities, maybe better ones. Jess…are you still thinking about that scouting position? Did Vic say something—"

"No…well, yes, he said something, but it was nothing bad. Actually, he asked the same thing you had, if the PWHL had made me an offer."

"And that's bad how?" Genuine confusion colored his tone. "You need to help me out here, sweetheart. I'm getting slow in my old age."

"You're not old and it's not you who has the problem. I have the problem. And I'm just not sure how to fix it."

"Well, then lay it out for me."

"What if there's this guy I've been seeing? And what if I suddenly have this great opportunity that suddenly doesn't seem so great anymore because I'd have to leave this guy behind? And what if I'm turning down an even bigger opportunity because I'm worried I'll fail?"

Silence from the other end that dragged on.

"Dad, you still there?"

"Didn't we have this conversation last week?"

A frustrated sigh slipped through. "Sort of. But…"

"But what?"

"What if I try to break that glass ceiling and find out I can't hack it? What if—"

"What if you're absolutely amazing? What if you don't do it and regret it for the rest of your life? And what if you give up this man for your job and realize in one, two, five years that you should've given up the job?"

He's talking about Mom.

From the other end, I heard my dad sigh. "I don't have an answer for you, sweetheart. I can only encourage you not to make the same mistakes I did. If you've found the right guy or even who you think might be the right guy, you need to give it a shot. Because sometimes you only get one.

"And if you don't take your shot at something you love, you will most certainly fail."

"And if you don't take your shot at something you love, you will most certainly fail."

505

Chapter 13

Will

"Dude, you're a fucking wet blanket. You kicked ass and took names tonight. You should be tearing a hole through this place. What the hell's wrong with you?"

Derek sat next to me at the bar and clinked his beer bottle against mine before taking another swallow. Most of the team was here tonight, hanging out around the pool table, being fawned over by a group of younger women in tight jeans, tighter shirts, and high heels.

I had absolutely no interest. I'd only come because the guys had insisted they'd wanted to buy me drinks and that had seemed like a great idea at the time. Now, though, watching the younger guys drink, laugh, and hook up…

I just felt old because what I really wanted was to be snuggled up on a couch watching TV or making out with Jess.

But I'd fucked that up royally.

And I must be pretty damn pitiful because even usually clueless Derek had noticed. Or he'd pulled the short straw and the rest of the guys had sent him as the sacrificial lamb to check on me.

I'd been nursing the one beer since we'd arrived an hour ago so I was clear-eyed when I turned to Derek. Who was surprisingly just as lucid.

"Why aren't you halfway to being plastered?"

Derek shrugged, his gaze flashing away for a second. "I'm driving. Doesn't matter. And stop trying to deflect."

"I'm not deflecting. I'm just…not in the mood."

"You and Miss Jess have a fight, huh?"

What the hell? Did everyone know we'd been dating?

Derek huffed out a laugh. "Dude, everyone knew. We're not totally oblivious. So what'd you do?"

"Why do you automatically assume—shit, no, you're right." I sighed and turned my chair so I could look straight at Derek. "I fucked up and I'm not quite sure how to fix it short of groveling. And I'm not opposed to that but…"

"But what?"

"But I'm not sure I was wrong."

"Oh, you were most definitely wrong about something." Derek laughed. "But maybe you just don't know what it is. So tell me what happened. Let's figure this shit out."

I wanted to laugh but Derek looked so damn sincere, I couldn't do it. The guy actually wanted to help.

"She's planning to do something, and I think she's making a mistake."

Derek's eyes widened. "You told her she was making a mistake? And she didn't immediately cut off your balls? Dude, you got lucky in my book."

"I walked out before she could."

Now, Derek's mouth dropped open. "Oh, man, you are *so* not as smart as I thought you were."

Grimacing, I took a sip of my warm beer. "Yeah, I'm thinking the same thing myself. The problem is, I still think she's making a mistake and I haven't figured out yet how to say that without getting into another fight."

Dammit, I wanted her to stay, to be with me. And I knew how amazing I'd be as a scout and—

"Holy shit, I'm an idiot."

Derek's expression was a whole lot of "No shit" as he sipped his own beer. "Apparently, I'm a miracle worker. You're welcome. So what are you going to do now?"

I shook my head. "Fuck if I know. But I think I need to get the hell out of here tonight. Can you give Justin a ride back to our apartment?"

"No problem, man. He can sit on Lad's lap. Lad needs a little pick-me-up with Jake out of the picture."

Rolling my eyes, I smacked Derek on the back of the head for being an asshole, which Derek took in stride, then headed for the door.

I needed some space to figure out how the hell I was going to making things right with Jess.

Jess

Thursday morning, I pushed away from my desk and headed for the lower level.

I'd had shit luck getting anything done since I'd arrived at my desk at 8:45 a.m. My brain refused to cooperate. Too many things crowding it and not enough sleep last night. But I'd come to a conclusion around three o'clock this morning. And now was as good a time as any to set it in motion.

I hadn't expected any of the players to be there for practice yet. Actually, I'd been counting on it. But I should've known it wouldn't be that easy. And of course it would have to be Will.

My heart gave a painful little thump in my chest as I caught sight of him walking through the door, duffel bag over his shoulder. He hadn't seen me yet but it'd only be a matter of time before he realized I was standing in the hall. I just wasn't prepared for the pain. It'd only been a few days but damn, I'd missed him.

Had he missed me? Would he even speak to me?

I got my answer a second later when his head popped up and his gaze connected with mine. Was he happy to see me? He didn't look happy. He didn't mad either. He just looked…like Will. The man I was about to do something very brave or very stupid for.

No, that wasn't right, either. I wasn't doing this for *him*. I was doing this for myself.

And if I was very lucky, I'd get him in the process.

"Hey, Jess. How are you?"

His voice wasn't filled with the warmth I'd gotten used to but it wasn't cold, either. And it still made me want to push him up against the wall so I could climb all over him.

But I couldn't. Not yet.

I smiled, hoping he might still want to let me later. "I'm good. You had a great game last night."

"Thanks. Tough game, but we pulled out the win."

An awkward silence fell. I hated that this was so hard. And that I had to go. I had to catch Cary before practice.

"Well, I need to get to a meeting but—"

"Sure, no problem." He cut me off but he still didn't sound angry or upset. "I'll see you around, Jess."

Then he faked a smile and continued down the hall to the locker room.

Okay, wow, that sucked. But it didn't change my mind. In fact, it actually made me more resolute. With a deep breath, I headed past the locker room entrance, down to Cary's office.

His head popped up as I knocked on his door, but he didn't look surprised to see me.

"Hey, Jess, got your message. What's up?"

I bit my lip. "Could I come in and close the door?"

His eyebrows rose but that was his only outward sign of curiosity. "I feel like I'm being called into the principal's office. Except this is my office."

My nose wrinkled. "Sorry. I don't mean to be so secretive about this. It's just… I know I said I didn't want to be considered for a scouting position. But… I'd like to reconsider."

Cary's eyebrows rose in shock. "Seriously? Of course you can reconsider. I'm thrilled, but I hope I didn't pressure you into something you don't want to do. That wasn't my intention."

"No, you didn't pressure me. And I need to thank you. I understand that you're going out on a limb for me on this."

"It's no limb when I know you can do the work. I realize picking up this scouting position means a whole hell of a lot of extra work on your part. But I have to confess I already talked to Philly's GM about this, and he's behind you one-hundred percent. If you take the job, you'll be supervised by Bobby Vigneau, who I believe you already know. When I mentioned your name, he was on board immediately. Are you going to encounter some assholes along the way? Of course. It's going to be tough. But I don't think for one minute that you can't handle the job."

My smile had grown as he'd spoken, my heart pounding a mile a minute. "Thank you, Cary. That means the world to me." Which was pretty stupid considering Will had said almost the exact same thing the last night we'd been together.

Shaking my head at the thought, I drew in a deep breath. "You know about Will and me, don't you?"

His amused grin spoke volumes. "I think everyone knows about you and Will." He raised a hand to stop my response. "And that relationship isn't going to be a problem. At least, not from a team standpoint."

"I'm not sure there's a relationship left to have a problem. We had a…falling-out."

Cary's brows rose. "Sorry to hear that. Will and I have had our differences, but we worked them out. Maybe you will, too. So…does this mean you're staying?"

I paused for several seconds before nodding, slowly at first and then faster, my smile becoming full-blown. "Yes. And Cary? Thank you."

Cary's smile stretched wide. "Welcome aboard but don't thank me. I just doubled your workload and probably made the next few months of your life complete hell."

No, the only way the next few months of my life would be hell was if I couldn't convince a certain tough defenseman to accept my apology for being a total basket case.

The question was how did I do that?

Will

"Tough game tonight, guys, but I'm proud of the way you played." Coach paced back and forth as the team gathered in the locker room just after our loss against Idaho. "The bounces didn't go our way, but you played a full sixty minutes and that's what I want from you. We're going to spend time on special teams tomorrow before the game so heads up. Get cleaned up and rest for the game tomorrow."

As the rest of the team headed toward the shower room, I dropped my head back and remained seated. I had nothing to rush out for and damn if my shoulder didn't hurt like a sonuvabitch from a wicked check in the second period.

"Hey, Mac, you okay?"

Opening my eyes, I saw Cary standing over me, frowning.

"Yeah, shoulder's a little sore. Nothing major."

"Make sure you have the trainer look at it. We need you at full strength tomorrow night. Wilkes-Barre's gonna be tough."

Nodding, I expected Cary to move off but the guy stuck.

"Something wrong?" I asked.

"Nope. One of the scouts from the big club is here tonight. Wants to talk to you before you head out. In the spare trainer's office."

I frowned. "What the hell for?"

Cary shrugged. "Just relaying a message."

Before I could ask any more questions, Cary turned to talk to the coach.

Well, damn. All I really wanted to do tonight was head back to my apartment, eat a shit-ton of food, and sleep until tomorrow morning at nine, when I had to get up for morning skate.

Shit, what I really wanted to do was go home with Jess, make love to her until we both passed out then sleep curled around her. I'd wanted to get on my knees and apologize this morning before practice. Had wanted to beg her to take me back. And when she took that job in Philly, I'd find a way to make it work. *We'd* find a way to make it work, even if it meant I only saw her one day a week until the end of the season.

That's what I should've told her this morning. What I wanted to tell her now. But first, I had to talk to someone from the main office so...

Fifteen minutes later, I walked through the silent halls to a small, out-of-the-way office and stopped dead in the doorway.

"Hi, Will."

Jess leaned back against the small desk, staring at me like she wasn't sure I wanted to see her.

Considering my heart had begun to pound against my ribs and my stomach twisted in on itself, I knew she was dead wrong.

And I knew exactly what I had to say.

"I was a complete ass. I'm sorry. And whatever job you want, I'm behind you. I think you can do fucking anything you want, Jess. I should've said that the other night. You're not a coward. You're the smartest person I've ever met and I hope you can forgive me for being a dick."

Her lips quirked up a little at the corners and her head tilted to the side, just enough to make her hair fall over her shoulder in that way that made me want to brush it over her shoulder and kiss the now-exposed side of her neck. And then I'd work my way down to the small vee of skin revealed by the silky blouse she wore tucked into one of those pencil-thin skirts I loved on her.

I stuck my feet to the floor, waiting for her to acknowledge my apology, ready to be sent packing if she didn't. She'd gone to the trouble of seeking me out tonight, but she needed to make the next move.

"Apology accepted." Her smiled widened. "But I owe you one as well. You were right."

I shook my head. "About what? Because from where I'm standing, I was wrong about so many things, I have no idea what you could be talking about."

"About me being afraid. You had more faith in me than I did. And I wanted to thank you for that."

Shit, was this good-bye? The pit that had pretty much taken up residence in my stomach the past week opened just a little wider. Then I remembered Cary had said someone from the big club wanted to see me. She must have taken the job in Philly.

I stepped closer until she had to tilt her head back to stare up at me. I clenched my hands at my sides so I wouldn't reach for her. But I so wanted to pull her against me and say I was sorry again with my mouth all over her body until she could do nothing but pant and say yes.

Instead, I nodded and forced myself to ask her, "When are you leaving?"

Another ghost of a smile crept over her lips, and I had no idea what the hell she was thinking.

"I have my first game in Norfolk next week."

What the fuck? "Philly doesn't play Charleston."

And that was the stupidest fucking thing I thought I'd ever said, but I had no idea what the hell she was talking about. She was making no sense at all.

"Philly has their eye on a couple of rookies playing for Norfolk."

Which didn't clear up a damn thing. "Jess, what—"

"I'll be gone Wednesday and most of Thursday, but I'll be back in time for our game Friday."

"Jess—wait." My brain began to work again, having finally made its way through the clues she'd already dropped. My gaze narrowed and I took another hard look at her. "You agreed to the scouting position."

Her mouth had a wistful twist to it as she nodded. "I told you. You were right. I was afraid. About the job. About change. But mostly I was a little afraid of you."

I took a step back. "Whoa, wait—"

"Sorry." She held up a hand and shook her head then reached for me, placing her hand flat on my chest. "That didn't come out right. I'm not afraid of you, Will. I'd never be afraid of you. But I *am* deathly afraid of losing you."

As I tried to catch my breath, my heart pounded hard against my ribs, right under her hand.

"I don't want to lose you." Her voice held so much sincere emotion, it cut straight to my heart. "I want to wake up with you in the morning and go to bed with you at night and fight with you over which game to watch before bed and—"

I closed the space between us and dropped my mouth over hers, sealing our lips together and kissing her until we were both breathless and clinging to one another, and I practically forgot that we were still in the arena. Otherwise I would've turned her around, pulled up her skirt, and pushed her down on the desk so I could prove to her just how much I wanted her.

As it was, I had a hard time releasing her even though I knew we both needed to breathe.

When I finally did pull away, I only allowed our lips to part enough to speak.

"I can think of a lot better things to do while watching a game than fight."

Her smile was a revelation. "I thought you liked a good fight."

"Only when I know we're both going to win. And right now, I feel like I won the fucking Stanley Cup."

Running her hand through my still-wet hair, she had to rise onto her toes to rub her nose against mine. "I'm going to be really busy for the rest of the season. There are going to be weeks that we might not see each other."

I pressed a kiss to the side of her neck, breathing in her scent. "It'll just make the time we spend together even better."

"I'll be traveling most weekends."

"I have games most weekends. We'll spend every day off together. In bed. We won't answer our phones or the door and we'll only get out of bed to eat." I trailed kisses up her neck to her ear and bit the tiny lobe until she shuddered against me. "Unless you wanna do it on the couch. Or against the door. Or on the kitchen table. I'm easy."

Her hands tugged at my hair and I lifted my head. "I'm serious, Will. I'm going to be away. A lot. My mom couldn't take that. It's what broke up her marriage to my dad."

I stared down in her worried eyes. "We're not your parents. We know how this game works and what it takes to win."

Her smile was back and it wiped the worry from her eyes. "Have you always been this sure of yourself?"

"I'm that sure of *you*. We'll make it work. Besides, I'm pretty sure I love you, Jess. No, not pretty sure. I'm damn sure."

Her smile got even wider. "I'm damn sure I love you too, Will."

"Then I'm pretty damn sure we should go the hell back to your place and fight over who gets to be on top."

Her laughter filled up all the little cold places in my heart that'd been there since I'd walked out on her. "That's a fight I think I can win."

"And I will gladly lose if I get to make you scream out my name when you come."

Heading for the door, she tugged on my hand. "I'll race you to the car."

"You go right ahead, I'll just follow behind, watching your pretty ass the entire way."

The look she threw over her shoulder made my heart beat double-time.

"Do you think you'll be able to keep up?"

"I maybe not be the fastest guy on ice but I will always be right beside you, Jess. Always."

Also by Stephanie Julian

OFFSIDE HEARTS

Netting the Goalie

Pucking the Grinder

Falling for the Enforcer

Tempting the Instigator

Desiring the D-Man

Taming the Machine

Gambling on the Ghost

DEVILS HOCKEY

Rowdy Hearts

Rainbow Kisses

Rebel Secrets

Rocky's story (Title TBA)

FAST ICE

Bylines & Blue Lines

Hard Lines & Goal Lines

Deadlines & Red Lines

SCANDALOUS DESIRE

Invite Me In

Reserve My Nights

Expose My Desire

Keep My Secrets

Rock My Heart

WICKED & CHARMING
Seducing Whitney
Claiming Ellie
Sharing Brianna

INDECENT
An Indecent Proposition
An Indecent Affair
An Indecent Arrangement
An Indecent Longing
An Indecent Desire

LOVERS UNDERCOVER
Lovers & Lies
Sinners & Secrets
Beauty & Brains

DARKLY ENCHANTED
Spell Bound
Moon Bound
Twice Bound

MOONLIGHT FANTASIES
Shadow Magic
Enchanted Magic
Dangerous Magic

MOONLIGHT LOVERS

Kiss of Moonlight

Visions of Moonlight

Edge of Moonlight

Temptation in Moonlight

Grace in Moonlight

Shades of Moonlight

DIVINE DESIRES

Dark Desires at Dawn

Rough Caress of Midnight

Double Fantasies at Twilight

Enchanting Temptations in Shadow

REDTAILS HOCKEY

(Third-person OFFSIDE HEARTS)

The Brick Wall

The Grinder

The Enforcer

The Instigator

The Playboy

The D-Man

The Machine

The Ghost

About the Author

Stephanie Julian is a USA Today and New York Times best-selling author of contemporary and paranormal romance. Make sure you sign up to receive all of her news here.